EMPEROR OF ROME

Robert Fabbri read Drama and Theatre at London University and has worked in film and TV for twenty-five years as an assistant director. He has worked on productions such as *Hornblower, Hellraiser, Patriot Games* and *Billy Elliot*. His lifelong passion for ancient history inspired him to write the Vespasian series. He lives in London and Berlin.

EMPEROR OF ROME

ROBERT FABBRI

CORVUS

First published in Great Britain in 2019 by Corvus, an imprint of
Atlantic Books Ltd. This edition published in 2019 by Corvus.

Copyright © Robert Fabbri, 2019

The moral right of Robert Fabbri to be identified as the author of this
work has been asserted by him in accordance with the Copyright,
Designs and Patents Act of 1988.

This novel is entirely a work of fiction. The names, characters and incidents
portrayed in it are the work of the author's imagination. Any resemblance to
actual persons, living or dead, events or localities, is entirely coincidental.

10 9 8 7 6 5 4 3 2 1

A CIP catalogue record for this book is available from the British Library.

Paperback ISBN: 978 1 78239 710 6
E-book ISBN: 978 1 78239 711 3

Corvus
An imprint of Atlantic Books Ltd
Ormond House
26–27 Boswell Street
London WC1N 3JZ

www.corvus-books.co.uk

Printed and bound by CPI Group (UK) Ltd, Croydon, CR0 4YY

To everyone who has taken the time to read the Vespasian series; I thank you all.

PROLOGUE

The Via Postumia between Cremona and Bedriacum in the Venetia and Histria region of Italia, 15 April AD 69

CHAOS WAS AN understatement. The shambolic deployment from column to line was in marked contrast to the neat cohorts drawn up, chequerboard, straddling the Via Postumia; with the River Po on their right flank, they blocked the way to Cremona. Tens of thousands of legionaries and auxiliaries stood in silence, burnished helms glowing soft in the dawning rays of sun, watching their enemy struggle to form battle order. But it was not because the deploying army was a mass of ill-disciplined barbarians that there was disarray, nor was it a lack of generalship; quite the contrary. It was a surfeit of generalship that this army suffered from, for, in the absence of the Emperor, Marcus Salvius Otho, no one man was fully in command. There was nothing wrong with the troops' discipline either, for they too, like their opponents, were Roman.

And this was civil war.

Titus Flavius Sabinus grimaced as he watched the centurions of the five Praetorian Guard cohorts, under his command, bawl and beat their parade-ground soldiers into a new position, the orders having changed for the third time since the sighting of the foe. How had it come to this, he wondered, raising his eyes and surveying the army of the Rhenus that had marched south, in a two-pronged attack, in support of the man they had hailed as emperor, Aulus Vitellius, the noted gourmand and Governor of Germania Inferior. How, in under a year since Nero's suicide, having been declared an enemy of the state by the Senate, had it reached the point that there were two emperors and Roman blood would be spilt?

Caecina Alienus and Fabius Valens, the two Vitellian generals, had surprised the forces loyal to Otho, the Emperor in Rome, by the speed of their advance and descent into Italia so early in the season. Otho's response had been to try to negotiate a settlement; however, he had been rebuffed.

Thus, civil war had become the only choice for Otho if he were not to immediately abdicate by committing suicide. And it was here, in the Po Valley, that the issue would be decided.

Sabinus' father and namesake, the elder Sabinus, prefect of the city of Rome under Nero, had been replaced by his successor, Galba, and then reinstated by Otho, who had also promised the younger Sabinus a consulship. And so the family found themselves on the Othonian side of the civil war.

But for how long? Judging by the army's situation, not long was the younger Sabinus' assessment; confusion had reigned all around him since he had started to bring his command across the Po before dawn to join the main body of the Othonian army. 'Otho should have stayed here with us rather than retire to Brixellum,' he observed to his second in command, mounted next to him, 'then, Nerva, we might have a clear command structure rather than this ... this ...' He indicated to the Legio I Adiutrix, recently formed from marines of the Misinium fleet, deploying directly onto the right flank of his own command and having difficulty forming the chequerboard, quincunx formation due to the baggage train being in the wrong position.

Marcus Cocceius Nerva, who at thirty-nine was three years Sabinus' senior, sucked the air through his teeth. 'Otho has been badly advised throughout this campaign; although, with no military experience, having him here wouldn't make much difference. He's great fun at dinner but on the battlefield he'd be worse than a man short. He's like his brother Titianus when it comes to organisation, but perhaps marginally more efficient.'

'And, as Titianus' brother-in-law, you should know.'

'It's because I made the mistake of marrying Titianus' sister that I'm obliged to be here witnessing this.' Nerva looked in disbelief at the shambles unfolding. 'Gods, but we could do with the infantry and cavalry Otho took with him; forty-odd thousand against our thirty; does he need that large a bodyguard so far from the enemy? It's lost us the battle before it's even begun.'

Sabinus shook his head and turned to the thin-stripe military tribune awaiting orders behind his superiors. 'Has our personal baggage been taken to the rear?'

The lad nodded, trying to keep the fear from his expression with a false smile. 'Yes, sir; and the spare horses you asked for.'

Sabinus nodded with grim satisfaction and turned back to his companion. 'We put up a decent show, then get out as fast as possible and surrender to Valens, hopefully.'

'That would seem the wisest course of action. And then we become the ardent supporters of Vitellius until ...' Nerva left the sentence hanging.

'Until what?'

Nerva lowered his voice and leant closer to Sabinus. 'I heard that your father made a trip to Judaea during the time that Galba relieved him as prefect of Rome.'

Sabinus kept his face neutral; Vitellian horns sounded their advance. 'Maybe; but it's no business of yours.'

Nerva was not to be deterred. 'He returned soon after Otho had assassinated Galba and the Senate declared him emperor, just before the news arrived that Vitellius had been hailed as such on the Rhenus.'

Sabinus concentrated his attention on the river where two thousand gladiators, making up the rest of his unlikely command, were in danger of being caught disembarking from the flotilla that had ferried them across.

Nerva pressed his point. 'It wasn't a sightseeing trip, I'm sure. Your uncle, Vespasian, commands the eastern legions putting down the Jewish revolt. That's a powerful force. My guess is that your father and uncle had some in-depth conversations about how this crisis would play out and, if I'm right in thinking, Galba, Otho and Vitellius aren't the only emperors that we'll see this year. The question is: who'll get the prize, your father or your uncle? But, just so you know, I'll support either of them.'

Titus Flavius Sabinus did not respond but, rather, busied himself by sending the tribune with orders to the gladiators to keep themselves positioned hard on the bank of the Po so as to prevent the Batavian auxiliaries, advancing towards them, from outflanking them. His mind, however, was elsewhere: he wondered how Nerva had come by this information and who else knew of his father's secret errand.

Otho slumped back in his chair and looked up along the line of sullen faces; none of his generals could meet his eye as they apprised him of the calamitous defeat. And calamitous it had been: the Vitellian forces had shown no quarter to their fellow citizens with different loyalties as, through the convention of civil war, they could be neither sold nor ransomed so were therefore worthless to them; thousands had been slaughtered. 'It's over, then,' Otho said, fingering the tip of one of the two daggers on the desk before him.

'The rest of the Moesian legions could still come to your aid,' Otho's older brother, Salvius Titianus, urged as he saw despair in his sibling's eyes and, therefore, probable execution in his own future.

Otho shook his head with regret; his face was handsome and melancholic but running to fat after ten years of luxurious exile as Governor of Lusitania. 'It was my mistake not to wait for them to arrive in the first place. I thought that delay would bring disaster; now I find the very opposite to be the truth.' He paused, reflecting upon his position, running a hand through the thick curls of his hair. 'Am I to expose your courage and valour to further risks? That would, I believe, be too great a price for my life. It was Vitellius who initiated our contest for the throne and began this war, but it is I who shall end it; let this one battle be enough. This is the precedent that I shall set and posterity shall judge me by it.' Otho stood, looking down at his two blades. 'I am not the man to allow the flower of Roman martial strength to be mown down senselessly and thereby weaken our Empire. So, gentlemen, I take consolation in the fact that you were prepared to die for me, but you must live. I will not interfere with your chances of pardon so don't attempt to interfere with my resolve.'

*

'And did he do it then and there?' the elder Sabinus asked his son.

'No, Father.' The younger Sabinus took a draught of warmed wine, draining the cup. 'It was rather embarrassing; he praised our loyalty, even though he knew that we had deserted him in our minds some time ago. Then he sent us on our way, saying that with his death and his mercy for Vitellius' family he was earning Vitellius' gratitude, thus buying our lives.'

The elder Sabinus grunted, refilling his son's cup. 'Very noble, I'm sure. Then did he do it?'

'No; he went to quell a disturbance amongst his remaining troops who had tried to stop some of us from leaving the camp.'

'Not you?'

'No, Father; I stayed as you had told me to, so as to see it done.'

'And?'

'And once he had calmed his men he returned to his tent, drank a cup of iced water, tested the sharpness of his daggers and then, choosing one, retired to bed with it under his pillow. Believe it or not, he slept deeply the whole night through.'

'That shows remarkable nerve.'

'It was impressive and made more so by the fact that as soon as he awoke at dawn he reached for his dagger and fell out of bed onto it without a sound.'

The elder Sabinus rubbed his near-bald pate and contemplated this as a light draught made the oil-lamp on the desk between them gutter, causing shadows to drift back and forth across his rounded face, dominated by a bulbous nose. Night had long since fallen; they were sitting in his study in the house on Rome's Quirinal Hill that he had inherited from his uncle, Gaius Vespasius Pollo, after his suicide at Nero's command, three years previously. 'And that was dawn two days ago?'

'Yes, Father; I rode fast, pausing only to change horses, to bring the news.'

'Good lad. So, at the moment, we're the only people in Rome to know?'

'I would think so; no one could've got here faster. Otho was warm when I left.'

The elder Sabinus steepled his fingers and brushed them over his lips. With a slow nod, he came to a decision. 'Very well. I'll assemble the Praetorian Cohorts remaining in the city as well as the Urban Cohorts and the Vigiles at dawn tomorrow and administer the oath to Vitellius; that will force the Senate to recognise him as emperor. Get yourself back north and surrender to the Vitellians; tell them what I have done to secure the city for them. That should keep us safe for the moment.' Sabinus winked at his son. 'Especially if you add that I have taken both the Vitellius brothers' wives and children under my protection. That will concentrate their minds.'

'You play a dangerous game, Father.'

'No one ever won by being nice. Tell the Vitellii, I'll be more than happy to send them their families if they write to me requesting it; they'll understand what that means.'

'Confirmation of your position as prefect of Rome and ...?'

'And you keep the consulship that you're due to take up at the end of this month.'

'What happens then?'

The elder Sabinus tapped his fingers against his lips. 'Then? Then we shall see.'

'Come here, my boy!' Aulus Vitellius' great bulk prevented him from reaching down too far and so a stool had been placed next to him on the dais. His six-year-old son stepped onto it to be enfolded into his father's many layers of blubber. Lifting the boy, Vitellius presented him to the ranks of legionaries, making up his escort, and the crowd of senators and equestrians, newly arrived in Lugdunum, the provincial capital of Narbonese Gaul, to hail their new Emperor as he processed in Triumph from Germania Inferior to Rome. 'I name him Germanicus after the province whence I launched my glorious bid for empire. I confer upon Germanicus the right to wear imperial insignia and confirm him as my sole heir before my victorious legions.'

Rapture greeted this statement as Vitellius' victorious troops hailed their Emperor – the fact that they had not taken part in the battle but had, rather, escorted Vitellius on his slow, gastronomical progress through Gaul was conveniently overlooked.

The younger Sabinus joined in the adulation; as the consul heading the senatorial delegation that had come to congratulate the new Emperor, it was only right that he should be seen to be most enthusiastic as this hippopotamus of a man wrapped himself in the dignity of the Purple.

'You might not believe it,' Sabinus whispered to Nerva, next to him, 'but my father met Vitellius at Tiberius' villa on Capreae when he was a teenager. He was lithe and beautiful and much prized by Tiberius for his, shall we say, oral skills, and I don't mean as an orator.'

Nerva looked at Sabinus, incredulous, as he kept up his applause. 'No?'

'It's true; he even offered my father a demonstration of his art. You wouldn't have thought it looking at him now; I suppose he must have learnt the joys of hedonism kneeling at the feet of Tiberius, so to speak.'

'Not only hedonism,' Nerva said, indicating to more than fifty prisoners, wearing only unbelted tunics, like women, being led out for execution, their heads, which they were soon to lose, held high. 'There was no need for this: making an example of the centurions who most vigorously supported Otho.'

With a solemn countenance Sabinus masked his satisfaction that Vitellius was acting to character. 'This will not please the Moesian legions.'

Nerva concurred. 'I was a part of the delegation of former Othonian officers sent to induce them to return to their bases and swear allegiance to Vitellius. They only did so grudgingly as they saw no alternative.'

They may see an alternative soon, Sabinus thought as the first head fell to the ground in a spray of blood, *and when news of this gets out, the Moesian legions will want their revenge.*

The silence of Vitellius' troops was almost physical as head after severed head rolled across the ground turned to mud by gore; the silence deepened so that it pierced, eventually, the thick skin of the Emperor, his face flushed with the joy of cruelty. As the last body slumped, Vitellius tore his gaze away from death and looked about him; gradually his eyes registered nervousness as he perceived the heavy atmosphere. He cleared his throat. 'Bring the generals!'

'I hope he decides to spare them after that bloodbath,' Sabinus whispered, wishing the exact opposite. 'We've had enough vengeance for one day.' And, in truth, as he watched the two Othonian generals, Suetonius Paulinus and Licinius Proculus, as well as Salvius Titianus, the brother of the dead Emperor, led forward and forced to kneel before Vitellius, Sabinus felt relief that he was not also in that position. It had been his father's shrewd offer of protection to Vitellius' family that had secured his pardon and consulship. Then he had been given the dubious honour, by Vitellius himself, of returning to Rome to escort his son north and deliver him to his imperial father; a task he had completed with great ceremony as if it had been the pinnacle of his career.

'And what have you to say for yourselves?' Vitellius demanded. Folds of fat wobbled beneath his clothing as he shook with indignation at the sight of the men who had opposed him.

'You should reward us, not accuse us, Princeps,' Paulinus said, his voice steady and loud so it carried over the assembly, 'for it is to us, not Valens and Caecina, that you owe your victory.'

Vitellius stared down at the prisoners, baffled; his mouth opened and closed as he struggled to comprehend just what had been said.

'It was us,' Proculus insisted, 'who created the circumstances whereby a victory for Otho was inconceivable.'

'How so?' Vitellius demanded, regaining his composure and control of his mouth.

'By insisting that Otho attack immediately, before the bulk of the Moesian legions arrived.'

Paulinus nodded in vigorous agreement. 'Yes, and then pushing our troops into a long march so as to arrive as quickly as possible into contact when there was no need to rush.'

'Our men were exhausted by the time we arrived,' Proculus confirmed, backing up the argument. 'And then we made the deployment from column to line a shambles by issuing counter-orders to each other's commands and then revoking them.' That, having witnessed it, Sabinus could believe. 'Plus, why else would we have placed wagons all through our lines if not to make forming battle order even harder?'

Vitellius studied the two generals and Titianus, who had remained silent throughout. 'Are you telling me that you sabotaged the battle? And what about you, Titianus? Did you betray your own brother?'

Titianus looked up with weary eyes. 'No, Princeps; I didn't need to. My innate inefficiency meant that, whatever I was given to do, I was more of a hindrance than a help.'

Vitellius nodded. 'I can believe that. I'm minded to spare you anyway as you cannot be blamed for supporting your own brother; and your ineptitude is legendary. I pity the man who would ask for your help.'

'I too, Princeps. Thank you.'

Vitellius turned his attention back to the other two defeated generals. 'As for you—'

'If you want real proof, Princeps,' Paulinus cut in, 'ask yourself why I placed our worst troops, a band of gladiators, opposite your Batavians on our extreme left flank and so doom our line.' Sabinus looked astounded at Paulinus as he made this claim that was so obviously untrue, as it had been his doing. 'Ask Titus Flavius Sabinus, who was in command of the left wing, whether I specifically ordered him to make that disposition after he crossed the river to join us.'

Vitellius turned his eyes to Sabinus as Paulinus looked at him, willing him to agree. 'Well, consul? Did he?'

Deciding that it would be better to have a live Paulinus and Proculus in his debt than dead ones owing him nothing, Sabinus nodded. 'Yes, Princeps, he did. I thought it strange at the time but he was insistent upon it; I now understand why. His heart was with you; as was mine, for I didn't argue.'

Vitellius grunted, thinking things over. 'Very well, Paulinus and Proculus. I believe your protestations of treachery and clear you of all suspicion of loyalty. You shall take me on a tour of the battlefield and show me just how this treason took place.'

It was a field of corruption; stench hung heavy in the air. In the forty days since the battle nothing had been done about the dead; Othonian and Vitellian decomposed together in the mangled heaps. Carrion-feeders had gorged themselves, stripping the corpses of man and beast alike, but now the remaining flesh was fit only for the maggots that writhed in their millions, in and out of cadavers, growing fat before metamorphosing to produce the swarms of flies whose endless buzzing was impossible to ignore.

Sabinus hid his rage at the sight of so many citizens left untended in death, doomed to roam dark paths that did not lead to the Ferryman. Seeing a pile of bodies, little more than skeletal, against the wall of a hut where they had been cornered and butchered, he swore to himself that, should his family one day be in the position to do so, they would take vengeance on Cremona whose citizens had lined the road to cheer Vitellius. No doubt they had stripped the dead of anything of value, indeed there was hardly even a helmet to be seen, but then they had been derelict in their duty to care for the bodies they had robbed.

Vitellius never once took his eyes from the piles of corpses as Valens and Caecina guided him across the field with Paulinus and Proculus in attendance as if it were a tour of a newly laid-out garden.

'It was here, Princeps, that the First Italica retrieved the Eagle that the First Adiutrix had managed to capture in their enthusiasm to prove themselves in their maiden battle,' Valens informed the Emperor as they approached the sector of the field that had been Sabinus'.

Vitellius surveyed the twisted bodies of the former marines who had been formed into a legion by Galba and had fought and died for Otho. With ostentation he sniffed the air. 'One thing smells better than a dead enemy and that is a dead fellow citizen.'

Tense, sycophantic laughter greeted this crass remark but even Valens and Caecina, Vitellius' most ardent supporters, could not completely conceal their unease. Noticing a shared look between them, Sabinus sensed their horrified realisation that Vitellius had no deference for these brave fellow citizens who had captured an Eagle only to lose it in a counter-attack. Vitellius had just lost all respect.

It was the moment his father had ordered him to watch for. 'Princeps,' he said, stepping from the crowd following the Emperor.

Vitellius turned, still chuckling at his weak and tasteless joke. 'What is it, consul?'

'Now that we have surveyed the scene of your triumph, I feel that it is time for me to return to Rome and prepare the city for your welcome.'

Vitellius' huge frame swelled even more at the thought of his Triumphal entry into Rome. 'Yes, yes, so you should, my dear Sabinus; and I look forward to seeing your father and thanking him for securing the city for me. We are old friends, you know; we go back a long way. But don't you want to show me the section of the field where your command lost the battle for Otho first?'

'I think it would be only right for Paulinus and Proculus to have the honour of showing you the gladiator dead; I take no joy in stealing other men's plaudits.' He glanced across to the losing generals and, by their countenances, understood that they fully acknowledged the debt they owed him. As Vitellius dismissed him back to Rome, Sabinus knew that he had made two important recruits for his family's cause.

It was the same enthusiasm with which they had acclaimed the previous two Emperors that the people of Rome welcomed Vitellius: as if he were the answer to their prayers, the Emperor they had always desired. Ten, twelve deep, and waving their racing faction colours, they lined the streets as Vitellius, mounted upon a straining horse, his unmartial frame incongruously clad in a general's uniform, led his legions onto the Campus Martius two days after the ides of July, two months after the younger Sabinus had taken his leave of him.

'He's not going to lead his troops right into the city, is he, Father?' the younger Sabinus asked as they stood, with the

Senate, outside the Theatre of Pompey waiting to welcome the victorious Emperor with the sacrifice of two white bulls.

'Why not? Galba did and billeted them here.'

'But they caused carnage: fights, rapes, murders; they thought they could get away with anything.'

'They did. But don't forget: Vitellius wasn't here to witness that; Galba sent him to govern Germania Inferior before he arrived in Rome so he doesn't know what a burden billeted troops are on the citizenry. Even if he did, I doubt he would care enough to do anything different.' The elder Sabinus took on an overly solemn expression. 'It's a shame, it really is.'

His son understood. 'And I'm sure that as the prefect of the city you're not going to do anything to alert him to the dangers of upsetting the people by allowing their daughters to be gang-raped by ill-disciplined legionaries.'

'It is not my business to tell the Emperor what he should or shouldn't do.'

The younger Sabinus suppressed a smile. As he and the rest of the Senate began applauding Vitellius who was drawing close at the head of his martial column that would bring misery to his subjects, he reflected on the dangerous game that he and his father would be forced to play over the next few months: living in the city with an emperor that they were seeking to undermine.

As the thought went through his head a man caught his eye, working his way amongst the senators towards him; he knew the man well for he was his uncle Vespasian's freedman, Hormus. He signalled Hormus to wait where he was until the end of the ceremony. With a nod, Hormus moved back into a doorway.

'Well, Hormus,' the elder Sabinus asked as they greeted the freedman once the prayers and sacrifices were complete.

Hormus grasped both their forearms in turn. 'It's happened, masters: Julius Alexander, prefect of Egypt, had his two legions proclaim Vespasian emperor on the calends of this month, seventeen days ago; Vespasian's legions did the same in Caesarea, two days later, as soon as they heard. My master sent me straight here to bring you the news and ask you to prepare the city for his army. Mucianus, Governor of Syria, and Cerialis, Vespasian's son-in-law, are marching overland to Italia, hoping to pick up the disaffected Moesian legions on the way.'

'Mucianus and Cerialis!' the elder Sabinus exclaimed. 'Why them? Why not Vespasian at the head of his army?'

'He plans to take Rome without a war by using the threat of one in conjunction with a greater menace. He's gone to Egypt to take control of the grain supply there and, also, if he can, in Africa. He'll threaten to starve Vitellius out; only if he refuses to go will he revert to war.'

Sabinus looked at his son. 'Let's hope that my fair treatment of Vitellius' family will stand us in good stead; it looks as if we may be hostages for some time.'

'Shouldn't we just leave and go to Vespasian?'

'I'm more use to him here.'

'What do you plan to do?'

'When the time comes, I'll take Rome and hold it until Vespasian's army arrives.'

'What do you mean: the people wouldn't let him abdicate?' The elder Sabinus slammed the palms of both hands down onto his study desk.

The younger Sabinus gestured helplessly. 'Just what I say: the senior consul refused to take the knife he offered in token of giving up his power; then the mob blocked him from going to the Temple of Concordia to deposit his Triumphal Regalia and, instead, forced him to return to the Palatine where he remains. He's technically still emperor, although he would rather take that private villa in Campania and the guarantee of a peaceful retirement that you offered him in Vespasian's name.'

Another double-handed palm slam. 'The weak-willed, fat glutton! Medusa's dry dugs, he's been pressured by rabble who know nothing of politics or what's best for them. I know the Saturnalia started yesterday but spare us from the poor playing "king for the day".'

'It's not just the Head Count; it's his friends and the remnants of the Praetorian Guard. They claim that what you offered

Vitellius in the Temple of Apollo was a bluff. They think that you and Vespasian won't keep your word; they don't see how you can let Vitellius and his son live, and, frankly, I don't blame them.'

'Just over a month ago his army was defeated and three days ago the remnants surrendered and Valens was executed! I've more troops with the three Urban Cohorts under my command than he does – not forgetting the Vigiles. What harm can he possibly do?'

'He can be a focus for dissent,' the third person in the room said, stepping away from the scroll-case against which he had been leaning. 'They're right not to trust the offer; I'll have him killed along with the brat as soon as I can.'

'You're not going to be the Emperor, Domitian,' the elder Sabinus snapped.

'Not in name; but I will be the Emperor's son. With my father in Egypt and my brother in Judaea, I would say that gives me a great deal of authority.'

'You're eighteen! You have as much authority as a whore-boy with a cock in either end. Now shut up and listen; perhaps you may learn something.' Sabinus turned back to his son. 'What about the Germans?'

The younger Sabinus grimaced. 'That's a bit of a problem, Father: the Germanic Imperial Bodyguard is also remaining loyal to Vitellius.'

'That's still only five hundred men. I'll send to Vitellius once more, saying that if he doesn't accept the offer he really is a dead man and he'll die having seen his boy's throat cut in front of him. Let him take that chance if he wants but he'd be a fool, whatever Domitian—' A knock on the door interrupted him. 'Yes!'

Hormus stuck his head around the corner. 'There's a delegation to see you; they're waiting in the street.'

'Tell them to come in and wait in the atrium!'

Hormus winced at the unexpected ferocity of the reply. 'I would do, sir, but they wouldn't all fit in.'

'And what do you expect me to do, Nerva?' Sabinus asked the head of the delegation as he took in the magnitude of the crowd waiting for him outside; over a hundred senators, thrice as many equites and the best part of the Urban Cohorts and the Vigiles, all crying out for Sabinus to lead them. 'Lead you where?'

'The Palatine; we have to force Vitellius out.'

'He's right,' the young Sabinus agreed, 'the longer we wait the more polarised the city will become and the more lives lost. Back in July, you said you would take the city for Vespasian when the time comes. Well, it's now December and that time has come.' He indicated to the armed troops of the Urban Cohorts and the club-wielding Vigiles of Rome's night-watch. 'And there's your army.'

'I don't want to be the one who brings violence to Rome, as it would be said that Vespasian came to power on a tide of blood.'

Domitian stamped his foot. 'It doesn't matter what people say; the important thing is to secure my father as emperor. Vitellius must die along with anyone who hinders that objective.'

'Hold your tongue, whelp!' The older Sabinus did not even look at his nephew. 'Vitellius is not going to die if he goes peacefully.' His eyes hardened into resolution. 'Right! We go, but no one's to offer violence unless provoked; understood?'

It was a single javelin that commenced hostilities; slamming through the head of the Urban Cohort centurion marching in front of the elder Sabinus, it lodged in the shoulder of the standard-bearer next to him. The standard toppled as its bearer staggered with the impact and was then dragged down by the dead weight of the man with whom he was coupled.

And then, as they approached the Fundane Pool towards the lower Quirinal, came the volley; scores upon scores of javelins rained down from the rooftops and upper-storey windows on either side of the street, in a well-set ambush. The younger Sabinus looked up and around him but could see only civilians on the roofs or in the windows, no one in uniform, as tiles and bricks began to pitch down in lieu of javelins. All about him his father's small army scattered for cover, those without shields taking shelter, if possible, with Urban Cohort troops as the improvised missiles continued to cause injury and death.

Bodies paved the road and shrieks echoed off the walls, but these were suddenly drowned by a savage cry that rose like thunder rumbling in from a distance. And then they hit; hundreds of bearded, betrousered and chainmailed warriors with long, hexagonal shields, legionary helmets and the slashing *spathae* swords favoured by tribesmen in Rome's service over the shorter *gladius*. The Germanic Imperial Bodyguard thundered out of a dozen side streets, striking the column at multiple points with the force of forked lightning, irresistible and shocking. Down went those nearest to the strikes whilst others struggled to flee, as the hail of improvised missiles intensified; Germanic war cries filled the senses of all as the killing began in earnest.

'Come, Father!' the younger Sabinus shouted, pulling his father's toga. 'I'd say that we've just been provoked.'

The elder Sabinus raced forward, holding his arms over his head against the deadly rain. 'Keep going!' he shouted as he ran. 'We'll take the Capitoline and hold out there until help comes. Keep going!'

A chill rain had fallen with the night but that did not deter people from making their way to the Capitoline: senators, equites and common people joined Sabinus and his small, much-weakened army holding out on Rome's sacred hill. Even some women came to endure the siege, which, due to the conditions, was not yet impenetrable.

'Arulenus Rusticus, my so-called husband, is hiding under the bed,' Verulana Gratilla informed the elder Sabinus, as she pulled back the lank strands of hair from her face. 'There are many who'd say that my place is with him. But I think: let them say what they will. I'll fight for an emperor whom I can respect; not a sluggard whom I despise.' Her dark eyes fixed Sabinus, daring him to send her back to the husband under the bed.

'You can throw a javelin or a stone as well as anyone, Gratilla,' Sabinus said, trying not to look at the way the wet stola clung to full and inviting breasts. 'I'll treat you no differently.' Admiring the contours of her posterior as she walked away, he knew that was not the truth. He turned to his son to clear his mind of the possibilities the well-formed buttocks had conjured. 'Still no sign of Domitian?'

'No, Father; he was last seen dragging a shield from a wounded Urban Cohort man and then running away.'

'The little shit never did show any spunk; he'll turn up, once it's safe, with tales of personal glory.'

'Two of them,' Domitian asserted, 'both with slashed throats.' He grinned at his cousin, showing the blood on his hand as proof.

The younger Sabinus knew better than to believe anything his cousin claimed but never to show his incredulity. 'You did well to get back; where were you since the ambush?'

Domitian frowned as if the question was beyond stupid. 'Getting supporters to join us, of course. Whilst you've been hiding safely up here, I've been around the city in disguise, urging people to support our cause.'

Hiding until night fell and it was safe to make a dash for the Capitoline, Sabinus thought as he clapped his cousin on the shoulder. 'Did you get a look at how many are down in the Forum?'

'Hundreds; all the Germanic Bodyguard and a good deal of the Praetorian Guard.'

Unless they had arrived undercover of night, Sabinus knew this to be a gross exaggeration. 'And what about behind us, on the Campus Martius?'

Domitian shrugged. 'I didn't come in that way.'

'Well, let's hope that there are fewer than in the Forum and that our messenger got through. With luck, Vespasian's army could be here in two days; his cavalry could even be here tomorrow evening. We can hold out until then.'

Domitian sensed Sabinus' unease. 'Will they attack?'

'Who knows? My father's sending Centurion Martialis to Vitellius at first light to complain about him breaking his agreement to abdicate. If he still refuses then I think … well, I think if they do attack, it won't be just a matter of a few lives being lost.'

*

'He says that he's too unassuming to cope with the overpowering impatience of his supporters,' Cornelius Martialis, the primus pilus centurion of the Second Urban Cohort, reported in a clipped tone.

The elder Sabinus widened his eyes in astonishment. 'Unassuming? The fat slob is one of the least unassuming men I know. If he thinks he has a chance of remaining as emperor with just the support of his bodyguard, a couple of Praetorian Cohorts and the rabble then he's seriously mistaken. Vespasian's army will be here within a couple of days.'

'If the messenger got through,' the younger Sabinus pointed out.

'Of course one got through; I sent a dozen.' The elder Sabinus turned back to Martialis. 'Did you point out that we agreed he should abdicate, and that if he goes back on that then he'll most certainly die along with his son and brother?'

'I did, prefect; and he seemed to be more interested in his breakfast than the danger he was putting himself in. He said it's out of his hands and then bade me leave by a secret passage in case his supporters decided to kill me because I'm an ambassador for peace.'

'It sounds as if he's emperor solely in name and has completely lost control,' the younger Sabinus said, looking out over the Forum Romanum to the far end where a body of troops was congregating near the Temple of Vesta. 'And here come the worst sort of soldiers: leaderless ones.'

'Now!' the younger Sabinus roared as the Germanic Bodyguard approached the gates to the Capitoline at full sprint.

Hundreds of broken tiles and bricks hailed down upon the attackers, forcing them to raise their shields and crouch under the onslaught.

With the relentless energy of those whose lives depended on it, the younger Sabinus, his father, Nerva and all those defending the Capitoline hurled missiles down into the Imperial Guards who had brought nothing but their swords and shields. Back they were forced as more of their number fell unconscious or clutching broken limbs.

'They'll be unable to threaten us even if they come back with a thousand javelins,' the elder Sabinus asserted as the last Germanic troops disappeared towards the Temple of Saturn and the safety of the Forum. 'They need siege equipment to get into here and there's none in the city.' He looked down at the iron-reinforced, wooden gates secured with two metallic bars across them and stout wooden logs wedged against them. 'They're not going to force those without a ram or some serious artillery.'

'Or fire, Father,' the younger Sabinus said, his voice low with dread.

The elder Sabinus looked up. 'Jupiter's great sack, even the Gauls, four hundred and fifty years ago, had respect enough for our gods not to destroy their temples.'

'The Gauls may have; but these are Germans.' His son glanced once more at the approaching enemy, each man bearing a flaming torch, before turning to his comrades. 'Get water! Get it from the cistern; as much as you can or we're lost.'

Water, however, was in short supply on the summit of the Capitoline but, even in December, dry wood was not. The younger Sabinus and his father urged their followers to greater efforts in emptying the cistern with the few pails that could be mustered along with brass bowls used for collecting the blood of sacrifices. But torches streaked over the walls continuously, firing everything combustible.

It was a sharp flash that made the younger Sabinus turn and stare in horror. 'The gates! Get water onto the gates; damp them down!' But even as he shouted he knew that it was too late, for the gates had been ignited from without and his nostrils detected a smell stronger and rarer than wood: Naphtha had been used, hence the flash, and Naphtha paid little heed to water.

His father had seen it too. 'Block the gates, tear down all the statues and pile them up, and then find some way to escape,' he ordered. 'The Capitoline is lost!'

'But that's sacrilege; many are statues of the gods.'

The elder Sabinus pointed up to the roof of Jupiter's temple; flames had begun to crack the tiles and lick through holes that multiplied rapidly. 'And that's not sacrilege? Germanic tribesmen in the Emperor's service setting fire to Rome's guardian god's temple! The statues will hold them back for long enough to get a lot of people away; if that adds a bit more sacrilege to what's already happened then it's worth it. Now get going and take that little shit Domitian with you, if he hasn't already scarpered. You should be able to climb down from the Arx into the Campus Martius.'

'What about you, Father?'

Sabinus looked at his son and namesake and, with a grim smile, shook his head as a thunderous crash and a burning jet of air issued from the Temple of Jupiter, heralding the collapse of the roof. 'I'm staying here. The prefect of Rome does not flee the city; if Vitellius wants to live then he needs to negotiate with me.'

'And if he thinks that he can live without negotiating with you?'

'Then we are both dead men. Now go!'

Smoke wafted across the Forum Romanum and over the Palatine from the blackened ruins of the Capitoline now a husk of its former glory. The younger Sabinus looked down from his hiding place, on the roof of the Temple of Apollo, to the palace built by Caligula and newly restored after the Great Fire five years previously. Below him, Vitellius hauled his bulk out of the main doors and stood at the top of the steps, surrounded by his loyal Germanic Guards. Waiting to greet him were senators and equites, many of whom had been up on the Capitoline that morning, but had escaped as Sabinus and the Urban Cohorts delayed the storming of the hill; now they had sneaked from their hiding places to support the Emperor they hated as he passed judgement on those who had opposed him and failed.

Sabinus' fingers squeezed the parapet, his knuckles white, as he looked upon a figure, weighed down with chains, being frog-marched up the steps: his father.

The elder Sabinus was thrown to the ground in a rattle of fetters, causing the crowd, which had hitherto remained silent, to jeer.

Vitellius indulged his audience for a while before raising his arms; he looked down at Sabinus, hawked and spat the contents of his throat over his head. 'How dare you bargain with the Emperor? How dare you tell me whether to come or to go; to offer me my life, as if it were yours to give, and deigning to grant me a patch of land in Campania when I have all this?' He indicated to the vast expanse of Rome before him, over the charred Capitoline to the Campus Martius with the Tiber and the Via Flaminia disappearing north, calm in the evening light. 'This is mine, all mine, and I see now that there is no need to give it up as the people love me.' Vitellius paused to allow the crowd to cheer and affirm their misplaced support. 'So what shall I do with you?' he asked, addressing the question to the crowd.

The answer was unequivocal. 'Death!'

'Death?' Vitellius mused, pulling at his many chins. 'What say you, Sabinus; do you not deserve death for your arrogance?'

The elder Sabinus looked up at Vitellius, squinting through swollen eyes. 'Kill me and you'll be dead by sunset tomorrow. Spare me and I'll see what I can do to save your miserable and copious skin.'

Vitellius tutted. 'More arrogance. I'll tell you what I'll do, Sabinus, seeing as we're old friends. Do you remember, all those years ago, on Capreae when I made you an offer, a generous offer and you called me a disgusting whore-boy? You said that you wouldn't suck another man's cock to save your life; I hoped one day you would be in the position to prove that. Well, here you are.' He lifted up his tunic and pulled his penis out of his loincloth. 'Here's my cock; suck it and live.'

The older Sabinus started shaking; for a moment the younger Sabinus feared that he was sobbing until thick laughter burst from him. 'Look at you, standing there proudly showing off a cock the size of my little finger. Is that the dignity of an emperor? Is this what it's come to? I remember that conversation; I was disgusted with you then, whore-boy, and I'm disgusted by you now so get it over with. I'll not suck your cock, even if I could find it.'

Vitellius' mouth opened and closed; he gazed around, seeing the ludicrousness of his position. Quickly adjusting his dress, he turned and waddled away. 'Despatch him and expose the body,' he called as he disappeared into the palace.

It was the silence that the younger Sabinus remembered most as his father voluntarily offered his neck to the executioner's sword: the silence of the crowd watching as the blade flashed in the evening light, taking his head from his shoulders in a fountain of blood that slopped over the swordsman's feet. Sabinus' head rolled down the steps, his body collapsed, disgorging its contents, and the crowd watched in silence. The younger Sabinus would always recall that silence, choking back his grief as his father's corpse was dragged off to the Gemonian Stairs, for it was because of that silence that he heard a faint call of a horn drift on the breeze. He turned, looking north whence the sound came, and there, in the distance on the Via Flaminia, were tiny mounted figures glinting in the setting sun.

Too late to save Sabinus but not too late to avenge him, Vespasian's army had come.

PART I

GABARA, GALILEE, MAY AD 67, TWO
YEARS AND SEVEN MONTHS EARLIER

CHAPTER I

Titus Flavius Vespasianus had the strange sensation that he had been here before. In fact, to Vespasian, the circumstances of the situation were so similar to an incident twenty-two years previously that he was not surprised by this sense of revisiting time. Almost every detail was in repetition: the legions and auxiliary cohorts drawn up awaiting the order to begin the assault; the objective itself: a small hilltop settlement of rebels holding out against Roman rule; and then the possibility that the leader of said rebels was trapped within the township. It was uncannily akin to the siege of a hill fort in Britannia, during the second year of the Claudian invasion, when he, Vespasian, had hoped to capture the rebel chieftain, Caratacus. It was all so similar; all, except for one detail: then he had been a legionary legate in command of a single legion, the II Augusta, and its associated auxiliary cohorts; now he was a general in command of three legions and their auxiliaries as well as other contingents supplied by friendly, local client kings, including Herod Agrippa, the second of that name, nominal tetrarch of Galilee, as well as Vespasian's old acquaintance, Malichus, King of the Nabatean Arabs. All in all he had over forty-five thousand men under his command. It was a huge difference; almost as big as the difference in the climate between that damp isle and this realm of the Jews, he reflected as he watched his son and second in command, Titus, ride, kicking up a cloud of dust, towards him and his companion sitting quietly upon his horse to his right. Vespasian could not remember the last time it had rained anything more than a light drizzle in the three months since he had arrived in this arid part of the Empire that had so violently risen up against Rome.

And it had been violent; violent and humiliating. For, but a year ago, Cestius Gallus, the then Governor of Syria, had come south to Galilee and Judaea, in an attempt to quell the burgeoning rebellion; with him he brought the XII Fulminata bolstered by contingents from the three other Syrian legions and their auxiliaries, upwards of thirty thousand men in total. His initial success in retaking Acre, in western Galilee, and then marching south to Caesarea and Jaffa in Judaea, where he massacred almost nine thousand rebels, was overturned when, citing threats to his supply lines, he withdrew, just as he was on the point of investing Jerusalem, and was ambushed at the pass of Beth Horon. More than six thousand Roman soldiers died that day, with nearly twice that number wounded; the XII Fulminata was almost annihilated and its Eagle lost. Gallus had fled back to Antioch in Syria, shamefully abandoning the remnants of his army to extract themselves from the province that, buoyed by this triumph, had now gone into a full-scale revolt. Now, however, the Jews' revolt was bolstered by their leaders who claimed that their singular Jewish god had brought about the victory and therefore their success in ridding their land of Rome was a foregone conclusion.

The Emperor Nero had turned to Vespasian to disabuse the Jews of this notion.

But it was not the help of the jealous Jewish mono-deity that caused Vespasian concern as he awaited the reports of spies, working for Titus, who had infiltrated Gabara, the first town he had targeted in his campaign: it was the fact that the dead at Beth Horon had all been stripped of their armour and weapons; many of the wounded, and, indeed, many not so, had also abandoned their arms as they fled. Vespasian was very aware that he faced a well-armed fighting force and no mere rabble of rebels. And more than that, their leader, Yosef ben Matthias, the rebel Governor of Galilee, had the ability to inspire men; this Vespasian knew from first-hand experience having met him when he was a part of a Jewish delegation to Nero three years previously.

'Well?' Vespasian asked as, with prodigious skill and much dust, Titus brought his mount to a skidding halt next to him.

'They refuse to parley and are keeping their gates closed.'

'And Yosef?'

'He's not in there, Father.'

'Not there? Then how did he get out?'

'He didn't; he was never in Gabara. Our informants were wrong.'

'*Your* informants.' Vespasian took off his high-plumed helmet and the cushioning felt cap and rubbed his bald, sweat-soaked pate; his strained expression, which was the default mode of his rounded face, gave the impression that he had been attempting to pass a stool which was putting up more of a fight than was the norm. 'So who is the commander?'

'Yohanan ben Levi, he's Yosef's rival for power in Galilee and every bit as fanatical; he leads the Zealot faction in Galilee.'

'Zealots?'

'They're zealous for their god, which basically means that they'll kill anyone who doesn't believe or think like they do, especially us; and, even more especially, any Jew who has a less fanatical view of their religion than they do. They were the people who destroyed all the art and statuary in Tiberias because they claimed it offended their god.'

'Barbarians!' Vespasian's disgust at such behaviour was plain. 'How many of the fanatics do *your* informants reckon this Yohanan has under his command?'

Titus, whose prominent nose, intelligent, quick eyes and large ears made him the image of his fifty-seven-year-old father, suppressed the petulant urge to point out that many of the spies had been recruited by Vespasian; he had taken on the role of chief intelligence officer upon his arrival at the rendezvous with his father in the port of Ptolemais, having brought his legion, the XV Apollinaris, from Egypt. 'Not as many as we first thought, *our* informants seem to have exaggerated somewhat.'

Vespasian shook his head and smiled. 'I'm sorry, Son; I learnt long ago not to apportion blame. They're as much mine as yours; more so, even, since it's my army.'

Titus returned the smile. 'Don't you mean "the Emperor's army", Father?'

'I do, of course. It's just that he has, very kindly, lent it to me at the moment and the question is now: how am I going to use it? Roughly how many men of fighting age do *our* informants think are inside the walls?'

'No more than five hundred.'

'And others?'

'At least two, but no more than three, thousand.'

'Good; I can give this to the auxiliaries and let them have the chance to show me what they're made of. It should provide the rest of the army with a bit of sport to whet their appetite for the coming campaign.'

Titus looked with regret at the stone walls of Gabara. 'It's a pity about that sly rat Yosef, though; it would have been good to have caught him this early on. Still, getting Yohanan ben Levi will be almost as good; that will be a great piece of news to have trumpeted around Rome. Nero should be very pleased to hear that we have made such a good start and captured one of the main rebel leaders.'

'What should please Nero and what you think would please Nero and what really does please Nero are three completely separate things, as you should know by now, my boy. Doing too well too quickly won't necessarily endear us to our Emperor; look at what happened to Corbulo.'

Titus sighed. 'Very true.'

And that was just the problem that Vespasian faced: considered to have been the greatest general of the age, Gnaeus Domitius Corbulo had been a victim of a combination of his own success and Nero's jealousy. Having effectively prosecuted a war with Parthia to wrest Armenia back into the Roman sphere of influence, it would have been thought a certainty that the Emperor would have sent Corbulo, his best general, to deal with the crisis, when news of Gallus' defeat had reached his ears as he was touring Greece entering every competition for singing, poetry and chariot racing and, unsurprisingly, winning them all – all one thousand eight hundred of them; indeed, the Olympic Games and many other religious festivals had been brought forward out of their normal cycles so that Nero could indulge his vanity, believing himself to be the greatest artist and the most competent charioteer of all time.

But it was not so in Nero's mind. It had been Vespasian to whom Nero had turned; and this despite the fact that he had angered the Emperor by falling asleep and then spluttering awake during one of Nero's interminable recitals.

Vespasian had been hiding from the Emperor's displeasure in the lands of the Caenii in Thracia having taken his long-time mistress, Caenis, home to visit her people for the first time since her mother had been sold into slavery whilst pregnant with her. It had been his old friend, Magnus, who had sought him out with the Emperor's summons, having guessed where he was; Magnus had been with Vespasian, Corbulo and Centurion Faustus when they had been captured by the Caenii forty years previously. A pendant that Caenis had given Vespasian had saved their lives just before the four of them were due to fight to the death; the chieftain of the Caenii, Coronus, Caenis' uncle, had recognised it as the emblem of his tribe. Upon their release, Vespasian had promised to, one day, reunite Caenis with her people.

Vespasian had known that if he did not obey Nero's order to return then he would be forever an exile and always on the lookout for the executioner that the Emperor would, inevitably, send. But one man's reprieve is another man's downfall as Vespasian found out when, having been forgiven, Nero charged him with suppressing the growing uprising in Judaea and to meet with Corbulo in Corinth on his way to the province. Vespasian had assumed that the orders that he carried from the Emperor for his old acquaintance were for the great general to brief him on the finer points of eastern politics and dealing with rebel guerrillas. It was not so: Corbulo had committed suicide there and then, in compliance with the imperial command and had died at Vespasian's feet.

It had been a salutary lesson in the workings of the imperial mind and it had left Vespasian in a dilemma: do too well in Judaea and he would attract the Emperor's jealousy and, most likely, be obliged to suffer the fate of Corbulo; do too badly and, if he was spared execution or enforced suicide, then a fate worse than death awaited: humiliation and the disapprobation of his peers. Either way, the rise of the Flavii, which he and his brother, Sabinus, had striven for throughout their careers, would certainly be put on hold if not terminated.

So how should he conduct this campaign now that it was about to commence? He cursed, inwardly, the cowardly, unmartial nature of the Emperor who craved military success but, fearing to attain it himself, punished those who procured it for him. He was the first Emperor never to have led an army in battle; granted, his great-uncle and adoptive father, Claudius, had only nominally led an army during his lightning visit to Britannia in the first months of the invasion, but this had been enough to secure him a Triumph with a certain degree of legitimacy. His Uncle Gaius Caligula's minor excursion into Germania Magna was still far more than Nero had achieved militarily and Caligula's mighty defeat of the god Neptune on the shores of the northern sea had earned him, too, a Triumph – although this had been more a private joke on Caligula's part as he had forced his legions to attack the sea after they had refused to embark on ships for the invasion of Britannia; he had much enjoyed the looks on the faces of the Senate as he had paraded scores of wagons full of seashells through Rome. Nero's own Triumph had been when he returned from Greece with his one thousand eight hundred victor's crowns; he would not want anyone to overshadow that. And yet if Vespasian were to crush the revolt with anything like the alacrity that was required then he would put himself in serious danger from the man who considered himself to be the only person of consequence in the entire world.

It seemed, therefore, to Vespasian that he had three viable choices and none of them were a guarantee of safety. He could do his duty to Rome and risk the wrath of the Emperor. He could deliberately fail and let the province erupt into violence and then slip from Rome's grasp and trust that his punishment would not be too severe. Or he could ... but, no, he did not want to dwell on that; he did not want to contemplate just what else he could do with the army that the Emperor had let fall into his hands.

And now here he was at the point of decision. He drew a breath and looked at Titus. 'To fail on purpose would get the family nowhere. Therefore, we must succeed and pray to our guardian god, Mars, that the situation in Rome will change and success is no longer rewarded by death.'

Titus frowned. 'What are you talking about, Father?'

'I'm saying that I've made a decision: we're going to prosecute this war ruthlessly and crush the rebellion as quickly as possible and then figure out how to proceed once we're victorious because I'll not be so compliant as Corbulo.'

'You mean you would defy the Emperor.'

'Someone at some stage has to. I'd prefer it not to be me but if it comes to the choice of certain death by suicide as the reward for good service or ... well, let's put it this way: whatever happens I shall not be choosing the first alternative.' He turned to the party of staff officers awaiting orders a short distance behind him. 'Gentlemen, the auxiliaries will handle this. Prefects Virdius and Gellianus, your two cohorts should be sufficient to take the walls supported by Petro's archers. I want no mercy shown; utter destruction. Kill everyone in the town over the age of five, with the exception of their leader, Yohanan – I want him alive; the rest can be sold as slaves as they'll be too young to remember and desire vengeance. See to it.'

'Always one with the eye to a profit,' his companion, who had been sitting in silence next to him, muttered. 'It would have been a terrible shame not to have got anything from the town. Not that babes fetch much, as the purchaser is obliged to invest quite a bit feeding them up so as they can stand on their own two feet, if you take my meaning?'

'And there was me thinking you had dozed off, Magnus; having your old man's morning nap. I'd been very much looking forward to the thud you would have made as you slipped from the saddle.'

Magnus scratched at the grey stubble swathing the lower half of his battered, ex-boxer's face and regarded Vespasian with his one good eye from beneath the wide brim of his leather sun hat – the glass replica in his left socket worked to its own agenda. 'No, I was very much awake, sir; I was just enjoying watching you come to a decision. It was like watching a Vestal take it up the arse for the first time whilst trying not to scream: all grimacing and grinding of teeth. I was almost surprised that your eyes didn't start watering with all that straining that seemed to be going on. I hope you haven't done any permanent damage.'

'Everything is just fine, thank you, Magnus; that truss you gave me last Saturnalia is holding up a treat.'

Cornua, the large G-shaped horns used for signalling on the battlefield, began their low rumblings as three cohort standards dipped, centurions bellowed and the auxiliaries began to move forward to provide a spectacle for the rest of the army and to raze a town to the ground.

'By the way,' Magnus said as the archers of the fourth Syrian auxiliary cohort commenced clearing the walls of defenders so that their comrades could more safely attempt an escalade, 'it's the right decision. Who knows what will happen in Rome whilst you try to sort this mess out.'

Vespasian nodded with approval as he watched the first Augustan cohort approach the town in centuries formed into testudo with the ladder-men in their midst; arrows hissed over their heads and the walls remained clear of defenders. 'Yes, well, I'm sure that my brother will keep us well informed; in the meantime, all I know is that I'm going to show these Jews just what it means to rebel against Rome. They're going to find out exactly what war is.'

Pity was not an emotion in which Vespasian could afford to indulge. As he, Titus and Magnus surveyed the smouldering ruins of Gabara and the hundreds of dead within, some no more than charred husks of humanity, he suppressed all feelings of compassion for the women and children who had been massacred alongside their menfolk. 'None of them were innocent,' he said, looking down at the tangle of corpses of both sexes and all ages, each with their throats cut, having been methodically executed. He nudged the head of a young girl with his toe, turning her face towards him to stare up with sightless, pale blue eyes. 'Had

Yohanan ben Levi seen sense and opened the gates to us I would have been lenient with them and this child would still be alive. But this is the message that we have to send to every town that contemplates defying us.'

'And if every town does?' Magnus asked, kicking a bloodied slingshot lying next to a dead auxiliary with a vicious dent in his shattered forehead.

'Then there will be very few people left to govern in Judaea,' Titus said, 'but it won't come to that. Sepphoris, twelve miles south of here on the other side of Jotapata, has already sent a delegation pledging their loyalty and we've sent a garrison there to help them remember their promise.'

'Ah, well, that's all right then; at least the procurator will have a few people left to tax extortionately.' Magnus retrieved a discarded leather sling and examined it. 'I think that was how this all started in the first place, wasn't it? Or was it just us being too nice to them for a change?'

Vespasian frowned at his friend in confusion. 'What are you suddenly taking their side for? I've never thought of you as the champion of the Jews, or any other race for that matter.'

'I ain't; it's number one who I look out for as you know and I've no wish to be the victim of a nasty piece of leather like this,' Magnus said, throwing the sling over his shoulder. 'My point is that because the last couple of procurators, no doubt both about as pompous as an arsehole can get, pushed these people into revolt, it resulted in six thousand of our lads getting theirs at Beth Horon because the pompous arsehole in command forgot to send out scouts to spring any ambushes. All I'm saying is that whilst people of your class come to shitholes like this to grub out every last sesterce from the local population that they can, it's the lads from my class who have to pay with their blood to sort it out.' He pointed to the dead auxiliary. 'Matey-boy here being a case in point, even though he weren't a citizen. Now, I understand that when you join the army you've got a good chance of ending up dead but that minor detail don't stop people from signing up. But there's ending up dead and then there's ending up dead unnecessarily, and I would say that ending up dead because some procurator wanted to have a few more golden goblets than his neighbour on his dining table is unnecessary. That's all; I'm just saying.'

'Yes, well, stop just saying,' Vespasian snapped. 'I don't like it any more than you do, but that's the way it is and there's nothing that you or I can do about it.' He turned to his son. 'Titus, have the dead counted; I want their exact number publicised. We'll make camp here today, fully fortified. Our next move is to see how the people of Jotapata intend to welcome us.'

'With open arms, hopefully, once word gets to them about what happened here.'

'Not if Yosef has his way with them. Send out a cavalry ala to ride to within view of the town to take a look and bring in any prisoners they can find. How many agents do you have in there?'

'Three reliable ones and two others that I know for sure are double agents. We may be able to put them to some use.'

'I'm sure we will. Have all the legionary legates and auxiliary prefects assembled in my tent an hour before sundown.'

'Here are the rest of the reports to have come in, sir,' Lutatius, one of the young, thin-stripe military tribunes attached to Vespasian's staff, said, depositing a dozen or so wax tablets on Vespasian's desk in the *praetorium*, the command post, for perusal. 'The only one outstanding is the Second Cappadocian Cavalry ala which was sent out scouting towards Jotapata.'

Vespasian rubbed his temples as he contemplated the pile before him. 'Is there any word from the prefect of the camp on how the fortifications are doing?'

'Prefect Fonteius sent a report saying that five miles of ditch have been completed and he is just waiting for the Fifth Macedonica to complete their last mile stretch.'

'The Fifth again, eh? They were last to finish yesterday; they seem to be making a bad habit of it. Thank you, Lutatius, you can go, but bring me the prefect of the Second Cappadocia as soon as he's back.'

With a smart salute, the young lad turned and marched from the room, if, that was, it could be called a room, being a curtained-off area within the huge tent that served as the headquarters of the army. Vespasian picked up the first of the tablets and studied its contents: a dry list of the battle-effectiveness of the X Fretensis, broken down cohort by cohort: number of sick or wounded, number on secondment, number on leave, number on garrison duty and other dull details. Methodically he made his way through the pile.

'Why do you bother with such trivialities, my love?' Caenis said, standing in the doorway as he put down the final tablet.

Vespasian glanced up; by her stillness and the way she was cradling a crystal glass of fruit juice in both hands, he guessed that she had been standing there watching him for some time. 'It helps me sleep.'

She returned his smile; her eyes, sapphire blue, glinted in the lamplight, as vivacious and beautiful as the day he had first looked into them just outside Rome forty-one years ago. Then she had been the slave and secretary to the Lady Antonia, who was sister-in-law to Tiberius, the mother of Claudius, the grandmother of Caligula and the great-grandmother of the present Emperor; now Caenis was a freedwoman and rich in her own right having spent her life navigating the politics of the Palatine. She moved across the room towards him. 'Sometimes I think you try to be too diligent a general.'

'Maybe so; but I believe that it's better to have too many facts than too few. Something I'm sure you can appreciate.'

'When it comes to your opponents in politics, yes; but when it comes to how many men in the ninth century of the fourth cohort have diarrhoea, then I beg to differ.'

Vespasian picked up the first report he had read and scanned it. 'Four, actually; at least there are four off sick but whether they're lucky enough to have just a bout of diarrhoea or something really disgusting that seems to be all the rage here, I don't know. But what I do know from this whole list is that the Tenth Fretensis have an effective number of three thousand six hundred and ninety-eight, almost a quarter under strength, and, as we progress through the campaign, that will only get worse, not better. Now, I'd say that was a piece of information that a good general should take care to know.'

Caenis stood over him and stroked his cheek. 'Point taken.' She bent down to kiss him on the forehead. 'Now *I* have an interesting piece of information for you that will take your mind off the diarrhoea sufferers of the fourth cohort's ninth century.'

Vespasian was immediately interested; he knew from having shared his adult life with Caenis, even when his wife, Flavia, had been alive, just how good she was at procuring information. Caenis had not survived for so long in the mire of imperial politics without the ability to winkle out interesting facts, through her Empire-wide network of informants and correspondents, and then be able to store them in her vast memory until they became pertinent. He placed the X Fretensis report back down on the desk. 'Go on.'

'Gaius Julius Vindex.'

Vespasian was at a loss. 'What of him?'

'He's of Gallic descent from Aquitania and is currently Governor of Gallia Lugdunensis.'

'Good for him.'

'Yes; very fortunate. It's a rich province and also has the imperial mint in Lugdunum. I'm sure he's doing very well for himself there, which makes it rather strange that one of my people should have intercepted and copied this letter.' She put down her glass and pulled a scroll from within her palla. 'It's written to Servius Sulpicius Galba.'

'The Governor of Hispania Tarraconensis.'

'Quite so. In it, in a rather roundabout way, Vindex is asking if Galba is happy with the way things are and implies that he is not.'

Vespasian shrugged. 'I'm sure if you ask most governors or senators if they are happy with the way Nero behaves the answer would be that they are not.'

'Yes, but would they go so far as to suggest an alternative from outside the imperial family?'

'Outside the Julio-Claudians?'

'Yes; Vindex hints to Galba that if he were to have any aspirations in that direction he could expect his support; although he didn't put it as bluntly as that. But what you have to remember is that when Claudius died there were more than a few whispers that it would be better to have a man of experience wearing the Purple rather than an effete youth of seventeen and I heard Galba's name muttered a number of times. I also heard that he did discuss the matter with his close associates and decided that it would not be the honourable thing to do; and honour is, as you know, everything for a man such as Galba who prides himself in his lineage.'

'Well, the Sulpicii are one of Rome's oldest families.'

'And, therefore, steeped in the traditions of the old ways; which is why, what with Nero behaving with such little regard for Galba's cherished old ways, I think Vindex might have found a sympathetic ear. I think that this may be the start and I couldn't think of a better place for it to begin, from our point of view, than almost as far away from us as it is possible to get.'

'What do you mean "from our point of view"?'

Caenis gave an exaggerated version of the look of a teacher who cannot believe the obtuseness of her charge. 'Do you think that everyone will think that Galba is a better choice than themselves?'

'Of course not; it'll spark the most violent jealousies.'

'But what will most people with a degree of intelligence realise?'

Vespasian was baffled and did not attempt to conceal it.

Caenis' teacher's look deepened. 'How old is Galba?'

Now Vespasian understood. 'Ahh! Well into his seventies, and, I think I'm right in saying, childless.'

'Well done, my love; I can see that the diarrhoea sufferers of the ninth century haven't completely monopolised your mind – quite yet. So aspirants to the Purple will have to judge whether to fight Galba or court him in the hope that he will adopt them and make them his heir.'

Vespasian tapped his fingers on the desk as he absorbed and played through this scenario. 'Whatever happens, there'll be war; it's unavoidable, isn't it?'

'That's my assessment too. Galba may take the Purple, but he won't last long; civil war will be inevitable either to get rid of him or between his nominated heir and someone who thought that it should have been them. But civil wars can't be fought without the legions; and you, my love ...' She left the sentence dangling.

'Have legions; in fact I have my own army. It makes you think, doesn't it?'

Caenis placed her hand on Vespasian's neck as she sat on his lap. 'It certainly does.'

'And you're right: the West is the best place for civil war as far as we're concerned. Let them slug it out for a while. Galba has his single Hispanic legion and will therefore have to get the support of the Rhenus legions or the Danuvius ones to make his bid for empire.'

Caenis pointed to the copied letter. 'Vindex hints that he is already in contact with the incoming Governor of Germania Inferior, but doesn't mention a name.'

Vespasian looked at her expectantly.

'Of course I know. Nero appointed Gaius Fonteius Capito; he should have already arrived in the province.'

'And Germania Superior?'

'That's different; Lucius Verginius Rufus would be unlikely to countenance a rebellion.'

'But would he counter one?'

'That remains to be seen.'

'Then there's a possibility of civil war already. And that's before we even think about the Danuvian legions in Noricum, Pannonia and Moesia.'

'I'm sure they'll all want to have their say and promote their own champion. You do well here and, who knows, but the diarrhoea sufferers of the ninth century and all their friends might think that they should also have a say in the matter.'

Vespasian cupped his mistress's face in his hands and kissed her full on the mouth, feeling a stirring in his loins as he did so. 'You, my love, talk a very dangerous game; treasonous, even.'

Caenis kissed him back. 'Then you had better not tell anyone, had you?'

A cough from the doorway interrupted Vespasian as he went to return the kiss with interest; he looked up. 'What is it, Hormus? Can't you see I'm busy?'

'I'm sorry, master,' his freedman replied. 'Titus sent me to tell you that the officers are assembling.'

'Thank you for coming, gentlemen,' Vespasian said, quite unnecessarily, as he stepped into the area of the praetorium housing the Eagles of the three legions present and the images of the Emperor, surrounded by an honour-guard, that was used for briefings; no one would ignore a summons from the commanding officer.

'All present, sir, apart from Prefect Calenus of the Second Cappadocian,' Titus barked in fine military fashion. 'I've left orders for him to report straight here as soon as he gets back.'

Vespasian acknowledged this with a curt nod before turning his attention to his prefect of the camp for the whole army, Fonteius. 'Well? Are the defences complete yet?'

Fonteius snatched a quick glance of disgust towards the legate of the V Macedonica. 'No, sir; the Fifth still had a couple of hundred paces to go when I left to come here.'

'What's the delay, Vettulenus?' Vespasian asked the legate. 'That's the second day in a row that your legion has been last, by a long way, in completing its share of the defences.'

Sextus Vettulenus Cerialis squared his shoulders. 'There's no excuse, sir. I'll have Primus Pilus Barea kick a few arses.'

'If I were you I'd order him to kick every arse in the fucking legion, including his own and yours, come to that! Otherwise he won't be a primus pilus any longer in my army.' He pointed to Marcus Ulpius Traianus, the legate of the X Fretensis. 'Traianus' legion is at three-quarters strength and it can still do its share faster than the Fifth; perhaps it's because they spend more time with shovels in their hands rather than their centurions' cocks!'

'It won't happen again, sir.'

Vespasian allowed himself a few moments glaring at the man. 'Good, Vettulenus, see that it doesn't.' He looked around the room full of the legates of the three legions, the prefects of the auxiliary cohorts and the commanders of the contingents donated by local client kings as well as his own personal staff. 'I will not have slackness on this campaign; every one of you will get the maximum amount of effort out of each one of your men at all times, even when they're taking a shit. A soldier with too much time on his hands becomes ill-disciplined and a menace to his comrades and a threat to morale and the cohesion of his century. I'll not have it in my army; do I make myself clear?'

Everyone in the briefing understood the point perfectly.

Vespasian deflated his chest and allowed his countenance to mellow. 'So, gentlemen, to business. That was a good start, this afternoon; my congratulations on the showing of your men, Prefects Virdius and Gellianus. Over the wall and the town taken in less than an hour with only thirty-three dead and one hundred and twenty-five wounded between you; excellent work. Please pass on my congratulations to your officers.'

The two prefects stiffened to attention, their expressions full of pride.

'What news of Yohanan ben Levi?' Vespasian asked Titus.

'Not good, sir. It seems that he wasn't amongst the dead; I've had every corpse examined. Somehow, and I don't know how yet, he got out of the town just before it fell.'

Vespasian slammed his fist into his palm. 'That's not good enough. We can kill as many of these people as we like and it won't make a scrap of difference if their fanatical leaders get away and take their poison to another town. They're the cause of this, not the average carpenter or shepherd. It's the minority of religious fundamentalists; kill them and the problem solves itself.'

'I've got patrols out scouring the country for Yohanan, sir; I hope we shall strike lucky.'

'I hope so too, but somehow I doubt it; any man who can get out of an encircled town just as it's falling is unlikely to let himself be caught out in the open.' Vespasian glared at his son for a few moments before turning to Petro. 'Your archers were exemplary, prefect; they saved a lot of our lads' lives by keeping the battlements so clear with very accurate shooting. Only one dead and he was shot from behind by one of your own men, you said in your report; how was that?'

'It was a feud; I've had the murderer executed. The idiot tried to make out it was an accident and it was a tragedy that he'd shot his own centurion.'

Vespasian rubbed his chin. 'Have that century excluded from the camp for ten nights to encourage others to keep an eye on their comrades to ensure that things like that don't get so out of hand.'

'Yes, sir.'

'Titus, make sure the whole army knows what happened and what the consequences were to the man's century. I will not have soldiers with a grievance killing their officers; every man in every century is responsible for his unit's morale and feuds like that need to be reported and stopped before they go too far.'

Titus nodded and made a note on a wax tablet.

'Jotapata, gentlemen,' Vespasian said, changing the subject and turning to a map pinned to a board behind him. He pointed to a place halfway between the coastline and an inland lake. 'We're here outside Gabara.' His finger moved southwards. 'This is Sepphoris, which has declared for us and accepted a garrison.' His finger went north to a point between Gabara and Sepphoris. 'And this is Jotapata; without it and the much smaller Japhra just to the east of Sepphoris, we cannot move forward to Tiberias, here on the Sea of Galilee,' he indicated to the inland lake, 'without our supply line to Ptolemais on the coast being threatened. Once we have Tiberias then Galilee is ours and we can concentrate our efforts south into Judaea itself advancing down the Jordan. So, as you can see, Jotapata is strategically vital. Having received no communication from the town elders I have to assume that it is hostile and will need to be taken by force; the Second Cappadocia are having a look at it as we speak. Now, the road there is almost non-existent, no more than a track; so at dawn tomorrow, Vetullenus, send the three most deserving of your cohorts ahead to level it enough for us to be able to get our siege train along. I think that might help with your legion's lack of enthusiasm for manual labour and give your admirable primus pilus an ideal opportunity for the kicking of arses.'

Vetullenus grinned. 'A perfect opportunity for him and me, sir.'

'Good. Traianus, I want you to take the Tenth and your auxiliaries and put on a show of strength at Sepphoris just to remind them who's in charge and then move on to Japhra; take it and destroy it if it doesn't open its gates to you. You may keep the women and children to sell, if you wish.'

'Very good, sir; we'll move at first light.'

'Sir?' came a voice from the door.

Vespasian turned to see Tribune Lutatius. 'What is it, Lutatius?'

'The Second Cappadocia has just come back in.'

'Well, tell the prefect to report to me at once.'

'He can't, sir; I'm afraid he's dead, as are over forty of his men. They were ambushed on the way to Jotapata and were only just able to fight their way back.'

Vespasian looked around his assembled officers. 'Well, gentlemen, I think we have our answer; rather than our friendship, Jotapata has chosen total destruction.'

CHAPTER II

VESPASIAN HAD KNOWN that Jotapata was built on a high promontory but no amount of briefing by Titus' informants could have prepared him for just how precipitous it was. Three sides of the town fell away, almost sheer, into scrubland between fifty and a hundred feet below, making a concerted assault all but impossible whilst leaving it just about accessible to a determined climber. The northern approach was defended by a twenty-foot wall that ran across the lower slopes of the mount upon which Vespasian had built his camp overlooking the town and thereby, he hoped, overawing the populace with the size of his force.

It was shortly before dusk on the fifth day after the fall of Gabara as Vespasian and Titus stood, looking down on the town that was, despite whatever obstinate opposition it put up, doomed. It had to fall for if it did not, it would not yield up the prize that, once again, was believed to be within its walls.

'Here he comes,' Titus said, gesturing to a manacled Jew being escorted, without much consideration, by four legionaries commanded by an optio.

'Is this the one that first told us the news?' Vespasian asked, squinting as the westering sun hit the corner of his right eye.

'No, this is another one; we caught him just now trying to get through the ring that we set up as soon as we heard Yosef had arrived.'

Vespasian still could not quite believe his luck; it had taken four days for Vettulenus' men to level a road sufficient to allow passage for the great engines of war hauled by lumbering oxen. As soon as it was complete, Vespasian had sent two alae of horse under the command of Sextus Placidus, the thick-stripe military tribune of the V Macedonica, to seal off the town whilst Vespasian brought the main body of the army up behind. Placidus had interrogated the few deserters who preferred to chance their luck as prisoners rather than face a siege. It had been with amazement at the stupidity of the move that Vespasian had received the news that Yosef ben Matthias himself may have slipped into the town just before the cordon around it was completed. Stupidity or, perhaps, bravery, if it were true; for it sent a loud message, to both besiegers and besieged alike, that the leader of the rebellion in Galilee was prepared to sacrifice everything to keep Jotapata from the foe. The stakes may just have been raised and Vespasian was relishing it.

'Tell him to repeat what he told you earlier, optio,' Titus ordered as the prisoner was thrown into the dust before them.

The optio kicked the Jew to get his attention and then shouted at him in what Vespasian assumed was Aramaic, the local language.

The man stuttered out a reply from bleeding lips; his long hair, loose and matted, clung to the sweat dripping from his face as his gaze remained firmly on the ground.

'Well?' Titus asked as the prisoner fell silent.

The optio stood to attention. 'Sir! The prisoner says that the rebel Governor of Galilee, Yosef ben Matthias, is indeed within the walls organising the defence of Jotapata.'

Titus looked down at the man. 'And he's completely certain of this?'

The optio barked some more before the prisoner replied wearily.

'He is, sir! He says that Yosef's vanity would not let him be eclipsed by the likes of Yohanan ben Levi, the hero of Gabara.'

'The hero?' Vespasian said incredulously. 'That's an interesting way of looking at the man who presided over the deaths of thousands of his own people. Ask him why he chose to get out when Yosef arrived.'

'He has a blood-feud with Yosef's family,' the optio translated. 'He had little choice but to leave when Yosef arrived, otherwise he would have surely died.'

'Just as surely as he's going to die now,' Titus said.

Vespasian put his hand on his son's shoulder. 'Keep him alive; he knows the layout of the town.'

'I've got agents in there who can tell us that.'

'They're more help to us on the inside; we may have use of an assassin.' Vespasian contemplated the town for a few more moments. 'What do we know about their supplies, Titus?'

'The three agents whom I trust, in as much as you can trust anything that these people say, tell me that they have a good supply of grain but very little salt. There is no well in there and they have to rely on rainwater stored in a public cistern, and, as we know—'

'There has hardly been any rain since we arrived,' Vespasian cut in. 'So the level in their cistern must be getting low. What do your double agents say?'

'They say that there is plenty of everything and that they have just dug a well and could hold out for a year or more.'

'Really?' Vespasian looked down at the prisoner. 'What does he say? Ask him if there's a well in the town, optio, and how long he thinks that the supplies will hold out.'

'There isn't a well, sir!' the optio announced, having shouted at the man for a while before receiving a muted reply. 'Just the cistern, which is about half full. He doesn't think that they've got food and water for more than forty days, sir!'

'Forty days, eh? Well, let's hope it doesn't come to that. In forty days I'd like to be negotiating the surrender of Jerusalem, not sitting and rotting in front of this shithole waiting for them to drop down dead. Bollocks to forty days; we attack at first light. Titus, you can win yourself some glory here; no point in giving it all to the auxiliaries: I want your legion to attempt an escalade; let's see what these Jews have got.'

'Thank you, Hormus,' Vespasian said, handing back to his freedman four letters, newly dictated, that he had just signed, before taking a sip of wine.

'Who are you writing to, my love?' Caenis asked as she walked into Vespasian's study, smelling of rosewater, having somehow managed to have a bath.

'I'm surprised that you don't know, seeing as nothing seems to escape your notice.' He topped up his wine and poured Caenis a fresh one.

'Oh, so we're playing a game, are we?' She accepted the proffered cup and took a sip, thinking theatrically. 'Your brother, Sabinus, for one.'

Vespasian raised his drink to her as she sat on a leather couch next to his desk, her skin glowing soft and her raven hair full of lustre in the lamplight. 'Very good, but an easy guess.'

'You want him to make subtle enquiries as to the mood of the Praetorian Guard prefects.'

'I'm impressed.'

'It's what I would do. The second is to Herod Agrippa refusing his demand that he join you and personally take command of his troops.'

Vespasian inclined his head. 'How did you know?'

'Because you dislike him as much as you did his father and you don't trust his motives for wanting to join the campaign.'

'Yes, the slimy little shit is hoping that when the rebellion is put down Nero will make him King of Judaea like Claudius did his equally untrustworthy namesake of a father. I'll not have him boasting to Nero that he sent troops to help and led them in person, putting himself in some danger; I'd rather have him sitting and festering in Tyre as he's doing at the moment. I won't have him trying to steal any of my glory and raising his standing in the Emperor's eyes. It will be interesting to see if he accepts my refusal or writes again begging to come.'

'He might just come anyway.'

'He might, but I get the feeling that since he lost Tiberias to Yosef and his rebels, Herod Agrippa prefers to remain safe within the walls of Tyre. The letters are just for form's sake so he can say to Nero that he wanted to join the campaign but I wouldn't let him because of the enmity that has always existed between his family and mine. Third one?'

'Mucianus?'

'Oh, you are good. Yes, I felt that I should smooth over my relationship with the newly appointed Governor of Syria. We're old friends, he was my thick-stripe tribune in the Second Augusta for a while, you know.'

'I do.'

'Well, I've apologised to him for not consulting him more about the coming campaign and asking his advice and that sort of nonsense, which should flatter him back to being amenable towards me after his lack of co-operation in handing over the Fifth and Tenth to my command.'

'Very wise, my love; a friendly governor of Syria is far better than a hostile one. But I have to confess, I have no idea who the fourth letter is to.'

'Hah! So you're not a goddess after all, you are fallible. Well, it was to Tiberius Alexander.'

'The prefect of Egypt?'

'That's the one.'

'He could be useful to cultivate.'

'I don't need to cultivate him; he owes me his life.'

Caenis was intrigued.

'When Caligula sent me to Alexandria to bring him back Alexander's breastplate so that he could wear it as he rode over his ridiculous bridge across the Bay of Neapolis, tensions were very high between the Jews and the Greeks.'

'When are they not?'

'Quite. Well, I had some private business with his father, Alexander, the Alabarch of the Alexandrian Jews, and got to like him immensely. When the massacres started he appealed for my aid and I led a unit into the Jewish Quarter and got the Alabarch and most of his family out. They had already started to flay Tiberius alive, a fate that his mother died from, but I got there just in time and only a couple of strips of skin had been torn from his back. So, you see, he does owe me.'

Caenis' eyes widened. 'That is most fortuitous. He has two legions in his province.'

'Which is why I've just written to him to say hello and remind him, gently, of his debt.'

'You're serious about this, aren't you, my love?'

Vespasian shrugged and took another sip of wine. 'I don't

know yet; but what I do know is that it doesn't hurt to have people from whom you can call in favours.'

'So true.' Caenis placed her cup down upon a table and looked at him with invitation in her eyes. 'And now, Vespasian, I'm pretty sure that you owe me a couple of favours and so I'm calling at least one of them in.'

'You look tired,' Magnus commented as Vespasian stepped out into the chill, pre-dawn air; Castor and Pollux, Magnus' two fearsomely muscled hunting dogs, strained on their leashes as they tried to welcome Vespasian to the new day.

'Really? Well, I don't feel it,' Vespasian replied, scratching the dogs' heads as they slavered over his knees. 'In fact, I'm feeling great.'

'Ahh, I see: looking tired but feeling great; horizontal wrestling always has that effect.'

'I'm surprised you can remember.'

'Now, don't mock, sir; there's plenty of fight and fuck left in me, as I always say.'

Vespasian looked around at the shadowy forms of legionaries quietly making their way, in centuries, out of the camp to form up beyond the gates. 'So you do; I can only hope that you've had time to do the latter as it's now the former of those two activities that we have to concentrate on. Although, considering your advanced years and the fact that you are a civilian, I give you full permission to sit this out and observe from a safe distance whilst having a nice cup of warmed wine and some freshly baked bread.'

Magnus grinned. 'That's very kind of you; I shall make notes of the action for your benefit.'

Vespasian waved away the suggestion as he walked off towards his horse held by a slave. 'You can't write.'

'Mental ones, then,' Magnus called after him, tugging his dogs away up the hill.

'What are they doing?' Vespasian asked, aghast, as the first rays of the sun hit high, slow-moving cloud and the town walls began to emerge from the gloom and solidify into their daylight form.

'Waiting for us,' Titus replied, his face as surprised as his father's as they sat together on their mounts at the command post of the XV Apollinaris; thin-stripe tribunes, legionary cavalry messengers and a cornicern waited to relay their legate's and their general's orders. 'They heard us coming and they won't yield the walls unfought. I can see that Yosef is a cannier general than we have given him credit for; he's not going to be content just to sit behind his defences and point his hairy arse at us.'

Vespasian surveyed the silhouetted ranks of rebels lined up before the gates of Jotapata, just over half a mile away, with each flank secured by a sharp drop. 'There must be a good three thousand of them and they're armed and armoured with our captured equipment.'

'But they don't know how to fight like us, Father,' Titus said, watching two men and a woman, all manacled, being hauled out of the Jewish line. 'Hardly any Jews have signed up to serve in the auxiliaries because they refused to sacrifice to the Emperor.'

Vespasian watched as the prisoners were thrown to the ground; he turned to Titus who was shaking his head with regret. 'Are they who I think they are?'

'I'm afraid so; with those three dead there is no one left in the town who will get reliable information out.'

A semi-circle of a couple of dozen men formed around the condemned who knelt calling out to their god. The first stone hit the woman on the side of the jaw, crumpling her down; even at this distance, Vespasian clearly heard the impact. Her scream drowned out the cracking of the men's skulls as a barrage of rocks crashed into them; the executioners carried on hurling stones at the recumbent bodies long after they ceased to move.

'We're blind, now,' Titus said as the bodies were dragged away. 'I'll have the two double agents killed next time they make contact as they're of no use to me any more; and it will make me feel better.'

'Do that,' Vespasian said, studying the Jewish disposition. 'With the way they've positioned themselves numbers don't matter, as we can't outflank them. They're five or six deep so all they need to do is hold their line in a shoving match, but I won't give them one. Let's see how good their shield discipline is.'

'Release!'

The dull thuds of wooden arms thumping into padded, restraining uprights and the faint whistling of speeding projectiles ran down the line of the XV Apollinaris' field artillery; they were screened from the enemy by three cohorts, two centuries deep, in line and well out of bowshot from Jotapata. As the order was repeated from piece to piece, scores of stones and bolts accelerated away, rising over the heads of the legionaries and then dipping in an arc towards the Jewish position.

Shields were raised, but raggedly so, throughout the Jewish formation; the front rank went down on one knee as the second rankers made a roof over their heads that was added to by the rear ranks. But this was more guesswork than the result of months of repetitive training and Vespasian felt a surge of satisfaction as stone and bolt ripped through the rebel Jews, skittling away files in explosions of blood and shrieks of agony as the gaps in the shield wall made the construction porous.

But Yosef was not a general of little or no experience and, as the last bolt left its housing and hurtled towards the defenders of Jotapata, a roar rose from the rebels and they leapt forward up the hill in an impetuous charge of the desperate.

'Lower the trajectory!' Vespasian yelled at the tribune commanding the artillery line before looking apologetically at his son. 'Sorry, I won't interfere with your legion again.'

'I was just about to give the same order, Father.'

The legionaries working the catapults and ballistae sweated as, with rolling shoulders, they wound the ratchets to pull the torsioned arms of their machines back as the captains of each piece hammered out the wedges to lower the aim.

But many quickening heartbeats passed while the lengthy business of reloading took place. Vespasian could see that his opposite number had timed his charge well and his men, despite the hill, were gaining quickly on the Roman position.

'Prepare to receive!' Titus shouted down to his cornicern.

A rumble of four differing notes caused centurions to bellow commands and standards to dip and sway in the three cohorts forming the XV Apollinaris front. As one, the men of each of the front rank cohorts stamped forward their left legs, holding their shields firm before them whilst slinging back their right arms, javelin-like *pila* gripped in fists. A silence fell over them as they waited for the next order, oblivious to the hatred being howled by the host hurtling towards them.

And then the torsioned arms flung forward again; a hail of missiles shot over the Roman line and on towards the incoming storm. But the Jews had judged their charge with almost perfection and it was but a couple of the more sluggish of the rebels, struggling to keep up with their fellows at the back, whose heads disappeared in sprays of gore, their decapitated bodies running on a couple of paces before collapsing to bleed out in the dust.

On they came, underneath the artillery volley, screaming their rejection of the hated invaders of the land, strangely arrayed with captured Roman chainmail and *lorica segmentata* over their calf-length tunics or long robes, some with legionary or auxiliary helmets, shields and swords. None were attired exactly the same and all were bearded, giving the impression of a Roman cohort long isolated in some remote outpost and gone to seed.

It was with pride that Vespasian watched his eldest son, fist in the air, judge the pace of the charge; many times as a legionary legate he had been in the same position and he could appreciate the finesse that it took to get it absolutely right so that the maximum amount of damage could be inflicted. Down went Titus' arm and the cornu rumbled a command. With a delay of a couple of heartbeats as the centurions reacted to the sound, the pila volley was launched like a black mist rising from the regimented ranks of Rome to fall and enswathe the incoming charge. Down they went in their scores, pierced, broken and screaming, teeth bared and arms flailing, punched back by the weighted weapons raining down upon them with all the fury of a sudden hailstorm. But the Romans did not pause to admire their handiwork as they pushed their weight back onto their right legs, whipping their short stabbing swords from their sheaths on their right hips and bracing their left arms for the shocking impacts on their shields. With the precision that could only come from mindless repetition over years, the entire front rank pushed forward onto their left legs an instant before the charge hit home. Shield rims cracked up under chins and bosses thudded into midriffs as the legionaries of the leading centuries rammed their shoulders behind the boards to help absorb the collision; comrades behind pushed up against them and the shock rippled down the files. The line undulated and heaved, but it held.

It was with little delay that the teeth of Rome's legions began to rip and tear; flashing from between, above or below shields, the wicked points of gladii thrust into groin, belly and throat opening them to spill their contents over sandalled feet. Relentless was the work-pace of the blades as the Jewish charge compressed their own ranks so that their leading men did not have room to wield their weapons. Their roars of hatred rising from their battle cries turned into bellowed anguish as iron bit flesh and tore through muscle and sinew leaving gushing wounds and, for many, certain death. But still they pressed on, the rear ranks unaware of the carnage being visited upon their comrades ahead of them. Such was the fanaticism with which they prosecuted the charge and such was the desperation they felt, to a man, that it was inconceivable for them to withdraw so soon after contact; and so the teeth of Rome bit on and the blood of the Jews drained into their native soil, providing it with the first moisture that it had seen for a month. Slowly the stench of death ate its way back through the Jewish ranks and soon, for many, its reality became apparent in the slack limbs and lolling heads of corpses held upright by the press from both before and behind. Gradually the defenders of Jotapata realised that to stay was to die and to die that day would leave their wives and children open to the brutal treatment that was to be expected from the victors of a siege. With almost a common consent they turned and ran, pell-mell, back towards the gates that had stayed open to receive them.

It was with difficulty that the centurions bawled their men back into line to prevent them from an ill-disciplined and disordered chase of their retreating foe, but order did prevail and a strange silence fell over the Roman formation as weary soldiers tried to catch their breaths and marvel that they were still in one piece. The wounded were pulled from the ground and carried to the rear as the three front rank cohorts withdrew through the open files of the next line to present fresh, unbloodied troops to the enemy.

Titus shouted over to the tribune commanding the legion's artillery. 'Aim at the top of the walls! Keep it constant as we advance with each piece shooting as fast as it can, so that the defenders don't get a chance to read the rhythm and shoot back in the gaps between volleys.'

The tribune acknowledged the order as Vespasian called over a cavalry messenger. 'My compliments to Prefect Petro of the fourth Syrian auxiliary cohort. Ask him to bring his cohort to form a screen for the Fifteenth as they advance. He's to keep the walls clear of archers and slingers as he did at Gabara. He's to act upon the orders of the legate of the Fifteenth for the duration of the assault. Understand?'

The rider saluted. 'Yes, general!'

Vespasian squinted, trying, but failing, to make out the cohort insignia in the XV Apollinaris' front line. 'Who have you chosen?'

'The pioneer century of the first cohort,' Titus replied, 'because Primus Pilus Urbicus wouldn't have it any other way, and then the fifth and sixth cohorts who both have two pioneer centuries each. The pioneers will lead the escalade; ten ladders a century so fifty ladders in total. One for every fifteen paces of wall.'

'That should give them something to think about. If Petro and the artillery can keep the walls clear until the ladders are up, then this may go smoothly.' Vespasian clutched his thumb in his fist and spat to ward off the evil-eye, having said something that was so tempting to the baser sense of humour of some of the gods. 'Here comes Petro now.'

Father and son watched in silence as the bearded archers, mainly in eastern-style scale armour and conical helmets, double-timed in two dust-raising files across the frontage, left to right, of the fifth, first and then sixth cohorts of Titus' legion, each with their pioneer centuries, ladders aloft on shoulders, to the fore.

Once the skirmish cohort was in position, two ranks deep across the legion's frontage, Vespasian leant over and slapped his son on the shoulder. 'I'll leave you in peace to get on with this, Titus. Don't do anything silly like trying to be the first over the walls; leave that sort of heroics for Primus Pilus Urbicus.'

Titus retied the leather chinstraps of his high-plumed helmet, checking that it was thoroughly secure. 'Don't worry, Father; I've learnt that, for the smooth running of the legion, it doesn't do to upset a primus pilus by killing the enemy before he's had a chance to.' He flicked his red cloak back to reveal bronze breast- and backplates and then kicked his horse forward to lead the assault.

The sun was gaining in strength and Vespasian felt driblets of sweat run from beneath his helmet to catch in his russet linen neckerchief as he pushed his horse on up the hill to get a better overall view of the attack; his staff followed him. Below, the horns of the XV Apollinaris rumbled through the air as the legion's first line began to advance with its screen of auxiliary archers out in front. As Vespasian turned his mount about, a volley of bolts and rounded stones rose from the artillery; he followed their flight and grunted with approval as they slammed into the top of the wall or flew just over it, taking more than a few of the tiny figures lining the defences to a bloody and broken death at its feet.

Shading his eyes against the strengthening glare he could make out Titus, still mounted, riding at the extreme right of the first cohort next to its primus pilus centurion with his transverse plume marking his position. Vespasian sucked the air through his teeth and inwardly cursed his son for making himself so conspicuous but at the same time felt a surge of pride for Titus' bravery. He knew that had he been in the same situation he would be doing the same; indeed, he had done so on numerous occasions, so that the men under his command would follow more readily. But the thought did not stop him from feeling more concern for the fate of the legate of the XV Apollinaris than he would have had he been just another privileged Roman clawing his way up the Cursus Honorum. He chided himself for allowing such feelings to circulate around his head and swore that he would be more dispassionate in future; Titus must be allowed to win renown and the respect of his men and that was not going to be done sitting in a tent well behind the rear ranks of his legion.

In vocal silence the assault marched forward; no cries, no horns, just regular, military hobnailed footsteps, over two thousand of them, accompanied by the chinking of as many sets of equipment. Another volley whistled towards the walls, this time more ragged as the artillery pieces vied with each other to release first. The second line of the legion, the four cohorts as yet uncommitted, formed up in square blocks, stood their ground so that the gap between them and their advancing comrades widened. Behind them the three cohorts already blooded that morning waited, at ease, supping from their canteens and watching their brethren's advance as the rest of the army, drawn up outside the camp, higher up the hill, looked on with relish at the spectacle now unfolding.

A single horn rumbled long and low and eight hundred bows were raised; but the Syrian archers did not break step. Two hundred paces out, their volley erupted from them, clattering into the walls and beyond, clearing the last of the visible defenders, shortly followed by a second and then a third and then more, all released on the march so that there would be no loss of momentum in the assault. On the cohorts pressed, raising dust so that soon the air about them became opaque and the individual legionaries were lost in the blur of their unit's formation. However, Titus remained discernible and Vespasian tried to stop his eye continually seeking him out.

One hundred paces to go and the artillery and archers kept up a relentless barrage of projectiles; if any shots were returned,

Vespasian did not notice them, nor were any casualties left lying in the wake of the cohorts whose shields were now up.

Fifty paces out and a few heads began to bob up from behind the walls, slings whirling above them; some managed a release, others were punched back never to reappear, but the damage they inflicted was negligible on the archers and non-existent on the cohorts.

Twenty paces to go and, at the rumble of many cornua, the auxiliaries turned and swarmed back through the legionaries' formation. Gaps opened between the centuries in each cohort to ensure that this was not a disordering process. The artillery continued to pepper the summit of the wall but, with the sustained influx of arrows now gone, more defenders braved the chance of releasing a slingshot, arrow or javelin at the enemy now arriving at the base of their defences.

Up and over in arcs swept the ladders of the pioneers as their comrades hurled their pila aloft at the many faces now raining down projectiles and abuse upon them. The tops of the ladders crashed against the wall and the artillery was forced to cease for fear of hitting their own. Vespasian held his breath as he saw the transverse plumed helmet of the senior centurion of the legion rise first, his legs powering him up; to either side the first cohort's pioneers flowed up their ladders, shields and swords in hand, adding much difficulty to the ascent, as they braved the missiles now pouring down on them with growing ferocity. Conspicuous to all, Titus, his horse rearing, held his sword on high, waving it in circles and bellowing his men up the ladders. On they went, the pioneers of the XV Apollinaris, one straight after the other, swarming upwards as all fifty ladders hit the walls; and it was but a few heartbeats thumping in Vespasian's ears before Urbicus' transverse plume crested the battlements. Vespasian's breath released in a long sigh as the primus pilus' ladder was flung back, pushed by a pole; the centurion and those following him jumped clear, landing Vespasian knew not where, but what could be certain was that their falls would have been broken by comrades below. The chaos mounted as more and more ladders were pushed back, the tops of walls being now infested with the defenders able to operate with relative impunity as there were very few supporting projectiles to threaten them, other than a few pila from those below who had not yet hurled theirs.

Vespasian's heart pounded faster as, to the left, three or four of the fifth cohort's ladders stayed in place long enough for more than a dozen men to scale the walls. Immediately they attracted a swarm of defenders coming at them from both sides, like flies to an exposed wound. The fight was obscured by the press of bodies around the centurion leading the party but more and more pioneers managed to scale the ladders as it progressed. Vespasian found himself digging his fingernails into the palms of his hands as he willed on the centurion and his men and then almost let out a wail as, one by one, the ladders were dislodged, leaving the Romans, already up there, stranded and easy prey for the defenders.

'It ain't looking so good,' Magnus said, walking up to stand next to Vespasian's mount as his dogs inspected a selection of the beast's recently released turds.

'That's not a helpful observation.' Vespasian did not take his concentration from the walls. 'But no, it's not looking like we're going to get over this time.'

As he spoke, piercing shrieks rose above the cacophonous din of battle, clear and brim-full of anguish, so that for a moment all seemed to pause in wonder that such pain could be expressed by the human voice.

'Fucking savages!' Magnus growled. 'What is it, oil or sand?'

Vespasian strained his eyes to see what was being poured from the iron cauldrons being emptied over the legionaries directly in front of the gate. 'I can't tell from here; but it's doing the trick.'

And it was: around the gate at least a dozen of the first cohort writhed in supra-heated agony, struggling to rip their segmented armour off, as their comrades retreated in the face of such a destructive weapon.

Vespasian could see Titus as he leapt from his horse and ran to the aid of the stricken men, calling on others to follow. 'Idiot!' he muttered under his breath, thinking that it was exactly this sort of action that would endear his son to his men and knowing that he too would have done the same. 'Hurry, Titus, hurry!'

As if in slow motion, Titus and a small band of legionaries braved the broiling rain and pulled the scalded men back towards the relative safety of the first cohort's front line now retreated, in a concave bulge, twenty paces from the gate. To either side, the fifth and sixth cohorts were making a second attempt at getting their ladders secure. Again, despite already suffering a reverse, the pioneers of the two flanking cohorts flung themselves up towards the summit, with shields over their heads, deflecting the missiles pummelling down on them. A bestial cry cut through the chaos; Titus' abandoned horse bucked and reared, shaking its head and bellowing shrill and long, before charging, with smoke issuing from charring flesh on its rump, towards its master.

Vespasian felt himself dodging to one side in his saddle in sympathy with his son as he jumped out of the way of the maddened beast thundering into the front rank of the first cohort. Cracking men aside and trampling under hoof those in its direct path, it continued its madness until a desperate thrust of a sword put it, rearing, out of its misery, crushing the wielder of the blade as it crashed to earth.

It was then that the gates opened, quicker than would have been thought possible for such a weight of wood and iron, and it was a plague of Furies that emerged. With nothing to lose, for it was all already lost should the sortie not drive the enemy off, the men of Jotapata stormed from their stronghold. At their head was a man Vespasian recognised: with oiled hair and long black beard, equally as well kept, and swathed in a black and white embroidered mantel, Yosef ben Matthias charged his already disordered enemy with all the wrath his jealous god reserved for those who threatened his people.

Out they swarmed, naturally forming a wedge with Yosef at the head, chainmailed and shielded and brandishing the spathae preferred by Rome's auxiliaries, both horse and foot. Down came his blade, slicing into the mob of legionaries still reeling from the rampant horse; blood sprayed from the neck of a hoary veteran just in front of Titus as more of the Jewish onslaught thundered into the disintegrating Roman formation, all intent on bloody slaughter whilst the main advantage of the invaders, cohesion, was absent.

'Get out of there, Titus, get out!' Vespasian found himself shouting and looked about in surprise. He turned to the cornicern awaiting orders behind him. 'Sound the withdrawal! Now!'

The instrument growled three repeated deep notes; its call was taken up by others in the XV Apollinaris.

Vespasian felt he was waiting far too long to see the result of his orders but eventually the fifth and sixth cohorts began to pull back from the walls and they and the flanks of the first cohort drew level with the embattled centre, thus straightening the frontage.

And now it was a fighting retreat, leaving the dead and the wounded behind for there was no energy left to be expended upon aiding one's comrades, so desperate was the situation. Step by step, Vespasian willed his men away from what had turned out to be a disastrous assault, all the while cursing himself for so blatantly tempting the caprice of the gods.

'There's only one way to remedy this, sir,' Magnus said as the trail of casualties thickened in the wake of the retreating cohorts.

'Yes, I know!' Vespasian snapped despite knowing that his friend was only proffering good advice.

'Then the sooner it's done the better.'

'Yes, I know!' Vespasian tried to calm himself as he still could see no sign of Titus; he consoled himself with the fact that there was no body on the ground with bronze cuirass and an extravagantly plumed helmet. 'I'll do it tomorrow.'

'It was sand, almost red-hot,' Titus said through gritted teeth as the surgeon stitched up a deep slice across the top of his right arm. He held out his left hand to Vespasian. 'Look!' The back of it was entirely covered with small round blisters. 'I was lucky that's the only place it caught me and then it just brushed my skin. Others got it down their necks and under their armour; one grain of it in the eye can blind; I know, I saw it happen and you should have heard the screams the men made.'

'I did,' Vespasian said, his voice subdued. 'All the way up here I heard them. So what happened the first time? They didn't start tipping the sand over you until you had already been repulsed once.'

Titus grimaced again with pain as the needle was pushed through raw flesh. 'There are more fighters in there than we thought. My sources must have severely underestimated the number of men Yosef brought with him. On top of that, each one is a fanatic and fights like two men. I'll tell you what, Father: we're not going to capture a single one of them alive. They've come here to keep the town or to die. There will be a lot of our blood spilt before this is over. I lost forty-three men today and some of them weren't dead when we were forced to abandon them.'

'What about your primus pilus?'

'It takes more than a little tumble from a ladder, a slash across the forehead and a close encounter with a maddened horse to stop Urbicus being ready to kick arse and kill; I got the impression from him that he thoroughly enjoyed his day. I lost two other centurions today, both from the first cohort; Urbicus is busy deciding which of the optios in the legion are unpleasant enough to get promotion. In the meantime, Father, what are we going to do? This is going to be tougher than we thought.'

'I know; so we're going to have to try even harder.'

'Harder! How much fucking harder do you think I could have tried today? Ow!' He jerked his arm away from the surgeon. 'Medusa's rancid arse, man; do you have to enjoy it so much?'

'I'm sorry, sir,' the surgeon muttered, retrieving his needle and taking a firm grip back on the arm. 'I'm almost done; or I could stop now and wait for the wound to become infected and then take the whole arm off, if you would prefer?'

'Just get on with it.' Titus winced as the surgeon plunged the needle back in. 'So how are we going to try harder, Father?'

'We attack again tomorrow and I shall lead it in person.'

Titus looked at his father, unable to keep the incredulity from his expression.

'It's called leadership, Titus! You showed a great deal of it today, and tomorrow it will be my turn. I shall be first over the wall.'

CHAPTER III

'Somehow news of our setback today will get about,' Vespasian said without any preamble as he strode into the evening gathering of his legates, prefects and other senior officers. 'And that sort of news will only incite more of the vermin into rebellion.' He paused whilst the assembled company grunted and mumbled their agreement with the assessment. 'Therefore, gentlemen, we need to bring this to a speedy conclusion. Legate Titus Flavius Vespasianus,' he said, addressing his son formally, 'I want you to march south out of the camp with your legion at dawn tomorrow in proper order of march, auxiliaries in the vanguard, trumpets blaring and all that sort of thing so that it looks like the army is on the move. Understood?'

Titus snapped to attention. 'Yes, sir!'

'Good. Now, it is vital that you're leaving at dawn: I want Yosef to see you marching away and I want you to pass within a hundred paces from the town's gate as you head south. I want him to think that we're all leaving so have your baggage loaded, your men with all their kit packed in their yokes, tents packed onto mules, everything that says the legion is going away. Is that clear?'

'Of course.'

'Vettulenus, I'll be with you and your legion; we'll be following the Fifteenth out and then, hopefully, we'll have a little surprise for our Jewish friends. Your legion will be ready for an assault and, all being well, by the time Yosef notices the difference in appearance between the two legions it'll be too late. Have the three cohorts best suited for the assault in the lead and then have all of your pioneer centuries interspersed throughout those cohorts and ready with ladders; but they're to keep them concealed. Carry them low. I want all your artillery pieces loaded onto carts, ready for action; cover them with sacking to disguise what they are.

'Prefect Petro, your archers are to come between the leading three cohorts and the rest of the Fifth. When the order to attack comes they will, once again, form a screen for Vettulenus' advance, keeping the walls clear along with the artillery mounted on the carts. And then, gentlemen, we go over the wall but this time I hope there will be less resistance because we shall have a diversion.'

Vespasian turned his attention to an older man swathed in black robes, sitting towards the rear of the gathering. 'King Malichus, are your Nabatean Arabs ready to play their part?'

Malichus smiled, betraying a set of gloss-white teeth in amongst a bush of a beard. 'I await your orders, general. I am much in your debt for your procuring me citizenship when I wished to appeal to Caesar to have the tax revenue of Damascus returned to my jurisdiction; the chance to repay that is welcome.'

'If you do what I require of you tomorrow then it will be me who shall be in your debt.'

Malichus rose and bowed, appreciating the courtesy.

'Your thousand horse shall lead the whole column out of the camp, riding south, as if all the Furies were after them; my hope is that this will make Yosef think that we are trying to catch a town by surprise and add credence to the fact that we seem to be leaving. You and your five thousand foot archers will follow them out at the trot and stay at the head of the column until you receive my signal; upon that you will peel off and take position at the southern side of the town. From there I want you to pump as many arrows over the walls as you have, as if you are covering an attempt to scale the cliffs.'

'Do you want my men to attempt to scale them? I have some excellent climbers amongst them.'

'No, the impression is all I need to create a diversion; but thank you for the offer, Malichus.'

The Nabatean king bowed again at the courtesy.

'Is that clear to everyone?'

Prefect Decius raised a hand.

'Yes, prefect?'

'What about the units that you haven't mentioned, sir?'

'I've no need of them tomorrow morning, so they may stay in the camp on make and mend until the assault is over and the town is ours. Then I'll probably leave an auxiliary cohort here to garrison the ruins as we move on to Tiberias.' He looked at Titus. 'Is there any news from Traianus on how he's doing at Japhra?'

'Nothing further than we had yesterday evening: the town has closed its gates and he's preparing an assault.'

Vespasian nodded. 'Very well, gentlemen; you have your orders. Reveille will be at the start of the eleventh hour of the night, two hours before dawn. I want everything ready to move the moment the sun breaks the eastern horizon.'

Vespasian dipped his face into the bowl of fresh water on a chest in his sleeping quarters, at the rear of the praetorium, spluttering as he did so and splashing the reviving liquid over the back of his neck. He opened his eyes and threw his head back, arcing droplets, glistening in the lamplight, behind him, before grabbing the towel laid next to the bowl and rubbing his face, wishing the tiredness away.

'You're as bad as one of Magnus' dogs, shaking water all over the place like that,' Caenis said, wiping drips from her arm. She was sitting in their campaign bed with her knees up and her arms clasped around them.

Vespasian turned to face her. 'I'm sorry, my love, I forgot you were there.'

'Thank you; it's nice to know just how important I am in your life.'

Vespasian did not react to the jibe but carried on drying himself.

'Are you going to tell me what's wrong?' Caenis asked after a few more moments of silence. 'You hardly said anything over dinner; in fact you've barely spoken a word to me since the attack faltered. Are you blaming yourself or someone else? Because either way you should stop acting like a child and sulking just because things didn't go right for you.'

Vespasian threw down the towel. 'Of course it's not that, Caenis; I've stormed enough strongholds in my time to know that they don't just roll over like a bitch on heat. This one is going to take some cracking.'

'So you think that getting yourself killed tomorrow will help?'

'I'm not going to get myself killed tomorrow! I'm going to lead my soldiers over a wall, that's all.'

'A wall that they failed to get over today; a wall that Titus almost got himself killed whilst attempting to take.'

'He was behaving like a reckless young fool! I was feeling sick just watching.'

'Ahh, so that's it, is it?' Caenis pointed at Vespasian. 'You've never watched your son in combat before and you didn't like it, did you? And what made it worse was that it was your orders that sent him to risk his life; so, to make up for that, you're going to risk yours even though you are thirty years older than him and half as fit.'

'I'm still fit; I thought I proved that to you last night. And yes! That is the problem: my judgement was swayed this afternoon because my boy was in danger and I don't like how that feels. I gave him the assault because I want him to win fame and glory without thinking about what the reality of that is. This is right at the beginning of the campaign, so does this mean that I will feel constricted, fearing to send my son into danger, or is it something that I'll just get used to and then never stop blaming myself for if my orders get him killed as they could have done today?'

Caenis patted the bed beside her, inviting him to sit next to her.

He paused and then sighed and complied.

Caenis took his hand. 'You have to do your duty to Rome just as Titus has to; and if that involves getting killed, then so be it. But what is not going to make things any easier for you or him during this campaign is if you make military decisions for personal reasons. So you just have to forget that Titus is your son when you issue orders because he won't thank you if he thinks that you are protecting him; that's not the way to win fame and glory. And then trying to get yourself killed as a way of saying sorry is just pathetic.'

'That's different, my love. I have to lead the assault tomorrow because the men must see that having failed to take the town once I'm not just going to sit behind the army and send more and more of them to their deaths against that wall, but I'm prepared to lead them over it myself. It's my responsibility to the men.'

Caenis' eyes glinted. 'And men who see you lead are more prepared to support you in other ventures?'

Vespasian shook his head in mock exasperation. 'Do you do nothing but plot and scheme?'

'Plenty of other things, as I think I proved last night; or were you too busy proving to me just how fit you still are to notice?'

It was the high-pitched warning notes of a *bucina*, the horn used for signals in the camp and on the march, which prevented Vespasian from essaying a repeat performance of his proof of fitness. He jumped from the bed and grabbed his tunic, threading his arms into the sleeves.

'What is it?' Caenis asked, seeing his urgency.

'We're under attack,' he replied as Hormus came rushing in with two body slaves bringing his armour.

'I didn't hear anything.'

Vespasian held a foot up for Hormus to lace on his sandals whilst holding his arms out wide so that his breast- and backplates could be attached. 'Nevertheless, that is what the call means and an attack doesn't have to be noisy. It's the quiet ones I fear most.'

'All of them, Petro?' Vespasian asked as they walked through the dead of the century of Syrian archers that had been excluded from the safety of the camp for allowing one of their own to shoot their centurion. Legionaries with torches guided their way whilst auxiliary horse and foot formed a perimeter to discourage a further sneak attack.

'I think so, sir,' the prefect replied, 'although we haven't conducted a full tally yet.'

Vespasian looked around the collection of ten eight-man tents, pitched as close to the camp as possible; there were no defences around them. 'What happened?'

Petro shrugged. 'I suppose the Jews must have crept up on the sentries, slit their throats and then set upon the men as they slept.'

'Well, that's the risk you run if you allow something to happen that disbars you from the security of the camp. I'm sorry for the loss of the men, Petro; but I can't help feeling that this is a good lesson to the whole army right at the beginning of the campaign. I will not tolerate indiscipline. Nevertheless, I'm sure the men will be only too willing to avenge their comrades in the morning.'

'I'm sure they will, sir. I for one will be looking for my share of Jewish blood. It's just a shame that there're seventy archers fewer to claim their shares.'

Malichus' cavalry, black-robed horsemen with curved swords, round shields and a fist-full of javelins, galloped away into the new morning with high-pitched ululations and much waving of weaponry. The foot archers followed, more of a rabble than a formation, the Nabatean Arabs evidently placing little importance on ranks and files or, indeed, jogging at the same pace.

But Vespasian was not going to judge the effectiveness of his diversionary troops by their appearance as he, Magnus and Titus sat on their horses outside the camp's southern gate watching Malichus ride towards them.

'Good morning, Vespasian,' the Nabatean king said, bringing his beautiful Arab stallion to a majestic halt.

'That is a beautiful animal,' Vespasian said in admiration. 'As beautiful as the team you gave me fifteen years ago.'

Malichus stroked his mount's neck with obvious affection. 'There are plenty more like him in my kingdom. How are my gifts?'

'They were the best team of their generation but they don't race any more; they're very active in the stud, though.'

A gleam came into Malichus' eye and his teeth sparkled in a grin. 'We're never too old for the stud, eh, my friend?' He leant over and slapped Vespasian on the thigh. 'I congratulate you on your woman; I admit that I saw her, although you Romans don't seem to cover your women as we do. Anyway, she is as beautiful as any one of my wives or concubines.'

'I shall tell her that you said so, Malichus.'

A look of horror passed over the king's face. 'For the love of all the gods do not do that, Vespasian; if it should reach the ears of my women that I complimented another woman's beauty the jealousy would be intolerable and I would hear of nothing else for months on end. Believe me, my friend, my life would not be worth living.' His face brightened. 'But come, we sit and talk of women when there is Jewish blood to spill.'

'Expect my signal within half an hour, Malichus,' Vespasian said as he noticed the first inquisitive heads poke over the walls of Jotapata, half a mile down the hill.

'I look forward to it. I will see you at the end of the day and we shall dine on Yosef's corpse.' With a flourish of his hand he spun his horse and rode off to take his place at the head of his archers.

'I hope he meant that we shall dine using Yosef's corpse as a table and not as an ingredient,' Magnus said as the first of the auxiliary cohorts marched with smart precision through the gate.

'We seem to be attracting the right sort of attention,' Vespasian observed, ignoring Magnus and gazing down the hill to the town. Malichus' Arabs were passing it by, now more than a couple of hundred paces from the gate, just out of bowshot. 'If I'm not mistaken, that is Yosef himself come to take a look at us.'

Titus grinned at his father. 'The sight of a retreating army should give him a nice feeling as he has his breakfast.'

'If he goes for the ruse, I'm sure it will. Now we just wait until the Fifth emerge.'

Titus squeezed Vespasian's forearm. 'Good luck, Father. I'll go and rejoin my legion now.'

'I'll be fine, Son. As soon as you hear the fight commence you can turn your legion round and bring it back to the camp; with luck you'll ... no, I won't say it. I tempted the gods with an incautious remark yesterday, I'll not do the same today.'

*

The final elements of the XV Apollinaris paraded through the gate, mules loaded with tents and legionaries weighed down with their full kit hanging in bags slung on the yokes they carried on their shoulders: the image of a legion on the move.

Vespasian kicked his mount forward, leaving Magnus muttering about climbing ladders at his age, and swung in beside Vettulenus, the head of the V Macedonica. Casting a look behind he saw with satisfaction that the leading cohort was, indeed, ready for action. Pila instead of yokes slanted over their shoulders and within their formation pioneer centuries concealed their ladders held low by their thighs.

'Ride ahead and give Malichus the signal,' Vespasian ordered one of the messengers accompanying him. He watched the legionary cavalryman race off towards the Arabs, who were now a mile away below the town, and then turned to Vettulenus, saying: 'This will take careful timing.'

It was as the Arabs began to stream from their path and head for the southern wall of Jotapata that Vespasian saw urgent movement on the defences as Yosef and his comrades, just a couple of hundred paces away, ran along the northern wall following the path of Malichus' archers.

'Now!' Vespasian said to Vettulenus who immediately gave the order to the cornicern striding next to him. Four rising notes sounded over the column to be repeated by musicians further down the formation. The effect was immediate: centurions bellowed and standards dipped and pointed towards the town as, from further down the column, the archers of the fourth Syrian double-timed along the leading three cohorts as they formed a line, eight men deep, facing the northern wall. Behind them mule carts bearing the legion's carroballistae, still covered in blankets, trotted forward, positioning themselves at the centre of the assault force before turning their aim to the walls. The blankets were ripped off and the crews jumped up to their weapons and furiously worked the ratchets.

'Forward!' Vespasian ordered as the Syrian archers completed their screen. The low notes rumbled, the order was relayed and, in silence, the three cohorts of the V Macedonica moved forward, at a jog, behind the archer screen. The thumps of artillery release and the whoosh of projectiles passing overhead gave more of a sense of urgency to each man in the attack and the pace increased as if by mutual consent. At a hundred paces out the Syrians let fly their first volley but, as yet, there was no one on the walls, which gave Vespasian the hope that they might reach them without serious setback.

On they went under the cover of carroballista projectiles and Syrian arrows. Vespasian held his excited horse back as he trotted in front of the central cohort next to Vettulenus, willing the defenders to keep their attention on Malichus' Arabs on the south side of the town. With fifty paces to go Vespasian muttered a prayer to his guardian god, Mars, to hold his hands over him in the coming engagement and to blind the Jews to the attack. At twenty paces out the Syrians loosed their last volley and turned to filter through the legionary files; ladders came to the fore and Vespasian's heartbeat quickened as a few defenders appeared on the walls and slingshot flew. He swung his leg over the rump of his horse and jumped to the ground as the pioneers rushed to the base of the walls arcing their ladders up.

The first one in place was going to be Vespasian's; no one was going to stop him. Pushing aside the pioneer erecting it, he set his foot on the second rung and began to climb, shield over his head and bellowing over his shoulder to those behind him. 'With me, lads! I was storming forts when you were sucking on your mothers' tits.'

Up he went, rung after rung, hauling himself up with one hand as his shield arm, held rigid above him, braced against the crack and thump of mighty impacts; stones, javelins, roof-tiles and slingshot rained down upon him, slowing his progress the higher he reached as the deadly hail thickened. A judder ran through the ladder and he felt it being pushed away from the wall. He glanced down; the next man was a few rungs below him and then the man after that had only just started to climb.

'Hurry, man, we need more weight on the ladder!' He doubled his efforts to push himself up another couple of rungs as the men below him came as close as they could, making room for another couple to add their weight to the ladder, which crashed back down against the wall, too heavy to be easily dislodged. A thrust of a spear jabbing against his shield told Vespasian that he was in range of hand-held weapons and therefore nearly at the summit; now came the hard part. Letting go of the ladder with his sword arm he pulled his gladius from its sheath and pumped his legs, one two, one two, hurling himself upwards as he punched his shield, repeatedly, blindly, to clear a way ahead. The lip of the wall came in view under his shield, he was there; he cracked his shield rim at the throat of the first defender who came into focus and worked his legs, taking care not to overbalance backwards. With a lightning thrust he sent the tip of his blade into the eye of the man replacing the defender with the crushed throat. On he climbed as, to the left and right of him, two centurions were also making the same hazardous transition from ladder to wall. With a final leap, he landed on the battlements, a spear narrowly missing his left calf; he jammed his shield on it to prevent it from being pushed up into his groin, which, as he looked down on the hate-filled, bearded faces below him on the three-pace-wide walkway, was feeling very exposed. He knew from past experience that there was only one viable alternative to standing on the wall to be a target for, and eventually succumb to, many spear thrusts: so he jumped. Shield and sword exploding out to either side, the boss breaking a skull, the blade cleaving into a jaw as he kicked the man directly before him in the chest to send him toppling back, arms windmilling as he teetered on the brink, before gravity got the better of him and he plunged onto his comrades, below, awaiting their turn on the ramparts.

Vespasian was up and he was exposed and now only fury could be his friend and keep him safe; and fury came willingly to him as only an old friend can. His blade leapt left and right, a blur of fluid motion, rending blood-spurting flesh, piercing organs and severing limbs as a roar, primeval and brutal, erupted from that deep part within him that was only ever exposed in the extreme danger and joy of battle. On he pressed, gore-slimed and howling, a thing barely recognisable as human, as he strove to link up with the centurion who had mounted the ladder next to him, just ten paces away. Behind him his supporting legionaries piled onto the battlements, killing the wounded and kicking their bodies down onto the defenders trying to mount the steps to reinforce the dwindling first line of defence.

'Centurion! To me!' Vespasian shouted to the leader of the assault group to his right who was beset by enemies on all sides. But too late, the transverse plume on the centurion's helmet jerked back as a spear thrust took him in the forehead and a flashing blade sent his right hand spinning away still gripping his sword. His supporting legionaries, jumping down behind their officer, bellowed their anger at his demise and waded into the men responsible. Eyes wide and rolling, filled with hatred, mouths inarticulate with guttural, bestial roars, they began to exact full retribution for the death of the man who had, in life, ruled them with fear and a vine-stick and now in death released in them a surge of loyalty so strong that they thought nothing of dying for their vengeance.

Vespasian's shield slammed into a young lad, barely bearded, cracking ribs and projecting him back into the comrade behind him, as he strove to join up with the legionaries avenging their centurion. How things were progressing further afield from his microcosm of violence he could not tell; all he knew was that they had to consolidate their line and so he fought on, with fury as his guide, to clear that crowded walkway and join up with the lads surging up the neighbouring ladder.

But the slaughter had left a ghastly residue, as treacherous as it was noisome: the fluids of ruptured bellies provided no purchase for iron hobnails and Vespasian's leading leg went from under him, forcing the other leg back to counterbalance and leaving him wide astride and attempting to push himself back upright with his shield rim and the clenched fist of his sword arm. The red cloak and high plume of his helm, conspicuous at the best of times, proved an irresistible draw as he floundered on the slick stone. A shield, thrust over his head from behind, took the first downwards blow aimed at his neck as another legionary stamped his left foot next to his general and presented his shield as protection for Vespasian's face. Pulling his feet together, Vespasian managed to rise as his two saviours parried the blows that sought to despatch him to the Ferryman; the sudden twinge of a pulled left thigh muscle caused him to grimace but, knowing that he had no time for such trifles, he rode over the pain and jabbed his shield forward, once again able to fend for himself.

'Thanks, lads,' he huffed as the two legionaries came onto each of his shoulders, presenting a three-man shield wall, swords flashing low as they stamped forward; defenders edged back as Vespasian and his new comrades advanced, death in their eyes and blood on their blades. With only a couple of paces to go to link up with the next ladder and no more than half a dozen Jews in the way, two of them fighting in the other direction, Vespasian gritted his teeth against the pain from his thigh and tried to blink the incessant sweat from his eyes, to no avail. As one, they stamped forward another pace, their swords jabbing out between their shields. But their opponents were not faint of heart and had already seen, with certainty, their own deaths; it was now just a matter of the manner of their passing to choose and for them the choice was obvious: with the intensity of the religious fanatics that they were, the four men facing Vespasian, with one accord, pounced forward brandishing captured shields and swords to crash into him with the intention of taking the life of the Roman general with theirs. And it was a torrent of slashing strokes that rained down upon Vespasian and his two comrades; there was no craft to them, only savagery, and the pounding of metal on leather-faced wood throbbed in Vespasian's ears, drowning out the rage of the fight behind and beyond. It was a shrill scream that broke through the reverberating din as Vespasian's shield arm began to buckle under the pummelling, and it was from next to him and not in front. Again he jabbed his sword out, only to hit another shield, and, in that instant, light appeared on his shielded side as the legionary to his left tumbled away, down off the wall, an arrow in his neck. The Jewish archers had been brought back from Malichus' diversionary attack to deal with the real assault.

In came the arrow storm, aimed at the legionaries but often hitting defenders as well, for the captains of the archers cared not if some of their own were cut down so long as Roman lives were reaped in abundance. Fletched missiles hissed up at the small groups of Romans on the wall who, as they had not yet managed to form a contiguous line by linking up, could not have their shields facing the incoming hail as well as defend themselves in the hand-to-hand combat that embroiled them still. To remain isolated was to die, or, worse still, be captured. With no one on his left shoulder, Vespasian was directly exposed to the deadly attentions of the archers whose numbers were growing all the time as they raced out of the tangle of narrow streets between Jotapata's chaotic and cramped buildings and formed along the road that ran the length of the wall. With nothing to lose but his life, he stooped down and swiped under his foes' shields; his blade bit into an ankle, almost taking the foot right off, to bring down one of the four Jews assailing him. The legionary to his right slammed his shield forward and up, catching a forearm on a downward stroke, snapping the bone so that the incoming sword fell from a useless hand, his blade then stabbed up into the vitals of the wounded Jew as the flashing pain of the shattered limb caused him to loosen his shield guard. With two of the four disposed of and the odds even, Vespasian pushed himself forward against one of the remaining two whilst stabbing his sword down into the throat of the screaming Jew clutching at his flapping foot, ending his noise and his life.

It was with a stinging pain and the inability to put any weight onto his left leg as he thrust his opponent over that Vespasian collapsed; down he went after the man, landing heavy on his chest, exploding the air from his body. Knowing he was hurt and almost helpless added yet more clarity to Vespasian's thought;

he pushed himself up with his left arm and drove the tip of his sword into the choking man's mouth. Blood sprayed out, coating Vespasian's face; he rolled aside, bringing his shield to bear to the archers. The legionary to his right stood over him as more came from behind to drag him away. His shield echoed with the juddering thumps of arrow hits as he stole a look down at his left leg: the pulled thigh muscle was in spasm.

'Pull me up!' he yelled at a legionary trying to drag him back.

As the man bent down he was spun around and sent crumbling to the ground, dead before he hit it, with an arrow in his cheek, its tip protruding from the side of his head.

Cursing and realising that their position was becoming even more precarious with every racing heartbeat, Vespasian crawled back, keeping his shield up, towards the ladder he had mounted what seemed like days ago but was, in reality, little more than the time it takes for a man to empty a full bladder. He reached the wall and managed to haul himself upright; keeping all the weight on his right leg he surveyed the length of the defences in both directions and groaned. In all but a few places the assault parties had failed to join up before the return of the archers, and his men were suffering from their storm of missiles whilst still fighting hand to hand with the defenders remaining on the battlements now bolstered by reinforcements pounding up the steps from below.

Not to admit it to himself would have been a foolish act of stubbornness that would have cost more lives of his men; their position was untenable. He drew breath and then with as much force as he had left within him roared: 'Withdraw! Withdraw!'

The cornicern at the bottom of the ladder heard his general's command and rumbled the notes that were soon echoing all over the front. The Roman attack had failed and now it was a matter of extracting as many men as possible alive from the walls of Jotapata.

It was with failure in his heart that Vespasian stood on one leg using his shield to cover the men heading over the wall and down the ladder away from the lethal arrow storm that had proved too much. Many did not risk the wait for the ladders and, instead, took their chances with the twenty-foot leap to the hard ground below, but for Vespasian, in his condition, this was not an option and the defenders, emboldened by the Roman retreat, were closing in.

'I'll hold them, sir!' an optio shouted, raising his shield in front of Vespasian. 'Get on the ladder.'

Vespasian knew it was no shame not to be the last man off the battlements as he heaved himself onto the wall; he had done all that had been required of him, leading from the front and being hurt in the process. Throwing his life away would serve no purpose and would be contrary to the greater good; with the second rebuff in as many days, leadership was required. The optio roared at a couple of legionaries to join him defending their general as he made his escape; their shields feathered with shafts, their faces were grim as they realised that they were to sacrifice their lives so that Vespasian could live.

With stabbing pain at every move of his left leg, Vespasian swung his body over the wall and felt his good leg hit a rung; he took one last glance at the interior of the town, hoping for a clue as to how to succeed in taking it, when a familiar figure bounded up onto the walkway, helmeted and shielded with captured equipment. 'Today you run, Vespasian,' Yosef shouted, 'and so it will be tomorrow and the next. We shall hold out until the relief that has been promised arrives from Jerusalem. Mark my words well; we shall hold.' He threw himself at the optio as other defenders took on the two legionaries, battering them down in a flurry of blows too numerous to parry all.

'That will be enough to give heart to every one of my people to rise against Rome,' Vespasian heard Yosef shout as he hopped down the ladder. 'Mark me well, Vespasian!'

Vespasian looked back up at the wall as he was carried away, his arms slung about two men's shoulders, to see the optio leap down and Yosef run forward to place his hands upon the wall and bellow: 'We'll break your women's hearts.'

Vespasian, vowing to promote the optio to centurion if he survived, turned away to see the cohorts retreating in good order and swore to himself to do everything within his power to prove

Yosef wrong. He could not afford for the leader of the Jewish rebels to be right, for with every day that passed without the fall of Jotapata the rebellion would find strength. He did not have enough time to allow Yosef's prediction to come true.

CHAPTER IIII

'WHAT ARE THEY doing?' Magnus asked as he and Vespasian surveyed the walls of Jotapata at sunrise on the twenty-second day of the siege, having endured a night of intense curiosity caused by the sound of construction that had come from the town.

Vespasian was as nonplussed as his old friend. 'I can only assume that they think that erecting ox-skins all along the wall will act as a screen stopping the towers from disgorging their cargo.' He looked at the four massive siege engines taking shape behind the earthworks that had grown every day to protect the legionaries from the numerous sallies that the Jews had made to try to halt their construction. 'Well, it won't; we'll just crush them down when we lower the ramps. Titus assures me that they'll be ready in five days, once the wood arrives, that is.'

And that had been the problem throughout the construction of the siege towers: wood. The entire countryside for a ten-mile radius had been scoured for trees and every one had been cut down, but that had proved insufficient so the search had been widened and for a further ten miles the landscape had been ravaged. Titus had now been forced to send wooding parties out thirty miles, more than a day's travel, and therefore the supplying of the works had slowed considerably. The longer supply line inevitably meant that the foraging parties were liable to ambush from the numerous bands of rebels roaming the countryside, so larger and larger units had to be sent out to ensure the precious timber arrived safely and without too much loss of life. Vespasian's patience was being sorely tried.

The day after his leg had rendered him incapacitated he had ordered another assault on the walls, this time following a fire attack in the hope that the extinguishing of the flames within the town would keep sufficient numbers away from the walls to force an entry. It was not to be: Yosef had let the buildings burn once they caught light, dousing only the infant fires so as not to use too much of his precious water. The attack had stalled in much the same way as the previous day. The two following days produced the same result and so Vespasian had been forced to admit that an escalade was not the way to bring Jotapata down. A full siege and all the work it entailed would be the only way, and he had cursed, for he knew that the time that it would take to bring it to a successful conclusion would be time for the radicals in the province to whip up more of their countrymen into revolt and the result would be more Roman deaths. And all the time he kept patrols roaming the south in search of the relief force that Yosef had promised was on its way; so far there had been no sight of it. Indeed, Titus' informants in Jerusalem had claimed that there was much faction fighting in the city between the radicals and more moderate factions who wished to negotiate with Rome and saw Yosef and his men as an impediment to that. So far, it seemed, the moderates had the upper hand but who knew how long it would be until violence erupted and the radicals seized control and a regime put in place that was more favourable to Yosef.

Yosef, for his part, had done all within his power to disrupt Vespasian's preparations, setting fire to the towers on a few occasions – one time destroying them entirely – and it had not been until the earthworks had been completely dug across the promontory, sealing off the town, that the raids had stopped and building could go on uninterrupted. Yet, despite the completion of the earthworks and the patrols around the base of the precipitous hill upon which Jotapata perched, Vespasian still knew that there was a deal of coming and going into the town as Yosef had read aloud, from the battlements, letters of support from the radical factions in Jerusalem and other Jewish cities. That was bad enough because it meant that Yosef was getting letters out as well, telling his side of the story and providing valuable propaganda for the revolt.

But it was Vespasian's fear that Yosef would escape that kept him searching for the secret way in and out of the town, so far without success.

Vespasian leant on the stick he had been forced to use to protect his weakened leg as he turned and started walking back to the camp that he would have wished to have vacated half a month ago. 'If Traianus hadn't captured Japhra I would be in an even worse position and looking very silly; my despatches back to Rome can't help but fail to conceal my lack of progress.'

'Yeah, well, I wouldn't worry too much; you ain't going to be replaced,' Magnus said with a certainty that surprised Vespasian.

'What makes you so sure about that?'

'Well, it stands to reason, don't it, sir?'

'Does it?'

'Course it does: you were sent here because Corbulo had been too successful for Nero's liking so he forced him into suicide. As far as Nero's concerned at the moment, just because you ain't done so well is no reason to replace you. I know you decided to try and finish this thing as quickly as possible because I watched you make that decision, but I would say that this delay has made you more secure in your appointment than if you'd made a roaring success of the whole thing.'

Vespasian shrugged as he limped back up the hill. 'Perhaps you're right, Magnus. Still, at least Traianus had the good sense to invite Titus to lead the final assault on Japhra; our family has had a bit of glory thrown at it, as I could legitimately claim in the despatch that it had been all Titus' work. I owe Traianus.'

'He knows; that's why he did it.'

Vespasian smiled, nodding. 'I know he does; he wants the plunder from one of the bigger cities. I'll probably have to give him Tiberias.'

'No harm in doing that, sir, seeing as the religious fanatics destroyed all the statuary and artwork in the city because it offended their religious sensibilities. You'll make enough out of Jerusalem; that's where the gold is.'

'If we ever get there.'

'We will; it's just going to take longer than we thought.'

*

'A ram?'

'Yes, Father,' Titus said, looking very pleased with himself as he stood before Vespasian's desk in his private quarters.

Vespasian put down his stylus, giving his son his full attention. 'But I thought there weren't any trees big enough in this gods-forsaken country.'

'I sent a couple of auxiliary centuries north to the cedar woods near Tyre. They've hauled a monster tree all the way back; a messenger just arrived saying that they're a day away; they should arrive tomorrow evening.'

Vespasian's eyes lit up with hope and, leaning on the desk, he pushed himself up from his campaign chair. 'How long will it take you to mount it on a swing and make a protective roof?'

'Once it's here, two days, if I can take the timber from one of the siege towers.'

'Do it; use two of the towers if necessary. Those walls are old; they won't stand a long battering. With a breach and two towers on the walls we'll finally get in. Get on with it, Son.'

'We'll be ready in the morning four days from now.'

'Oh, and Titus,' Vespasian said as his son turned to go.

'Yes, Father?'

'Well done.'

'Thank you, Father.'

'You're very lucky to have him,' Caenis said, looking up from the letter she had been reading at her desk.

'*We're* very lucky to have him,' Vespasian said, sitting back down.

'*Rome's* very lucky to have him,' Caenis corrected. 'He has to be the most promising man of his generation; which is hardly surprising, seeing as he is your son. He'll make a fine heir; at least you have one.'

'One? I've got two, as you know.'

Caenis pointed at the letter. 'It's from Nerva.'

'Nerva! What's he doing writing to you?'

'He's not; he's writing to both of us, he just sent it to me. I think he believes that I'll be able to make what he has to say more palatable.'

'Domitian?'

'I'm afraid so.'

Vespasian sighed and wondered how he could be cursed with such an antithesis to Titus. 'Go on, then.'

Caenis took a deep breath and looked at Vespasian apologetically. 'Well, I'm afraid that Domitian has refused to take up the military tribune post that Nerva has managed to procure for him with the First Adiutrix; he says that it's beneath him as he is the son of the general commanding the Roman forces in Judaea and he should, therefore, be serving there with his father like his older brother is doing.'

'Titus is the legate of the Fifteenth Apollinaris, not some snotty-nosed little thin-stripe tribune.'

'And that's another complaint that Domitian has: he says that being a thin-stripe is an insult to his rank and he should be a thick-stripe tribune and—'

'Be technically the second in command of whatever legion he's attached to! Minerva's tits! Can you imagine it? Someone who has never considered anyone else in the world other than himself, potentially looking after the welfare of five thousand men if the legate should manage to get himself killed. Who does he think he is?'

'He thinks he's your son.'

'And I am just a New Man with a Sabine burr; a first generation senator. What expectations can he conjure from that?'

Caenis put the letter down and looked at Vespasian with exaggerated patience. 'You are the commander of the East; the most powerful man out here. If we Romans didn't hate the idea of kings, you would be compared to one because you are in effect the King of Rome's East. Domitian is not stupid; whatever else you might think he is. No, he's far from that and he can smell the possibilities for his family and wants to be a part of that. He's jealous, Vespasian, face it. He's jealous of Titus and he can't understand why you haven't asked him to come out here and serve with his brother and you.'

'Because I know what he'll do: he'll act as if he was in charge of everyone, refuse to take orders from anyone but me; and then he'll only do that grudgingly. He'll be a danger to the command structure and morale of the whole army because he'd have an even more overinflated view of his own importance, which is exactly why I asked Nerva to get him a posting with a legion where he knows nobody.'

'I know that, my love, you know that and Nerva knows that, but does Domitian? Perhaps you should have been honest with him and told him your reasons for excluding him.'

'Domitian wouldn't understand it even if I did. No, I'll just have to write to him and command him as his father to take the post that Nerva is offering.'

'I don't think that will work.'

Vespasian looked downcast, his expression more tense than usual. 'I know; he very rarely does what he's told.'

'It's not so much that, my love.' Caenis looked at the letter again.

'Well?'

'Well, Nerva says here that, the day before he wrote, he tried ordering Domitian, in your name, to take up the post, as did your brother. But it was no good as it is too late, the situation's changed and Domitian says that whatever happens he refuses to leave Rome at all. Ever.'

Vespasian struggled to understand the concept. 'Ever? Why? What could possibly make him think such an absurd thing?'

'It seems that he's fallen in love.'

'Love! The only person he loves is himself.'

'And Corbulo's youngest daughter.'

'Domitia Longina? I admit that I once entertained the possibility of their getting married but put off all thought of the match once Corbulo had committed suicide. He hasn't even met her so how can he be in love with her?'

'She got married to Lucius Aelius Plautius Alienus.'

'Even more reason for him not to be in love with her.'

'Domitian was at the wedding and fell in love with her at first sight.'

This was too much for Vespasian; he slammed his fist onto the desk. 'Well, he'll just have to fall out of love with her, won't he! I'll not have him ruining the chance of a career by sulking about in Rome drooling after another man's wife. He's sixteen! How can he be in love at that age? It's ridiculous!'

'You were sixteen when we met.'

'Pah!' Vespasian spluttered, shaking his head. 'That was different.'

'In what way?'

'Firstly, you weren't another man's wife.'

'I wasn't any man's wife; I was a slave.'

'Well, at least you were available.'

'I've never been available to you, either as a slave or after Antonia manumitted me, as it's forbidden for a senator to marry a freedwoman. If that law didn't exist and I had really been available then we'd be married now and I would have had your children and not Flavia. So you can't argue that, as Alienus might die or divorce her and then she would be available to Domitian. No, the only way it was different is that you didn't refuse to go and serve as a military tribune in Thracia for four years after we met. If anything, it would seem to me that Domitian is far more in love with Domitia Longina than you were with me as he's refusing to go.'

'That's a ridiculous thing to say.'

'Is it? Well, my love, all I mean to point out is that you shouldn't dismiss Domitian's professed feelings out of hand just because you don't think him capable of them.'

'All right, imagine he really is in love: is that any reason to dis- obey his father and refuse to do his duty to his family and to Rome?'

'Of course it isn't.' Caenis paused in thought and then looked back at Vespasian. 'But consider this: Domitian is cunning and devious, by your own admission, so if things develop and Galba does go into revolt at Vindex's instigation and a civil war is triggered, where would it be best to have Domitian? In a legion fighting for one contender or another without much say in the matter; no more than an insignificant tribune, prey to the political inclination of the legate or the populist sentiments of the rank and file. Of absolutely no use to you whatsoever and quite likely dead in his first battle—'

'Oh, I'm sure he'd find a way of avoiding going into battle.'

'Stop putting him down at every opportunity.' Caenis raised her hand as Vespasian went to argue. 'And quite likely dead in his first battle, or would you prefer him to be in Rome where he may at least be of some use to us should things develop in our favour? Think about it, Vespasian. Perhaps it's not worth arguing the point with him on this occasion as he will, no doubt, defy you anyway.'

'Whereas if I was ordering him to stay in Rome?'

Caenis smiled. 'There you have it: he'd be running off to the legions whether he was in love with Domitia Longina or not. No, much better to save the argument and have him somewhere where he may just be of use one day.'

'And let him think that it was all his own idea.'

Caenis walked over and kissed him on the cheek. 'How well you know your own son.'

'How true, my love; the trouble is that I don't much like what I know.'

'Father, come quickly,' Titus said, running back into Vespasian's quarters. 'We can hear the sound of construction.'

'Construction?'

'Yes, from behind the ox-hide screens.'

Vespasian followed Titus out into the camp, a sea of leather tents swathed in the smoke of thousands of cooking fires as each eight-man contubernium not on duty prepared the evening meal. The smell of crisping pork – an outrage to the Jews – filled the air and woodsmoke stung the eyes as they walked, at speed, along the Via Praetoria to the main gate facing Jotapata. The centurion of the watch saluted and his sentries snapped to attention as they passed through the Porta Praetoria.

Titus returned the salute. 'Thank you for bringing this to our attention, Primus Pilus Barea.'

Barea stood at ease. 'It was a patrol that first heard it, sir. They were on the other side of the siege works, but you can hear them well enough from here if I get a bit of hush. They're still at it, sir; I can definitely hear hammering and chipping as if they're shaping blocks.' He strode forward, bearing down on the earthworks just a few score yards away filled with men on duty in case of a sortie from the town. 'Shut the fuck up for the general, maggots! Next man who so much as farts will spend a month in the latrines as my personal arse-sponge!'

'They must be using the ox-hide screens to cover the men working on the walls,' Titus said as he and Vespasian stood listening to what was clearly the sound of blocks of stone being shaped and then laid on the walls.

'The devious bastard,' Vespasian muttered. 'He's probably using the material from the burnt-out houses to raise the battlements. Those screens have to be at least ten feet high. Do you know what, Titus? I'm beginning to have a grudging respect for the man, even though he's a disgusting fanatic. With just a few thousand men he's held up a Roman army for more than half a month. The sooner we have your ram the better.' Vespasian turned to go, having seen and heard enough. 'Oh, and add another ten feet to the siege towers.'

The ram did indeed arrive early the following day, trundled to the siege lines on a series of carts, hauled by many oxen and with the men of the centuries sent to get it taking it in turns to lend their shoulders to the effort.

It was a tree of such girth, at least seven feet in diameter and fifty feet in length, that all stopped working as it passed to admire its magnitude and cheer its arrival, calling it their saviour, the colossus that had come to ease their toil and batter their enemies into submission.

'That should do it,' Magnus observed as the monster passed him and Vespasian by. 'A few taps with that and in you go.'

'You're not coming then?'

'There'll be nothing in there worth having; my bet is they'll kill all their women and children and then finish themselves off so there won't be a lot of fun to be had. I can't imagine that they're swimming in gold or silver, seeing as it's because we taxed them too much that they're in there in the first place. No, I'll sit it out, thank you.'

'What do you think, Father?' Titus asked, walking up to Vespasian, followed by a contubernium escorting two Jewish prisoners.

'I think you'll have a lot of trouble making a frame strong enough to support it as it swings and sturdy enough to roll it to the walls.'

'We'll manage, Father; in the meantime I think we've found out how they're getting in and out undetected.' Titus turned to the optio commanding the prisoner escort. 'Bring them here.'

The two Jews were pushed forward, their hands tied behind their backs. Despite being brought before the man who was the arbiter of life and death for them, they showed no fear and held their heads high and looked with insolent directness into Vespasian's eyes.

'Tell the general, optio,' Titus ordered.

'We found them trying to sneak into the town along a gully on the far side, sir,' the optio informed Vespasian. 'It was shortly before dawn. We often patrol in this area and, recently, in the last ten days or so, we've been noticing that there seem to be the occasional sheep in there, leastways that's what it looked like in the dark. Well, I never paid it no mind, seeing as we are very well supplied with pork here and I didn't want to risk me or one of my lads breaking an ankle chasing a tough piece of meat over rocky ground—'

'Yes, yes,' Titus interjected. 'Get on with it, man.'

'Sorry, sir. Well, to cut a long story short, just before dawn this morning we saw a couple of sheep down in the gully again, I could just make them out, they were standing still. Anyway, one of the lads, Primus, here.' He pointed to a young legionary, no more than a year in service, looking very proud to be brought to his general's attention. 'Well, Primus thought it would be a laugh to try and wake the things up so he lobs a stone at them. Now, this is where it got strange: he hits one, fair and square on the side, but the beast doesn't move or even bleat, and I knew it wasn't dead because it hadn't been there when we patrolled past the gully an hour earlier. So I gets to thinking and become suspicious and I lead the lads down into the gully as fast as I can and would you believe it but—'

'The sheep got up and ran on two feet?' Vespasian said, finishing the sentence.

The optio looked disappointed. 'Oh, so you've already heard the report, sir?'

'No, optio, you just set the scene so well I could visualise it.' He looked at the two prisoners. 'Turn them around.' Vespasian was not surprised to see fleeces stitched to their robes made of undyed wool. 'What did you find on them, optio?'

'This, sir.' The optio handed him a scroll-case.

Vespasian opened the case and unrolled the scroll; it was written in Aramaic. 'Take them away and lock them up; I may well need to question them once I've had this translated.'

As the optio turned to go, Vespasian asked: 'How often have you noticed these *sheep* in the gully in the last days?'

'I would say, every night at some point.'

'Thank you, optio. Get some rest; I want you to show me this gully tonight.'

'What do you think, Hormus?' Vespasian asked as he and Caenis waited whilst his freedman studied the scroll.

'I think it's an appeal to Yosef not to surrender,' Hormus said, putting the scroll down on Vespasian's desk. 'It's not clear who it is from, although there is a line at the end which translates as: "Master of the Anointed." But there is no name.'

'Master of the Anointed?' Caenis repeated. 'That could be anyone in this country; they all seem to feel that they have some sort of religious position or standing. So what does it say?'

Hormus picked up the scroll again. '"We have known each other a long time and I feel that we have come to trust one another's judgement. This is not an easy letter for me to write but I feel that for the sake of our people I must make this appeal to you. Do not lay down your arms and walk out of the gate as a member of my family has begged you to do. That person believes that Titus Flavius Vespasianus is a reasonable man, and if you were to appeal to him now, as they would have you do, they think that he would be merciful. I am not so sure, my father never trusted him, in fact Vespasian caused my father many difficulties during his life and proved himself to be a vicious enemy and I don't believe that clemency is one of his faults. However, now that the rebellion is spreading, more than ever we need martyrs. I beg you, in the name of the Lord, hold out until the last and then, once the town falls, make sure that not one of our people comes out alive. I know you will think it easy for me to ask, I who am a hundred miles away and safe behind my walls; I whom Rome counts as a friend and therefore have no need to fear her wrath. But believe me when I say that, were our positions reversed, I would happily sacrifice my life for the cause"—'

Vespasian scoffed, interrupting Hormus. 'That's very easy to say when the positions quite evidently cannot be reversed. Whoever is the author is a disingenuous coward who wants other people to do his fighting for him. A friend of Rome with a member of his family who's trying to make peace and a father who hated me; who could that be, I wonder?'

Caenis thought for a moment. 'Master of the Anointed? Herod Agrippa was recently granted by Nero the right to nominate the chief priest in Jerusalem. He and his sister, Berenice, both tried to contain the rebellion in Jerusalem and only just managed to escape from the city with their lives last year. She could be the member of Herod's family evidently still trying to make peace when Herod seems to have changed his mind.'

'So it would seem,' Vespasian agreed. 'And his father, the first Herod Agrippa, had no reason to like me: I was, in part, responsible for him being thrown into prison by Tiberius and then, after Caligula released him, it was me who he blamed for having his grain stockpile in Alexandria confiscated. No, I can see that, in private, the younger Herod Agrippa would be very hostile to me, no matter what he professes to my face, especially since I've forbidden him to join this campaign. The question is: why is he now secretly supporting the rebellion having originally tried to quell it and then sent me troops to help fight it?'

'I would have thought that was obvious,' Caenis said. 'He tried to stop the rebellion before it started because as ruler of his small tetrarchy based around Tiberias it served no purpose for him to see Judaea, to his south, rebel against Rome. If it was successful then he would be seen as a collaborator, as Rome gave him his position, and would no doubt suffer the consequences; if the rebellion wasn't successful, and that is the only acceptable outcome, then he would almost certainly find himself less independent as Rome strengthens her grip on the region.'

Vespasian grunted to show that he was following the logic of her argument.

'So,' Caenis continued, 'once the rebellion started to spread up here into Galilee and into Herod's tetrarchy he finds himself in a completely different situation: he is now the victim of the rebellion as he has been forced to flee his domain. He then sees how he could benefit himself by becoming a part of the solution to the problem, and the bigger the problem the bigger the solution needs to be.'

Vespasian put a hand to his forehead. 'Oh, my love, that is so cynical.'

'He's a cynical person.'

Knowing the man, Vespasian could but agree. 'Once the rebellion has been crushed, he's going to offer Nero to govern Judaea in Rome's name as a sop to the Jews so that they'll feel that they are, at least, being subjugated by one of their own. To make the idea appealing to Nero, the rebellion has to be widespread and long so that the idea of it happening again is just so appalling from the financial point of view, a view very dear to Nero's heart, that Herod Agrippa seems like a saviour and is completely acceptable as he is a Roman citizen anyway. This is all about how Herod Agrippa plans to get his father's kingdom back.'

'Precisely. So now he's busy playing both sides: supplying troops to us to help tackle the rebels whilst imploring Yosef to fight to the last man so that the rebellion goes on as long as possible.' Caenis looked back to Hormus. 'Was there anything else in the letter?'

'Just one more line: "And don't forget; if our fortunes fade we can always look east." That's all.'

'Look east?' Vespasian said, not liking the sound of that at all. 'Parthia? He wouldn't try to bring Parthia into the rebellion, would he? That would be exchanging one master for another, and from a Jewish point of view Parthia would be the worse choice as it would guarantee war in this land until Rome had reclaimed it. We could never allow the Great King access to Our Sea again.'

Caenis shook her head. 'No, my love, I don't think he means that; he would never ask for Vologases' help as he knows what the price would be. Hormus, is there another way to translate "fortune" from Aramaic?'

'I suppose one could say "treasure".'

'There! You see, Vespasian, he's talking about money. If they start needing more cash then they'll look to the East; not so far as Parthia, but slightly closer to home. Who is between Judaea and Parthia?'

'The Kingdom of the Nabatean Arabs,' Vespasian replied, unconvinced. 'But Malichus fights for us, and fights very well; why would he supply the rebellion with money?'

'I suppose you'll just have to ask him.'

The smile was broad and full of gleaming teeth as Malichus scratched his bush of a beard. 'General, you have me at a severe disadvantage.'

'I'm sorry to hear that, Malichus,' Vespasian said, leaning across his desk and giving the Nabataean king an uncompromisingly stern look. 'Perhaps you would care to explain what benefit you were trying to get from this severe disadvantage that you didn't report to me?'

Malichus frowned with a pained expression and put his hands in the air as if it were all too trying. 'General, I was not seeking a benefit just for myself, you must understand that; I was seeking an advantage for you as well, my friend.'

'You were willing to support the rebels financially to help me fight them better, Malichus? Is that how it was?'

'If necessary, of course; I'm your good friend.'

'I can't see how aiding my enemy makes you my good friend.'

'I haven't given them any aid – yet. I just agreed with Herod Agrippa that should he need a loan to pass on to the rebels then I would be willing to provide him with one. It seems a very straightforward arrangement; and would benefit you considerably.'

'How?'

Malichus' grin became even wider; he reached over the desk and patted Vespasian's hand. 'My friend, surely you don't want the rebellion to be over before we've even got going. Jerusalem is rich, so rich; I know, I've been there. We've all heard the stories of the wealth that the Jews hoard for their god in his temple. Remember tell of how much Pompey Magnus removed when he was here over a hundred years ago. A hundred years, my friend! Imagine how it's built up again in that time. No, if we allow the rebellion to peter out before we have a chance of taking Jerusalem as a spoil of war then we will miss the opportunity to become very wealthy men. And you, my friend, will be the wealthiest of us all. So what's a small loan to Herod, should he need it, compared to all that wealth we stand to gain?'

Vespasian sat back in his chair trying to get his head around Malichus' logic. 'I see what you mean,' he said after some reflection. 'But prolonging the fight until we take Jerusalem will cost many Roman and Nabataean lives; not to mention the Jews.'

Malichus shrugged again as if it were of little import. 'More lives will be lost if the rebellion finishes here. Do you think the Jews will meekly settle down again under Roman rule, even if Nero does make Herod Agrippa governor or client king?' His eyes twinkled. 'Yes, I know what Herod's motives are and what his strategy is, that's what makes it so enjoyable, pretending to be his friend covertly fighting against Rome when all the time it's to help you become rich on Jewish gold – and me of course; I trust you shall give me the honour of sacking some part of the Temple complex?'

It was as much as Vespasian could do to keep a straight face and prevent himself from laughing. Malichus' logic was faultless and he found himself admiring the king's callous pursuit of riches. 'Very well, Malichus, I'll try to ensure that you get some considerable gain from Jerusalem, if it comes to that. Although, personally I think that if we do our job properly here and in a few other towns along the way, the carnage we'll cause will make the people of Jerusalem less keen to risk the destruction of their city.'

'Let's hope not, general; the only logical conclusion to all this is the complete destruction of Jerusalem and the Jewish Temple, otherwise this will happen again and again and again.'

'Yes, well, we'll see. As to Herod Agrippa, I want you to keep me informed of all contact that you have with him and I want to know as soon as he asks you for a loan, as I may veto it if I don't think the circumstances are suitable.'

Malichus inclined his head in silent acquiescence.

'In the meantime, I want to bring Herod here without him knowing for sure whether I am aware of his duplicity. I think that having him close to me and unsure of his position would be a satisfactory situation to have him in, rather than just reversing my previous decision and granting his request to join his troops and giving him no cause for concern.'

'I completely agree, general,' Malichus said, his voice rich with understanding. 'May I make a suggestion as to how that may be achieved?'

'Go on.'

'I would surmise that the two messengers would not give away the identity of who sent them, even under the most rigorous questioning.'

'I imagine you're right.'

'Therefore have them tortured, maybe have a few fingers clipped off or even a hand each, and then contrive it so that they can escape.'

Vespasian's liking for Malichus grew as he saw the beauty of the scheme. 'They'll make their way back to Herod, who will know that his message has been intercepted but will think that I don't know who sent it, as he has two mutilated messengers before him, both swearing that they said nothing, as proof of my ignorance.'

'Exactly. Obviously he'll kill them both, so they don't become an embarrassing inconvenience, and then he'll make his way to you to judge by your reception of him exactly what you know of his schemes.'

'Which, my dear Malichus, is absolutely nothing.'

Malichus beamed, his face alight with pleasure. 'He will be *so* relieved.'

*

The plaintive tewoo of an owl, somewhere above him, made Vespasian wonder whether it was a genuine bird call or if they had been spotted by watchers in the night. The moon, not yet a quarter full in its cycle, was intermittent, the night sky being flecked with fast-moving clouds, sailing on a warm breeze that grew with every passing hour. He sat, swathed in a dark cloak, hunched next to a rock, overlooking the gully where the optio had found his sheep. Magnus sat next to him with Castor and Pollux lying by his side, the models of well-behaved beasts. Behind them, lying flat on the ground, were the optio and his men, again wearing dark cloaks and divested of all metal equipment other than swords wrapped in cloth to prevent chinking and reflecting moonlight.

Conversation, for obvious reasons, had been forbidden, and, as they waited for what Vespasian hoped would be a messenger coming in or out, he cast his mind back to the interrogation of Herod's two men. They had, he freely admitted, been exceptionally brave and endured the knife and the fire without divulging Herod's name or, indeed, any other name in its place. They had, for the three hours they had endured, kept up a stream of muttering which, Hormus had informed him, was a recitation of the Jewish holy book.

It had not been until one of the men had died – a modification Vespasian had added to Malichus' plan to better justify in Herod's mind why the questioning had been suspended – that Vespasian had ordered the survivor, who, although hurt, had not been incapacitated, to be placed in the hospital tent, ostensibly so that his wounds would not get infected and he would be fit to resume questioning on the morrow. An hour after night had fallen he had disappeared from the hospital. Vespasian had been told by the centurion commanding the 'guard' that he had told his men in Greek to go and get something to eat as the man was too hurt to attempt going anywhere; he had slipped out of the camp disguised as an old man, his wounds making a stooped walk with a limp not a matter for serious acting. Vespasian had calculated that he should be expecting Herod Agrippa's arrival in ten days.

A nudge from Magnus brought Vespasian out of his reverie; his eyes followed the direction of Magnus' pointed finger aimed up at the darkling mass of Jotapata's precipitous mount. Taking a few moments to let his eyes focus in the gloom, he slowly began to make out a dim blur of slightly lighter shadow slowly descending. Vespasian turned to the optio and signalled for him and his men to be ready for swift action.

Some loose scree, tumbling from above, confirmed the arrival of a messenger. Magnus clamped his hand over Castor's snout as a growl began to rumble in the hound's throat upon hearing the falling stones; obedient to his master's wish the beast ceased its noise.

Vespasian's heart quickened and he found himself holding his breath; the figure stilled as if listening intently to the night around him. No one moved. Even the dogs detected the tension and remained motionless.

After a score or more pounding heartbeats the man resumed his descent, more scree heralding his coming. As he neared the bottom, he paused to listen again and, satisfied that there was no one about, raised his head and did a soft imitation of an owl hoot before getting down on all fours, pulling a fleece over his back and beginning a slow crawl along the gully floor in Vespasian's direction. With caution he came on until he was directly below the Romans, no more than fifteen feet away and, to the uninitiated, easily mistaken for a sheep in the dark. Vespasian raised a palm and shook his head, guessing that, because of the owl signal, there was a second man following the first down who would certainly turn back at the slightest noise from below.

Letting the first man crawl past, Vespasian stared up into the darkness, praying that he was right in his hunch. Just as he began to lose hope and was about to order the pursuit of the messenger, now disappeared into the night, another fall of scree confirmed that he had been right. He pointed at the dogs and then out into the night after the first man; Magnus understood. It had been for this eventuality that they had risked bringing Castor and Pollux along. Vespasian would take the second man quietly whilst the dogs would hunt and catch the first, many paces away from the gully; if the chase was heard up on the ramparts of Jotapata, Yosef would guess that one of his men had been caught out in the open by a patrol, but being so distant from the gully he would deem the route still safe.

It was with a sudden lurch forward that Vespasian hurled himself down the wall of the gully as the second man was directly below him; the optio and his men followed him down as Magnus launched his dogs out into the night on the trail of the fugitive.

Already on all fours the second man had no time to make a bolt for freedom as Vespasian crashed down upon him, pinning him to the ground. With a couple of right jabs into the man's face, he halted his squirming and the optio and his men were able to restrain him and stuff a gag into his mouth as from out in the darkness came the sound of canine excitement and human terror.

Working fast, Vespasian frisked the messenger and within a few moments had retrieved a note secured beneath the man's belt.

Still keeping as silent as possible, Vespasian signalled for a couple of the legionaries to drag the man away before setting the optio and the rest of his men after Magnus and his hounds.

'There ain't much left of him, I'm afraid,' Magnus whispered as Vespasian caught up with him.

'I wasn't expecting there to be,' Vespasian said, prodding the mangled and blood-slick corpse with a toe and trying to ignore the sound of Castor and Pollux tucking into some tasty treat they had ripped from the carnage. 'Did he have anything on him?'

'Just this.' Magnus handed him a note similar to the one he had already retrieved.

'Under his belt?'

'Exactly.'

'Come on, let's get back; I'm curious as to who our friend Yosef chooses as his correspondents.'

'"To Yohanan ben Levi, greetings,"' Hormus said, translating from the Aramaic.

Vespasian was immediately outraged. 'That slippery bastard; where is he? Did the messenger say where he was bound?'

Titus shook his head. 'I'm afraid the messenger died whilst being severely questioned; he gave nothing away. My agents haven't reported any sighting of him either.'

'I'm beginning to lose all faith in them; not that I had much in the first place. Go on, Hormus.'

'So Yosef is appealing to Yohanan to stir up his supporters in Jerusalem and usurp power from the priests,' Vespasian summarised after Hormus had finished. 'If that happens then there will never be a chance of a negotiated settlement.'

Caenis frowned in thought for a few moments. 'Perhaps, but I imagine that should that happen, there will be civil war between the factions, which will be of great benefit to us.'

'In that they'll be doing our job for us? Yes, I suppose so.'

Titus waved away from under his nose a trail of smoke from one of the oil lamps. 'It would be far more complicated than that, should it happen. There are so many different factions, all hating one another, it's amazing that there isn't a civil war in Jerusalem already. Eleazar ben Shimon, for example: he commanded the Jewish army that did so much damage to the Twelfth at Ben Horon. He's also a Zealot, but Yohanan can't stand Eleazar because he's considered to be the greatest hero for defeating a legion, and Eleazar can't stand Yohanan because he won't acknowledge him as such. If Yohanan's faction of Zealots were to take power then you can be assured that Eleazar will fight him.'

'Well, perhaps we should hasten that eventuality. Do you think you could find a way of getting this letter to Yohanan without him suspecting it came through our hands?'

Titus took the letter from Hormus. 'Leave it with me.'

Vespasian turned back to Hormus. 'Who is the second letter addressed to?'

Hormus glanced at the parchment. 'Ananus, the chief priest in Jerusalem.'

'What does it say?'

'"Since you asked me to hold out for a week to give you time to organise a relief force, twenty-two days have passed."'

Vespasian put up his hand, halting Hormus. 'What's a week?'

'Seven days,' Titus said. 'It's what they call the six days of labour and then the Sabbath on the seventh; like our market interval of nine days.'

'So, Yosef must have been asked by the authorities in Jerusalem to hold out for seven days from the time we arrived and he slipped into Jotapata. He's been a disappointed man for fifteen days then.' He signalled his freedman to continue.

'"We have done our part of the bargain, where is yours? We held out for the seven days that you asked for and we shall hold out for forty more, but I warn you, Jotapata will fall on the forty-seventh day; I have seen it. And with Jotapata falls Galilee and once Galilee is gone then so will fall Transjordan and it will be just a matter of time before you see a Roman army before Jerusalem's walls. How long will the Lord preserve you for then? Remember, the forty-seventh day; after that Judaea will be lost and the blame will be laid at your feet for not keeping your word and relieving Jotapata."'

Vespasian rubbed his chin as Hormus put the letter down. 'The forty-seventh day, eh? That's another twenty-four from today; we can't have them holding out for that long – it'll inspire other towns. Titus, you had better hurry with your ram.'

CHAPTER V

IT WAS A mighty engine of war: magnificent in size and awesome in power; Vespasian felt that the end of the siege must surely be in sight. The Brute, as the ram was affectionately called, rumbled forward. Suspended within a latticework of sturdy beams by a web of ropes and protected by a roof of dripping, soaked hides, The Brute presented a fearsome sight with its burnished iron ram's head gleaming in the sun; its beauty belying its capacity for destruction.

But Vespasian knew that its deployment would not be an easy affair. If he were in Yosef's position he would not yield the open ground, between the siege lines and battlements, unfought; for it was there, out in the open, that the chance to set fire to The Brute best presented itself – although it was, at most, a forlorn hope. So it was that as the two centuries, one on either side of the engine, pushed the great beast forward on many wheels across the ramp spanning the trenches, Titus' entire legion moved in support with them, hauling the two siege towers, their extra height making them rock precariously on rougher ground.

It was to be, Vespasian hoped, the final play in the agonising fall of Jotapata that had now been almost a month and a half in coming. Ever since the discovery of the gully and sheep ruse, the town had grown weaker by the day for it had not been just messages that had been getting through, but also much-needed supplies in the form of barrels of water and salted beef rolled along the gully by the 'sheep' and then hauled up to the town by cranes with, Vespasian assumed, greased pulleys for they were noiseless. For a couple of nights after the discovery the Romans had apprehended at least a dozen men either leaving with messages or coming with victuals, until, by the third night, the flow dried up as Yosef realised that his courier system had been discovered. However, during that time five more messages had been intercepted and Vespasian wondered just how many more there had been and whether the ones his men had seized were duplicates or originals; somehow his suspicion was that they were the former. This time they were to Eleazar ben Shimon urging him to have a rapprochement with Yohanan and take on the conservative priesthood together, and then to Yohanan begging him to do the same with Eleazar, and finally to the Jews of Alexandria, Antioch and, more alarmingly, to the fifty thousand or so Jews in Rome, imploring them to stand firm with their eastern cousins and defy Rome. He had written immediately to all the governors concerned – his old friend Tiberius Alexander, the prefect of Egypt, and Mucianus in Syria, as well as his brother Sabinus, the prefect of Rome – advising them all to stamp down hard and swift on any signs of discontent and nail up a few scapegoats as examples to the rest. This had been almost half a moon ago and he was still to receive replies and did not know yet whether the Jewish rebellion had spread beyond the confines of Judaea and Galilee.

But this concern was now pushed to the back of his mind as he watched Jotapata's bane finally moving towards its walls. Finally. And it had been a long time, far longer than hoped. The four days that Titus had promised to rig the ram had turned into twelve due to the suicidal raids of the Jews. Realising that they had nothing to lose in delaying the readying of the ram as, with its arrival, their death warrants were already signed, it made little difference to them whether they died trying to burn it or as a result of it making a breach for the legionaries to storm. And so, night after night, attacks, each more daring than the last, were made on the workshops of the carpenters and smiths attempting to complete the rigging. Many lives had been lost, mainly Jewish, and Vespasian had marvelled at the pointlessness of the exercise: Yosef's men were sacrificing their lives for an already lost cause and yet they were queuing up to do so. It was madness; as if the whole race had made a mutual pact of self-annihilation in an attempt to get their strange god to prove his existence by saving them from themselves. As far as Vespasian was concerned he was going to do as much as he possibly could to help push this obstreperous people into oblivion.

And, as the gates of Jotapata opened to disgorge the expected sortie, Vespasian felt a surge of vicious joy that yet more of the fanatics were going to die. 'Gods below, I hope they throw every man that they've got against us now, then the ram will become redundant because we can slaughter each one of the bastards before the gate.'

Titus, on a horse next to him, looked weary of the endeavour. 'If only, Father; but, knowing Yosef, as we have come to know him over the last month and a half, I guarantee you that he will send no more than five hundred of the fanatics with torches and pitch, maybe even some Naphtha – if they have any, which I doubt – to try to set The Brute alight and die whilst failing to do so.'

Vespasian sighed. 'I'm afraid you're right and we'll be obliged to have a few hours battering the walls whilst they throw all manner of shit down at us.'

It was with resignation that father and son silently agreed the truth of the matter and watched a few hundred Jewish fanatics, all bearing torches, swarm out of the gates and head straight towards the ram to throw their lives away in an impossible quest.

And die they did, many before they had even raced fifty paces, as Malichus' Arab archers and the Syrian auxiliaries let fly volley after volley, supported by the legion's artillery shooting over their heads, into the mass of men, screaming at one another to urge each other on, hurtling towards The Brute. Down they tumbled and Vespasian's sense of vicious joy melted into a feeling of bored resignation at the futility of it all; battle, he knew, could be glorious – terrifying but glorious – but what he beheld was naught but stupidity, aimless stupidity. He felt that if he had to watch one more of these fanatics give their life for a doomed cause he would ... well, what more could he do? He was killing them anyway. And so he sat and watched as the sally was thinned out the closer it got to its objective until just a couple of hundred made it to the cohort that protected the ram. They threw themselves onto the blades of their enemy as they tried to hurl their torches over the legionaries' heads towards the ram; none managed to. So as the ram came within bowshot of the walls, crushing the limp bodies of the Jewish dead and wounded under its huge, solid wheels, Vespasian's bitterness at Yosef's complete disregard for the lives of his men felt sour in his throat. He prayed that if one man survived within the town, it would be the Jewish leader so he could have the pleasure of nailing him to a cross.

Flaming arrows in volleys, smoke trails grey beneath the clear sky, flew from the town to thump, staccato as hail, into the wet hide roof, there to fizzle to extinction as The Brute pressed on.

'I'd better be joining the legion, Father; we're nearly there.'

Vespasian nodded, trying to keep the fear for his son's safety from his mind. 'Take care and remember, don't bring the towers onto the walls until there is a viable breach. With three points of entry at once we'll have them, finally.'

Finally. That word again, Vespasian ruminated, watching Titus gallop away as ballistae projectiles whistled overhead, keeping the walls of Jotapata clear of rebels but unable to halt the constant stream of smoke-trailing arrows that were now being aimed more randomly, as they were being released from behind cover. Finally. But was it really? Of course it was not: there were many towns that had closed their gates to Rome as Traianus had reported in the last month. All the while that Vespasian had been delayed before the walls of Jotapata, Traianus, having taken Japhra, had progressed with his legion through southern Galilee, from town to town, investing most of them and forcing their surrender with far more alacrity than Vespasian had enjoyed. Nazareth and Tarichaea had been the most stubborn but their populations were now either dead or being herded west as slaves; six thousand were being sent to Corinth where Nero had instigated the building of a canal to cut through the isthmus and revolutionise shipping in Greek waters.

But, whatever the relative rates of success between Vespasian and Traianus, one thing was certain: the rebellion was strengthening on the back of Jotapata's success in holding out for so long. So this 'finally' was for Vespasian just the first of what would have to be many 'finallys', for it was now clear that he would have to fight every pace of the way to Jerusalem.

With Traianus' success in the south, the way to Tiberias was now secure and it was with a feeling close to nausea that Vespasian contemplated a possible recurrence of recent events. It felt like far more than two months ago when he had resolved to end the rebellion quickly as he stood before the rebel town of Gabara. As The Brute closed on the walls, and Titus, his red cloak still visible despite the rising dust and falling smoke, joined it to take up command, Vespasian counted the days since Gabara in his head; it did not take long for him to arrive at fifty. He then subtracted the days between that victory and his arrival at Jotapata and frowned when he realised the answer was forty-six.

This was the forty-sixth day of the siege.

Forty days' worth of supplies was what the prisoner had told them upon their arrival; but men could fight on without sustenance, at least for a little while, so there had been no reason to assume that the town would fall immediately the last bushel of grain had been consumed. No, it had been Yosef himself who had predicted in his letter to Jerusalem that the town would fall on the forty-seventh day, and he had been insistent that the chief priest mark his words with care; but at the time he, Vespasian, had dismissed them. It had not been until now that he had considered them again. Forty-seven days? Am I destined to fail again today, Vespasian wondered, but will triumph tomorrow? Did that mean that Yosef had always planned to allow the town to fall and had chosen the forty-seventh day to do so in the hope that it would induce Vespasian to deal more leniently with him should he survive? But no, that could not be, as Yosef was unaware that Vespasian knew of his prediction and, besides, it was pure coincidence that The Brute, after much delay, had been ready by this, the forty-sixth, day. So, therefore, had Yosef really seen into the future and known that the town would fall on the forty-seventh day because he was in possession of the power of foresight? But if that were so, why had he come to the town in the first place, seeing as he already knew that it was lost? Shaking his head,

Vespasian put these thoughts from his mind and drew his eyes back to the unfolding events of this, the forty-sixth day of the siege of Jotapata.

The low grumbling of cornua rose up from the field above the crashing footsteps of a legion marching in time, steady and measured, despite the arrow storm cracking down on upturned shields. No shouts or war cries came from the XV Apollinaris, thus making their advance all the more threatening for their resolve needed no bolstering by bravado.

And so The Brute crossed the killing ground between the siege lines and the walls; but apart from the occasional unlucky legionary it was only Jewish dead that were left in its wake. It was with a renewed storm of stones and bolts, targeted by the artillery crews at the stretch of wall directly above The Brute, that it reached its destination. Titus' conspicuous cloak flashed in and around the centuries wielding the huge engine and his, and the centurions' and optios', shouted commands rose over the still-silent legion, stationary to either side of the ram. Back the great tree was hauled, slow but fearsome on its straining ropes; safe beneath the overhanging roof, its handlers sweated as muscles strained to gain every possible inch of swing. And it was with the first collective shout ejaculated by the Romans that, at Titus' shrill command, they thrust The Brute forward. Down the great tree swooped, its shining bulbous ram's head to the fore, reaching its lowest point as its ropes became vertical, its velocity ever increasing; its momentum, now Titanesque, forced it into the wall of Jotapata. The earth shook with the report of the blow, as if Vulcan himself had beaten on the stone with his hammer; its echo resounding around the hills as splinters of stone exploded from the impact. The frame upon which the great siege weapon was mounted juddered and jolted back, sending many of the crew toppling to its wooden floor. The Brute rebounded, its ropes thrumming with contrary forces as it reached a lesser apex from which to dive forward again. With a further deep concussive shock, the ram's head gorged out another spray of shards to leave a wound the depth of a fist in the ancient walls of Jotapata. But the walls were ten-feet-thick and The Brute would have to strike many a time before the stone would weaken and then begin to tumble.

The frame was pushed back to its original position so as not to lose any part of the strength of the weapon. With the roars of the officers urging them on, the men of The Brute grabbed hold of their charge by its many looped handles and steadied the great engine before, again at Titus' command, they strained to withdraw it to its maximum before thrusting the head back into Jotapata.

'You make progress, general; how pleasing it is to see that you do.' The voice behind him oozed obsequiousness in a tone more suited to falsehoods than to the truth.

Vespasian did not turn around. 'I thought that I had forbade you from coming here and leading your men in battle, Herod Agrippa.' He paused as another reverberating boom issued from the focus of all current martial endeavours. 'In fact, I had the distinct impression that you were happier hiding in your temporary bolthole rather than coming near the army that you sent to aid me.' The second, lesser crash sounded. 'It was, after all, over forty days ago that I wrote to you refusing your presence in command of your men. In the absence of a follow-up request from you, I had developed the distinct impression that you had decided that you had done enough for honour's sake and could legitimately stay safely away from the fighting.'

'My dear Vespasian,' Herod said, as his shaded litter was borne level with the general, 'I would never in normal circumstances ignore an order from you. To do so would be as if to disobey the Emperor himself as you are his representative here.'

'But you did so in this case.' Vespasian turned and smiled with exaggerated warmth at the tetrarch. 'And why now? Did it just take you a month and a half to pack?'

Herod returned the smile with equal insincerity, his dark eyes, either side of his hawk's beak of a nose, the legacy of his father, betraying an inner worry that pleased Vespasian. He gestured around the field of struggle. 'There is much that needs to be organised before one joins an endeavour such as this.'

Vespasian could not be bothered to goad the man any further as the work of his army was of far more interest. The Brute again collided with solid stone as the artillery kept up its barrage on the wall above it so that, still, none dared risk their head above it in order to rain missiles and fire down on the engine.

'I trust that I find you well, general,' Herod said after a while when it had become apparent that Vespasian would be venturing little in the way of conversation.

'You do,' Vespasian replied, deliberately not enquiring after Herod's health.

'That is most gratifying.' Herod cleared his throat as if he were building himself up for a difficult question and arranged his loose, exquisitely woven white robes over his slender frame so that they hung to best show his form. 'And Titus, your son, he is in good health too, I hope.'

'Yes, as far as a man can be if he's standing beneath the walls of a besieged town wearing a bright red cloak.'

Herod gave a supercilious little laugh and then quickly corrected it to another clearance of the throat. 'Indeed. Well, I shan't take up any more of your time, general. I shall go to the camp and summon my captains for a briefing on the situation.'

'You do that, Herod.'

'I will; perhaps you will be kind enough to share my table this evening?'

'This evening I intend to be feasting with my men in Jotapata. Perhaps you will join us instead?'

Herod's expression remained neutral. 'It would be my pleasure; provided, of course, that you manage to take it by dinner time. My constitution is such that I cannot delay my repast. But, before I go, may I ask something?'

Vespasian set his face in preparation for the question he knew to be coming. 'Go ahead.'

'I was wondering whether there had been any prisoners captured recently; I was thinking that if there had been it might be helpful for me to interrogate them as I know the way they think and would be able to question them subtly.'

And find out whether they know of his communications with Yosef, Vespasian thought with an inner smile as another mighty boom of The Brute echoed around the hills. 'There are a few,

Herod; they were caught sneaking in and out of a gully disguised as sheep. But I don't think that your kind offer is necessary as I believe that we've got everything out of them that we can; you know how persuasive we can be.'

'But, general, you know how brave a Jew can be.'

Vespasian made a show of considering this for a few moments. 'I suppose you could be right, Herod; we did have a couple a few days ago who were less than keen on talking. One even went to the trouble of dying rather than revealing anything of interest; like who he was delivering his message from, for example.'

Herod seized upon the bait that Vespasian had dangled. 'There you are, general; give me the other one and I shall have all he knows out of him very quickly, before he dies.'

'Would that I could, Herod,' Vespasian said in a tone laced with regret, 'but unfortunately the man escaped.'

'Escaped! How could that happen?'

Vespasian paused as he watched another brutal blow from The Brute shake Jotapata's walls. 'Very easily: I let him.' He was careful not to look at Herod but felt the tetrarch cast a worried, sidelong glance at him.

'Why did you do that?'

'To see to whom he ran.'

'And?'

'And the idiots who were meant to be following him lost him; I had the optio in charge broken back down to the ranks.' Vespasian felt Herod's relief as he let out a long breath. 'The prisoner managed to give them the slip just to the north of here so we assume that's the direction in which his master lives.' Vespasian turned to Herod with a look of baffled innocence. 'You live that way, Herod; you wouldn't have any idea who would be communicating with the rebels from up there, would you?'

'Ohhh,' Herod blustered as the sound of another impact thundered up from the head of The Brute. 'It could be a number of people. I've heard that the Jews of Damascus are getting restless as Malichus keeps on increasing the taxes they have to pay him. It might even be Malichus himself.'

'Malichus is here, with his army, and, unlike you, has been since the beginning, because I deem him to be a useful man to have by my side. Interestingly, he said that it might have been you.'

'Me? What would I want to have communication with Yosef for?'

'Yosef? Who said the message was for Yosef? I didn't.'

'Well, I just assumed that it would be, seeing as he's the leader of the rebels.'

'I suppose so; although it could just as easily have been to the town's elders or rabbis that the message was addressed. But, anyway, I told Malichus not to have his prejudices and antipathy against you colour his judgement. It was you and your sister, after all, who tried to stop the rebellion right at the beginning. I think he accepts that you would never betray Rome.'

'Quite. What did it say, this letter?'

'Well, it was from someone calling himself "The Master of the Anointed"; he was very keen that Yosef should continue to hold out despite what a family member had said. It went on to say that the rebellion could always look to Parthia for help.'

'Parthia?'

'Yes, the actual wording is something like: look to the East. Anyway, it's treasonous and I imagine the Emperor will want the balls of whoever sent it.' Vespasian looked over to Herod, concerned. 'You will put your mind to who it might be, won't you, Herod? The Master of the Anointed sounds Jewish to me.'

'I shall have my network of agents look into the matter with utmost urgency. Anything to help Rome, general.'

Anything to help yourself, more like, was Vespasian's unarticulated thought. 'And ask your sister, Berenice; she seems to have a good grasp of the politics of the region.'

'You can ask her yourself, general; she is on her way here. Although, naturally, as a woman she is unable to travel at the same pace as we can, being so encumbered with her baggage.'

'Indeed, Herod. I'm still in shock at the speed with which you got here. Now, if you would excuse me, I have a town to capture.'

*

Again the ground shook as The Brute crunched into the walls of Jotapata and again the report resounded over the field and echoed back from the hills. Fiery substances poured down from the newly extended walls onto the soaking hides of the engine's protective covering, here and there causing it to smoulder but, in general, they rolled or poured off the pitched roof causing little harm to those beneath its gables. Vespasian rode forward, with his staff in attendance, as much to rid himself of Herod's company as to be closer to the breach when it opened.

But the defenders had no intention of letting The Brute penetrate their town with impunity and, despite the continuous hail of missiles strafing the top of the wall, they managed to lower a device to counter the awesome power of the engine. It was an elegant solution, Vespasian had to admit to himself, as he realised that the huge bundle that Yosef's men were deploying on two chains was nothing more than an enormous cushion, the size of four men in a row. With one man risking his head, peering down over the wall to shout guidance to the teams on the chains, the cushion descended. Three such spotters in quick succession fell back, their skulls shattered by multiple impacts as archers and artillery turned all their attentions to them; but each time one disappeared with a cry of agony and a spray of blood a new spotter replaced him to shout invaluable directions back down to his comrades. As The Brute surged forward for yet another thrust, the counter-measure, at a screamed order from the latest spotter a moment before two shafts powered him back, jolted down and the ram's head thudded into the mass of blankets and straw. No noise emanated from the impact, deadened as it was by the cushion, and the wall suffered no damage. Its momentum stunned, The Brute did not recoil but, rather, remained embedded within the depths of the cushion.

'Cut it down!' Titus roared as all seemed to pause in shock at the effectiveness of such a simple gambit.

An instant later, the centurions commanding the legionaries on either side of The Brute regained their focus and bellowed commands at the men closest to them. Forward they dashed, swords flashing, to hack at the device that had so easily nullified the mighty engine of war. However, it was chain that the cushion was suspended on, not rope, and so it was impervious to blades and the legionaries were forced to hack at the material itself, trying to separate it off. And this was what the defenders had been waiting for: boiling oil and supra-heated sand flowed down through the gap between the wall and the protective roof, slopping onto the cushion and splashing onto the faces and clothes of the men attempting to destroy it. With screeches of anguish they fell back, burning or blinded, as the cushion itself burst into flame with an explosion of fire. Fuelled by so much heat falling from above the straw and cloth within it combusted with the rage of Vulcan, igniting the boiling oil that had fallen through to the floor of The Brute's housing. Within moments, a conflagration raged that set fear into the hearts of all who beheld it.

Vespasian kicked his horse forward, knowing that indecision would lead to failure and thence to disgrace. Leaping from the saddle, he pushed his way through the scrum of men all desperately trying to get clear of what was now searing heat. 'The hides! The hides!' he shouted, pointing up at the protective roof. 'Tear down the rearmost of the hides!' He jumped up and grabbed the overhanging edge of one of the soaked hides at the back of the engine's housing; pulling with all his strength he managed to dislodge it a fraction as an optio with a few men came to his aid. Together they heaved and tugged, pulling the hide from its nailed fixings; down it fell, sending Vespasian and his comrades tumbling to the floor as the two centurions realised what was being attempted and bawled their men into imitating their general.

With the hide held before him, protecting him from the furnace, he ran forward and threw it down onto the burning floor. Within a few heartbeats, more of the fire-dampeners had been thrown onto the blazing wood, smothering the flames and quelling the heat so that hides could be flung over the head of The Brute to quench the fire that threatened to consume it.

With the cushion destroyed, the chains were hauled up, their links too scalding for an attempt to pull them down, and Vespasian knew that it would not be too long before another counter was deployed. 'Now man The Brute!' he bellowed, seeing that the fire still raged on the oil sticking to the wall but no longer threatened the structure of the great engine. 'Keep it working!'

Reacting with military alacrity to the order, the centurions shouted their men back to their positions on the ropes. Back the huge ram was hauled; back as far as it could be, before, with a mighty grunt of exertion, it was hurled forward with rage and hatred. Almost majestic, it swung in a downward arc on its cradle, its massive weight accelerating it, bolstering its momentum until, with a glorious inevitability, it struck the wall once again through the fire that still clung to it. And it was with intense and concentrated power, through a billow of exploding flame, that it hit and Vespasian felt the shock course through his entire being and his eyes closed involuntarily. As they opened and The Brute rebounded, he peered through the fire to the point of collision; the heat had expanded the stone, weakening the wall's construction, and a crack had appeared; not large but a crack nonetheless. Once more the brazen-headed war machine surged forward and thumped into the newly made wound; this time Vespasian kept his eyes open and was rewarded with the sight of the crack jagging further open.

'Keep them at it, centurions!' he shouted, his excitement at the imminence of the possible breakthrough raising his voice.

The centurions exhorted their men to further effort; they hauled The Brute back even more than they had thought possible before flinging it forward with all their might and a massed roar of effort. With another fierce back-waft of roiling flames, the ram's head thundered into the wall, crunching the loosening stone; chunks, large and small, still ablaze with raging oil, burst from the impact, hitting the legionaries at the front of The Brute and causing them to hunch and turn away, cheering as they did so, arms flung protectively over their heads. The great cedar of Tyre recoiled, leaving a deep rend that Vespasian could see was certainly the beginning of the end. He turned to seek out his son. 'Now, Titus, now for your towers!'

Titus acknowledged his father's shout and, with his horse rearing and sword flashing over his head, summoned the two other great beasts of war from where they had been waiting out of bowshot. And forward they lumbered, hauled on by teams of lowing oxen and sweating legionaries as the archers and artillery kept a continuing flow of projectiles pounding the top of the wall, giving bloody execution to all foolish or brave enough to try to shoot down the trudging animals. But with only their lives to lose, lives that they deemed already lost, the Jews heeded not death and defied the missiles strafing them to launch shaft and stone at the oxen, as they came into range, felling a couple. With speed born of practice, their drovers cut the floundering beasts from their traces and put them out of their misery as the great towers rumbled towards them. Built on wheels the height of a man, the towers, wide at the bottom and tapering to the top, passed over the stricken oxen as, repeatedly, The Brute dealt carnage to the stonework of Jotapata's weakening defences.

In grim, silent ranks, the assault cohorts marched behind either tower, each man steeling himself for the ordeal to come, for they knew what to expect: they knew the claustrophobic confines of the narrow staircases within the engine, up which they would clamber, fleet of foot as speed would be crucial to the endeavour. They knew the dizzying height of the ramp that would be dropped across to the wall; there were no rails, just a sheer drop to the Ferryman or, worse, a life of crippled ruin. They knew, moreover, all too well from bitter experience, the ferocity with which the Jews would attempt to repel their assault and the soaring death toll of those first to storm the town; and they knew, too, that none of these factors would prevent them from entering the towers once they were rammed up against the walls.

And Vespasian knew, as he watched the siege engines progress forward over ground flattened especially for them, that victory was now within his sights, although he did not fully form the thought for fear of the black humour of the gods that had afflicted him the last time he had done so. Another booming report took his attention back to The Brute; the fire on the wall was dying but it had done much self-inflicted damage. Masonry cascaded down as the bulbous, brazen head delved deep into the opening of its own forging. In it drove, each thrust widening the wound as the housing was moved, foot by foot to the right, in order that new segments of stone would suffer its attentions, so now the whole length of wall visibly shuddered with each virile plunge.

Again a cushion was lowered on chains, the spotter above yelling directions; but this second was not as robust as the first and nor was the guidance equally accurate as, in their haste to deploy it, it fell uneven and swinging. With another thundering resound and a judder of freshly laid stone, the lip of the newly extended wall, directly above The Brute, collapsed, spilling the spotter from his perch to crash down amidst the falling stone onto the roof of the housing; off he rolled from the steep, oil-slick hides to pitch to the ground, his head crushed under jagged rock. The men of The Brute cheered his demise as proof of the effectiveness of their weapon and hauled all the harder on their ropes and the new, quickly constructed extension continued to tumble.

Stone and shaft still whispered overhead as Titus ordered forward the men of his legion's first cohort, who had the honour to storm the breach. On they came, at the double, led by the redoubtable Urbicus, primus pilus of the legion's élite unit. Battle-worn and grizzled, his numerous *phalarae*, awarded for bravery, clinking on his harness, and his transverse, white horsehair plume marking his position to his men, Urbicus advanced past Vespasian's position, now to the rear of The Brute, with the eagerness of a voyage-weary sailor approaching a brothel. At Urbicus' bellowed command, the first century of the first cohort formed into testudo as the original wall now crumbled freely and the breach became viable. Positioning his men to the right of The Brute, as the second century did the same on the left with the rest of the cohort waiting behind, Urbicus, impervious to missiles hurled down from above, waited for the great ram to be withdrawn from the gash in Jotapata's defences. And as the two towers rumbled up to the walls, The Brute was pulled back, foot by foot; a century of archers, now brought forward to beneath its protective roof, pumped shaft after shaft into the breach to stop a shield wall from forming or a sortie taking the offensive to the attackers. But the latter was what Urbicus and his men were determined to prevent and the moment the gap between the ram's head and the wall was wide enough for one man, Urbicus leapt through with an inchoate roar that rose above the cacophony of strife to which Vespasian had long since become accustomed. An instant later, the centurion of the second century followed his senior officer into the breach; hobnails gripping, shoulders rolling, lips snarling, the two centurions pumped their legs with vigour to climb the tumbled stone, dust and smoke obscuring their passage, swords drawn and shields raised. Without pause, their men stormed in behind them, determined to be deemed worthy of a place in the two senior centuries of the legion.

It was with pride that Vespasian watched Urbicus lead his men into the dust and smoke of the breach and it was with fear and pride that he saw Titus jump from the saddle and follow them in. Such considerations were forced from his mind as, with a grinding of wood on wood and the rattle of loosened pulleys, the two towers dropped their ramps to crunch down upon the defences. Even as the wooden ramps still quivered with the impact, the senior centurions of the assault cohorts charged across. A slingshot to the forehead snapped one back to plunge headlong, dead before he hit the ground. His men, incensed at his demise, their hatred boiling, took their wrath to the enemy and flung themselves forward as, at the rear entrances to the towers, men queued to mount the internal steps and follow their comrades over the wall and on into the town that had defied them for so long.

With great satisfaction and much relief, Vespasian swung his right leg over the rump of his mount and jumped to the ground. Jotapata was falling and this sack was one he would relish.

However, there are peoples who will never admit defeat, no matter how crushing the odds against them, and Rome found her match in that virtue in the Jews of Jotapata. All had been prepared in advance and all went according to plan.

Three legionaries plummeting headlong, screaming to the ground, from the right-hand tower, no more than thirty paces from him, was the first inkling Vespasian had that something was wrong. He glanced up to see two more men slipping from the ramp whilst others whirled their arms in the air, trying to retain their balance as their feet slid from under them. More men disgorged from the bowels of the tower and rushed onto the ramp in their haste to make contact with the enemy, colliding with their comrades floundering on a slick surface and losing their footing as, from the wall, defenders threw buckets full of greasy liquid onto the wooden surface. More legionaries fell into the void – two clinging on for a few moments with their hands until their fingers were kicked away or trodden on by struggling mates as the pressure from behind continued to grow.

In panic, Vespasian looked to his left, over The Brute, to see the mirror image played out on the second tower as legionaries skidded along the ramp, failing to get purchase on the wood, and then dived into the chasm below. Heartened by the effectiveness of the stratagem, the defenders thrust long spears into the chaos, dislodging many more of the hapless soldiers of the assault cohorts until the ramps were clear. The danger filtered back to those waiting in the towers and the aerial attack faltered.

Vespasian ran to the breach and clambered over the rubble, crowded with legionaries; on the other side of the walls hand-to-hand combat raged as more and more of the first cohort streamed through the gap. But the defenders had been ready for them in the narrow streets, along a frontage of no more than a hundred paces, opening out onto the wider thoroughfare that ran the length of the wall. Here, where close confines negated their numerical inferiority and protected by their captured armour and shields, they fought toe to toe with the élite, professional soldiery hurled against them, their refusal to acknowledge defeat giving them the edge that they needed.

The Jewish line was holding.

'With me,' Vespasian shouted at a centurion leading his men down the rubble in a column, four abreast. The man acknowledged his general's command and fell in behind him. 'We go for that flank,' Vespasian instructed, pointing at the right-hand side of the fight straddling the thoroughfare itself and abutting, fifty paces away, stone steps leading up to the walkway on the wall; Titus' distinctive helmet plume bobbed at the heart of the melee. 'We need to help your legate break through to those steps and then clear the wall so that the tower assaults can restart.'

The centurion nodded, understanding exactly what was expected of him and his men; he looked over his shoulder and, waving his sword in the air, urged his century on, past the bloodied body of Urbicus, staring with sightless eyes up at the empty ramp of a siege tower, thirty feet above him.

Running next to the centurion, Vespasian grimaced at the pain in his side and struggled for breath, feeling each one of his fifty-seven years weigh heavy upon him and envying the relative youth of the centurion pounding along beside him. Perhaps age was telling on him more than he cared to admit to either himself or Caenis. Her image flashed across his inner vision, highlighting his mortality as he had a moment's thought that he may not see her again. He thrust doubt from his mind and hurdled a fallen legionary. Ten paces away, the extreme right of the fight raged with the acute violence of bitter foes giving and expecting no quarter. It was here that Vespasian flung himself, to support his son and to save the faltering assault. With the wrath of a man who has seen the prize he thought he had won being snatched away from him, Vespasian barged through the rear ranks of legionaries, bellowing at them to make way for the fresh troops behind him. Through he drove, his sword held at shoulder height as the legionaries gave way to him. With an explosive punch of his shield into the chest of a manic-eyed, blood-spattered youth, Vespasian burst through the front rank of the Roman line. A sharp jab down to the throat sent the youth, already reeling and winded, back in a spray of gore from a gaping wound. Incoherent rage spewed from Vespasian as he stamped his left foot forward and lowered his shield to block a low spear thrust. Next to him, he felt the centurion press against his left shoulder as his men relieved the tiring legionaries of the first and second centuries. New strength gave new impetus and the Jews, lacking the ability to relieve their line, fought on with weakening arms against the fresh troops. On Vespasian worked his blade, on and on as he strove to reach the steps; stroke after stroke he dealt, supported by the century he had brought with him, every man striving for the same objective. And back the defenders fell in the face of such heated violence; tired and weakened by more than a month and a half of the deprivations of a siege, they retreated foot by foot, but they did not waver; their formation remained solid.

'There they are!' Vespasian shouted as the steps came into focus within the violent microcosm of reality that was his present existence. 'One more effort!'

Resurgent were the thrusts of blades darting from the Roman line as they reacted to their general's appeal; explosive were the punches of the shields that accompanied them. Forward they pressed, closing on their objective; a Jew fell dead at the foot of the steps and then another stepped backwards, over his fallen countryman, defending himself against the relentless thrusts of his veteran opponent. Back and up the man went, the legionary pressing him all the time; Vespasian mounted the steps after them, shouting at the veteran to finish the job. But as they rose they cleared the scrum of the melee and became a target for a new force. Unable to enter into the fray for fear of hitting their own in such close quarters, the Jewish slingers and archers had remained concentrating on targets to the other side of the wall. Now with the enemy isolated and exposed within the walls they took their chance. With at least four shafts appearing simultaneously in him, the veteran plunged off the steps onto the defenders below, breaking them and providing a gap through which the centurion powered, pulling his men with him. Cursing at his conspicuousness, Vespasian pushed on up the steps praying that the man behind him would hold his shield over him. Lunging at the retreating Jew, he sliced through his calf and then pounded him off the steps as he screamed and hopped on one leg. With the walkway in sight, Vespasian surged forward, feeling the presence of men coming up behind him. It was with a bellow of achievement that he took the last step, shafts and slingshot fizzing past from many angles. A searing pain shot up his right leg; he faltered and stumbled. Down he went to his knees, visible to all. A cheer rose from the defenders as they saw the Roman general fall and cries of concern stuck in the gorges of the legionaries as many turned to see the enemy surging towards their stricken leader.

Vespasian looked down at his foot: an arrow pierced it through and blood flowed freely from both entry and exit wounds. 'Help me up!' he shouted at the nearest legionary. 'I can't walk.'

Sheathing his sword, the legionary grabbed Vespasian's hand as his comrades held their shields over their general. Using his one good leg, Vespasian pushed and pulled himself up, wrapping an arm around the man's shoulder. With the protective shields cracking to the impacts of arrow and shot, Vespasian hobbled back down the steps.

'Are you all right, Father?' Titus asked as he pushed through the crowd to aid Vespasian.

He grimaced with the pain. 'I'll be fine, I think. Now get the lads out of here; without the towers we haven't got the walls and without the walls we are in a death trap. Unpleasant as it is to admit it, we've failed again today.'

CHAPTER VI

'I WILL NOT WITHDRAW, nor will I offer them terms for surrender so that they can walk away and do the same thing again elsewhere.' Vespasian was adamant; the pain inflicted by the doctor administering to his wound added to his vehemence.

'I didn't say that you should do either of those things,' Magnus said, as soothingly as his gruff manner would allow. 'I just said that you're going to have to rethink what you're doing here, as in: "how you are dealing with the situation here" rather than "whether or not you should be here at all".'

Vespasian winced as the doctor continued to swab out the two wounds, although the pain now was nothing compared to what he had endured during the extraction of the shaft; he had almost crushed Caenis' and Titus' hands as they held him down. 'Yes, well, how do you rethink taking a town by siege when the whole place is filled with religious fanatics so treachery isn't an option, especially since they stoned to death the only three agents we had inside?'

'But it *is* an option now, Father,' Titus informed him from his seat in the corner of Vespasian's private accommodation.

Vespasian frowned, interested in his son's statement. 'Go on.'

Titus took a sip of his warmed wine and then rolled the cup in both his hands. 'One of my double agents slipped out through the breach as we retired.'

'One of your double agents?' Vespasian dismissed the news with a petulant wave of his hand. 'What use is that? He's bound to betray us so you might as well just nail him up and perhaps we'll all feel a little better.'

'No, Father, he's far too useful. He's decided that his best chance of survival is to throw himself at my mercy, which, if what he says is true, may well be forthcoming.'

'What does he say?'

'I'll send for him once the good doctor here has finished putting you in an even worse mood.'

'And you're sure he's speaking the truth?' Vespasian asked Titus once they had finished listening to Hormus' rendering of the deserter's words.

Titus looked uncertain, hunching his shoulders. 'I think so, but who can ever be sure with these people? However, it does make sense if you do the arithmetic. When we first arrived here we were told that there were between three and four thousand defenders inside Jotapata and look at just how spendthrift they've been with their lives since. It could easily be that they were forced to use every last man to stop us from getting through today, even though they were only containing us across a hundred-pace front and probably had a similar number of men on the walls.' Titus pointed at the deserter. 'He maintains that Yosef sent half the men remaining to him out on the sortie against The Brute this morning and they all died. So I should say that it's perfectly possible that there are no more than four hundred fighting men left in the town at most.'

'And their women and children?' Caenis asked. 'From what you've told me, they can be as deadly as the males.'

'With slings from a distance, yes, perhaps.' Titus looked at Hormus. 'Ask him.'

A brief conversation in Aramaic ensued before Hormus replied. 'He estimates there to be no more than twelve hundred women and children left. Many slipped out through the ravine before we discovered it, to ease the burden on supplies.'

Vespasian thought for a few moments, contemplating his newly bandaged foot. 'And he is sure about the exhaustion, that none of the guards can stay awake at night any more through lack of sleep and malnourishment?'

'Look at him, Father; I think his appearance speaks for itself.'

Vespasian had to admit that the deserter did indeed look as if he was on the verge of laying himself down to die. Gaunt, pale and with dark sagging sacks under his eyes, the Jew looked even worse than he smelt – which was saying a considerable deal. 'And this unguarded door that he claims is the back way into the citadel, you believe him?'

'We'll find out when we get there, won't we? We'll take him with us, and if it's not exactly how he says it is, he'll die.'

Coming to a decision, Vespasian looked at his son. 'We'll go in at the beginning of the twelfth hour of the night.'

Titus looked confused. 'We?'

'Yes, we. I'll lead the assault.'

'Father, you can barely walk; you'll be worse than a man short, since someone will have to help you. And, besides, how can the slowest member of the unit lead from the front without gravely slowing the whole operation down?'

'I'll manage.'

'No you won't, my love,' Caenis said with a degree of firmness that surprised Vespasian. 'I realise that you feel today was an affront to your *dignitas* and an insult to Roman arms in general, and so it was, but that dent to your pride doesn't give you the right to act like a fool.'

'Act like a fool, woman! Me? How dare you talk to me like that?' Vespasian jumped to his feet and immediately regretted it, slumping back down to his couch with clenched teeth.

'I dare because somebody has to,' Caenis snapped. 'Look at you: you're practically a cripple and you talk of leading a century on a night assault, scaling the walls, creeping past sleeping sentries and then capturing the citadel, before the Jews are awake, just as the rest of the legion pours through the breach at the crack of dawn. Please be sensible.'

Vespasian checked a biting retort that he would probably regret and looked at the people around him; apart from the kneeling prisoner, who spoke no Latin, he was surrounded by those closest to him: his eldest son, his oldest friend, his long-time lover and his freedman. Those who loved him best; there was no need to feel obliged to save face with Titus, Magnus,

Caenis and Hormus and, indeed, he felt shame at having acted so ridiculously. Of course he could not lead the attack. Again he cursed the stubbornness of the Jews, and Yosef ben Matthias in particular, for holding out so desperately just when he thought he had triumphed. 'Boiled fenugreek!' he spat. 'We were defeated by fucking boiled fenugreek. I've never even heard of boiled fenugreek becoming impossibly slippery; imagine my despatch back to Rome when I say that I lost over twenty men to boiled fucking fenugreek? I'll be a laughing stock.'

'You'll be a laughing stock if you try and lead a night assault hopping on one foot,' Magnus pointed out. 'And, what's more, I'll wager that you'll be a dead laughing stock.'

Vespasian relented. 'You're right; you're all right: I'm just being foolish because I want to be there at the death and have my revenge of these bastards who've defied me for the last, how long is it?'

'Forty-six days,' Caenis said.

'Forty-six days? And we go in tomorrow just before the dawn of the forty-seventh; it looks like Yosef's prediction will come true, after all.'

'I'll make sure that it does, Father,' Titus said, smiling with relief that his father had not proved to be obstinate in the matter. 'I'll take the first century of my first cohort to do the job. They are raring to avenge Urbicus, although none of them had any reason to love him personally.'

'I would hope not. We can't have the men liking their centurions, especially the primus pilus. Who's his replacement?'

'Labinus from the third century as Centurion Fabius of the second is now without his right hand.'

'I expect Labinus will be anxious to get a grip on his new command; this will be an ideal opportunity for him. I look forward to hearing how it goes.' Vespasian winked at his son. 'You may have banned me from the night assault but I can assure you that I'll be there when the rest of the legion come through the breach, even if I have to swallow my pride and have Magnus and Hormus carry me.'

'You'll be swallowing something all right, if you ask me to carry you,' Magnus muttered. 'And I can assure you that it won't be your pride.' He cast Vespasian a wicked grin. 'It'll be *my* pride, if you take my meaning?'

Before Vespasian could say whether he did or not take Magnus' meaning, the centurion commanding the guard snapped to attention in the doorway.

'What is it, Plancius?'

'Sir! Herod Agrippa is here, sir!'

'Herod Agrippa? What's he doing here?'

'Sir! He says he's here at your invitation, sir!'

Vespasian had a sick feeling bubble in his stomach as he realised that he was about to have his face rubbed into his failure by the oily oriental; to refuse him admittance would be the act of a coward. 'You'd better show him in then.'

'And so, my dear general,' Herod Agrippa oozed, 'determined as I was to take up your gracious offer of dining with you in Jotapata, I readied myself, as you can see, in my finest attire.' He indicated to the long robe of delicate linen, embroidered with gold and silver thread and girded by a belt of golden chain; over his shoulders, he sported a black and white patterned mantle, the work of many hours of intricate knitting. A bejewelled turban and golden-toed calfskin slippers completed the apparel. He looked with sympathy at Caenis. 'Alas, my good lady, you can imagine my consternation when I approached Jotapata only to find myself being shot at as, despite Vespasian's admirable confidence this morning, the town seems to remain in the hands of the rebels.' He spread his arms in a gesture indicating his total bemusement at the situation.

Vespasian suppressed his urge to slip a dagger between the tetrarch's ribs; he gave his most ingratiating, false smile. 'I'm very sorry to have put you to such inconvenience, Herod Agrippa; I'm sure it must have come as a complete surprise to find that we had failed to take the town today. Why, you are a man of such importance that I'm sure you were weighed down with so many of the affairs of state of your vast domains as to be oblivious to all that was going on around you, despite being nominally in command of a large contingent of my army.' He indicated to the couch next to him. 'But please, do recline and drink some wine; I'm sure my cook will be serving dinner very soon.'

Herod's return smile was equally as hollow and even more sickly as he took up Vespasian's offer. 'That is most kind of you, general. My sister has just arrived in the camp; may I send her a message to join us?'

'It would be my pleasure to meet her; I shall send her an invitation at once.'

'You are most kind, general. Now, tell me, as a person of little martial experience, I should be pleased to hear the insights of one so practised in the ways of war – what went wrong today?'

Vespasian indicated to Hormus to escort the Jewish deserter, still kneeling on the floor, out of the tent. 'And tell the cook to serve dinner as soon as he can and then bring some more wine on the way back, Hormus.' He turned his attention back to Herod. 'What went wrong, you ask. I'll tell you what went wrong, Herod: nothing went wrong. In fact, it is all going according to plan as tomorrow is the forty-seventh day of the siege, the day that Yosef himself predicted for the fall of Jotapata. And knowing you Jews and your predilection for prophecies I thought that I would oblige him.'

Dinner had been a strained affair as Herod bluntly refused to let go of the failure to capture the town that afternoon, always returning to the subject whenever possible in whatever roundabout way he could think of. Vespasian responded by either ignoring the change of subject and striking up another conversation with Caenis, Titus or Magnus, or deliberately misunderstanding Herod's intention and apologising for not having invited him to take a personal part in the action and offering him and his men the honour of storming the breach first at dawn the following morning.

'Again, I must refuse your kind offer, general,' Herod said, with deep regret in his voice, in reply to Vespasian's third invitation to lead the attack, this time with the reasoning that the tetrarch could take his place due to him being incapacitated

ROBERT FABBRI

by his wound. 'I know that the army would benefit from having a man of my rank, and undoubted importance, leading it, but I fear that my paucity of military knowledge would in some way detract from my other qualities.'

'Then, my dear Herod Agrippa,' Vespasian said, his voice melodramatically earnest, 'this would be an ideal opportunity to expand that knowledge.'

'Alas, I think not; if only you hadn't failed to take the town this afternoon, then this conversation would not be happening. Such a shame; and you were so sure that you would, weren't you? Never mind; but it must be playing on your thoughts.' Herod shook his head with regret and helped himself to another fillet of salted fish. 'However, I would consider having a more forward role in the retaking of Tiberias; I believe that would be greatly suited to my talents.'

'Don't you mean your purse, Herod?' Titus said, his face barely disguising his dislike of the tetrarch. 'You would dearly love a chunk of the proceeds from selling the prisoners.'

Herod's expression was one of complete innocence as he picked at his salted fish. 'The financial considerations have nothing whatever to do with it, my dear Titus. Tiberias was, or is, my capital. It was the destruction of my palace there that was the ignition of the revolt. All my artwork and statues destroyed because the religious fanatics that we're dealing with take quite literally the injunction not to forge graven images. All that art and beauty destroyed in the name of religion.'

Vespasian gave an unamused laugh. 'All that art and beauty that you would, no doubt, wish to replace, at great expense, once you've rebuilt your palace at even more expense. I'm sure the proceeds from the sale of any slaves would be very welcome; especially if you've done nothing to deserve it.'

'*We* can afford to rebuild *our* palace, General Vespasian,' an imperious female voice said.

All in the room looked towards the doorway to see a woman, in her late thirties, of exquisite refinement and great beauty.

'Sir! She wouldn't wait, sir!' Plancius reported from over her shoulder.

The woman winced at the loudness of the voice in her ear but disdained to look at its origin, so far beneath her did she, evidently, deem the centurion to be.

'That's all right, Plancius,' Vespasian said, knowing who the new arrival was. 'You may go.'

'Sir! Yes, sir!' Plancius snapped a salute and turned sharply on his left foot before marching away at the double.

Vespasian looked to Herod. 'I believe it should be you who makes the introductions, my dear Herod.'

Herod rose to his feet, his eyes staring at the vision of womanly perfection with greed. He walked over to her and kissed her on the lips and then, taking her hand, presented her to the company. 'This is my sister, Queen Berenice.'

Dark-haired and pale-skinned with a full figure and adorned with sparkling jewels and a couple of hours' worth of makeup, she was, indeed, a vision to behold, especially as she eschewed the traditional dull and shapeless dress of a Jewess and was clad in a far less concealing manner and far more expensively than her brother.

'The general, Titus Flavius Vespasianus, commander of the army of the East,' Herod said, indicating to Vespasian.

Pushing aside the temptation to ask Berenice just where she thought she was queen of, Vespasian inclined his head towards her. 'It is a pleasure to make your acquaintance, Berenice. You'll excuse me if I don't get up.' He gestured to his bandaged foot and neglected to say that he had no intention of getting up, with or without his wound.

Berenice looked down her pronounced nose at Vespasian, her pale blue eyes assessing him with evident disappointment. 'I imagined you to be—'

'To be what?' Vespasian cut in, instantly disliking this haughty faux-queen for the way she looked at him. 'More refined, perhaps? Less of the Sabine farmer in my appearance?'

Berenice checked herself. 'No, general, that is not what I meant; what I meant was that—'

'I wouldn't say what you meant, my dear,' Caenis said, getting to her feet and approaching Berenice. 'It might be misconstrued and then we might all say that we imagined you to be more polite.' She held out her hand, smiling with what Vespasian took to be genuine warmth.

There was a pause before Berenice took Caenis' proffered hand. 'You must be Caenis, the former slave of Antonia the younger.'

Caenis' smile remained fixed. 'I am, although I prefer to think of myself as the freedwoman, Antonia Caenis, wife in all but name of the most powerful man in the East. Indeed, one could almost think of him as a king, which would make me his queen. Where did you say you were queen of, my dear? As I believe your second husband, King Herod of Chalcis, died twenty years ago and then you abandoned your third, King Polemon of Pontus, soon after marrying him. You're not married to your brother, are you?' Gripping Berenice's hand firmly, Caenis led her to the couch. 'Please won't you join us; we're only on the third course.'

Vespasian felt a deep love for Caenis as she helped settle the bristling Berenice on the couch next to her. He glanced over to Titus to see if he had enjoyed the demonstration as much. One look at his son caused Vespasian to start; he knew the expression written all over Titus' face, he knew it only too well for it had been on his face one time too: it had been on his face all those years back on the day he had entered Rome for the first time. It had been the day he had first set eyes on Caenis.

One look at Titus, slack-jawed, soft-eyed and head tilting, and Vespasian knew that, despite being at least a decade younger than Berenice, his son was hopelessly in love.

'You take care, Titus,' Vespasian said, as the first century of the first cohort of the XV Apollinaris formed up in the shadowed Via Principalis, at the beginning of the eleventh hour of the night, two hours before dawn. 'If the deserter was lying and they are alert in there, fall back immediately. Don't take any unnecessary risks.'

'Father, stop acting like a mother hen,' Titus replied as, behind him, Centurion Labinus and his optio silently counted their men off with the aid of a flaming torch. 'I have every intention of coming back alive; in fact, I've never felt more alive.'

The gleam in Titus' eye told Vespasian exactly what was making his son feel so vivacious. Vespasian had watched as Titus made, at first halting and then more fluent, conversation with Berenice over the last couple of courses at dinner and how he had hung on her every word in reply, agreeing far too readily and enthusiastically with her assertions as to the progress of the war. He had noted with interest how her brother had seemed to grow more attentive to Berenice the more she favoured Titus with her attention. But most of all he had noticed the soft brush of his arm that Berenice had favoured Titus with upon withdrawing for the night and the thrill that it clearly gave him; so much so, that Vespasian had observed his son caressing the skin that she had touched on a number of occasions since. 'She's eleven years older than you; she's going to be forty next year, I checked with Caenis.'

Titus looked at his father in surprise. 'What do you mean?'

'I mean that the non-queen Berenice was born eleven years before you. She has been married three times, has two grown-up sons. She's Jewish – although, granted, not rabidly so – and is, if the rumours that Caenis has heard are to be believed, a frequent and enthusiastic visitor to her brother's bed and is also no stranger to liaisons less close to home. He, you will note, is not married and never has been. All in all, I would say that she is the most unsuitable woman for you and I advise you to forget her.'

'What makes you say that?'

Vespasian put his hand on his son's shoulder. 'Titus, I saw the way you ogled her, all doe-eyed and drooling; don't tell me that you don't know what I'm talking about. Cupid sent an arrow right into your heart and it's my job to persuade you to pull it out because it will cause you nothing but grief to love that woman.'

'She's beautiful, Father.'

'So are countless other, far more suitable, women; women who can give you children, an heir. Berenice is most probably too old to bear children safely and besides, even if she did, she's Jewish and Jewishness passes down through the mother. Do you want your children to be Jewish? Just look around you, look what we're fighting; would you want your offspring to associate themselves with all this?'

'They would be brought up Roman with Roman gods.'

'Ah! So you've already considered the matter, have you? That was quick. Well, let me tell you something: whether you bring your children up to be Roman and respecting the Roman gods is irrelevant as you will spend much of your life away from them in the service of Rome, whereas Berenice, if you are foolish enough to make her a mother to your offspring, will be with them for far more of the time and who knows what sort of poison she will drip into their ears. No, Son, you can't trust a woman like that. And if in the unlikely event that she did return, or, more likely, pretend to return, your affection, I can guarantee that it would be for selfish reasons; she would be using you to further her own ends.'

'What could she use me for, Father? I'm just a legionary legate.'

'At the moment you are; but you are also the son of the commander of the army of the East at a time when the West is starting to look more and more unstable. Now you think about that when you've finished capturing the citadel and ask yourself this: if the West does flare up and the Emperor is deposed, how many legions could an eastern army muster if it were to join the dash for power that would inevitably follow?' Vespasian leant on both his crutches and kissed his son's forehead. 'Now, go and take care of yourself. I'll see you later when Jotapata is finally in our hands. And, if you can, take Yosef alive.'

'We think he's down there, Father,' Titus said, pointing to the entrance of a cistern, as Vespasian hobbled towards him on his crutches, across a small agora. Breathing hard, having climbed the citadel with Magnus and his dogs and Hormus, Vespasian scented the stench of death. All around, in the dawning light, lay the aftermath of a surprise attack: bodies, some intact and some not, piles of offal, discarded weaponry, spent shot or arrows, doors and shutters hanging loose where hiding places had been breached, and all swathed in the mixture of smoke and steam from fires still burning or recently extinguished. Legionaries roamed the streets, searching for what spoils of war they could find as was their right having taken the town. The wailing of children and the cries of ravaged women filled the air as the customs of siegecraft were adhered to and the victors took their pleasure; the fact that so few women were found alive meant that their ordeals were protracted.

'Are you sure it's him?' Vespasian asked, catching his breath before leaning forward and peering down through the opening into a cavernous interior; there was a faint flicker of torchlight and the sound of voices coming from within but no one was visible.

Titus shrugged and again touched his arm, involuntarily, where Berenice had brushed it. 'We haven't found his body and Malichus assures me that no one slipped through the cordon that his Arabs set at the base of the hill, so that leaves either in here or in another hiding place that we've yet to discover. But I think he's down there with another twenty or so.'

Vespasian grinned. 'We really did catch them by surprise, didn't we?'

Titus returned the smile. 'We were over the walls and in the citadel without being challenged once; the deserter was right, they were too exhausted to stay awake and the door was exactly where he said it would be, unguarded and unlocked.'

'Yes, the rest of the cohort went through the breach with hardly any opposition, just a few sentries, most of whom were dozing. Ironic, isn't it, that after forty-seven days of the toughest siege I've ever conducted, it should fall with hardly a whimper.' Vespasian looked back at the cistern and then signalled to Hormus. 'Have a listen and see if you can understand what they're saying down there.'

The freedman bent down to put his ear to the opening and closed his eyes. 'It's an argument, master,' Hormus said after a few moments; he listened on. 'It seems that there are three different points of view. One party is insisting that they should come out and fight to the death and take as many of us with them as possible. Another says that is too risky and they run the risk of being captured and humiliated and should therefore just commit suicide immediately. And then there is a third point of view, which seems to be held by just one man, that they should surrender and throw themselves at your mercy, because, surely, as a soldier, you would appreciate the bravery they have shown and grant them mercy as one soldier to another.'

Magnus gave a grim chuckle. 'Whoever that is doesn't know you at all well.'

Vespasian agreed with that assessment. 'Yes, the men are all going to be nailed up and the women and children are headed for the slave markets of Delos.'

Hormus waved his hand, trying to listen closely. 'I think it's Yosef, master; all the others are now shouting at him, accusing him of leading them into this disaster and then showing no honour at the end.'

'Well, I'd say they have the measure of the man.'

'He's now saying that if they are wary of coming out fighting and risking being captured and if they are unwilling to throw themselves at your mercy, the only option left is killing themselves. But, he says, suicide is a sin in their god's eyes.'

Vespasian shook his head. 'These people never fail to amaze me.'

'He's saying that they should take it in turns to kill one of their number and then only the last one alive will risk their god's wrath by killing himself.'

'Ahh! This Yosef is a cunning bastard,' Vespasian said. 'We're just about to see how good his arithmetic is.'

Magnus frowned and tugged his dogs away from a lump of flesh of dubious provenance. 'What's arithmetic got to do with it?'

Vespasian held up his finger, quietening him, so that Hormus could carry on listening.

'He says that there are twenty-three of them. Yosef has given the sword to the man two places away on his right, the third man and he will kill the man two away from him, the fifth man. The sixth man will then kill the man two away from him, the eighth man, and so on. They've agreed.'

Vespasian did a quick mental calculation. 'I'm beginning to have a grudging respect for this Yosef. He's worked it so that he's going to be one of the last two left alive along with the tenth man.'

'How can you respect someone who's so obviously a coward?' Titus asked. 'And a dishonourable coward at that, seeing as he's deceiving comrades with whom he's fought shoulder to shoulder for the last month and a half.'

'Let's just wait and see what he has to say for himself when he comes out, before we make any such judgements about him, shall we?' Vespasian said as the sound of the first body slumping to the floor, amidst the muttering of many prayers, emanated from the cistern.

'Toss me down a rope,' a voice called from within the cistern. 'I wish to throw myself at the mercy of Titus Flavius Vespasianus.'

'And you are?' Vespasian asked, knowing perfectly well what the answer would be.

'I am Yosef ben Matthias, priest of the first rank and the Jewish Governor of Galilee.'

'What a surprise,' Vespasian muttered before shouting back down, 'And what about the tenth man?'

There was a pause. 'The tenth man?'

'Yes, the one who would survive with the way you set it up; very clever, I thought.'

'We made a pact and he too lives.'

Vespasian nodded to a waiting legionary to throw down a rope. 'Then you had both better come up.' He turned to Titus. 'Bring Yosef to me back in the camp. I'll see him in public in the *principia*; I want the men to witness what this Jew has to say for himself.'

It was a bitter and bedraggled column of more than a thousand wailing prisoners that filed into the compound built to house them until they could be assessed, categorised and then sold to the many slave-dealers that followed the army along with the merchants and whores. Most of the women were naked having been stripped during their defilement; as they could not, therefore, rend their garments they had torn at their skin with their nails and wrenched out clumps of their hair before they could be manacled to stop them from reducing their worth. A couple had managed to strangle their children to prevent them from suffering a life of slavery, so now the women had been separated from their offspring as a precaution against such unnecessary financial loss.

Vespasian stood with Magnus, contemplating the scene, calculating how much the entire batch would be worth and what percentage he could expect to get from it. 'They're not going to fetch much,' he complained. 'There's hardly any flesh on any of them after such a long siege.'

'You've only got yourself to blame,' Magnus pointed out. 'Seeing as you was in command.'

Vespasian looked askance at his friend. 'Are you being serious?'

'Of course. You can't go moaning about the state of the captives if you allow them all that time to get out of condition. Next time, I suggest that you bring things to a speedier conclusion. Although, I would say that with the way things are going, your inability to conclude a quick siege may be a good thing.'

Vespasian shook his head in disbelief. 'You really are turning into a cantankerous old man, Magnus. Nothing ever seems to be quite right for you, lately.'

'Yeah, well; can you blame me when I'm being dragged around this armpit of the Empire with fuck all to do?'

'Well, no one asked you to come.'

'And no one's asked me to leave.'

Vespasian squared up to Magnus. 'Is that what you want then? Me asking you to go?'

'No, sir. I'm just saying that I'm bored and when I get bored I get crabby. I don't mean nothing by it. But you have to admit that I do have a point: if you want the captives to be in a better condition, you should capture them before they've had time to go to seed. And, after all, it may well be that you will be needing money soon; a lot of money and quite soon.' Magnus' good eye took on a shrewd aspect. 'And don't pretend that you don't know what I'm talking about. I know you, sir, and I know that you've always been obsessed by all these omens that have beset you throughout your life: the signs at your birth that no one will tell you about; the Oracle of Amphiaraos; Thrasyllus' prediction that should a senator witness the Phoenix in Egypt then he would go on to be the founder of the next dynasty of emperors, and I was there with you in Siwa when you saw the bird's rebirth and Siwa may not be part of our province of Egypt but it used to be a part of the Kingdom of Egypt. All that stuff, even Antonia bequeathing you her father's sword after her suicide when it was well known that she would give it to the grandson who she thought would make the best Emperor, has made you think that maybe, just maybe, if you take my meaning?'

'Well, of course with the way things seem to be going in the West, it would be foolish of me not to consider my options. Although Caenis hasn't heard any more about Vindex's or Galba's intentions, there is certainly evidence of discontent with the current regime growing and then, well, who knows?'

'I know, sir. I know that you would be foolish to relinquish your army with the rumours that we're getting from the West. That's why I say that perhaps it's a good thing that this is taking longer than you hoped.'

Vespasian considered his friend's words. 'It has crossed my mind a few times in recent days; the trouble is that the longer the rebellion is allowed to rage unquashed, the worse it will get and then the longer it will take to defeat to the extent it might prevent me from doing anything else with this army, if you take *my* meaning?'

'I most certainly do, sir. So, my advice would be to stop complaining about the state of the captives and just make sure that you get more of them and eke out the whole campaign. No one should be in a hurry to give up an army.'

'You sound like Malichus. He's also very happy to have this thing last as long as possible so that he can achieve maximum profit out of it.'

'Then he's a sensible man, sir.'

'Yes, well, I suppose it's some consolation to make money out of a bad situation.' Vespasian caught sight of the last two prisoners being led into the compound. 'And there's the man who started the whole thing. This could be an interesting interview; I shall dress for it.'

Legionaries jostled one another to get a view of the man who had caused them so much hardship over the last forty-seven days, and beyond. Indeed, it had been Yosef who had instigated the destruction of Herod's palace at Tiberias, which had been the act of violence that had catapulted Galilee into joining the rebellion that had, until then, been mainly confined to Judaea and centred upon Jerusalem.

Tall and proud, despite his fetters, Yosef ben Matthias walked through the jeering crowd. He cast his eyes around and showed nothing but disdain for their derision, even as a good many of them called for his death.

Vespasian sat on a curule chair that had been set up on a dais in the centre of the principia, the main meeting place of the camp, on one side of which was the praetorium. With all the dignity of his rank, togate and wearing the Triumphal Insignia he had won in Britannia, he watched his prisoner approach. All hushed as Yosef reached the foot of the dais steps and then knelt in supplication before them; yet he did not grovel. Rather, he held himself proud upon his knees, his eyes looking directly into Vespasian's, the image of a brave man defeated in fair and open combat.

Vespasian contemplated the leader of the Jews in his leg-irons and manacles, kneeling before him, and was reminded of the way Caratacus, the rebel King of Britannia, had comported himself when he had been brought before Claudius; there were, he reflected, many similarities between the two men: not least the dignity with which they suffered defeat. 'So, Yosef ben Matthias, we meet again in very different circumstances,' Vespasian said after a few moments of thought. 'Circumstances that do not seem to be at all to your advantage; circumstances that have been brought about by your own actions. I would be curious as to how you would justify those actions.'

Yosef drew a long breath. 'Titus Flavius Vespasianus, I have done no more than any man who valued his liberty would. Now that I have lost that liberty I do not mourn it for I did not give it up without fighting to the utmost limits of my strength. In the end it was the failure of the priests in Jerusalem to support me that led to my downfall; I spit upon them.'

These words set a stir around the watching legionaries as they understood well the martial sentiment behind them and had witnessed the determination with which Yosef had fought. Murmurs of appreciation could be discerned and the mood against the rebel prisoner began to soften.

Vespasian recognised the change in atmosphere and, indeed felt it within himself: who would not resist subjugation? 'What do you expect me to do with you, Yosef ben Matthias?'

'What I expect is Roman justice, seeing as I have given myself up to Rome.'

Vespasian had to refrain from smiling; it was a clever answer, he had to admit. Roman justice in this case could mean one of two things: summary execution on his orders or being sent to Rome to appear before the Emperor, and Vespasian could guess what Yosef was asking for. He looked around the faces of his men, which were now all turned to him, awaiting his decision; he could see what they wished for. 'Very well, Yosef ben Matthias, Roman justice is what you shall have; I will send you to Rome for Caesar to decide your fate.'

The legionaries broke into rapturous cheers that grew as news of the pronouncement filtered back through the crowd. Vespasian stood, favouring his good leg, and extended an arm to the crowd as they hailed him. For longer than he would have normally deemed safe he allowed his men to continue the applause and he noticed Titus raise a quizzical furrow in his brow at the length of the Ovation. However, he had, he felt, earned this praise and it was a few score more heartbeats before he brought the men to order. 'You may take him away and keep him in close confinement,' he told Yosef's guards.

'Before you lock me up, Titus Flavius Vespasianus,' Yosef said as he got to his feet, 'may I request the privilege of a private audience?'

Vespasian looked at the Jew who had with such accuracy prophesied the fall of Jotapata, and his curiosity as to how that had come about got the better of him; and anyway, what had he to lose? 'Very well.'

'Whatever you have to say,' Vespasian said, reading the expression on Yosef's face as he looked at Caenis, Titus and Magnus, sitting with Vespasian in his private quarters, 'you can say in front of these three people. Not that you have any choice, I would remind you, seeing as you are my prisoner.'

Yosef tilted his head in acquiescence and then, again, looked Vespasian straight in the eye as if dealing with an equal. 'You may suppose, general, that in capturing me you have merely secured a prisoner, but I come as a messenger of the greatness that awaits you. I come from God himself. I know the Jewish law and I know how a defeated Jewish general should die; but I fixed things in that cistern so that I would not. You say that you would send me to Caesar; how so, when I see him before me?'

Vespasian's hands gripped the arms of his chair; Yosef had his full attention.

'Do you think,' Yosef continued, 'that Nero will remain in power for long? Do you think that the few who will follow him before your turn comes will reign more than months? You, Titus Flavius Vespasianus, are Caesar and Emperor, you and your son here. You are the one who was foretold: the messiah to come out of the East and save the world.'

This was too much for Vespasian. 'Messiah! Me? Bollocks! Now it's obvious that you just saying all this to try to save your life.'

'Then clap me in your heaviest chains and keep me for yourself and see what comes to pass, for I tell you: you are master of land and sea and of the whole human race – and then kill me if you find that I'm taking the name of God in vain.'

Vespasian thought for a few moments as within him his heart raced. 'How did you know that Jotapata would fall on the forty-seventh day?'

'Who told you I said that? I only made that prediction in a letter.'

'We intercepted that letter.'

'Ah, of course you did.'

Vespasian leant forward in his chair. 'How did you know?'

'I can do these things. I can see.'

'Then why did you go into Jotapata,' Titus asked, 'if you could see that it would fall and that you would be captured?'

'I always said that it would fall after forty-seven days and I also said that I would be taken alive and now I say that you will be emperor.'

'Centurion!' Vespasian called towards the entrance.

'Sir! Yes, sir!' Plancius shouted, coming into the room and saluting.

'Take this man away and keep him in close confinement.'

'Sir! Close confinement. Yes, sir!'

'But he's to be treated well; do you understand me?'

'Sir! Well treated. Yes, sir!'

'Good, you may go.'

With military precision, Plancius marched forward and then, taking Yosef's arm, turned him and marched him from the room calling out the steps.

'Well, what do you make of that, Father?' Titus asked once Plancius was a sufficient distance away to make conversation possible once again.

Vespasian was dismissive. 'I think he's a clever man who can see what's happening in the Empire and who is trying to gain favour with me by making a wild guess.'

'But you were implying exactly the same thing to me this morning.'

'Yes,' Magnus put in, 'and you know perfectly well, sir, that this idea has been growing in you for a while.'

'But I'm not certain,' Vespasian argued. 'At least, not like Yosef seems to be.'

Caenis put a hand on Vespasian's arm. 'Then, my love, perhaps it's time that you became certain. When the inevitable happens and Nero is deposed, all the evidence, both prophetic but mainly practical as in who is in the best position, points to you.'

Vespasian took a large intake of air and exhaled slowly, shaking his head as if unable to comprehend a concept. 'I can't believe it; I can't be certain. Surely it doesn't all point to me becoming the … the …' But just like his late uncle, Gaius Vespasius Pollo, all those years ago when Vespasian was sharing his suspicions with him, he could not quite bring himself to say the word.

PART II

JUDAEA, JULY AD 68 TO JULY AD 69

CHAPTER VII

'OUR ESTIMATION IS that there are about fifteen thousand of them,' Tribune Placidus reported to Vespasian as he stood on the walls of Jericho gazing east, towards the Jordan River, just six miles away. Between the river and the town was a mass of people, a smudge on the well-irrigated landscape that had been trampled and ruined by their flight.

Vespasian studied the herd of humanity as it was driven towards the river by four alae of auxiliary cavalry and six cohorts of foot, both legionary and auxiliary, in what he hoped would be the final subjugation of the rebellion outside Jerusalem.

It had been a year since Jotapata had fallen and every day of that year had seen bitter fighting. His men, hardened now to the fanaticism and excesses of the rebel Jews, killed without compunction or mercy; it was now difficult to get them to spare even the peaceful villagers who were caught up in the conflict through no fault of their own, for many a rebel had masqueraded as such and used the cover to perpetrate murder on their captors. No Jew could be trusted in Roman eyes and the brutality with which Vespasian and his legions were prosecuting the war only added to its ferociousness.

After the relatively easy capture of Tiberias it had been one long list of sieges: Gishala, where Yohanan ben Levi had been cornered, had fallen to Titus who had made the mistake of agreeing not to enter the town on the Jewish Sabbath, in the hope that this concession would be seen throughout the land as an indication that Rome was considerate of Jewish sensibilities. Yohanan had taken advantage of Titus' goodwill gesture and slipped away in the night with hundreds of his followers; the mistake was never made again. Tarichaea, Gamala, Gadara, the list went on as Vespasian had subdued first Galilee then Peraea and then Idumaea in the south and now, finally, Judaea. Now, once these fugitives from Gadara had been dealt with, just Jerusalem remained.

Just Jerusalem.

And this is what had been playing on Vespasian's mind of late as he had waded through the laborious and distasteful process of killing or enslaving all who would not willingly submit to Rome, more than a quarter of a million people, by his reckoning: Jerusalem. What to do about Jerusalem?

Jerusalem. After Yohanan ben Levi had escaped from Gishala he had made directly for the city of the Jews and here he had proceeded to do what Vespasian and Titus had hoped he would: cause division within the populace. In fact, so successful had he been in causing division that one of Titus' agents estimated that over half of the population had been killed. He had joined forces with other radicals and called upon the people of Idumaea, the Jewish kingdom to the south of Judaea, to come to their aid. Twenty thousand answered the call and swarmed into the city, treating the local population as hostile, looting, raping and murdering; with savage brutality the Zealot and Idumaean alliance fought its way through the city and on up into the Temple itself, leaving the complex awash with blood.

Not being satisfied with the booty they plundered from the common people they then turned their attention to the priests and aristocracy, murdering all they could find and enriching themselves on their property. The morning after the storming of the Temple, eight and a half thousand bodies lay in the dawn light, untended in a sacrilege that had shown just how far this takeover of the city had got from religious principles. Ananus was murdered on the basis that he had been in contact with Vespasian, something that Vespasian knew all too well had not been the case, and a puppet high priest, who knew nothing of the rituals, was put in his place. An extreme form of the law was imposed, using the harshest interpretations of the Jewish Scriptures, and fear lay over the whole city whilst those who professed to be fighting in the Jewish god's name enjoyed the power they had seized and conducted themselves in any way that they saw fit.

In other words, the rebels were doing his job for him, and Vespasian could not help but feel that, for the time being, it was best to leave them to their own murderous devices. But, having said that, Jerusalem still defied Rome; at some point it would have to be broken and the Temple, that monumental symbol of their intolerant religion, would have to be razed to the ground. Vespasian felt it vital that it be shown that the invisible god of the Jews was not only invisible but also non-existent, seeing as it could not prevent the destruction of its people and its Temple.

'What are your orders, sir?' Placidus asked, bringing Vespasian out of his reverie.

Vespasian looked again at the thousands of fleeing refugees from Gadara and felt no pity for them. 'Kill all that do not wish to subject themselves to slavery. There is no mercy, not now; things have gone too far for that.'

Placidus saluted and went to carry out his orders as Vespasian continued to gaze east, his hands resting on the ancient walls of Jericho, a town almost as old as Arbela where he had been imprisoned for two years over fifteen years ago. He thought of that time, living in the depths of that ancient city with no light, little food and less hope, and reflected that, even in the depths of the despair that he had wallowed in, he had been more attached to life than these people who were happy to throw their lives away for some god whose very existence was impossible to prove. At least, he reasoned, the fanatics who worship Yeshua, the Jew who had been crucified, like so many of his countrymen, had something tangible to believe in, since Yeshua had existed. Vespasian knew that for certain for it had been his brother, Sabinus, who had been in charge of crucifying the man, here in Judaea.

No, it was time to bring this whole rebellion to a halt and crush the fanaticism out of the Jews; it was time to make them see sense and join the rest of humanity in respect for all gods and tolerance for those who worship differently from others. It was time, and Vespasian felt steeled by the thought after so long fighting a belief that he could not understand.

He turned and walked along the ancient battlements of the town that had, firstly, refused entry to the fleeing rebels and then had, secondly, flung its gates open to the pursuing Romans in a sure sign that the tide of opinion in Judaea had turned in favour of Rome; the ordinary people had begun to turn their backs on the fanatics who had blighted their lives and brought ruin to their land. Yes, Jericho's submission was an indication that it was finally time.

They lined the west bank of the Jordan ten deep, caught between the river, swollen by unseasonal rain, and the blades of their pursuers. A great wail rose from them and many rent their clothes or tore at their hair for they saw the impossibility of crossing the usually placid river as a sign that their god had forsaken them. And, after all the atrocities that had been committed by the Jews in their god's name, Vespasian was not surprised that he had deserted them – if that god existed in the first place, he mused, as he and his staff pulled their mounts up on a knoll to witness the final destruction of the last rebel force outside Jerusalem.

Placidus did not waste time sending forward messengers in a futile attempt to parley; neither side expected that any more. Although outnumbered by more than three to one, Placidus showed no fear of what was a poorly armed and badly led rabble. To either side of the Roman formation, two alae of cavalry moved forward at the trot as the central infantry cohorts began a steady and silent advance formed in great blocks.

Many of the trapped Jews, both male and female, fell to their knees beseeching their absent god for deliverance, but most controlled their anguish, drew their weapons and waited in grim expectation for what was to be visited upon them: death.

And death was swift to find them. With fifty paces between the sides, the cavalry charged. Facing only a ramshackle line with hardly any long-reach weapons, the horses did not shy but carried their assault home. Both flanks of the Jewish line buckled and split asunder, allowing the mounted troopers to penetrate and then overwhelm them. Down fell many beneath the trampling hoofs of maddened horses; back the rest were pushed before the stabbing and slashing of swords from above as they suffered the inevitable fate of infantry overrun by cavalry. The centre began easing back as they felt their comrades to either side giving way, threatening to expose their flanks, as the Roman war machine bore down on them. In silence the cohorts marched, their measured steps threatening in their steady repetition, until, with the release of thousands of pila, hurtling low towards the foe, they broke into a run, shields in advance, and slammed as one into the broken frontage of the rebels. It could not even be called a fight, Vespasian thought with satisfaction as the Jews were propelled back with the shock of multiple impacts. But there was nowhere to go other than the river; its current surging and swift, it swallowed them whole. In they fell, those who had not perished to pila or blade, their long robes pulling them under as they struggled with unpractised strokes to stay afloat; but even those few who could swim floundered amongst the mass of bodies, dead and alive, packed so close in such a fast-moving stream. And the Romans stood on the bank and laughed as they hacked at those trying to wade out, forcing them back to certain death in a river already clogged with corpses but ever greedy for more.

'That should do it, gentlemen,' Vespasian said to his staff, and turned his horse, having seen enough. 'When the Jordan disgorges all those bodies into the Dead Sea they'll float there for days for all to see; that should focus their thoughts in Jerusalem. I'm returning to Caesarea; send out orders for all legions and all auxiliary cohorts, other than those on garrison duty, to assemble there by the full moon. And send a message to Mucianus in Antioch to ask whether he wants to be consulted, as well as to Tiberius Alexander in Egypt. And then, gentlemen, when we're all gathered, we shall see what to do about Jerusalem.'

'How did it go?' Magnus asked through the steam as Vespasian walked into the hot room of the baths in the Governor's palace overlooking the modern harbour of Caesarea.

'I thought I might find you in here,' Vespasian said, throwing a towel over the stone bench next to Magnus and sitting down; warm droplets of water dripped from the domed roof, decorated with an aquatic-themed mosaic of fierce sea creatures battling in a startlingly blue environment. 'It was as expected: a futile waste of life, which, seeing as they seemed determined to die anyway, hopefully brought them some satisfaction; I was certainly pleased to see them dead. I'm told that Placidus managed to capture a couple of thousand alive so that should make us a little money.'

'Not as much as a year ago seeing as you've been flooding the market with all the slaves you've been sending to Delos, and the same thing is happening in the West with all the Gallic captives after Vindex's failed revolt a couple of months ago.'

Vespasian wiped the sweat from his bald pate and contemplated the recent news from Gaul: Vindex, the Gallic Governor of Gallia Lugdunensis, had revolted against Nero's tax policy and declared his support for Galba as emperor. But the rebellion had failed to take root and had been joined only by three of the sixty-four Gallic tribes. No other governor had supported him with their legions as it looked to be nothing more than a Gallic revolt with Galba as an unlikely figurehead. Nero had responded by making preparations to travel north to confront the rebels and weep and then lead them in paeans of victory after his tears had melted their hearts; it had, however, been Lucius Verginius Rufus, the Governor of Germania Superior, who had spared the Empire from witnessing Nero's novel military tactic by defeating Vindex, who had promptly committed suicide.

What was uncertain, here in Judaea at the other end of the Empire, was Galba's position, for news of him and his actions had only been sketchy. However, it had been rumoured that he had raised a second legion in addition to the one that was already under his command as a part of his province of Hispania Tarraconensis, and it had been further rumoured that he had named it the VII Galbiana, which in itself was a statement of intent. But more than that Vespasian did not know despite Caenis' attempts to gather information.

What was certain, though, was Magnus' assertion that the price of slaves had tumbled because of the huge number of captives as a result of revolts at either end of the Empire; but Vespasian was sanguine about the result of market forces. 'Well, that can't be helped; and, anyway, it doesn't bother me. Just because I'm getting thirty per cent less per individual, the fact that I've been selling in bulk means that overall I haven't made any less than I would have expected.'

'Fair point, if you look at it that way. Mind you, if you carry on like this, there won't be a Jew left in Judaea.'

'Would that be such a bad thing? We could settle the land with veterans or give some of it to reasonable people like Malichus and his Nabataean Arabs; we could make it governable again.'

'And what about the Jews?'

'What about them?'

'Well, there'll still be thousands, hundreds of thousands of them alive throughout the Empire.'

'But they'll be slaves.'

'Only the ones who you captured; not those living in the big Jewish communities of Alexandria, Antioch and Rome, to name but a few. Now, the way I see it is that to the Jews this country is sacred because they believe that their invisible god lives here and that they are his people. You take that away from them and what will happen? They'll want it back; *demand* it back, knowing them.'

'Well, they won't get it back.'

'Someday they might well get it back, you've seen for yourself just how stubborn they are; and then what will happen to all the other people that we settle here, Malichus and his Arabs? They'll fight to keep what they see as now being theirs; that's what'll happen and then we'll have another problem on our hands.'

Vespasian let out a long sigh and, resting his elbows on his knees, hung his head, enjoying the heat as he contemplated what his friend had said. 'I don't know, Magnus,' he said eventually. 'And frankly, I don't care because it'll be somebody else's problem. I've had more than my share of it and I've still got Jerusalem to deal with.'

'And when are you going to do that?'

'I don't know at the moment, but I've summoned a council to debate the matter; it should convene in three days' time.'

'My instinct is not to rush into a full-scale siege of Jerusalem whilst they are still fighting each other; but, gentlemen, the problem is so complex and the stakes so high that I would appreciate the benefit of your opinions.' Vespasian looked around the large, circular table set in the exact centre of a bright, airy room on the first floor of the Governor's residence; tall, open windows with white marble surrounds looked out over the harbour, bristling with ships, with lighters and other small craft rowing between them, as beyond, the sea glistered in the afternoon glow of a hot August day. Curtains billowed, filled with the soft, warm breeze that flowed through the windows bringing with it the sounds and smells of the fish market lining the south quay, the civilian side of the harbour; to the northern side, the military half, the triremes that had brought Mucianus from Antioch and Tiberius Alexander from Alexandria bobbed at anchor amongst the many other vessels of war that were at Vespasian's disposal.

For a while, no one spoke as Vespasian studied each man in turn. The effete Mucianus, who, judging by his colourfully flamboyant dress, was, after eighteen months, adapting well to his post as Governor of Syria, tapped his finger on the table and glanced, rather too lingeringly, at Titus. Seated next to Titus was Tiberius Alexander, one of the three Jews in the room, although only two were accorded a place at the table; swarthy and ruggedly handsome with oiled black hair and beard, he did not look like a Roman prefect of Egypt, but this, Vespasian surmised, was the secret to holding in check that delicate province, so finely balanced between the Greek, Jewish and indigenous populations. Malichus, scratching at his bush of a beard with one hand and fanning himself with the other, sat next to the prefect with Herod Agrippa to his left; Vespasian had not wanted to invite the tetrarch for personal reasons but had been persuaded by Caenis to overcome his antipathy on the basis that Herod might prove useful in any negotiated settlement, in the unlikely event that one could be achieved. It was for that reason too that Yosef was present, standing next to the door; still a prisoner and still wearing his shackles, Yosef had been a source of good background information to the intelligence that Titus had gleaned from his various sources over the year. Vespasian had grown to like him, thinking of him as his pet Jew, and had decided to keep him rather than send him to Rome.

And then there were the legates of the other two legions, Traianus and Vettulenus – Titus still being in command of the XV Apollinaris. Finally six auxiliary prefects, including Placidus, filled the other places around the table. It was, Vespasian mused, a meeting of the men with the most experience of Judaea and the Jews in the Empire; if they could not come up with sage counsel then no one could – but that was also a likely outcome, for who could say anything sensible about such a nonsensical land?

'We should attack, Father,' Titus said when it became apparent that no one was going to give their opinion before the general's son and second in command. 'They are weak and divided; my sources tell me that, ten days ago, the Idumaeans in the city rampaged through the lower town, killing everyone they could find. The people would surely join us and rise against the Zealots and Idumaeans if we attack.'

'That is something that will never happen,' Tiberius Alexander said with certainty. 'No matter what wrong a Jew has been done by a fellow Jew, they will unite in the face of a Gentile enemy. If we lay siege to Jerusalem, we will be fighting almost the entire population.'

'Almost?' Vespasian asked, leaning forward.

'There'll always be a few who will see Rome as the answer to the problem of religious fanaticism; fair-minded businessmen from the better-off families in the main, but not more than a few.'

'Then perhaps we should try to contact them. Herod Agrippa, do you have any way of getting messages in and out of the city?'

Herod considered the matter for long enough to convey the complexity that doing such a favour would involve. Vespasian hid his exasperation by leaning back in his seat and admiring the graceful manoeuvrings of a trireme entering the harbour, hauling down its main- and foresail to dock using just its oars.

'It may well be possible,' Herod said, bringing Vespasian back from things nautical. 'I have contacts with a few of what is left of the priestly and aristocratic families, although most of them have been murdered; I shall put my mind to who might be open to negotiation.'

'That is very good of you,' Vespasian said without a trace of irony. He turned back to Tiberius Alexander. 'So, you say if we attack we will only succeed in uniting a divided people against us. That would be the height of folly when they appear to be doing so well at slaughtering each other without the loss of one Roman life; it would seem that we should let them get on with doing our work for us for a while. However, they cannot be allowed to defy Rome indefinitely; so the question is: for how long do we let them slaughter one another?'

The prefect of Egypt did not need long to consider the matter. 'It's now August; the Zealots and the Idumaeans have held the Temple and both the lower and upper towns for most of the year; if even our roughest estimates are correct, then with the number of people who have fled the city and the number who have been slaughtered, there cannot be more than a hundred thousand people left inside. The harvest is coming in now; throw a loose cordon around the city and start to deprive it of supplies.'

'Not a full siege, just a blockade,' Vespasian said, almost to himself, as he watched the trireme glide into dock and discharge mooring ropes. 'Yes, as soon as word gets about that anyone taking produce into Jerusalem will have it commandeered by us the traffic will dry up very quickly and the city will begin to starve.' Vespasian looked across to Yosef. 'What will they do?'

'The Zealots will ransack the city looking for supplies and keep them all for themselves,' Yosef said, his chains clinking as he gesticulated. 'They see themselves as doing the Lord's work in defending the Temple from us and therefore have a right to be fed; whereas the common people are just there to obey the law as the Zealots interpret it.'

'And what will the common people do when they start to starve?'

'They will try to leave but the Zealots will prevent them from doing so.'

'Why would they do that?'

'Their ideology is such that they cannot allow people to have free will. You see, everything is about their interpretation of our religion; if they say that the common people must starve so that they can eat and be strong to protect the Lord's House, then it amounts to a religious command from God himself.'

Vespasian saw the implication. 'Therefore if you try to escape, you are going against God and the only punishment for that in their eyes is death.'

Yosef raised a dismissive hand, chain chinking. 'The punishment for most things they consider to be a sin is death.'

'Yes, it seems to be that way.' Vespasian turned to Mucianus. 'Governor, how is our border with Parthia? Have they taken advantage of our having three legions and their auxiliaries fully occupied here in Judaea?'

Mucianus pouted slightly as he phrased his reply in his mind. Gone was the athletic military tribune that Vespasian had known from his time in the II Augusta; the man whose actions had helped to save the legion the night that Caratacus had surprised it as it formed up. It was a different man who now sat at the conference table: elegantly coiffured and stylishly dressed in eastern fabrics, he was a man who exuded a love of pleasure and a desire for power; he was a man whom Vespasian had once trusted with his life and been rewarded by his trust, but could he still do so now, he wondered?

'There has been very little incident on our border,' Mucianus said, his voice silky, his expression serene. 'Vologases is happy with the settlement in Armenia and his attention is now turned to the East where there are a couple of troublesome satraps who used the Armenian war to try to assert their independence from the Great King. I believe that one of the satraps died wishing that he could assert his independence from the stake up his arse and the other one has fled to India; Vologases won't be looking this way again until he has finished his settlement of the East, next spring at the earliest.'

'Then that gives us our timeframe,' Vespasian said. 'We begin the blockade now and keep it up throughout the winter before moving to a full siege on the weakened city at the beginning of the campaigning season, which we will try to conclude in two months, before Parthia sniffs an opportunity.' He looked around the table but no one made to argue against him.

'In the meantime,' Titus asked, 'what do you have planned for the army?'

'Apart from enforcing the blockade, just the usual: punishment raids, garrison duty and generally keeping our presence noted amongst the locals. Why?'

'There is an issue that has developed in the last few days and has just been reported to me this morning. Another group of fanatics called the Sicarii, after the curved knives they use to kill all who don't agree with them, have taken advantage of the Idumaeans coming to Jerusalem; they've taken the mountain fortress of Masada and occupied it with at least a thousand men as well as their women and children. My spies report that they've raided all the surrounding villages and taken all the supplies they could. By stripping the country dry, they now have enough to hold out for at least a year up there.'

'What harm can they do sitting up on the top of a mountain?'

'Nothing; but they're going to have to be dealt with sooner or later, so why not sooner?'

Vespasian was dubious. 'I've seen Masada, and it is almost impregnable. The only way an army could take it is to build a ramp up to the top; think how much earth would need to be moved and how many slaves you would need to move it. No, we wait until after we have Jerusalem and use the captives that we get there to deal with Masada. Meanwhile we let them sit on their mountain.'

'Do we blockade it like Jerusalem?'

Vespasian shook his head. 'What's the point? It would be a waste of effort: let them have as much food as they like up there as, when we build the ramp, we will take the fort in less time than they already have supplies for. So their bellies are going to be full when we kill them anyway.'

Caenis walked into the room, carrying a scroll and cutting off the discussion. 'I'm sorry to disturb your council, gentlemen, but a ship has just arrived from Rome bringing news that I deemed could not wait.'

All eyes were on Caenis; Vespasian signalled for her to speak and she indicated to Yosef.

'Leave the room,' Vespasian ordered.

As the door closed and the clinking of Yosef's fetters diminished, Caenis unrolled the scroll and looked at Vespasian. 'It's a letter from your brother; he says that Nymphidius, one of the prefects of the Praetorian Guard, has persuaded the Guard to swear allegiance to Galba who, since Vindex's failed revolt, has been titling himself as legate of the Senate. This emboldened the Senate to declare Nero an enemy of the state.' She paused and looked around the room; all were holding their breath. 'Nero has committed suicide.'

There was a mass exhalation as all took in the enormity of the consequences of Nero's death without a male heir.

Caenis' eyes delved into Vespasian's; excitement burned within them. 'It's started, my love. Servius Sulpicius Galba has claimed the Purple and is marching on Rome. The Senate have confirmed him in his title; Galba is the new Emperor of Rome.'

CHAPTER VIII

SILENCE PERVADED AS all calculated and contemplated their positions. The vendors' cries from the fish market, mixed with the hustle and bustle of port activity, both military and civilian, continued to rise through the windows as the life of the common people went on, unaffected by such momentous news – the price of fish was hardly likely to be influenced by an old man, whom few had heard of, becoming emperor. Vespasian envied them their certainty of life whatever way the political wind blew, as he took a few moments to assess what he must do to keep both himself and his family safe.

'Do we know anything else?' Vespasian asked Caenis, breaking the silence.

'Marcus Salvius Otho, the Governor of Lusitania, has joined forces with Galba; not that he has any soldiers, but his long association with Nero, before they fell out over Poppaea Sabina, does give a degree more legitimacy to Galba's claim.'

Vespasian looked across at Mucianus. 'What do you make of that?'

'I would have thought that it was obvious,' Mucianus said, a smile flickering on his lips. 'Galba is childless and seventy-two; Otho is a very well-connected member of the aristocracy and aged only thirty-six, young enough to be his son ...' Mucianus left the rest of the thought unspoken.

'That's how I saw it.' Vespasian cast his eyes around the table. 'So, gentlemen, where does this leave us?'

Herod Agrippa pushed back his chair and rose. 'I have no doubt where I stand. I'm leaving for Rome immediately to congratulate the new Emperor and swear loyalty to him in person.' Without waiting for a response, he turned and left the room.

Vespasian allowed himself a thin smile. 'No doubt he hopes that by prompt sycophancy he can persuade Galba to grant him more lands. Well, Herod has his own agenda, as does each one of us here. However, gentlemen,' he looked up at Caenis and indicated that she should sit in Herod's vacated chair, 'and lady, we represent the real power in Rome's eastern provinces. My assessment would be that a combined reaction from us would be far better for all our positions than if we act individually.'

'What makes you so sure of that?' Traianus asked.

It was Caenis who, with a glance to Vespasian who nodded his agreement, replied: 'Because, legate, Galba is going to want to split up the four main concentrations of power outside Rome: the Rhenus frontier, the Danuvius frontier, the Britannic legions and the eastern army. Sabinus also said in his letter that he has heard a rumour that Galba has immediately replaced Rufus, the Governor of Germania Superior, despite the fact that it was him who defeated Vindex. Rufus's legions hailed him as imperator but he rejected the title. Obviously Galba can't keep Rufus in position, even though he did refuse the chance of power from the army.'

'Who did he replace him with?' Mucianus asked.

'That seems to be uncertain at the time Sabinus wrote, which was fourteen days ago. He says that there is rumour and counter-rumour coming out of Galba's entourage and as the new Emperor has not yet crossed into Italia from Gaul no one knows what to believe. However, he says that Aulus Vitellius was very quick to leave Rome to travel to Galba to swear allegiance to him.'

Mucianus examined a well-manicured hand. 'A fat gourmand with no military experience and an arse as flabby as a sow's belly: an ideal choice, in Galba's mind, to entrust to the security of the Rhenus border.' He carried on examining his fingernails to avoid looking at Caenis as he addressed her. 'So you would conjecture that if we send a letter with a united greeting and profession of loyalty from us all together then he would think twice before trying to remove anyone of us from our very lucrative posts.'

'Yes, Galba knows that if Syria, Egypt and the army of the East choose to do so, they can name their own candidate for the Purple and so ignite the civil war which has only just been avoided by Rufus' refusal to accept the accolade; and with control of a major part of Rome's grain supply in Egypt, that is a position in which he would not like to find himself. Therefore he is far more likely to leave a united East alone to carry on putting down the rebellion and keeping Parthia at bay. A divided response for you, however, gentlemen, will give him the opportunity to pick you off one by one.'

There was no argument at this assessment by Caenis, as all present knew her for the sharp politician that she was, albeit with only freed status.

'Tiberius Alexander?' Vespasian said, giving the prefect an opportunity to voice his opinion.

'I agree; one of the first things that he will try to do is remove me and put someone far more to his liking in my place. I can avoid that by an alliance with you, Vespasian, and you, Mucianus. We three must stand as one so that Galba will have little option but to confirm us in our posts. I will return to my province, swear my two legions to the new Emperor and ensure that the grain fleets sail on time whilst we send a combined message to Rome professing our undying loyalty to the new regime and our support for Otho should Galba choose to adopt him as his heir.'

Mucianus nodded, placing his hands on the table, evidently satisfied with the state of his cuticles. 'And I shall go back to Antioch and keep sending regular reports on how well it is going for our puppet regime in Armenia; how far away the Great King is in the East and just how well Vespasian is doing in Judaea. The Emperor will be made aware that the East is not a place that he should waste any care over.'

Vespasian inwardly congratulated himself on writing that conciliatory letter to Mucianus the previous year; a little humility had been a justifiable expense to get Mucianus to the point whereby he could support him without rancour. 'And for my part,' Vespasian said, 'I shall make my army swear the oath of loyalty immediately, so that whoever carries the letter can report to the Emperor that they have seen it with their own eyes, and then carry on containing the rebellion.' Vespasian grinned. 'So, "business as usual" is what we shall say to Galba in our joint letter. The question is: who is of sufficient status to deliver it to him?'

Titus caught his father's eye. 'It obviously can't be you, Father; nor could it be either Mucianus or Tiberius Alexander—'

'No, you are not going,' Vespasian interrupted. 'I need you here. Besides, I won't risk putting you in Galba's power so that he can use you as a hostage to my behaviour; he could force me to accept him recalling me by threatening your life.'

Titus frowned. 'I wasn't going to suggest me, Father; I was about to say that the three legionary legates, one being me, cannot be spared with the state of the rebellion as it is, therefore we have to look elsewhere. We could give the letter to Herod Agrippa but I imagine that he would try to make out that he personally was delivering the East into Galba's hands and should be greatly rewarded for it.'

'I agree,' Caenis put in. 'He cannot be trusted to be anything other than slippery; he'll make political gain out of the mission for himself whilst implying that perhaps things aren't all as they seem in the East and Galba would be wise to give him more say in the governance of the area.'

'And if he comes back with extended territory then he could make trouble for all of us,' Vespasian observed.

'Exactly,' Titus said. 'So I propose that we ask King Malichus here to deliver the letter.'

Vespasian looked across at the Nabataean king in his white flowing robes and could not imagine anyone less Roman-looking; Malichus looked delighted at the idea.

Titus read the confusion on his father's face. 'He's perfect, Father. He's a Roman citizen of equestrian rank. He's a king, in his own right, of a people who are loyal to us and we would want to keep it that way as the kingdom is a good buffer between us and Parthia. And, furthermore, he would be very happy to bear the letter because it would associate him with us and make it far more likely that Galba would confirm him in his kingdom.' Titus fixed Malichus with a stare. 'But, unlike Herod Agrippa, he won't play selfish politics with the task that we give him because he can see that his best interests lie alongside ours.'

Malichus rose and bowed his head with one hand across his breast. 'It would be an honour to bear the letter for you, gentlemen; I shall be most anxious that the new Emperor confirms Damascus upon me again, even though it would be the fifth time that I have received the same gift. Me delivering your letter to him will put him in a far more generous frame of mind towards me, I am sure; especially as Herod Agrippa is likely to make as much mischief as possible.'

Vespasian looked first at Mucianus and then at Tiberius Alexander.

'An elegant solution,' Mucianus said.

Tiberius Alexander nodded. 'Agreed.'

Vespasian put both his palms flat on the table. 'Well, I think that concludes matters for the time being, gentlemen.' He looked at the military officers. 'I'll be issuing orders concerning the blockade of Jerusalem in the morning. Dismissed.'

The three legates and six auxiliary prefects stood and saluted, before making their way from the room.

Vespasian turned to Malichus. 'If you wouldn't mind waiting in the reception room whilst we three compose our letter.'

'It would be my pleasure, general,' the king said, again bowing his head. 'I shall leave for Rome as soon as you have finished.'

'Why didn't you want Titus to go?' Caenis asked as she, Vespasian and Magnus sat on a terrace on the third floor of the palace, drinking chilled wine and watching the golden reflection of the sun lengthen on a slow-moving sea. A flotilla of small, night-fishing boats, escorted by cawing gulls and preceded by a larger, well-manned vessel, made their way through the harbour mouth, silhouetted by the westering light and putting Vespasian in mind of ducklings following their mother across a pond. Public slaves cleared away the tables and swept clean the detritus of the fish market as its traders sailed out to restock.

'For exactly the reason I said: I didn't want to offer Galba a hostage.'

'Galba has already got a hostage, two in fact: Sabinus and Domitian. You know that perfectly well. That's not the reason you wouldn't countenance Titus going.'

Vespasian raised his cup from the oval marble table around which they sat. 'He didn't even suggest that he should.'

'Don't try to avoid the question that way. It was you who said that he couldn't go without anybody suggesting it in the first place. He would have been a very good option because it would have shown Galba that you are so loyal as to not worry about sending him a third hostage; that would have impressed the Emperor far more than sending a Nabataean king. So tell me: why didn't you want Titus to go?'

Vespasian hesitated to respond, taking a sip of wine and enjoying the way the rich light reflected off the sea and played on the fishing boats' sails as they caught the breeze outside of the harbour walls. 'It wouldn't have been safe for him,' he muttered eventually.

'Bollocks,' Magnus growled, 'and you know perfectly well it is; so give us the truth or I'll do it for you.'

Vespasian looked at his friend, surprised at his sudden vehemence. 'Well then, I think you'd better do it for me seeing as you evidently have such a deep insight into my motives.'

'You're scared.'

'Scared?'

'Yes, scared.'

'Of what?'

'You're scared that you may end up in conflict with your son.'

Vespasian grunted and turned his attention back to the boats.

Caenis shook her head as Vespasian studiously avoided her gaze. 'He's right, isn't he? Of course; I should have seen that. It's a different sort of hostage that you meant, isn't it?'

Vespasian still could not meet her eye. 'Is it?'

'Yes; it's a move that would make Galba's position much safer for he would guarantee the support of the whole eastern Empire. Otho may have been close to Nero and of as high birth as Galba, but he brings nothing with him other than that. No army and no power; whereas Titus, well, Titus would be a far more attractive prospect as Galba's heir: Galba promises to make him emperor, and his father, you, my love, suddenly finds himself having to support the new Emperor because it would guarantee his family's rise to the very top.'

'And that's just the point,' Magnus said, 'his family's rise and not *his* rise. You don't think that I can't see through you, sir? You know that this is the beginning of a series of events that may just give you the chance you've been wondering about for a long time. Go on, say it! Say what you've been mulling over.'

Vespasian said nothing and continued staring at the boats as the sun deepened from golden into shades of red.

'Emperor! Say it, sir. You've started to believe that you could be Emperor of Rome and, frankly, I do too; and I'm sure Caenis feels the same way.'

'I do,' Caenis said in response to Magnus' questioning look.

'But if Galba adopts Titus,' Vespasian said, his tone quiet, 'then that becomes very unlikely. I will still be the founder of the next dynasty as Thrasyllus predicted any senator witnessing the rebirth of the Phoenix in Egypt would be, but it would be my son who would be emperor, I would just be the Emperor's father.'

'Unless you rebelled against Titus' adoptive father and overthrew him and your own son. That's what the problem is, isn't it, sir?'

Vespasian sighed and downed the rest of his wine. 'Yes, and yes and no.' He looked at his two companions, his eyes sorrowful. 'That is a part of the problem but only a part. Yes, if you insist on me coming right out with it, then I do see Nero's suicide, Galba's elevation and my command of the eastern army as being the beginning of events that could, could mind you, lead me to ultimate power. But if I allowed Titus to get into the position whereby Galba would see that it would be well within his interests to adopt him, then my ambitions would be all but over unless I fought my own son. That's just one scenario, but it's not just that: say I do decide that I have no such aspirations to the Purple and that all of the prophecies surrounding me do nothing but point to me being the father of an emperor and not emperor himself, what then? Should I allow Galba to make Titus his heir? Of course not. Am I the only one with an army in the Empire? No, there are three other large armies and a couple of smaller ones. Let's not deceive ourselves into thinking that Galba's going to die a natural death and his adoptive heir is going to inherit the Purple peacefully. No. Now, I'm not a prophet, but I'll give you this prediction: Galba and whoever he adopts as his heir, whether it be Otho or anyone else, will end up lying dead on the Gemonian Stairs and his murderer will gloat as he takes the Purple. Either way, I'll not have Titus go anywhere near Galba.' He picked up the pitcher and filled his cup to the brim.

Caenis and Magnus both contemplated his words as he drained his wine and then slumped back into his chair with a deep sigh.

'You're right,' Caenis said after a companionable silence. 'Galba would do that if he had the chance. Domitian's too young to adopt but Titus is approaching thirty, a good age. Yes, it would be a death warrant for him. I hadn't thought that through carefully enough.'

Vespasian grunted in amusement. 'Is that the first time I've seen through a political problem before you, my love? I must be getting sharper in my old age.'

'No doubt; but the fault is my ambition. I have only ever considered your prospects compared to the other men of power around the Empire. Titus I have seen only as your son and not as a potential rival. But you're right, he is, and from now on I shall think of him as such, no matter what love I bear for him.'

'Much as I hate to admit it, I can't help but feel that it's crossed his mind more than once. He must at least realise that he's a contender.'

'Yeah, well, I would trust him,' Magnus said. 'He's a good lad and surely he can see that supporting you and being your heir, should you succeed, is a far more reliable way of achieving any aims he has in that direction. As you say, he's not even thirty and look what happened to the last two Emperors who came to power young. I would think he's sensible enough to bide his time. Power is not a commodity that the Ferryman allows on board, if you take my meaning?'

'I do, Magnus, and I hope that Titus does as well.'

Caenis reached over and squeezed Vespasian's arm. 'Then you should ask him, my love. You need to have this conversation with him as soon as possible, before it starts to eat away at you and spoil what is, at the moment, a very good father and son relationship.'

Vespasian turned to Caenis, knowing that she was right. 'I'll do it after the swearing-in ceremony tomorrow.'

'We swear that we shall obey all that Servius Sulpicius Galba Caesar Augustus commands and we shall never desert his service nor shall we seek to avoid death for him and the Roman Republic.' Cohort by cohort, the Sacramentum was administered; and willingly the legions and auxiliary cohorts took it for they had hopes of a large donative from the new Emperor, larger than normal as he was not from the Julio-Claudian line and therefore would surely be wanting to secure his position with silver.

Smoke rose from the many altars set up around the parade ground outside the impressive military camp beyond the northern walls of Caesarea; breakers crashed onto the adjacent beach pushing driftwood to and fro and gulls circled above in hope of titbits from so much human activity. Each cohort was taking its turn and marching into position before one of the altars; with the cohort's offering of a lamb despatched and its heart burning on the fire the senior centurion administered the oath. Once complete, they marched away so that another could take their place.

And so it went on, hour after hour, as Vespasian oversaw the entire process, seated on a curule chair on a rostrum under a canopy against the burning sun. He had been the first to take the oath along with Mucianus, Tiberius Alexander and Malichus. The three legionary legates, along with the auxiliary prefects, had followed, leading the entire army in professing their loyalty to one who had seized power. It was that simple, Vespasian thought as yet another set of cohorts came stamping onto the parade ground ready to bellow out their allegiance.

As the first cohort of each legion arrived the primus pilus snapped to attention in front of Vespasian and, with great ceremony, was presented with the images of the new Emperor to attach to the legion's standards. Although they were but crude depictions of a man of whom few had any certain idea of his appearance, they were different to those of Nero, now discarded, and therefore worthy of reverence.

Finally the last anachronistic shout of 'Roman Republic' died away and the ceremony was complete. Vespasian stood and, placing an arm around the shoulders of Mucianus and Tiberius Alexander, led them down from the rostrum. 'We will keep in close touch as the situation will need to be watched carefully. All developments will have to be reacted to in concert; remember, gentlemen, it's only by supporting each other that we can hope to keep our positions safe. If one of us is false then he shall also go down with the other two, and I can guarantee that the punishment won't be as simple as banishment.'

'We both understand that, Vespasian,' Mucianus said, taking Vespasian's hand from his shoulder and turning to face him. 'Before we go there is one last thing that the three of us should discuss.'

'Go on.'

'If and when the time comes, which one of us should challenge for the Purple?'

Vespasian's heart jumped, and the surprise told in his eyes.

'Come now, my friend,' Tiberius Alexander said, 'of course each of us has put some thought into this. So in your mind, who should it be?'

Vespasian looked between his two allies; neither gave any hint as to what he was thinking. He took a deep breath. 'Well, in all honesty, I feel that it should be me; if and when the time comes, that is.'

'If and when the time comes, indeed,' Mucianus said with a hint of a smile. 'Well then, that settles it. Tiberius Alexander has ruled himself out because he's a Jew and would never be accepted in Rome and I've ruled myself out because, due to my preferences, I have no son.'

Vespasian frowned. 'You could adopt one.'

'I could, but then we would be back in the same place where we find ourselves now; no, whoever re-stabilises the Empire must be a man with a legitimate heir, and, from the East, that can only be you, Vespasian.' Mucianus took Vespasian's arm. 'If and when the time comes.'

'We will back you,' Tiberius Alexander confirmed as he took Vespasian's arm in turn. 'I suggest we arrange to meet back here at the close of the campaign season to discuss developments in Rome and the state of the Jewish revolt.'

Vespasian squeezed his friend's forearm. 'I think that would be a sensible thing to do. Until November then, gentlemen.'

Vespasian watched Mucianus and Tiberius Alexander go with Malichus to escort him to the ship that would bear him and their joint letter to Galba to Rome before turning to the three legionary legates and the auxiliary prefects awaiting his dismissal. 'You have your orders, gentlemen; I expect Jerusalem to be feeling the pinch within the next couple of months and I want any rebel town still holding out, even the smallest of them, obliterated and their inhabitants dead or in chains. You may rejoin your units.'

The officers snapped salutes and turned to leave.

'Not you, Titus Flavius Vespasianus,' Vespasian said formally. Titus turned back to face his father.

'I need to have a private word with you, my boy.'

'Yes, Father, but to be honest, I don't really think it's necessary.'

'What do you mean you don't think it's necessary? How do you know what I want to talk about so that you can judge it to be unnecessary?'

'Because, Father, I'm not stupid and I've worked out why you snapped at me yesterday forbidding me to go to Galba without anyone even mentioning it, and I can tell you that it is not necessary for us to have this conversation. But since you seem to feel it is so, then let me start by saying: yes, I have thought of making my own bid for power if the time should prove right, and on each occasion I have rejected the idea because it would involve fighting you and I don't think that a man who came to power having killed his father would last very long.'

Vespasian took a step back. 'Is that the only reason?'

Titus laughed. 'You should have seen your face, Tata; no, it's not the only reason, in fact it's not the reason at all. The real reason is that only a man of your experience can have a chance of becoming emperor and staying in place for more than a few months. I'm twenty-eight, there's plenty of time for me once you've had your turn and done the hard work. So don't worry about my loyalty; I'm with you should the opportunity arise, not against you.' He took Vespasian by the shoulders and pulled him close and kissed him on the lips.

Vespasian looked into his son's eyes. 'Thank you, Titus. This might all come to nothing; we shall just have to wait and see. I think we will have a better idea of what to expect by the end of the summer, beginning of autumn.'

'I think you're right, Father; the end of the summer, beginning of autumn. That will be our time, if it is to come at all.'

CHAPTER VIIII

EMITTING GUTTURAL SNARLS and slavering from lolling tongues, Castor and Pollux bounded through an olive grove, zigzagging around trees without loss of pace as they gradually gained on the two fleeing men pushing their cruelly used horses to the limits of their endurance. Keeping a steady thirty paces behind the hounds, Vespasian and Magnus husbanded their mounts to preserve their energy for what would be a long ride back to Caesarea. Behind them, the *turma* of Syrian auxiliary cavalry fanned out as they entered the olive grove so as not to fall foul of one another as they negotiated the trees; breath pumped from their horses' nostrils in the crisp, late November air.

Vespasian ducked under an overhanging bough as his mount hurdled a dead branch lying across its way. He had been enjoying the chase ever since they had spotted the two Jews, down in a valley, whilst hunting in the rough hills inland of Caesarea. They would not have interrupted their sport to pursue had not the two men fled at the sight of Roman uniforms. Now, four miles later, they were on the verge of capturing the fugitives and, by whatever means necessary, satisfying their curiosity as to the cause of the men's reluctance to come into contact with members of the occupying power.

With a final burst of speed, Castor and Pollux cleared the last of the olives just a few paces short of their quarry as the Jews' horses began to stumble from fatigue and lose the will to respond to the savage beating of their riders with the flats of their swords. Another couple of mighty bounds brought Castor up to the hindmost and with a roar he sunk yellowing fangs into the beast's rump; up it reared, its forelegs beating the air as it whinnied its anguish to the sky. With the desperation of a doomed man, the rider yanked on its mane in an effort to remain in the saddle, but to no avail and, as the beast fell backwards, he jumped clear towards the open jaws of Castor. With a scream that drowned out the noise of his thrashing horse, he crashed to the ground with the maw of the hound clamped into the forearm shielding his face. With feral savagery Castor tore at the limb as Pollux downed the second rider, sinking teeth into his ankle and heaving him off as his terrified horse sped away to the safety of distant scrubland.

'There's a good boy,' Magnus said as he drew up his mount and jumped down next to Castor who stood, snarling with intent through bloodied teeth at the terrified Jew lying, not daring to move, as he cradled his lacerated arm in his hand. 'That's a very good boy, Castor. Magnus would have been very cross with you had you eaten him before we could have words with him; very cross indeed.' He pulled at the thick leather collar around his pet's neck and eased him off the downed man. 'Now, Matey-boy, just why do you feel it necessary to run away from us when, as you can see, we're such nice and friendly folk at heart?'

As the decurion sent a couple of troopers on to apprehend the second fugitive, Vespasian dismounted and picked up the man's discarded sword. 'Perhaps it has something to do with this, Magnus.'

Magnus took one look at the weapon. 'Oh dear, sir, a Roman auxiliary spatha; what a naughty boy our Jewish friend here is. Just being caught in possession of this is enough to have him nailed up; or perhaps that's too nice for him, seeing as he probably killed one of our lads to get it, and we should send him to Greece to break rock until his back breaks cutting that canal through the isthmus.'

Vespasian turned to the auxiliary decurion. 'Search them, bind them and bring them back to Caesarea; I want to question them personally.'

'And you're sure of this, my love?' Vespasian asked, not wanting to believe what she had just told him.

'I'm afraid so,' Caenis replied, rubbing oil into his shoulders. 'Since our discussion, and despite Titus' professed loyalty to you, I've made it my business to know what he gets up to and for the last month he has not been with his legion but, rather, at Tiberias sharing Berenice's bed.'

'But he sends me regular reports from his legion.'

Caenis took up the strigil and began to scrape the oil from Vespasian's back, wiping the residue on a cloth. 'That's easily done: his thick-stripe tribune sends him reports of how the legion has been doing in stifling the flow of supplies from Samaria into Jerusalem. He then lifts himself off Berenice for long enough to write his report to you and sends it back to his second in command who then forwards it by a normal military courier to you here in Caesarea. The point is, Vespasian, not so much that he's going behind your back seeing this woman after he promised to give her up, as that is between you and him; who he sleeps with is no concern of mine. What does concern me, however, is that Berenice is a very ambitious woman, one just has to look at her past husbands to realise that. She will have seen what is happening in the Empire and she will know full well Titus' potential and the possibilities for her should he claw his way over you to the prize.'

'But she is a Jew; Rome would never accept her in the unlikely event that should happen and Titus betrays me.'

'Cleopatra was Egyptian of Macedonian origin; that didn't stop Caesar – or Marcus Antonius for that matter.' She shifted her attention to the small of his back and buttocks, oiling and scraping, as he lay on the upholstered leather couch in the warm room of the palace baths. 'But whether or not Rome accepts her is beside the point; it's what sort of poison she is dripping into Titus' ear as he ploughs her.'

'If any at all.'

'Oh come now, do you really believe that she isn't trying to get something for her own ends out of Titus? Of course she is; she's an eastern … well, not queen, but she thinks she is and I'll wager that she would dearly love to be empress and doesn't see why her Jewishness should be a barrier to that.'

'Well, it is.'

'You know that, I know that, but does she? No.'

Vespasian grunted with enjoyment and let Caenis continue working in silence for a while. 'Why didn't you tell me about this earlier?' he asked as she moved on to his thighs and calves.

'I've only recently found out and then I wanted to have it confirmed before I worried you with it. It's bad enough that you haven't heard anything from Galba either one way or the other without unnecessarily being concerned about your own son.'

Vespasian continued with contented grunts as Caenis finished off her work. He contemplated the situation. She was right, he was concerned about the lack of news from Rome; he had expected Galba either to have confirmed him, Mucianus and Tiberius Alexander in their posts by now or to have tried to recall them. But nothing had been heard from the Emperor. News of him had arrived, though, and it had not sounded good for Galba: Malichus had written saying that he had joined the Emperor's entourage in southern Gaul in late August and had presented Vespasian's letter but had received no reply from him although he, Malichus, had been confirmed in his kingdom with half the revenue from Damascus at his disposal. Galba had processed slowly through his new domain, arriving in Rome in October where he had massacred more than a thousand legionaries of the I Adiutrix at the Mulvian Bridge in a dispute over his recognising their newly formed legion. He had then gone on to cancel the donative that had been promised in his name saying that he chose his soldiers, he did not buy them, thus alienating the Praetorian Guard, the Urban Cohorts and all the army. He had also executed various senators and equestrians whom he considered to be suspect in their loyalties. Now it was being said that everybody thought Galba would make the best Emperor until he actually became so. If all these things were true, it would not be long until the fight to replace him commenced, and Vespasian did not want Titus being coerced into doing something stupid by an oriental faux-queen using all the charms of her, admittedly, very desirable body. 'Very well, my love, I'll write to him at Tiberias asking him to come and report immediately to me here as soon as I've questioned those two Jews.'

'They both had these on them, sir, hidden in their robes.' The decurion held out two vicious-looking curved-bladed knives.

'*Sicae*,' Vespasian said, recognising the weapons instantly and knowing exactly what they signified. He looked down at the prisoners, both lying strapped onto a table. They were young, with full black beards; their faces were burned by the sun whereas their bodies were pale having always been covered. One's arm was still bleeding from shredded skin and the other's ankle was mangled and punctured with many teeth marks. The dark, piercing eyes of fanatics gazed back up at him with unconcealed hatred. 'I don't suppose we'll get anything out of them even if we chop all the bits off them, one by one.' He took hold of the nearest man's circumcised penis and looked at it in curiosity. 'Such barbarism.' He turned back to the decurion. 'No, I think this calls for a different sort of questioning; have my pet Jew brought here along with Magnus and his dogs.'

The decurion gave the order for Yosef to be found as Vespasian smiled coldly at the prisoners. 'Ask them, whilst we wait, decurion, where they were going to and whence they came.'

The decurion shrugged, evidently aware that questioning without inducement was a waste of time. He framed the question in Aramaic and repeated it several times as the Jews stared back at him with dumb insolence.

'Show them a blade,' Vespasian ordered.

'The decurion did as he was told, taking a sica close to each man's face, threatening their eyes and nicking their ears, but this produced no outward signs of fear in the Jews.

'No matter,' Vespasian said, 'I'm sure we won't have to wait long.'

It was Magnus who arrived first, a few moments later; Castor and Pollux sniffed the air and immediately started growling as they recognised the scent of their two victims from earlier. The Jews looked sidelong at the beasts, their fear of them real in their eyes.

'That's better,' Vespasian said, 'that should put them off their guard.' There was a knock on the door. 'Enter.'

Yosef, still manacled, was escorted in by a guard.

'Ah, Yosef ben Matthias,' Vespasian said, slowly enunciating each name as clearly as he could.

The effect was instant: a stream of Aramaic invective poured from the gorges of the two prisoners, their outrage at being put in the same room with such a traitor clear.

Yosef stepped back, taken by surprise by the verbal abuse.

'What are they saying to you?' Vespasian asked.

Yosef looked down at the two men as they spat their hatred at him. 'They are saying that Shimon bar Gioras will punish me for my treachery and that I have already been excommunicated and will be shunned like a leper or a woman taken in sin. No Jew will ever come voluntarily within seven paces of me unless it's to kill me; I am rejected and I will soon be dead.'

'So they are Shimon bar Gioras' followers,' Vespasian mused as the tirade continued. 'That is interesting seeing as he's still holding out on Masada. I wonder what they are doing so far from him? Ask them, Yosef. Magnus, I think Castor and Pollux should give them a little encouragement.' With his head he indicated to the men's genitals as Yosef asked the question.

Magnus encouraged his hounds up onto their hind legs with their forelegs resting on the tables; drool dripped from loose lips and low growls accompanied their close, nasal perusal of the areas in question.

The two Jews raised their heads to stare, petrified, at the two beasts slavering so close to their crotches.

'Repeat the question, Yosef.'

As he did so, Vespasian nodded at Magnus, who clicked his fingers in front of Pollux's muzzle as he sniffed at a penis; the dog snapped its teeth, narrowly missing the shrivelled organ. A stream of Aramaic spewed from the terrified Jew; his eyes remained fixed on the hound as it continued to inspect his genitalia, bestowing the occasional lick.

'Well?' Vespasian asked when the Jew became silent, his chest heaving with fear as his comrade looked over at him in disgust.

'Shimon has come down from Masada, a few days ago, leaving Eleazar ben Ya'ir and his followers garrisoning it. He has marched on Jerusalem; Yohanan and his army came out to meet them and they fought an inconclusive battle. Yohanan has withdrawn back behind the city's walls and Shimon has turned south to invade Idumaea to punish them for what their army did in Jerusalem last year.'

Vespasian looked down at the Jew; his eyes flicked between Pollux and Magnus and then looked up at Vespasian, pleading. 'He doesn't seem to be lying but point out to him that he hasn't answered my question, Yosef: what are *they* doing so far from Shimon?'

'They were coming to Caesarea to assassinate me,' Yosef translated after a brief conversation. 'Shimon wants to make an example of me; he wants to show the Jews that anyone who has dealings with Rome will die, without exception.'

'Does he now?' Vespasian smiled to himself. 'Then I would have thought he should order his own murder seeing as he seems to be doing Rome a great many favours. Attacking Jerusalem and now Idumaea, that's very helpful to Rome. It's completely justified my policy of having just a loose blockade around Jerusalem and letting them get on with it by themselves without interfering. What an obliging people these Jews are. Ask him when this battle was.'

'He says that it was yesterday; they rode all night to get here.'

'Were there many casualties?'

'About ten thousand in all, from both sides.'

Vespasian shook his head in amazement. 'They kill each other as quickly as we kill them.'

'It's amazing that there are any left,' Magnus observed, pulling his dogs away from the prisoners. 'What shall we do with these two?'

Vespasian looked at Yosef and then held out one of the Sicarii. 'They were coming to kill you, Yosef, for betraying your people; this is your decisive moment: use the blade on yourself or on these two. If you kill yourself I will let these men go so that they can tell the Jews that you repented in the end; if it is you who walks out of this room then I shall know that you are completely loyal to me.'

Yosef looked at the two prisoners strapped to the tables and then at Vespasian; with a slight inclination of the head he took the knife.

Vespasian walked from the room with Magnus and the dogs; the decurion closed the door behind them.

It did not take long before the door reopened and Yosef walked out with his guard; the decurion followed.

Vespasian glanced at the decurion, who nodded, showing him the bloodied knife; he wiped it, placed it back in its sheath and handed it to him. Vespasian tucked the knife into his belt and then looked with approval at Yosef. 'So, you have made your choice and I shall reward you with your freedom. Guard, take off his chains.'

The guard took a large ring of keys from his belt and unlocked the manacles and the leg-irons; they clunked to the ground.

Vespasian took Yosef by the shoulders. 'You are now my freedman; I will prepare the necessary papers to show that you are a freed citizen of Rome by the name of Titus Flavius Josephus.'

'Hormus!' Vespasian called as he entered the atrium of the palace. 'Hormus!'

His senior freedman scuttled out from his study, a smaller room off the atrium next to his master's far more spacious working space. 'Yes, master.'

'I need you to make out the manumission document for Titus Flavius Josephus,' Vespasian said, pointing at his new freedman.

If Hormus was surprised he did not show it. 'Yes, master.'

'And then write a brief note to Titus, in Tiberias, summoning him to see me immediately; I want him here by the day after tomorrow. Bring them both to me for signature when you've finished.'

'Yes, master. And, master?'

'What is it?'

'Three messengers have arrived from Rome; they have the Emperor's mandate.'

'Finally. Where are they?'

'The mistress is entertaining them in the courtyard garden.'

'Now we get to see exactly where I stand with the new regime,' Vespasian said to Magnus as he turned to go.

Magnus tugged at Castor and Pollux's leads to prevent them from following Vespasian. 'Well, I hope you're still standing after you've found out, if you take my meaning?'

Vespasian did; he had been waiting a long time for this message, too long for comfort.

'I advise you to do exactly as we say, general, or the lady will be taking her last breaths through a gash in her throat.'

Vespasian stopped still as he looked at the Praetorian centurion holding a dagger to Caenis' throat, clamping her mouth shut with the other hand. Two Praetorian Guardsmen stood at their leader's shoulders; both had a slave lying dead at their feet. 'What do you mean by this?' Vespasian kept his voice calm, despite the turmoil that surged within him.

The centurion's eyes were killer-cold. 'Stay still and receive the Emperor's orders and she will live.'

The two Guardsmen walked towards Vespasian, drawing their swords with a ringing flourish; Vespasian saw his death approaching. 'Is this the Emperor's orders? Am I not, at least, allowed the mercy of suicide?'

'No, he was quite clear upon that point. Neither you nor Clodius Macer, the Governor of Africa, were to be given that benefit ... Ahhgg!' He pulled his hand away from Caenis' mouth, blood dripping from a deep bite to the forefinger.

'Defend yourself, my love!' Caenis screamed, struggling in her captor's arms. 'I'm dead whatever happens.'

The two Guardsmen paused to look back at their officer; a snarling black streak thumped into one spilling him to the floor. Vespasian grabbed the sica from his belt and threw himself towards the centurion as another blur hurtled past him.

Caenis screamed again; blood appeared on her throat but Castor's jaws closed over the centurion's face and he brought his dagger away from her flesh to defend himself and she dropped to the floor. Without thought, Vespasian plunged his blade, just below the scale armour, into the centurion's groin as he fought the hound savaging his face. All three toppled back to the ground, crashing onto the body of one of the dead slaves as shrieks came from behind them mixed with the bestial roars. Forcing his knife further in and up, Vespasian twisted it, with a hatred never before felt, as the centurion howled his pain to the gods. In a final act of violence, the centurion raised his blade and brought it flashing down as Vespasian rolled away; with a butchering thump and a canine screech it clove into Castor's shoulder. The beast arched back, its maw clamped firm, tearing off the centurion's face as if pulling the mask from an actor. Vespasian pushed himself up to see Caenis, lying, holding her throat with blood seeping through her fingers. Silent was his scream as he looked down at her paling face.

'Behind you!' Caenis croaked.

Vespasian turned and just dodged the sweeping blade of one of the Guardsmen as Magnus despatched his mauled comrade, strangling him with bare hands, tears flowing down his face as he looked at the lifeless body of Pollux. Vespasian grabbed the Praetorian's arm as the stroke went wide, spinning his body as he did and bringing the arm round behind the Praetorian's back; with a sudden brutal motion he forced it up, popping the shoulder. The man shrieked and dropped his blade. Vespasian forced him down to his knees, pushing on the dislocated shoulder; he stooped and grabbed the discarded sword. It was with a savage joy that he pressed the tip into the junction of neck and shoulder and, without pause, plunged it deep into the man's vital organs and then pushed the twitching body forward in disgust.

Vespasian pulled himself up and staggered, sobbing, over to Caenis. He knelt by her side and stroked her cheek, not knowing what to say or do.

'I'll be fine, my love,' Caenis said, rubbing her throat. 'It's just a flesh wound. Castor hit him just as he was about to do it; he saved my life.'

Vespasian's sobs turned into choking tears of relief as he touched the wound and saw that it was not fatal; he put his arms around Caenis and cradled her as he looked over to where Castor lay, whining pitifully.

'I'll help you, boy,' Magnus said, walking up to his wounded dog and sitting down next to it. He took Castor's head in his hands and laid it in his lap, stroking the cheek with a bloody hand; the centurion's face slopped to the floor. 'I'll help you, boy.' He reached out and pulled the centurion's dagger from Castor's shoulder, tears tumbling down his face. 'I'll help you; you can join Pollux now, boy.' Magnus leant over to kiss his dying pet and sank the dagger deep into Castor's heart. With one spasm, Castor went still and Magnus collapsed over his body, convulsing with grief.

'I heard the swords ringing as they were drawn,' Magnus said as Vespasian came back into the garden, having left Caenis in her room being seen to by the doctor. 'I had a nasty feeling about the whole thing anyway, so I just hung back to listen.' He looked down at the bodies of his two dogs and sighed, shaking his head in disbelief, misery carved into his face. 'The sound is unmistakable so I just let the boys go and ...' Magnus could not go on.

'And you saved mine and Caenis' lives,' Vespasian said, placing a soothing hand on his friend's shoulder.

'I didn't,' Magnus replied, looking between Castor and Pollux's corpses, 'they did.' He glanced down at the faceless body of the centurion and stamped down on his featureless head repeatedly. 'Bastard! Goatfucker! Cocksucker! What did they ever do to deserve that, eh? They never hurt anyone.'

Vespasian knew that was not strictly true but refrained from saying so as he pulled Magnus away from the corpse of the man that Galba had sent to kill him.

Hormus came out into the garden with Josephus.

'Burn the bodies here, privately, Hormus,' Vespasian said, indicating to the three Praetorians, 'and then take the remains in a sack and throw it into the sea. Make sure that none of the household see you doing it; I don't want any evidence that they were here at all. If anyone should ask what the burning flesh smell is then let it be known that poor Castor and Pollux died of an illness and we're cremating them here in the garden.'

'Very good, master,' Hormus said, looking around at the carnage. 'And what about the two slaves?'

Vespasian had forgotten about them. 'Did they have any family?'

Hormus bent down to identify them better. 'No, they were both garden workers, no privileges.'

'Good, burn them too and get a couple of replacements. I want it to seem as if nothing happened; those Praetorians were never here and if you hear that any of the slaves know they were, get rid of them.'

'Yes, master.' Hormus turned to Josephus. 'Order the steward to lock all the slaves away until we tell him otherwise. No one is to come near the garden. I'll start getting some wood together.'

'Come on,' Vespasian said to Magnus as the two freedmen went about their tasks, 'let's build a pyre for your two boys and show them the respect they deserve for sacrificing their lives for Caenis and me.'

It was a mournful little group that gathered around the dogs' pyre at the further end of the courtyard garden. Caenis, her neck bandaged and the colour returned to her face, held Magnus' hand as he thrust a torch into the oil-drenched wood upon which lay the stiffening corpses of Castor and Pollux.

Vespasian stood back, watching the flames grow as his mind raced, wondering what his next move should be. The Emperor had sent men to kill him; it was a stark reality. But why? And was he the only one to incur Galba's displeasure? And then he remembered that the centurion had said that the Governor of Africa, Clodius Macer, had also been targeted and he wondered how many more governors were to be assassinated. Mucianus, perhaps, or Tiberius Alexander or, indeed, both of them; he would send urgent messengers as soon as he was finished here, he decided.

The fire caught and the dogs' fur burst into flames and soon Castor and Pollux were slowly being consumed as Magnus looked on with unrestrainable tears coursing down his cheeks.

When it was done, they walked back into the palace past the smoking pit where the bones of the Praetorians and the slaves hissed with steam as Hormus tipped water over them to cool them sufficiently to collect, and on into Vespasian's study.

Taking a pitcher of wine from the sideboard, Vespasian poured three cups and passed them round, unwatered. 'I need a drink and then we have to think about what to do.'

'So, just act as if this never happened?' Magnus said. 'Is that really what you're suggesting?'

'I think that it's the only way that I can safely proceed,' Vespasian said, pouring himself a third cup of wine. 'If we pretend that the assassins never reached here, I won't have to defend my honour by rebelling against the man who sent them. I can't afford to do that now, it's too early; the West is still strong.'

'He's right, Magnus,' Caenis affirmed. 'If Galba hears that his assassins arrived and were thwarted, he will keep on sending more. So Vespasian's only options would be either to run to Parthia and, no doubt, be sent back to Galba by Vologases so as to avoid a diplomatic incident, or to take his legions and attack the West to remove Galba in a war where Vespasian would be seen as the aggressor. He would not stand a chance; no matter how unpopular Galba is, most of the western legions would back him.'

'Doing nothing buys me at least a couple of months before Galba realises that something went wrong, and if half the rumours coming out of Rome are true, a lot could change in that time.'

'What about the ship they arrived on?' Caenis asked after a short while thinking the scheme through.

'Torch it at its moorings in the harbour.'

'And the crew?'

Vespasian shrugged. 'If they survive, it would be a while before they could get back to Rome. The chances are that they didn't know what the Praetorians' mission was anyway.'

'Yes, I suppose you're right: we act as if this never happened.'

'You try telling that to Castor and Pollux,' Magnus said with more than a trace of bitterness.

'Yes, well, I'm so sorry, Magnus,' Vespasian said, topping up his friend's cup. 'I've a feeling that you are going to have to forgo your revenge for the time being. Indeed, you may not get the chance to have it at all.'

Magnus scowled and took a mighty swig.

'In the meantime, I'll send warnings to Tiberius Alexander and Mucianus for them to be on their guard. I'll also order the harbourmaster here not to allow any ships to dock until he's found out who is on board and has sought my permission; if Galba sent more than one party of assassins I want them arrested as they disembark.'

'You realise that if you were to do that, it would put you in direct defiance of the Emperor? It would be an act of rebellion.'

'I already am a rebel; I'm just trying to keep it hidden until the time is right for me.' Vespasian looked up as Hormus put his head around the door. 'Well?'

'You have visitors, master.'

Before Vespasian could ask who it was, Hormus opened the door fully.

'Thank my Lord Mithras that we've come in time,' Sabinus said, walking into the room with a large leather bag slung over his shoulder and Malichus following, beaming as always. 'Galba has sent assassins.'

CHAPTER X

'You've had a narrow escape then, brother,' Sabinus said after Vespasian had told him what had occurred. 'We've travelled non-stop since we heard that they had been despatched in the hope of overtaking them; I didn't think we would make it.'

'Well, you didn't,' Magnus pointed out.

'I'm sorry to hear about your boys, Magnus,' Sabinus said.

'Why did *you* come, Sabinus?' Caenis asked. 'Surely Malichus alone would have been sufficient?'

Sabinus considered the question for a few moments, his face grave. 'Well, there are two reasons, I suppose. When Galba arrived in Rome at the beginning of October one of the first things he did was replace me with Aulus Ducenius Geminus. I expected to be executed promptly but, despite that, I stayed in Rome. It was Tigellinus' inability not to gloat that saved me by letting it slip to Malichus that the new prefect of the Praetorian Guard had sent one of his centurions, on Galba's orders, to deal with you, as he put it. I realised that the reason I hadn't been executed yet was that Galba was waiting for news of Vespasian's death before killing me. He feared that if I was murdered first, you would rebel if the news reached you before the assassins, or that if the attempt on your life was botched, as it was, I would be killed anyway as you would've been forced into rebellion anyhow. Staying in Rome therefore seemed a stupid option and, as I was no longer the prefect and so no longer obliged to be within a hundred miles of the city, I left with Malichus the night he told me.'

'Why did Tigellinus tell you, Malichus?' Vespasian asked.

'Ahhh!' Malichus beamed, his teeth shining like many miniature moons from within his bush of a beard. 'Because he and his colleague, Nymphidius Sabinus, had turned the Guard against

Nero, Galba obviously wanted such untrustworthy men dead. Nymphidius tried to make himself emperor but failed and was executed at Galba's feet; but Tigellinus managed to survive by grovelling to him and his general, Titus Vinius, apparently claiming that he had saved Vinius' daughter's life by hiding her when Nero had ordered her death upon hearing of Galba's rebellion and Vinius' part in it. The daughter confirmed it and he was allowed to remain alive but was replaced in the Guard by Cornelius Laco.'

Caenis tapped the table, applauding in appreciation. 'Very clever; Tigellinus was always one for backing both chariots.'

Malichus beamed even more broadly in agreement. 'Yes, he was boasting to me about just how he had done it and how he, now that he had the Emperor's ear, was hoping that Galba might send him to be the new procurator of Judaea, a position that he would be highly suitable for seeing as he is an equestrian. He said that I would be advised to be courteous to him as he could well be in a position to make life very difficult for me in the near future. I pointed out that I was high in your favour, Vespasian, and he laughed, saying that you wouldn't be of any use to me before long and that's when he told me about the assassins.'

'Tigellinus coming to Judaea would be a fine act of justice,' Vespasian mused. 'They deserve each other. Did Tigellinus tell you who he planned to replace me with?'

Malichus' radiance faded.

'Well?' Vespasian insisted.

Caenis raised her hand, stopping Malichus from replying. 'I can guess.'

'Can you? I can't.'

'Mucianus.' Caenis looked at Malichus, who nodded.

'Mucianus?' Vespasian exclaimed.

'Of course, my love, he's the obvious choice: if you, he and Tiberius Alexander are all working together, the sole way that Galba could change things and make himself slightly more secure in the East is by getting one of you in his debt.'

Vespasian understood the line of Caenis' thinking. 'Therefore get rid of one of us and give his responsibility to one of the others, thus securing him into Galba's debt and keeping the third quiet as he has little choice but to co-operate with his very powerful colleague, unless he wants a visit from a Praetorian centurion with a knife. Yes, it would work.' Vespasian looked between Sabinus and Malichus. 'The question is: did Mucianus know?'

Sabinus shook his head. 'I wondered that and I think the answer is no. Galba had no need to warn Mucianus in advance; Mucianus wouldn't have refused having his command doubled after your murder but he might have decided he would be better off siding with you if he had advance warning of it.'

Vespasian considered this awhile. 'But we don't know for certain. I need to have a meeting with Mucianus to look into his eyes and find out for sure.'

Caenis agreed. 'Yes, my love, you're right: we need to be confident that we can trust him.'

Vespasian looked back to Sabinus. 'You said there were two reasons for you coming in person; what's the second?'

'I can't discuss it here, Brother, not in front of Caenis, Magnus and Malichus.'

Malichus got up. 'I will leave you in peace.'

As the Nabataean king left the room, Sabinus indicated to Caenis and Magnus.

'Oh, come on,' Vespasian said, 'you know perfectly well that you can say anything you like in front of them.'

'I know I can; but not this. I need to have a private chat with you, Brother. I believe that the time our father foresaw all those years ago has come and although the oath that he made us swear to, the day before we left for Rome, allows me to overcome the one which our mother made the whole family swear sixteen years previously, it only allows me to talk to you. I'd be breaking the original oath if I discussed in front of Caenis and Magnus the auspices that were read at your naming ceremony, and you need to hear about them now.'

Vespasian's heart beat fast as Caenis and Magnus left the room and Sabinus refreshed his throat with another cup of wine.

'Well?' Vespasian asked, unable to conceal his excitement at finally being told the nature of the prophecy that he had first overheard his parents discussing forty-three years before on the day his brother had returned from his four years' service as a military tribune with the VIIII Hispana.

Sabinus looked at his brother and for the first time in Vespasian's memory gave him a warm, fraternal smile. 'Well, Brother, it has come to this; you need my help. Our father, may Mithras warm his soul with his light, was right to make us both swear that oath together; it means I can tell you what I remember of that day. It's very clear, although I didn't understand what it meant at the time; however, just recently, I've put it together.'

Vespasian could barely contain the urge to hurry Sabinus along as he paused and refilled his cup.

'Do you remember the prophecy read to us by the priest at the Oracle of Amphiaraos all those years ago?'

'Of course.'

'How did it go?'

Vespasian thought for a couple of moments and then smiled slowly as it came to him.

'"*Two tyrants fall quickly, close trailed by another,*

In the East the King hears the truth from a brother.

With his gift the lion's steps through sand he should follow,

So to gain from the fourth the West on the morrow." Or something like that.'

'That's exactly how I remember it. Well, I worked out its meaning when I considered the marks on the livers of the three sacrifices at your naming ceremony.'

Vespasian wanted to slap the cup from Sabinus' hand as he paused for another sip.

'Well, Galba is not going to last; that has become obvious. People are already calling him a tyrant for his attitude to the army and potential rivals, and cancelling the donative to the army means that he has few friends. He replaced Nero whom everyone in their right minds agreed was a tyrant. So if Galba falls quickly, soon after Nero, then there'll be a third and, shortly after that, a fourth; so whoever that is will be the eighth Emperor.'

Vespasian mentally tallied up. 'Yes, so?'

'So, little brother, look at you; here in the East with one of the largest armies entrusted to anyone at the moment. Here because Nero thought that our background was too humble, too lacking in distinction, for you to be a threat, but in reality you are the power in the Roman East, the king even, and I'm your brother, here to tell you the truth.'

He paused to gather his thoughts, took a deep breath and then began: 'I remember our father's expression being one of incredulity as he examined, first, the liver of the ram and then the boar and finally that of the ox; he kept on staring at them and then held them up for all to see. I came forward and saw that there was clearly a strong mark on each of them and I was happy because I was jealous of you and thought that blemishes on all three livers were a sure sign that Mars had rejected you. But then I looked closer and even at that age I knew what the first one of them, the one on the ram's liver, looked like: it was clearly half an eagle's head, the eye and hooked beak. The other two I just memorised as they meant nothing to me at the time. Not until Galba entered Rome, and it became obvious that he would not last, did I remember the Oracle of Amphiaraos and realised that it had been predestined that you would be the ninth Emperor. I could not withhold that from you because, armed with that information, your actions may well be different.'

Vespasian's throat felt mightily constricted. 'What makes you think that I will be the ninth?'

'Because the second liver, that of the boar, contained two marks where three veins had come to the surface; one was on its own, a straight line, next to the other two which had crossed: an "I" and an "X". Nine. An eagle, the imperial sign, and a nine. I had to tell you.'

Vespasian put his hand across the table and squeezed that of his brother. 'Thank you, Sabinus, thank you. But tell me, what was the third mark?'

'That was the hardest one to work out: it was a slightly curved vertical line with four or five little bubbles hanging off it very close together. It took me the whole journey here to come up with the answer. Remember you told me how, after witnessing the rebirth of the Phoenix, you were taken to the Temple of Amun in Siwa; you said the god spoke to you? But he told you that you had come too soon to know what question you should ask and you should come back when you had a gift that could match the one laid across the god's knees?'

'Alexander the Great's sword. Yes. The god said that a brother would know how to match it.'

'"With his gift the lion's steps through sand he should follow." You need to go back to Siwa, and then I saw what the mark was: it was grain. Your route to the Purple will be by taking Egypt and controlling the grain supply to Rome and whilst you're there you must go to Siwa and consult the god.'

'But how can I match that gift then?'

'I've brought it with me.'

'What is it?'

Sabinus picked up the large leather bag from the floor and handed it to Vespasian. 'It was something that you gave to Caligula: Alexander's breastplate that you stole from his mausoleum in Alexandria.'

Vespasian opened the bag and pulled out the breastplate; it was exactly how he remembered it: dark brown boiled leather, moulded to the muscles it concealed and protected, inlaid with a silver prancing horse on each pectoral; not an ostentatious parade-ground ornament with protruding decoration that could catch a spear-point but, rather, practical battlewear that had once belonged to the greatest conqueror who had ever lived. And there it was: the stain on the left side, the blemish that reassured Vespasian that it was genuine for he had recreated it on the replica that he had replaced it with, which, as far as he knew, still lay on Alexander's mummified body under the crystal lid in his mausoleum. 'Where did you get this, Sabinus?'

'After Caligula drove over his bridge wearing it he must have just forgotten all about it; anyway, Claudius found it soon after he became emperor, recognised it for what it was and, wanting to keep it in Rome but, at the same time, needing to avoid causing an incident with visiting Alexandrians, he placed in it the treasury. I knew it was there from my time as prefect of the city so, when I realised what it could be used for, I called in a favour from one of the three vigintiviri who oversee the treasury – as prefect I'd used my influence to get him that position. He simply walked out with it in this bag and handed it to me. And there you have it.'

Vespasian admired the breastplate again, running his fingers over the silver inlays and then smelling the ancient leather. 'Thank you, Sabinus; this might persuade the god to speak to me again but it doesn't solve the problem of what to ask him so that I can "gain from the fourth the West on the morrow". Assuming that I'm going to, that is.'

'I think it's right to assume it, Vespasian: the Phoenix, Amun, Amphiaraos, the livers, Antonia giving you her father's sword that she had always said she would give to the grandson she thought would make the best Emperor; and when you told me the story I said: "and why not?" I've always had the suspicion in the back of my mind; that's why I didn't want to hear the prophecy of Amphiaraos.'

'I remember you saying that you didn't want to be left behind.'

'Yes, and I meant it at the time; I was thinking that if you heard what the priest had to say then that suspicion would grow into a certainty and you would eclipse me, the elder brother, and I would be left behind. I couldn't bear that thought. Remember how jealous I was of you? How much I hated you? How I always called you "you little shit"? Well, it changed after Amphiaraos when you turned on me and insisted the priest read the prophecy aloud; I saw a will within you and from that day on I started to respect you.'

'And to lose your fear of being left behind?'

Sabinus smiled. 'You little shit; yes, if you want to know. It's receded over the years; I can cope with it now, and especially now as I see it as being inevitable that you will eclipse me and leave me behind.'

'I'll not leave you behind, Sabinus; if what you, and perhaps I, believe comes to pass then you will always be the prefect of the city in my Rome. But anyway, none of what you say absolutely confirms my destiny.'

'How much more do you want? And then, of course, there's Myrddin, the immortal druid of Britannia, who said that he had seen your future and it scared him because one day you would have the power but fail to use it to bring an end to whatever he thinks is going to kill true religion.'

'That doesn't mean that I'm destined to be emperor.'

'Well then, what does it mean? He put enough effort into luring you, on your own free will, to the place that he had chosen for your death so that the prophecy that he had seen would be void because you had voluntarily chosen to die. But anyway, whatever you might think of Myrddin, everything else points in your favour, so, if I were you, Brother, I would start planning what course of action to take as soon as there is a change on the Palatine, because there will be one soon.'

'I have.'

Sabinus was visibly surprised. 'I thought that you just said that none of what I've told you confirms you will become emperor.'

'I did. But that's different from thinking it possible. Mucianus, Tiberius Alexander and I have an understanding: we have agreed that should the eastern legions make a move against the West, I am the obvious figurehead, as Tiberius Alexander is a Jew and Mucianus is ... well, he doesn't have a son. Planning it is different from believing that it will happen. Making a bid for power is one of the most dangerous things anyone can attempt and it often ends up in death, not only for the person in question but also his entire family; remember Sejanus? Remember that I was in charge of his children's garrotting? Do you remember that, because it is unlucky to execute a virgin, I had to order the gaoler to rape the seven-year-old girl? Do you remember, Sabinus?'

Sabinus' face was dark with the memory. 'Yes, I do, Brother; and I imagine it's not a deed that you are proud of nor is it a memory that you cherish.'

'Right on both counts. But I saw then at first hand just what a failed bid for power can do. I remember Sejanus giving me some advice just before he died: he told me that if I was ever in a position to attain power, seize it with both hands, do not wait for it to be given you as someone else may grab it first and they will kill you for coming so close to the thing they now own and covet.'

'That was good advice.'

'I know; and that's why I will take it. I shall make sure that I don't put myself in a position whereby I can attain power without knowing that I can seize it before someone else does; I have no wish to be the cause of the extinction of our family, Sabinus. Either I immortalise it or I stay as an unremarkable New Man from an undistinguished background with no ambition to go any further than the, frankly, surprising heights that I have already achieved; a safe pair of hands in other words. Vespasian the mule-breeder with the Sabine accent and the manners of a bumpkin; that's how many people see me; Corvinus used to taunt me with it at every opportunity. Well, that's how I'm going to stay unless there is a clear chance that I can surprise people and be something completely different.'

'Titus Flavius Vespasianus Caesar Augustus, for example.'

'Shhh, Sabinus; don't say that, it'll bring bad luck; but yes, something like that. But I have to be sure that I really can do it and that I can trust the people around me; Mucianus, for one: did he know of the assassins? Titus, for another.'

'Titus? But he's your son.'

'Yes, he is. But he's under the influence of a very ambitious eastern woman who seems to have taken up with him despite being eleven years his senior and also coming from a family with whom I certainly have a feud, having thwarted her father Herod Agrippa's ambitions on a number of occasions, a couple of which involved you. So what is she doing with Titus other than trying to further her own purposes by using someone who, after careful consideration, is a contender for the Purple, should we spend next year in civil war?'

'He wouldn't, would he?'

'He said he wouldn't but now I'm not too sure; I don't know what he's thinking of being with Berenice. But what I do know is that I need to be sure of him if I do go to Rome. However I do it, I need to leave behind someone whom I can implicitly trust with three legions to finish off the rebellion, take Jerusalem and destroy the Temple once and for all. And the only man I could trust to do that would be him.'

'Or me.'

It was Vespasian's turn to be surprised. 'I hadn't thought of that.'

'Now I'm no longer the prefect of the city there's no reason that I couldn't help you out should Titus not prove to be the son you thought he was.'

'Yes, thank you; but let's hope that it doesn't come to that. I'm summoning him here; he should arrive within the next couple of days. In the meantime we should find Caenis and draw up a list of senators and equestrians upon whose support we might rely and which legions might proclaim me ...' He left the word unsaid.

'That won't take long.'

'Yes, I suppose you're right; still, there'll be a few who are in our debt.' Vespasian reached over and put his hand on Sabinus' shoulder. 'As I am in yours, Brother; thank you for coming.'

'You have to have faith in yourself, Vespasian,' Caenis said yet again.

'You've told me that at least a dozen times over the last couple of days, my love, and repetition doesn't necessarily make a thing true. It's not a question of faith.'

'What is it a question of, then?' Caenis slapped the balustrade in frustration.

Vespasian affected not to notice as he stood on the terrace looking down into the harbour at the burnt-out remains of the ship that had brought the Praetorians to kill him. 'It's a question of numbers, my love; pure and simple arithmetic. It's the sort of thing that I'm very good at. There are two legions in Egypt: the Third Cyrenaica and the Twenty-second Deiotariana; then there are my three legions here: the Fifth, Tenth and Fifteenth.'

'Yes, I know; and then there are Mucianus' three legions in Syria.'

'The Sixth Ferrata, the Twelfth Fulminata, or what's left of it, I don't know how well up to strength it is yet. And then there is my old legion, the Fourth Scythica, which was moved there from Moesia. And finally there are the Moesian legions: the Third Gallica which was moved there from Syria just recently and would still be expected to be loyal to its former comrades in the East; plus the Seventh Claudia and the Eighth Augusta. That's a total of eleven. Since Galba formed his new legion and Clodius Macer formed his in Africa and the marines were made into the First Adiutrix there are thirty-one legions in total in the Empire; do the arithmetic.'

'I have done the arithmetic, you maddening man; we've both done it together for the last two days; just like we've worked out that there are around eighty senators who have ties with either your family or Mucianus and who could therefore be expected to look upon your challenge favourably. And don't say do the arithmetic again to me or I shall scream and then slap you; I'm well aware there are over five hundred senators still living. Well aware!'

'So you just expect me to have faith in myself and that will protect me from the numbers? Come on, Caenis; you were the one who counselled caution.'

'Caution, yes; inaction, no. If we can get a suitable promise out of Titus, when he arrives here anytime now, then you must think of preparing the ground, and one of the things that you must do is send Malichus as an emissary to Vologases to ask for a commitment from the Parthians that they leave our eastern border alone for the duration of the civil war. You know the man, you've dined with him. You like each other; he may well do that for you; and if he does, you will be able to afford taking more troops from Syria than would otherwise be deemed prudent.'

'And Armenia?'

'Armenia will look after itself if Vologases gives you his word; King Tiridates is, after all, Vologases' younger brother and has sworn an oath to Rome anyway.'

'And should I trust Vologases' word?'

This was too much for Caenis and she shrieked in his face, her chin jutting and her bunched fists pushing back behind her.

'I'm sorry, my love,' Vespasian said in a conciliatory manner. 'I know that the Great King would never lie as it is a fundamental tenet of his religion: fighting the Lie with Truth, I seem to remember him saying; so yes, if he does give me his word I should be able to trust him. It's just that the magnitude of what is starting to appear on the horizon is so big that it terrifies me.'

'Then rousing yourself and doing something, rather than pondering on the sheer scale of the undertaking, is the best way to combat that.'

'Have faith in myself despite the arithmetic, you mean?'

'Oh fuck your fucking arithmetic!' Caenis squeezed her eyes tight shut and breathed deeply.

Vespasian looked at her astounded; he had never before heard her swear, at least not that he could remember and certainly not with such passion.

'Yes, you made me swear at you, Vespasian. I lost my temper; can you believe it?'

'I'm struggling to.'

'That's just how difficult you are being. Now, the arithmetic will look after itself as things progress, think about it: if the Oracle of Amphiaraos is correct then there are two more to come before you, the seventh Emperor and the eighth; Galba's legions will support the eighth one because the seventh one will be seen as being responsible for their leader's death. The seventh Emperor's legions will support you for that very same reason: the eighth Emperor will be seen as responsible for the seventh's death. So, you see, numbers will come to you; so please stop talking about arithmetic and send Malichus to Vologases now; you need to have an answer by spring next year at the latest.'

Vespasian turned and took her in his arms. 'Very well, my love; I'll do as you suggest.' He squeezed her tight and held her for a few heartbeats. 'I'm terrified,' he admitted as he released the pressure. 'Absolutely terrified.'

'I know, my love; and so am I. But we need to move with everything in place and an eastern settlement is one of the most important things to have.'

'Malichus will leave tomorrow.'

As he embraced her again Hormus came to stand discreetly in the double doorway; Magnus hovered behind him. 'Master?'

'What is it, Hormus?'

'I have just heard from Tiberias.'

'Good, when is Titus arriving?'

Hormus paused and looked at Vespasian with nervous eyes.

'Go on, out with it.'

'He's not coming, master.'

'Not coming! What does he mean by not coming?'

'I don't know, master, he didn't reply in person. When my messenger arrived to deliver your letter he wasn't there; he had left a few days previously.'

'Left? Left to go where?'

It was Caenis who stepped forward to answer. 'I'm afraid, my love, that there is only one probable explanation: he and that Jewish bitch, Berenice, must have left to pay their respects to Galba in Rome.'

'What more do we know?' Vespasian asked once he had got over the shock.

'Not much, master,' Hormus said, wringing his hands as if the whole matter was his fault. 'It seems that Herod Agrippa returned and then, within a day, he departed back to Rome taking Titus and Berenice with him.'

'The bastard! What did he say to Titus, do we know?'

'No, master; that's all the messenger managed to find out.'

'It's a trap, my love,' Caenis said, sitting back down at the table. 'Galba's using Herod Agrippa to lure Titus back to Rome in return for enlarging his domains, I shouldn't wonder.'

'What do you think he said to him that made him be so reckless as to go?'

'The only thing that he could say to convince him that it was safe and right to go.'

Vespasian was incredulous. 'That Galba was going to adopt him? Surely Titus knows that would be a death sentence.'

'Why? Did you tell him?'

Vespasian thought back to the conversation he had had with his son. 'No, not as such.'

'Perhaps you should have.'

'But anyone can see it's a death sentence.'

'Perhaps not; not if he was told that the offer comes from both Galba and the Senate. Titus has been promised the Empire in a way that he may have a chance of keeping it without having to come into conflict with you. For him it's a sensible decision because, as he sees it, the East will be secure because you would never move against him, firstly because you are, obviously, his father and secondly because he has been given legitimacy by the backing of the Senate.'

'That stupid idiot! Why didn't he consult me?'

'Because he knows that you would have forbidden him to accept and he would have gone against your will and caused a rift between you.'

'And going behind my back hasn't?'

'My love, calm down; now is not the time to get worked up. Titus has been lied to, and Herod Agrippa knows it was a lie; he knows that he is being used as Galba's instrument to lure Titus to Rome now that he thinks you are dead; and don't forget that as far as he's concerned you should be by now. Titus is going to his death urged on by Berenice who has no idea of her brother's duplicity. Titus needs to be saved, not railed against.'

'Well, I'd better get going, then,' Magnus said, surprising everyone.

'You? What do you mean by that?'

'Well, it stands to reason, don't it: you can't leave without seeming to disobey your orders, which would be just what Galba would want you to do once he finds out that you're still alive; it will give him, or whoever has succeeded him, a good excuse to recall you and, seeing as you've abandoned your post to chase your son around, no one will have any sympathy for you, either in Rome or in the legions here. So I've got to go.'

'You? You're far too old for something like that. You had difficulty mounting your horse yesterday.'

'I'll go,' Sabinus said. 'As a senator I'll be able to move much more freely and quickly, and besides, whoever finds Titus has got to persuade him back in front of Herod and his sister.'

'Meaning I couldn't do that?'

Vespasian ignored Magnus as the answer was so obvious. 'Thank you, Brother.'

'I'll get going immediately.'

'But you've only just arrived; at least stay for the night to rest.'

'I can sleep on the ship. If I go now I'm no more than three or four days behind him; I've a chance. I'll bring him back within a month, Vespasian; that I promise.'

Vespasian pulled Sabinus to him and embraced him for the first time in their lives and, to his surprise, Sabinus returned the hug and it seemed natural. 'Thank you, Brother, you have been a true friend to me.'

Sabinus stepped back, holding Vespasian's shoulders, and smiled, his eyes wide and curious, as if he were seeing something for the first time. 'And you, Brother, have always been a little shit to me. I'll see you soon and then together we shall ensure that the auspices of your birth come to pass.' He kissed Vespasian on the cheek, turned and walked out of the room.

Vespasian watched him go, content that, after all this time and all that had passed between them, they had finally been able to talk to each other with affection.

CHAPTER XI

'I SWEAR THAT I shall obey all that Marcus Salvius Otho Caesar Augustus commands and I shall never desert his service nor shall I seek to avoid death for him and the Roman Republic.' Vespasian's voice was high and clear so that it carried to the ears of every man of the two legions and four auxiliary cohorts witnessing him taking the oath; the first man in Judaea to do so.

And he had been quick to take it. From the moment that he had received Sabinus' letter from Corinth informing him of Galba's assassination and Otho's elevation, Vespasian had known that it was the prudent course of action because his brother had been right: Galba had been murdered in the middle of January, barely two months after Sabinus had predicted he would soon be dead and a seventh emperor would take his place, and this one would not last either. Swear loyalty to Otho, as Caenis had pointed out, and when he too is dead then his supporters would support whoever opposed the man who had overthrown him. The name of that man was now known and it had come as no surprise to Vespasian: Aulus Vitellius, or rather, Aulus Vitellius Germanicus Augustus, as he had styled himself since the army of the Rhenus had refused to renew its oath to Galba on the calends of January and had proclaimed Vitellius emperor the following day. And now that army was marching south to invade Italia in Vitellius' name, despite it being, at the time of Sabinus writing, only the last days of February.

It was Vitellius whom Vespasian would face if he were to make the bid for empire, that was slowly becoming clearer in his mind. Vitellius of all people; Tiberius' catamite, whom Vespasian had first met on Capreae, now grown into a hedonistic gourmand with no discernible talent for public service, unlike Otho who had been regarded as a very competent governor during his ten-year tenure in Lusitania. No, it was clear that, of the two of them, Vitellius was by far the least worthy of the Purple and the man most likely to attract fierce opposition; a man against whom Vespasian was beginning to think he may have a chance of succeeding. And so now, here he was, standing before the army of Judaea drawn up in cohorts beneath a forest of standards, his army, taking an oath of loyalty to a man over twenty years his junior; a man whom, if Sabinus was right, was destined to die within a few months.

As the last word of his oath faded over the vast crowd witnessing it, Vespasian reflected that if Sabinus' letters to Mucianus and Tiberius Alexander had not gone astray then they too would be doing the exact same thing, and Sabinus would be able to tell Otho upon his arrival back in Rome that he had secured the East for him thus ensuring his safety and perhaps, even, his reinstatement as prefect of Rome. For Sabinus had decided to go back to Rome, as, with Galba dead and civil war now inevitable, he had judged that he would be safe if he returned as a vociferous supporter of the new young Emperor. Titus had not gone with him.

Sabinus had first written to Vespasian back in December having tracked down Titus, Berenice and Herod Agrippa in Corinth where they were waiting for the weather to improve sufficiently to continue their journey. He had written that Titus was not convinced that he should refrain from presenting himself to Galba and the Senate; he did not believe Sabinus that Herod Agrippa was lying to him. Berenice, her brother's unwitting confederate in the lie, had a far more persuasive tongue than he, Sabinus had observed, although he was not sure that it was just because of the eloquence of her rhetoric, and he had not been able to persuade Titus back to Judaea.

It had not been until news of Galba's death had arrived in Corinth, just as they were preparing to leave, that the truth of what Sabinus had put to Titus became apparent, for not only had Galba been assassinated but also Piso Licinianus, the man whom

Galba had adopted as his heir whilst Titus was still obeying his fictitious summons. It was then that Herod Agrippa's duplicity had been exposed and the tetrarch had departed immediately, fearing for his life at Titus' hand. Berenice, however, had justifiably claimed innocence of all knowledge of her brother's treachery and was still installed in Titus' bed; although her tongue, Sabinus had gone on to observe, may still be in service, it was now not listened to quite so attentively. For this at least Vespasian was grateful but his gratitude would be complete if he only knew where Titus was. Sabinus had written with news of Galba's death towards the end of February; Vespasian had received the letter on the ides of March, the previous day, and if a letter could arrive that quickly then so could a person. And yet, despite all that had happened, Vespasian had had no news directly from his son, and so, as he sat and watched the legions take their oath to the seventh Emperor, Vespasian worried that he was going to be obliged to commence the campaign without Titus by his side and with the nagging doubt ever present that maybe he could not trust his firstborn as much as he would wish.

'The Fifteenth Apollinaris have completed the oath, sir,' Silius Propinquus, Titus' thick-stripe military tribune and temporary commander in his absence, announced in the lazy drawl of a young man ruined early in life by excess of wealth and privilege.

'Thank you, tribune,' Vespasian said, snapping out of his reverie. 'You may take them back to the camp. We march to Herodium at the second hour tomorrow; have them ready. I want no delay as we must do twenty-two miles a day to make it there in two days and, hopefully, take them by surprise.'

'And then it carries on like this: "Now that I have had the army of Judaea take the oath of loyalty to you, Princeps, which they did, following my lead, with great enthusiasm, I will restart the campaign against the Jews, which had stalled during the confusing times that Galba held power, unless I receive a specific request from you not to do so. I believe that we can take the last two towns holding out, Herodium and Machaerus, and then move to invest Jerusalem, which is now so wracked by internal fighting and so short of supplies that I expect it will fall by the end of the campaign season. After that it will only leave the fortress at Masada, in the south, to crush, which, because of its position on a plateau whose only access is a goat track, will involve the building of a siege ramp. I believe that this should be done after Jerusalem is back in our hands as, because the winter months that far south are warm and rain scarce, it would be a far more conducive time for heavy siege labour. In addition, I would hope to have sufficient manpower for the task with the legions supplemented by a good number of slaves captured in Jerusalem. I would appreciate the wisdom of your advice on this matter, Princeps, as it is only you, with your overall view of events who can judge the sagacity of the actions I propose. You have my absolute confidence and loyalty.'" Caenis lowered the scroll and raised her eyes. 'Well?'

'Well, I think that should flatter and reassure in equal measure, my love,' Vespasian said as a body slave finished washing the dust from his feet. 'You were right to start it with such praise on his past achievements and how fitting it is for him to have been elevated to the Purple. You are also absolutely right to make no mention of Vitellius. And as for asking his advice on the campaign: that was fawning in the extreme; Uncle Gaius would have been proud. Have the clerk draw up a fine copy and I'll sign it and it can go tomorrow.'

Caenis rolled up the scroll and tied it with a ribbon. 'Are you sure that restarting the campaign without the express permission of the Emperor is wise?'

Vespasian held out his hands in a gesture of helplessness as the slave removed the basin and began to dry his feet. 'What can I do? If we are assuming that at some point I have to send an army west to stake my claim then I can't afford to leave a simmering Judaea behind it, especially as I don't yet know Vologases' intentions.'

'Malichus should be back very soon; he's been away for nearly four months.'

'I hope so. No, I have to start the campaign again now; I haven't got time to wait until Otho authorises it. And anyway, if Vitellius marched early enough, he could be through the passes in the Alps as soon as the snow melts, which, if the weather is kind to him, could be very soon. There may well be the first battle of this war in April, my love, sometime around the time that this letter will reach Otho; in fact he may never read it – he may well be dead by then.'

Caenis nodded slowly in agreement whilst thinking. 'And if Titus doesn't come back to join you, what then?'

Vespasian eased his feet into the slippers that the slave held in front of each foot. 'Then I'll have the problem of who to leave in charge of Judaea and complete the destruction of Jerusalem. It may even be that I can't risk leaving until I have done it myself, if that's the case.'

'Would that be too bad a thing? The Emperor proclaimed in the East putting down the rebellious Jews, destroying their Temple. The fighting Emperor; a man of action.'

'I would prefer to secure Rome by making Egypt mine and sending an army north and on into Italia. Assuming that I do make a play for the Purple, that is.'

'Of course you will; with all that Sabinus told you it's obvious that you have to.'

'So you say, and so I'm coming around to believing; but it is still a terrifying prospect, and with Titus' loyalty being suspect, well, it makes my position less certain. I need him with me.'

'The Fifteenth Apollinaris are refusing to form up until you've received a delegation from them,' Silius Propinquus informed Vespasian at dawn the following morning in a tone that implied it was no concern of his.

Vespasian restrained himself from rising from his desk and slapping the imp. 'And how have you allowed it to come to the brink of mutiny, tribune? What is it about command that you don't understand? You order, they obey; I would have thought that was quite straightforward.'

Propinquus' jaw muscles tightened as he was forced to swallow the insult from a man whom he considered to be from a family far beneath his. 'It is not mutinous; they just wish to speak to you before they form up.'

'Well, tell them that I won't speak to them until they form up.'

'Marcus Ulpius Traianus is here to see you, master,' Hormus said, putting his head around the door.

'Show him in,' Vespasian snapped, venting his anger on his freedman and immediately regretting it.

Traianus walked in and gave a leisurely salute.

Vespasian half returned it. 'Well?'

'The Tenth Fretensis have asked me to request that you admit a delegation into your presence.'

'And they have refused to form up as well?'

'I haven't given them the order to form up, general; I thought it prudent not to as, with the mood they're in, I could see that they would have refused and I didn't want to create a confrontational situation.'

Vespasian looked at Propinquus. 'There; learn from your betters. Traianus won't have to punish any of his men but you will have to.'

Propinquus' expression showed that he clearly did not see the Ulpii as being a better family than his.

Vespasian sighed and, slapping both his palms on the desk, leant back in his chair, looking at his two senior officers. 'How many are in these delegations?'

'Ten from my legion,' Traianus replied. 'One from each cohort.'

'And the same number from the Fifteenth,' Propinquus confirmed.

'Have you any idea what they want?'

Traianus and Propinquus shared a quick look and then both shook their heads.

Vespasian could tell that they had just formed a conspiracy of silence and decided that it would be better not to force the issue. 'Very well. I'll see them in the praetorium; alone.'

'I want one of you to speak for you all,' Vespasian said as he walked into the praetorium where twenty legionaries waited; not one, he noticed, was a centurion, optio, or even a standard-bearer; they were just rank and file mules. 'Be quick about it and I might just forgive your impertinence.'

Vespasian sat at a desk and waited as the delegations had a hurried and muffled discussion amongst themselves.

Eventually one man, tanned, broken-nosed and bull-necked in the mid-term of his service, stamped forward, stood to attention and saluted. 'Opius Murena, sir! First century, first cohort of the Fifteenth Apollinaris, sir!'

'Well, Murena, what seems to be so important that you refuse an order to form up until you have spoken with me? I could have you executed for refusing an order, as I'm sure you're aware.'

Murena's expression did not change at the implied threat. 'It's all of us, sir! Both legions here as well as the Tenth in the south, and all the auxiliaries, sir!'

Vespasian smiled inwardly and wondered how this man was not a centurion, with the deft manner he had pointed out that the whole army of Judaea was equally guilty and all risking execution. 'And what is it that has upset all of you, Murena?'

'It's like this, sir. We all knows what's going on in the West. Yesterday you made us swear to Otho but we knows them cunts on the Rhenus have declared for Vitellius and we knows why.'

'How do you knows why?'

'We knows because it's common knowledge: any of the lads who have been back to Rome recently will tell you, sir.'

'And you have been back, I take it, Murena.'

'I was there on leave six months ago, sir! And, like every one of the lads who goes back, I drinks with lads from other legions also back in Rome on leave. Well, it was always the same with them cunts from the Rhenus, they keeps on saying that it's only a matter of time before their legions are transferred to the East and it's our turn to freeze our bollocks off keeping an eye on them hairy-arsed savages which lurks in the dark forests on the other side of the river. And we don't wants that, sir; no, we don't wants that at all.'

'I'm sure you don't, Murena; but what's that to do with me?'

'Well, sir, we knows them Rhenus cunts will try to make Vitellius really emperor and we knows that they'll ask him for a reward, and we knows just what they'll ask, and we reckons that he'll say yes. And we don't wants to go; we don't likes the forests and we prefers to fight the Jews not them hairy-arsed Germanic savages – although we have heard their women are worth closer scrutiny. But we got women out here in the East and this is where we wants to stay. So why should our lives be ruined by them Rhenus cunts? Why should we let them declare an emperor and then get the reward? Why shouldn't we have the reward? And we thinks that if you—'

'That's enough, Murena,' Vespasian cut in, knowing exactly what the man was about to suggest. 'Be careful before you add treason to mutiny.'

'It ain't treason, sir!'

'It is; we have all taken the oath to Otho.'

'But we ain't taken one to Vitellius and them Rhenus cunts are hard cunts and they'll knock the shit out of Otho's Italian turds and Praetorian piss-drinkers and then the fatman will be emperor. And we heard that the Moesian arseholes and the Pannonian pricks have crossed the Danuvius to deal with the horse-fuckers that have just appeared from the East, so who's going to come to the Italian turds' aid once the Praetorian piss-drinkers have run away, sir? Fuck all, that's who; and fuck all never helped anyone.'

'Yes, thank you, Murena.'

But Murena was in full flow. 'It's only us eastern lads what can deals with the Rhenus cunts, even if the Britannia bastards comes with them; and don't forget we could rely on the Egyptian wankers to throw their lot in with us and maybe even the Moesian arseholes if they manage to get their fingers out and deal with them horse-fuckers; and, who knows, maybe even them African buggers will pull their boys off their cocks for long enough to join in; they weren't impressed by Clodius Macer getting his and they might fancy a nice ruck.'

Vespasian concealed his surprise as to just how well informed Murena was, and therefore no doubt the whole army too. Vespasian had heard of the arrival of the Sarmatian Iazyges and Roxolani tribes on the Danuvius the previous year but had not heard that a campaign had been ordered against them; by whom, he wondered, Galba or Otho? Not that it mattered, for the result was the same if it were true: the Moesian and Pannonian legions were busy and could not be expected to come to Otho's aid. This man, Murena, was right in his assessment that fuck all was going to come to help Otho and he did not have the benefit of the Oracle of Amphiaraos to predict that Vitellius would be emperor before very long. 'I can't help you, Murena.'

'The Hispanic cock-suckers chose Galba; the Italian turds and Praetorian piss-drinkers chose Otho and now we wants *our* choice of emperor, not the Rhenus cunts' choice. Why should they choose and then nick our billets and condemn us to the freezing north? I've heard the Rhenus cunts even have to wear trousers under their tunics because it's so cold in the winter.' The look of outrage on Murena's face was palpable. 'Trousers, sir! How can you air your balls if you're wearing trousers? It ain't right.'

'They're not trousers, Murena,' Vespasian informed him, enjoying the man's indignation, 'they're knee-length britches.'

'Well, we don't wants them. We don't wants them at all; we wants to stay here where we're happy killing Jews. We knows you're a fair man, sir. We knows that you leads us from the front. We sees that you looks almost like us, sir, no fancy uniform or nothing; we hears that you eats the same tuck and drinks the same slurp. We likes you, sir; and we chooses you. What do you says?'

'I says, Murena, that we haves had enough of this conversation. I know that it is your right to bring grievances to me and I am obliged to hear you out, but in this case there is nothing that I can do. I know what you are asking of me and at the moment the time is not right.'

Murena's face lit with hope as his comrades behind him muttered to one another. 'So you're saying that there may be a time that is right, sir?'

'Murena, I'm not saying anything. Now, I'm willing to put behind us this insubordination of the Fifteenth Apollinaris refusing to form up, if you deliver one man from every century for punishment before we march, which will now have to be tomorrow. Each man will receive a dozen strokes of the vine-stick.'

Murena saluted. 'Yes, sir. And I shall be proud to be one of them.'

The other nine delegates from Murena's legion also snapped to attention and volunteered their backs for punishment.

'Dismissed!' Vespasian ordered.

As he watched the delegation file out, Vespasian wondered how long it would be until the fact that he had not entirely rejected the men's demands out of hand got around the rest of the army. He felt his throat constrict as he realised that he was slowly approaching the point of no return.

He shook his head to clear his thought. 'Traianus and Propinquus!' he shouted at the open door.

His two senior officers marched in quick enough for it to be obvious that they had been listening.

'We will not be marching today,' Vespasian informed the two men. 'By the time we've formed into an order of march it will be at least the fourth hour, which means that we won't stand a chance of coming to Herodium in two days. We'll leave tomorrow.'

'Yes, sir,' Traianus and Propinquus replied in unison.

'Propinquus, have your legion formed up to witness punishment an hour before sunset. Sixty poles to be set up. And remember, every stroke administered is because of your ineptitude. Dismissed.' Propinquus, looking as if he smelt a particularly virulent fart, saluted and sauntered out.

Vespasian looked at Traianus. 'Can we trust him?'

'You mean with what the men asked of you?'

'Yes.'

'No.'

Vespasian sucked the air through his teeth, his countenance more strained than usual. 'I'll keep a watch on him and have his correspondence intercepted.'

'A wise precaution, general.'

'And you, Traianus, what do you think?'

Traianus pointed to a chair on the opposite side of the desk. 'Please do.'

'Thank you, general,' Traianus said, sitting. He paused as he arranged his thoughts and then looked Vespasian in the eye. 'I think it is your patriotic duty to do this, general. They may come from families of great lineage but neither Otho nor Vitellius have the temperament, the self-control, to be emperor; you, on the other hand, you have that self-control, that reserve that it takes to wield power responsibly.'

'Without having the lineage.' Vespasian smiled to show that he had not taken the implication as an insult.

'Speaking bluntly, no; but then I don't make judgements like that as my family, the Ulpii, is not exactly venerable. We're both New Men, general, and I say it is the time for the New Men; the old families have had their time and now it must be ability that is the deciding factor. You have the ability and you have a son with the same qualities; a combination that could ensure at least thirty years of stable rule, which, after the profligacy of Nero and the expense of the ongoing civil war, is what the Empire needs.'

'Patriotism?' Vespasian mused. 'That's a new approach. Self-preservation has always been my main motivation.'

Traianus nodded and leant forward in his seat. 'Supported by the self-interest of others. Mucianus, for example, he can sniff power but knows he can never hold it in his own right because he hasn't earned the respect; he'll support you to get as much from you as possible. He's no different from the delegation who came to see you; they don't care who has the Purple as long as he's their choice and he'll reward them and it just so happens that you seem to them to be that man; pure self-interest, but useful for the right cause. I, on the other hand, look further ahead and I realise that the Empire may not survive long enough for my fifteen-year-old son to thrive in and take the Ulpii further than I have, unless the right man takes control now. And so I agree with Murena and his mates, but for different reasons: that man, general, is you.'

Vespasian leant his elbows on the desk and rested his chin on his clasped hands. 'You make a powerful case, Traianus: patriotism? Who'd have thought it?'

'Think on it, general. I imagine that you must be in some turmoil as you weigh in your mind the risks of bidding for power and the chances of success. It is not just you and your family who would suffer if you fail, it's every citizen; Rome's very existence could even be threatened and I believe that it is your duty to heal her and it is my duty to help you, whatever the personal risks.'

'One!'

The crack of vine-sticks thumping down onto the backs of sixty men tied by their wrists to posts, with their hands above their heads, reverberated along the frontage of the XV Apollinaris. Silent, the legionaries stood and watched the volunteers from each century receive punishment on their behalf.

'Two!' the primus pilus roared.

Sixty of his brethren in the centuriate brought their sticks down in unison onto their victims' exposed backs, this time just a fraction above the new welts of the first impact; none of the men cried out as their bodies tensed with the pain and their wrists pulled against the leather binding them to the posts.

'Three!'

Vespasian sat on a dais before the XV Apollinaris, with Propinquus standing at his side, watching the sticks come down and making sure that there was genuine effort in each blow. He had sent a message to the primus pilus that there was to be no leniency with the punishment as he wanted the legion to understand in no uncertain terms that they could not refuse an order, even if it was to send him a delegation pleading for him to make a bid for power. If that were to happen, Vespasian had reasoned, it was even more important that the legions at his back should be of the highest discipline. One rogue legion out of control and sacking a town or committing other atrocities would ruin his reputation before he had even achieved his goal. Discipline was all.

'Ten!'

Now the strikes were almost up to the shoulder blades; blood was flowing from the wrists of those men who could not help but strain on their bindings.

'Eleven!'

And still none cried out and their watching comrades remained silent.

'Twelve!'

For the last time the crack of wood on flesh broke the hush; as it died away there was a rush of air as if all four and a half thousand men in the legion had been holding their breath and they had exhaled as one.

As the men were cut down from the posts and led off, all standing erect, proud to have done their duty to their comrades, Vespasian stood, feeling pride in the legion and knowing that its morale was better for what it had just witnessed. 'Men of the Fifteenth Apollinaris,' he declaimed, his voice carrying over the regimented blocks of ten cohorts. 'Your comrades have purged the shame of your refusal of an order this morning. It shall never happen again, not in my army, not if you wish to remain a part of my army.' He paused to let the implication of what he had said sink in. 'Now, go to your duties and we shall talk no more of this matter.' He turned to Propinquus, leaving the ambiguous statement hanging. 'Tribune, you may dismiss them.'

'What are you doing punishing my legion, Father?'

Vespasian looked around to see Titus standing behind the dais. 'Just where the fuck have you been?'

'I was a fool, Father,' Titus said as they walked back through the town to the Governor's residence.

'Well, that's one way of putting it,' Vespasian observed. 'Quite a kind way, at that. Another way of looking at it is that you were a naïve, pussy-whipped idiot with as much political nous as my arsehole and without the loyalty that it feels towards me.'

Titus looked suitably chastened. 'I fell for it, Father, and now I realise that I would have been killed had I got to Rome. It was an act of the gods that sent such bad weather that we had to wait in Corinth.'

'Why didn't you listen to Sabinus?'

'Because I thought that he was just saying things so that the way to the Purple would be kept clear for you. Herod Agrippa was so persuasive; if I ever get my hands on him, I'll rip his circumcised cock off and stuff it in his mouth.'

'There you go again being an idiot. You will see Herod Agrippa again and you will do nothing to him as he may well be very useful to us in the future. You just never trust a word he says again; do I make myself clear?'

'Yes, Father.'

'And where's that woman?'

'I sent her back to Tiberias.'

'Is it over between you?'

'No; I'm sorry, Father, but I have put her aside for a while whilst we finish this thing.'

'Which thing are you referring to?'

Titus took his father's arm as they walked. 'I came back the long way from Corinth, Father, via Cyprus. I went to the Temple of Aphrodite to sacrifice and ask for guidance; Sostratus, her chief priest, declared all the omens to be most favourable for great undertakings, those were his very words. He then took me into his private chamber and spoke to me in confidence; a confidence that I cannot even break with you, Father. But suffice it to say that I will never try to overreach myself again.'

'We'll see; although I am pleased that is how you feel at the moment. So I've got you back then, Titus?'

'Yes, Father, I'm back.'

Vespasian slapped Titus across the shoulders as they walked up the main steps of the Governor's residence. 'That is one major worry off my mind, my son.'

Caenis stood at the top of the steps showing no surprise at seeing Titus. 'He came here first,' she said by way of explanation. 'They both arrived together.'

Vespasian frowned. 'What do you mean: both?'

'Malichus is back. He's waiting for you in the formal reception; he has an emissary with him from the Great King.'

Vespasian's mind went racing back over fifteen years as he tried to haul from the past the name of the man standing next to King Malichus, waiting for him in the formal reception room of the residence. But his very presence gave him hope that the reply from King Vologases would be favourable. 'Gobryas!' Vespasian spluttered, retrieving the name just in time; to have forgotten the name of the man who had vouched for him to Vologases himself when he had been falsely accused of plotting the Great King's murder, all those years ago in Ctesiphon, the Parthian capital, would have been discourteous to say the least. 'I am delighted to see you after such a long time.'

Gobryas placed his hand on his chest and bowed; his slim, sharp-nosed, Persian face was now lined with age but his hennaed beard still grew strong. 'And I too am delighted to see you, my friend. I am much in your debt as, because of my friendship with you, the Great King, Vologases, the Light of the Sun, has conferred upon me the honour of being his mouthpiece.'

Malichus chuckled, scratching at his beard as his face lit up. 'It would seem that you have a good friend in the Great King, Vespasian; when he learnt that I had come with a message from you I only had to wait two days to be called into the royal presence; two days! I'm told it's not unusual to wait two months; in fact there was a delegation of Ethiopes who had been waiting for almost a year.'

'The Light of the Sun has always favoured the man who fights the Lie with Truth,' Gobryas agreed. 'And what Vespasian did for my family by returning the gold of my brother, Ataphanes, who had been his family's slave and then freedman for thirty years, greatly impressed him; his view is that most Romans would just have kept the gold, especially as there was so much of it.'

'Ataphanes had been a very loyal servant of our family and deserved to have his last request honoured. But come, let us recline and take some refreshment. But first, please, Gobryas, I insist that you refresh yourself after such a journey: make use of the bath house and change from your travel clothes; and then we shall talk.'

'The Light of the Sun commands me to wish you well with all your endeavours,' Gobryas said as they reclined to a meal as the sun fell towards the western horizon, washing the sea with a soft red glow. 'He has watched with interest as your prediction of Nero bringing an end to the Julio-Claudian line has come true and how you are now in a position to replace them. He says that when he met you he felt the potential within you and asks me to remind you that he stated, in jest, that had you been one of his subjects he would have removed all your extremities to ensure that you were no threat to his position.'

Vespasian smiled at the memory. 'Yes, I remember him saying that when I hunted with him in his paradise.'

'In normal circumstances my master would take full advantage of a civil war in the Roman Empire,' Gobryas continued, taking a pork and leek sausage and looking at it quizzically. 'He says to tell you that it is for the respect that he bears you that he will take no action that could prejudice your cause; therefore there will be no incursion across the border and Armenia will remain in the Roman sphere of influence.' He bit into the sausage, his expression showing that it pleased him

'He is very gracious, Gobryas,' Vespasian said. 'Please pass on my thanks to him for such restraint.'

'The Light of the Sun has gone further than that: should you wish it, he is willing to provide you with forty thousand of his finest horse archers to aid you in your campaign. He does, however, realise that you may not be able to accept the offer for the way that it might look to your opponents in using foreign troops to gain power. But should you wish them for garrison duties, for example here in Judaea, in order that you can take more troops west with you then he would be only too pleased to help one so enamoured of the Truth. This offer the Light of the Sun makes without expectation of it being accepted; therefore do not feel that you would be insulting him if you do so.'

'The Light of the Sun is generous indeed to make such an offer and he is wise in acknowledging that it cannot be accepted for the reasons that he has stated. But thank him, Gobryas, thank him with all my heart.' And Vespasian's heart was beating fast for now he knew he had the final piece in place: he had a promise from the King of Kings of the Parthian Empire not to attack his rear whilst he went west.

Now it was just a question of if or when he should make that move.

CHAPTER XII

'WITH THE BLOOD of this lamb, I beseech you, Carmel,' Basilides, the chief priest of the god, called in a clear voice to the peak of the deity's sacred mountain, 'send guidance to the supplicants who stand before your altar.'

Vespasian watched the blood flow from the sacrifice's throat as the creature's back legs thrashed; the old priest held it steady and soon the struggling subsided. The lamb went limp, its life given up to help three men come to a decision.

Basilides, with the aid of a couple of acolytes, opened the carcass on the unadorned, open-air altar, and, with practised hands, removed the liver and examined it as his assistants placed the beast's heart on the small fire.

Vespasian glanced at Mucianus, Tiberius Alexander and Titus, all staring intently at the proceedings; he felt Caenis clasp his hand and squeeze it as Magnus muttered to himself somewhere behind him.

Basilides continued his perusal of the liver, methodically going over every part of the surface, his expression increasing in astonishment with new observation. He turned the organ over and inspected the reverse side before looking once more at the front. Finally he placed it back down on the altar and regarded his small congregation. 'Whatever it is you have in mind, Vespasian, whether it is to build a house or enlarge your estate, or to increase the number of your slaves, there is granted to you a great building, vast plots of land and a multitude of men.' Basilides looked back down at the liver. 'In all my years as priest to the ancient god Carmel I have never seen the like; you are blessed by all the gods.'

Vespasian heard Magnus spit behind him and assumed that he was clenching his thumb between his forefinger and middle finger to ward off the evil-eye that might be drawn by Basilides' bold pronouncement.

'I had the same sort of reading at the Temple of Aphrodite, Father,' Titus said as the priest turned and walked away towards the cave in which he spent his days in contemplation of the mysteries of the god Carmel in the heart of his mountain on the Syrian border.

'Well, gentlemen,' Vespasian said, addressing Tiberius Alexander and Mucianus, 'what do you think? For my part I would value your advice as I cannot bring myself to jump either way, such are the consequences both of rebelling against Vitellius and not doing so.'

The two men shared a glance; it was Mucianus who spoke for them: 'Since Otho's defeat at Bedriacum in April and his subsequent suicide, two months have passed and you have done nothing, Vespasian, other than make your legions swear allegiance to that fat prig, Vitellius.'

'That is not fair,' Vespasian protested. 'We only heard the news in May and it has taken us a month to be able to organise this meeting between the three of us here. And don't tell me that you haven't taken the oath to Vitellius, or you and your legions, Tiberius. Eh?'

'Yes, we both have,' he admitted.

'And how did they take it?'

'Not well.'

'No, nor did my legions, but they did it for me; they can understand my indecision.'

Mucianus pointed to the mounted escorts each of the three had brought with them, waiting in the encampment at the bottom of the hill. 'Our men require leadership; not indecision. Now we have come to the point where we either go or not. One way or another a decision must be made today as we're coming towards the end of June; if we plan an invasion of Italia this year then we need to leave very soon or risk being defeated by the weather.'

'Which is why I called this meeting,' Vespasian reminded him. 'I know our men need leadership and I know that time is running out this year; but I was not going to act without consulting you both face to face, and this is the earliest opportunity we have had. Now, let's not bicker. Do we or do we not rebel?'

'I think you need to put the question another way, my love,' Caenis said, stepping forward into the masculine conversation. 'Rebellion is an act of treason that automatically puts you on the wrong side of the law. If you rebel, you pull your men behind you; if, however, you are proclaimed then you are pushed forward by your men and are doing their will. That gives you a mandate.' Caenis looked around the small group, searching the eyes of all three. 'Now that you are all together, if you are really going to do this, and I would be disappointed in all of you if you didn't, then I suggest that you frame a timetable, because this has got to look like a spontaneous uprising of the legions and not a planned grab for power.'

Vespasian thought that he had never loved Caenis more than at that moment: of course she was right and she had shamed them into seeing the correct way forward.

'I'll start it,' Tiberius Alexander said. 'If it begins in Egypt, the wealthiest province in the Empire, and technically the Emperor's personal domain, then that will add weight to the cause.'

'It will also mean the uprising will travel from south to north,' Vespasian said, his throat dry with the realisation that they had come to a silent, mutual decision, 'gaining momentum as it goes through Judaea and then on into the Syrian legions, so that the Moesian army may well declare for us as well.'

'For you, Vespasian,' Caenis reminded him. 'For you. You are the one they are going to make Emperor of Rome; you and you alone.'

The reality of what she had said hit him like a slingshot and he almost staggered back: he was going to be proclaimed Emperor of Rome; this was the reality that they were now discussing. If that was really the case, he would have to start acting the part. 'How soon before you can be back in Egypt, Tiberius?'

'Three days,' he replied with little thought. 'Today is eight days before the calends of July; if my ship sails tomorrow, that would give me four days to make the necessary arrangements

ROBERT FABBRI

with certain key men in the two legions and I could have them declare for you on the calends.'

'Good,' Vespasian said simply, as if Tiberius Alexander had just announced a mutually convenient date for a dinner party. 'That would mean that news of that event could safely arrive with my army three days after that. Titus, you will make the arrangements along with Traianus. It must be spontaneous and I will be taken by surprise and refuse at first; choose some officers and men to draw their weapons on me so that all can see that I did not seek this for myself but, rather, had it forced upon me.'

'Three days after that, so on the sixth day after the calends of July,' Mucianus said, 'I'll have the Syrian legions take the oath and then send messengers up to the boys in Moesia so they can see what's happening in the East; I'm sure the Third Gallica will support their former Syrian comrades and they'll bring the rest of the Moesian legions with them ready to join you when you take the army north and into Italia. All that support should, in turn, get the Seventh Galbiana in Pannonia to declare for you, as their new legate, Antonius Primus, is an opportunist with an eye for the turning of the tide.'

'So long as he supports us his reasons can be his own; but apart from that, it should work – but with one exception: I will not be leading the army north into Italia.'

Mucianus looked confused. 'But then who does?'

'You do, my friend, you do.'

'Me?'

'Yes, you.'

'But what will you do?'

'Firstly, I'll leave Traianus in command in Judaea and come to Syria with Titus to give you an imperial mandate before the whole army to take it to Italia; whilst I'm there I'll take oaths from all the client kings in the East and then I'll go south to Egypt. If I'm able to, I want to make this a bloodless coup; if I march at the head of an army, that shows aggression on my part, just as Vitellius did. I need to stress the difference between Vitellius and myself: I do not conquer Rome, Rome comes to me. And Rome

222

will come to me if I have Egypt and offer Vitellius his and his family's lives. He's fat and lazy; he'll be happy to live out a quiet retirement, knowing that if he refuses my terms, I can turn off the grain supply from Egypt, and the mob, who see no further than their bellies, will blame him and turn upon him.'

'And the army?' Mucianus asked, his voice quiet.

'You are to take it to Aquileia on the Italia–Dalmatia border and await my instructions; I hope not to have to use it. I want to be seen as a saviour not a conqueror.'

'It's the messiah prophecy,' Tiberius Alexander said.

Caenis looked interested. 'What's the messiah prophecy?'

'It's an ancient prophecy that the saviour of the world will rise out of the East. The Jews have their own version of it, which in their self-centred way applies only to them, the messiah coming to set them free from bondage; Herod Agrippa's father was the last one in a long line to make that claim and he was dead within five days of doing so, eaten from the inside out by worms. But if we project the idea that the Empire is tottering on the brink of collapse and you, Vespasian, the star of the East, have arrived as prophesied to save it then we could get a lot of traction for the cause very early.'

'And how will you do that?' Caenis asked, liking the idea.

'Firstly, we'll need miracles.'

Vespasian burst into laughter. 'Miracles! Me? What am I meant to do? Lay my hands on people and cure some vile disease that afflicts the poor?'

Tiberius Alexander's look was serious. 'You leave it to me, Vespasian; I'll get you your miracles and you'll be the eastern messiah that the world has been expecting.'

Caenis smiled. 'That will give you legitimacy, my love; it'll give your claim value.'

'It will give your claim comic value,' Magnus muttered, not all together to himself. 'I don't hold with miracles, they ain't natural.'

'All I'm saying,' Magnus insisted, 'is that if you want to be taken seriously you don't pretend to be some sort of a god.'

Vespasian leant on the rail of the trireme speeding them back to Caesarea, enjoying the salt breeze on his face. The shrill, intermittent whistle of the stroke-master's pipe interspersed with the grunts of one hundred and twenty oarsmen pulling on their sweeps had lulled him into a mellow humour and he felt a great weight had fallen from his shoulders. 'And why not? Augustus is a god; he's got priests and temples to prove it.'

'And Caligula claimed to be a living god, and look what he was like.'

'Caligula was just having a massive joke at everyone's expense. Claudius was worshipped as a god whilst he was still alive. If it helps the more ignorant and superstitious of my subjects to accept me as their Emperor then it has to be a good thing. Look at it this way, Magnus: whatever can be done to keep me in power in order to stabilise the Empire has to be the sensible choice and if it means projecting me as the prophesied messiah, then so be it.'

'But it's bollocks.'

'Of course it's bollocks, I know that and you know that; Caenis knows it, as do Tiberius Alexander, Mucianus and Titus, but does the common peasant in Egypt know it? Or a goatherd in Cilicia? Or, more importantly, the average citizen of Rome who does nothing apart from accept handouts and attend the free games? It doesn't matter what *you* think, it's what *they* think that counts.'

'But you're going to look really silly in front of your peers.'

'Since when have you been worried about what the pompous arseholes – as you term them – think? Besides, they will know that it's just a conceit; I've got far more pressing problems with my peers than worrying if they think that I think I really am the messiah. I've got to get them to realise that they are better off with me as emperor than without me and embarking on another civil war.'

Magnus turned his good eye to his old friend. 'You are really going through with this, aren't you?'

'What, being the messiah?'

'You know perfectly well what I mean.'

'I'm sorry, Magnus; yes, I do. And yes, I am going to go through with it; now that I've made the decision I've come to accept the inevitability of it. Everything has pointed to this moment and although inside I'm terrified, I can't see how to fight it. If I refuse to take it then I'm dead; just as Sejanus said to me all those years ago when he didn't grab power when he could but, rather, waited for it to come to him. Who would have thought that it would have been Sejanus of all people who gave me such a valuable piece of advice? But there it is, and so I'm starting to get an inner calm about the whole thing; within a few days I'm going to be hailed as Emperor of Rome and there is nothing that I can do to stop it: if I say yes, me and my family live, and if I refuse, we all die.'

'It's pretty bleak either way you look at it.'

'Why do you think that? Don't you want me to be the Emperor? Just imagine all the favours I can do for you.'

'It's just that I can't really picture you as emperor, you know, all pompous, patrician and dignified, looking as if you're dealing with an even bigger turd than you normally look like you're trying to pass, if you take my meaning?'

Vespasian chuckled. 'First of all I'm not a patrician, and secondly, I'm not pompous, at least I hope I'm not. And as to the turd, whatever its size, somehow I will always manage to pass it but I'll invariably look as if the strain could kill me. No, Magnus, I'm not going to change if that's what you are worried about. I'm going to remain the New Man, with a country burr from the Sabine Hills, who appreciates a good arse-joke and enjoys running his estate. The only difference will be that my estate will be the entire Empire, which, when I inherit it, will not have sufficient cash to keep it going. And that is the real reason that I'm taking this on, Magnus: because I know how to run an estate, it's in my blood. I'm the right man to get the Empire back on its feet after the madness of Nero and the tragedy of civil war. That's why I've come to accept my fate; it's so obvious to me that it has to be me. But it won't change me.'

Magnus looked dubious. 'Well, I hope not. I used to say that change pleases, but now the older I get, and I don't suppose I'll get much older than this, I've come to appreciate that stability pleases. And what with poor Castor and Pollux now gone I wouldn't want ... I would hate it if ... well, you take my meaning, I'm sure?'

Vespasian was touched by his friend's clumsy attempt to say how much he valued their friendship and would be loath to lose it. 'I do take your meaning, Magnus, I always do; and there is no need for you to worry, we'll ... well, you know.' He gave Magnus a playful punch on the arm to cover the embarrassment of such an intimate moment.

Magnus wiped his good eye. 'Bloody salt's making it water.'

'Yes, it does sting,' Vespasian agreed, running a finger under his own eye. He cleared his throat and then, looking out to sea, pretended, as did Magnus, that he felt no emotion.

'"Titus Flavius Caesar Vespasianus Augustus—"'

'Wait a moment,' Vespasian said, holding up his hand, turning from the terrace balustrade and halting Caenis. 'I haven't taken those names.'

Caenis looked at him from her chair, set in the shade, with infinite patience. 'My love, you haven't even been proclaimed yet, but when we arrived back here in Caesarea you asked me to draft the letter to Vitellius that you'll send once you have been.'

'But why "Titus Flavius Caesar Vespasianus Augustus"? Why not "Titus Flavius Vespasianus Caesar Augustus"?'

'If that's what you want then I'll change it.'

Vespasian narrowed his eyes. 'Why did you choose that form?'

'Because apart from Vitellius, who didn't take the name Caesar, all emperors have been Caesar Augustus going back to Caligula and I thought that it might be a wise move to disassociate yourself from them whilst still retaining the names that symbolise imperial power.'

'You're getting to be quite shrewd in your old age.'

'I don't call sixty-two old; now if I might proceed?'

Vespasian waved her on and turned back to watch the night-fishing boats dock below him accompanied by hundreds of gulls wailing in anticipation of breakfast.

'"Titus Flavius Caesar Vespasianus Augustus greets Aulus Vitellius."' Caenis looked up. 'You'll notice that I omitted the "Germanicus Augustus" part of his name.'

'Very good.'

'"And invites him to retire on a pension of one million sesterces a year to a villa of his choice in Campania as his services to the state are no longer required. There he may live, without fear of molestation, with his wife and children as well as a household that he sees as being commensurate to his dignity. In the course of time his sons will be free to enter public office without let or hindrance. Failure to take up this offer will have military consequences which I would hope that we both wish to avoid. Furthermore, it should be noted that I myself am proceeding to Egypt to take command of the grain supply. The bearer of this letter, my freedman, Titus Flavius Hormus, has my authority and therefore his person is inviolate."' Caenis rolled up the draft. 'Well? What do you think?'

Vespasian did not respond.

'My love, what do you think?'

Still Vespasian said nothing but continued staring out across the port.

Caenis rose to join him. 'What is it?'

Vespasian pointed to a sleek and fast little liburnian under full sail, speeding up from the south. 'There, that ship; I'll wager that's coming from Egypt with news.'

Caenis gripped Vespasian's arm. 'So, it's to be today, my love. It's time to get ready to be surprised.'

Vespasian said nothing; his stomach lurched and he felt sick.

Vespasian held his arms out for Hormus to tie the straps on his breast- and backplates, burnished to a dazzling degree, as a body slave knelt behind him, securing his greaves, which were equally as polished. 'You will leave with the letter for Vitellius immediately, Hormus.'

'Yes, master.'

'And there is one for Sabinus too.'

'Yes, master.'

'Stay with him; his position as prefect of Rome should protect you, as Vitellius hasn't dismissed him. With luck you will be in Rome before the calends of next month around the time that I shall arrive in Antioch. Send word to me there and then the following month I should be in Alexandria.'

'You don't wish me to come in person, master?' Hormus asked as he changed sides, kicking the slave out of the way.

'No, I need you to be my eyes and ears for a while in Rome; Sabinus and Domitian are too conspicuous and may have their correspondence intercepted, and if Vitellius does refuse my offer their positions could become untenable. You on the other hand—'

'Are insignificant, master?' Hormus cut in.

'In Vitellius' eyes, yes.'

Hormus beamed at the implied compliment and kicked the slave again as he fastened the last strap. 'The cloak!'

The slave scuttled off as Hormus began to tie the red sash around Vespasian's midriff.

'But I'll need you to do a greater service, Hormus,' Vespasian continued, 'because if it should come to war, it will be vital to get a message to Mucianus at Aquileia so that it is waiting for him there when he arrives, which, with luck, will be in late September. That cannot just be a written message; it has to be delivered in person by someone Mucianus can trust.'

'I am honoured, master. You can rely on me.' Hormus snatched the cloak, brilliant scarlet, from the returning slave and draped it over Vespasian's shoulders.

'I know I can; you're one of the few in whom I can have complete trust and it will not go unrewarded when this is all over.'

Hormus flushed with pride as he secured the cloak with a silver clasp engraved with the image of Mars.

Vespasian looked down at the engraving. 'An appropriate choice, Hormus.'

'I thought so, master.'

'Today, of all days, I pray that he will hold his hands over me and that, with his good help, success will crown my work.'

Vespasian picked up his high-plumed helmet, rubbed an imaginary smudge away, took a deep breath and then strode from the room.

It was Traianus who waited at the top of the steps of the Governor's residence and behind him were arrayed all the tribunes of the X Fretensis and the XV Apollinaris, as well as many of the centurions from both legions; to the side stood Caenis, Magnus and Titus. Beyond, covering the whole forum, was a multitude of faces; hard, legionary faces, waiting in absolute silence.

'Good morning, gentlemen,' Vespasian said in what he hoped was a nonchalant tone.

'Imperator!' Traianus bellowed.

The officers followed his lead. 'Imperator! Imperator!'

Vespasian stopped still as if hit by an invisible wall.

The legionaries joined in the acclamation. 'Imperator! Imperator!' It travelled like a wave back through the crowd and then beyond the forum so Vespasian realised that the whole army was present, out of sight in side streets, filling the whole of Caesarea. 'Imperator! Imperator! Imperator!' And so it went on as Vespasian stood still, neither acknowledging nor denying the chant.

For a few more heartbeats he let it go on as he adjusted himself to the reality that his life had changed in a seismic manner; and then he remembered that he had a part to play. He held up his hands for silence. It took a long while coming. 'What is this that you confer upon me?' he asked, his voice cutting through the last faint shouts from the distance. 'What is it you want of me?'

Traianus half turned to the crowd for them better to hear his reply. 'We, the army of Judaea, follow the lead of the Egyptian legions who proclaimed you imperator three days ago in Alexandria. We, like they, choose you. Caesar! Augustus! Imperator!'

And again, the shout was deafening as it rose from thousands of throats.

And again, Vespasian raised his hands for quiet.

And again, it was slow to manifest.

'Do we not have an existing oath to an emperor in Rome?' Vespasian asked as soon as he could be heard. 'Have we all not sworn to Aulus Vitellius Germanicus Augustus together? I cannot accept this proclamation.'

But Traianus was insistent. 'The army of Judaea choose you, Caesar, over the fat prig in Rome. Imperator!'

Once more the cry thundered around the forum and Vespasian stood, his hands over his ears as if trying to block it from his consciousness. For a few more heartbeats he let it continue and then, with a dramatic gesture, turned his back on the crowd. The steady chant turned into an angry roar until Traianus' voice rose above it, shrill and piercing. 'Do you refuse us, Caesar Augustus? Do you refuse the wishes of the army of Judaea?'

'I cannot accept what is another man's; a man to whom I am sworn,' Vespasian replied without turning around, his voice equally as forceful.

'We insist, Imperator; we, the army of Judaea, will have our Emperor.'

Vespasian heard the ringing of a drawing sword.

'And we have chosen you.'

Vespasian turned to see Traianus approaching him, armed; behind him the tribunes were unsheathing their weapons and mounting the steps. 'Do you threaten me with violence should I refuse your request?'

'We will have our way or our shame at rejection will be great indeed.'

Vespasian extended the palms of his hands. 'Hold there!' He waited until all had stilled. 'I do not seek this title, nor do I voluntarily accept it, as you have witnessed, but if you wish to confer it upon me under pressure, threatening me with naked weapons, then I have no choice but to accept. If you push me forward then I have no option but to lead you. Is that the wish of you all?'

And the shout went up again, this time louder than before; a cacophony of 'Caesar! Augustus! Imperator!' Vespasian extended his arms and received it, his eyes closed. Lifting his face to the sky, the image of Mars burning in his mind, he turned left and then right, wallowing in the accolade. Caenis, Titus and Magnus looked on with tears on their cheeks for the man they loved; the man who had just been proclaimed the ninth Emperor of Rome.

PART III

Egypt, Autumn AD 69

CHAPTER XIII

How word had spread Vespasian knew not, but that it clearly had was evident from the masses of people, crammed around the base of the towering Pharos lighthouse, waiting to greet their new Emperor. And it was for them an occasion indeed, for an emperor had not come to Egypt since Augustus and they cheered themselves hoarse as the ships bearing Vespasian and his considerable escort drew near to the Great Harbour of Alexandria. Despite the rages of an Egyptian September sun, more crowds of locals greeted him from the concrete moles that protected the harbour, each over half a mile in length. Waving and calling him 'Caesar Augustus', they danced and jigged as the flotilla, led by the imperial quinquereme, glided through the harbour mouth, bringing their Emperor home to his own personal fiefdom.

'It don't seem any less impressive the second time around,' Magnus observed, standing behind Vespasian's chair, looking up at the Pharos topped with a statue of Poseidon over four hundred feet above them.

Vespasian, his gold-plated breastplate and greaves gleaming, peered from under the cotton canopy shading him, as he sat in regal state on a curule chair, his bald pate adorned with a laurel wreath; Caenis sat next to him, slightly set back, and twelve lictors stood in a phalanx in front of him. 'You remember the last time we were here, Magnus, when Caligula wanted to drive across his bridge wearing Alexander's breastplate?'

'Yeah, young Ziri was alive, the fuzzy little desert-dweller.' Magnus' face lengthened as he remembered his long-dead favoured slave. 'I still miss him, especially now that Castor and Pollux ...' He stopped himself from going into a maudlin reminiscence.

'Anyway,' Vespasian carried on, used by now to Magnus' depression, 'I said that's how to make people remember you: build something that is of use to everybody and not just a three-mile-long bridge as Caligula did.'

'Yeah, and I asked you who built the Circus Maximus and you didn't know, thus proving that your theory don't always work.'

'Yes, well, be that as it may, that is what I'm going to do in Rome.'

'What? Build a lighthouse?'

'Of course not; what good would that be?'

'That's what I was wondering.'

'No, it has to be something that everyone would enjoy. Pompey has his theatre, Caesar has his forum, Agrippa his baths, Claudius his port, Augustus, well, Augustus has countless buildings, so what should I have?'

'Don't forget Nero's Golden House with his statue the size of a colossus, my love,' Caenis said. 'I'll tell you what people would remember you for and that is tearing that monstrosity down because it reminds them of the fire he started to get the land on which to build it.'

Vespasian again held a dignified hand in the air to acknowledge the greetings of the citizens of Alexandria. 'Yes, that's an excellent idea; I'll do that and then I'll build something in its place using the bricks and stone.' Vespasian's eyes brightened at the thought. 'That will make it much cheaper if I don't have to buy all the materials; and, what's more, I'll have plenty of free Jewish slaves to work on it.'

'Nice and cheap,' Magnus scoffed, 'just how you like it. So, what's it going to be, then?'

'What?'

'The thing we're talking about, the thing you're going to build.'

'Oh, I don't know yet; I'll have to see how much space there is when the Golden House comes down.'

'Well, if you want my opinion, the thing that everyone would appreciate best would be an amphitheatre like we saw in Cyzicus, you remember, that huge one built over a river so that it could be flooded and you could have sea battles in it. That would be great and we'd all love it, all of us apart from the gladiators and those idiots who get themselves damned to the wild beasts, that is.'

Vespasian contemplated the idea, acknowledging the crowds as the city opened up before him. It was exactly how he remembered it with its grand waterfront, a mixture of private villas, temples and warehouses running from the Heptastadium, the mole that joined the Pharos Island to the mainland thus dividing the harbour into the Old Port and the Great Harbour, to the Palace of the Ptolemys to the left, now the prefect's residence. He squinted up at the elegant structure, built by a dynasty of untold wealth, and could make out the terrace on the second floor from which he, Magnus and Flavia had escaped by rope to avoid the attention of the then prefect, Flaccus, on the night that they had stolen Alexander's breastplate from his mausoleum. And here he was again, he reflected, returning with the breastplate to Alexandria; but this time he was coming not as Caligula's thief but, rather, as Caligula's successor.

In the, almost, three months since his proclamation as emperor, Vespasian had grown accustomed to the title and the sycophancy that it attracted.

Once he had received the oath of the army of Judaea, administered that very afternoon of his proclamation, he had proceeded north to Berytus in Syria where he had rendezvoused with Mucianus who had brought with him the entire VI Ferrata and detachments from the other Syrian legions, a force of around eighteen thousand men. With great ceremony he had taken their oath and handed Mucianus the imperial mandate authorising him to march to Rome and secure the capital for the rightful Emperor should the city not be surrendered by Vitellius. Mucianus had departed promptly on his mission, promising to make good time and to wait at Aquileia for instructions one way or the other. Vespasian had then remained in Berytus for the many client kings of the East to come to him and swear their loyalty; and they all came: the client kings of Commagene, Cilicia, Pergamon as well as lesser tetrarchies and other domains. Messengers from all the governors of the East:

Asia, Bithynia, Cappadocia, Galatia and Achaea, stated that all had taken the oath to Vespasian, whilst rich gifts from Tiridates of Armenia and Vologases greatly increased his treasury and he was able to dispense a degree of largesse. But it was not only the powerful who came to pay homage but also the ordinary folk; many flocked to him to bring, as was their right as citizens, petitions, appeals and pleas for him to rule on. And so he spent many days wading through the grievances of those less fortunate than himself: adjudicating on property disputes, rights of ownership of slaves, contracts of supply to the army, wills, inheritance, citizenship, accusations of corruption and all the other things that affect the lives of the common man, including whether he should live or die as those condemned to death put their lives in the Emperor's hands for confirmation of the sentence, or commuting to a lesser forfeit or, perhaps, acquittal. He had then moved north to Antioch, the capital of the province, and had gone through the same procedure there and thereby securing the complete support of the most powerful province in the East.

On his second day in Antioch, Hormus' letter arrived with the not unexpected news that Vitellius had refused Vespasian's offer; it was now inevitable that there would be civil war, East against West.

It was after news reached him that the Moesian and Pannonian legions had sworn to him and that they too were marching west, that he had decided that the time had come to travel to Egypt in order to place his hand around Vitellius' throat by taking control of the grain supply. And so here he was finally beginning his roundabout journey to Rome, with the support of the two kings who could have made trouble for him, Vologases and Tiridates, and having spent valuable time securing the eastern half of the Empire to leave it united behind him – time very well spent. There was only one problem, at least only one that he knew of, and that was Jerusalem; but that was something that he would send Titus to deal with once his son had been feted by the Egyptians and his position as heir apparent accepted by the people and legions alike. In the meantime, Traianus was slowly tightening the blockade on the holy city of the Jews still riven by the murderous faction fighting of fundamentalist fanatics.

Vespasian smiled to himself as he contemplated the ease, so far, with which he had managed to take the East and prayed that the West would be as straightforward; but that was perhaps for Amun to guide him. Although he was still unsure of the question he should ask, he intended to consult the oracle as soon as his business with the Alexandrians permitted. And, as the quinquereme started slowing in preparation for docking, he hoped that his business would not take too long; but however quick it was, Vespasian knew that, with winter approaching, he would not be able to sail to Rome until at least the spring.

With a stream of incomprehensible nautical jargon from the trierarch and his subordinates, the great quinquereme lowered its mainsail, shipped its oars and, with majesty befitting of the cargo that it bore, slid under the power of a half-furled foresail into its berth; cables flew, uncoiling, through the air, to be caught and fastened to stout posts by scuttling, barefoot dockworkers. With the creaking of straining rope and wood, the ship's momentum eased until it rested, with a slight jolt, on the sacks of hay hanging from the posts to protect its hull from the grating of the rough concrete of which the quays in the Great Harbour were constructed; for it was here that Vespasian had ordered his flotilla to dock and not in the private port of the royal palace, a place hidden from view from the common people. And it was the common people, who lined the quays in their thousands and cheered and waved, who he now needed to awe, since the province's two legions, the XXII Deiotariana and the III Cyrenaica, were his already, their oath taken by Tiberius Alexander in payment for the debt he owed Vespasian for saving his life more than thirty years before. It was not so much that he cared for the common people but more because the Alexandrians were amongst the most volatile populations in the Empire and Vespasian had witnessed at first hand just what happens when the Alexandrians riot. He had, therefore, realised that to truly control the city, and thereby the province along with all its wealth, especially the grain, the people needed to love him.

Vespasian did not move as deck-hands raced about, securing the vessel whilst the ship's complement of a century of marines formed up, facing Vespasian and his lictors, on the foredeck; whistles blew and shouts were raised until all was in place and the gangplank lowered.

Titus appeared on deck from the cabin below and Magnus, along with Caenis, moved away from the Emperor sitting in state beneath his canopy. Vespasian signalled to his son to stand at his right shoulder as a man in an equestrian toga walked, with high-nosed dignity, up the gangway accompanied by a togate escort of equal decorum.

'It's a good start,' Vespasian observed to Titus, as, with a bark from their leader, the lictors parted so that the reception committee might have direct access to the object of their reverence. 'It seems that the whole city has turned out to welcome us.'

Titus stifled a yawn and looked around at the crowd made up of both men and women with their brats in tow, dressed mainly in the Greek style. 'Not many Jews,' he said after scanning the faces for a while.

'Well, at least the most important one is here.' Vespasian turned his attention to the leader of the delegation as it halted ten paces from his chair.

'Hail, Titus Flavius Caesar Vespasianus Augustus,' Tiberius Alexander declaimed, his voice high and carrying. 'The citizens of Alexandria and the whole of Egypt welcome their new Emperor with a joy not felt since the coming of your predecessor, Augustus, more than sixty years ago.' Tiberius turned and took a small chest from one of his attendants and then presented it to Vespasian. 'Princeps, please receive this, your rightful possession, from the safe-keeping of your servant and representative in this province.'

Vespasian took the chest, set it upon his knees and opened the lid. Reaching in, he pulled out a key, a golden key that glistered in the sun.

'The key to the treasury of Alexandria is now returned to its true owner. Hail Caesar!'

With a mighty shout all those in hearing distance joined in so that soon the cry spread throughout the city; palm fronds were waved aloft and the air was filled with incense and the smoke from many sacrifices. Vespasian rose to his feet and stepped out from beneath the canopy, holding the key above his head. He waited as the cheering subsided and people became aware that he was about to address them.

'Your Emperor thanks you, Prefect Tiberius Alexander, and the people of the province of Egypt, for delivering to me my property and having faithfully watched over it in my absence.' This drew a second resounding roar as all conveniently overlooked the fact that Vespasian had not yet been recognised by the Senate, the Praetorian Guard and the western half of the Empire; mere trivialities like that were not about to spoil everyone's day.

As the cheering continued, Vespasian took Tiberius Alexander's forearm in a firm clench of greeting. 'What do you have planned, my friend?'

'Cohorts from both the legions are here waiting to escort you to the Caesareum for a sacrifice and then on to the forum where I've had a rostrum set up for you to publicly receive petitions and listen to appeals and pleas.'

Vespasian smiled as if this was the very thing he desired; having already presided over many such sessions in Antioch and Berytus he was coming to realise that the burden of the Purple lay more in the mass of the minutiae rather than in a few grand schemes and ideas. 'Very good, prefect; how many days do you estimate?'

'How many days have you got, Princeps?'

Vespasian sighed as he suppressed the urge to give an untruthful answer. 'I won't be able to sail to Rome until at least May next year so that I can arrive with the grain fleet and be seen as the bringer of sustenance.'

'That should just about give you enough time, Princeps.'

*

On a white horse of proud bearing and great beauty, Vespasian processed through the wide thoroughfares of Alexandria, his back straight, his thighs gripping the beast's flanks and his feet hanging free. Preceded by his twelve lictors and followed by Titus and the stamping of four thousand legionaries, taken from both of the Egyptian legions, he acknowledged the crowd, sometimes ten to twelve deep, cheering themselves hoarse; Vespasian, however, had no illusions on the subject, he was a man they had absolutely no knowledge of other than through the propaganda that had been peddled by Tiberius Alexander. He was equally under no illusions that the prefect had paid off the debt he owed him by delivering Egypt so comprehensively into his hands.

And so, after sacrificing a white bullock in an emotional ceremony at the Caesareum, built by Cleopatra in memory of her dead lover, Vespasian came to the forum, larger and grander than any built so far in Rome, and there he dismounted. As the lictors formed up along the base of the rostrum and the cohorts stood to attention, still in column, carving the crowd in two, he ascended the steps, and, to the mightiest roar of the day, he received the acclamation of Alexandria.

On it went, pulsating as a combination of Greek, Latin, Aramaic and Egyptian blended, lauding him in different forms of words so that nothing was clear; and yet all was clear, for the meaning of the cacophony was in no doubt, and Vespasian was left in no doubt that the province was safe. With an extravagant opening of his arms he looked down at Titus and called him up onto the rostrum. In marked contrast to the dignity with which his father had mounted the steps, Titus leapt up them, taking them two at a time, in the spirit of a young man of action. As he reached the top, Vespasian took his left hand in his right and punched the air; the din increased still further.

Vespasian turned to Titus, as they thumped their arms up and down to the beat of the cheer, and grinned with uncontrolled glee.

'Well, Father,' Titus said, his enjoyment of the moment only too self-evident, 'it looks like we've founded a new dynasty.'

The smile faded on Vespasian's face; he turned back to the crowd as he realised the full implication of his eldest son's statement: how would his younger son, Domitian, react to not having a leading role in that dynasty?

Finally Vespasian knew what question he would ask of Amun.

It was with disgust that Vespasian watched the effete young Greek grovelling on the ground before him, screaming. He had not liked him at first sight and after three hours of listening to various degrees of truth and lies from many different citizens on many different subjects, Vespasian had not been in the mood to entertain the palpable falsehoods that the man, a spice merchant by profession, had levelled against Tiberius Alexander. Each accusation the prefect had disproved with clinical care and had proven beyond doubt that the merchant had attempted to blackmail him by killing a rival and falsifying the evidence so that it looked to be the prefect's doing.

'And see that he gets a clean death,' Vespasian said to the magistrate overseeing the day's legal proceedings. 'He may be an odious, lying little toad but he is still a citizen; now take him away.' Howling, the man was dragged from Vespasian's presence.

'Thank you, Princeps,' Tiberius Alexander said, his expression one of relief that the verdict had been in his favour.

'I can tell when someone is trying to get out of paying the lawful import tax on valuable spices by threatening to ruin the reputation of the man who collects those taxes, Tiberius. He was being greedy, and I'll not have that.' Vespasian raised his voice so that all the spectators around the open-air court could hear. 'I'll not have people trying to defraud my revenues and I wish all to see that.' He consulted the scroll giving the order of the hearings, drawn by lot. The two names up next meant nothing to him; he gestured to the magistrate. 'Bring the next case forward.'

'The two men coming now, Princeps,' Tiberius Alexander said, moving closer to the dais in order to lower his voice, 'are not here to plead a case before you, but, rather, to ask for your help.'

'Help in what?'

'Help to cure them of their afflictions.'

'Afflictions? I'm not a doctor.'

'No, Princeps, but perhaps you have other powers.'

Vespasian looked at the two men approaching him; one, his eyes bound, was being guided by the other, his two gnarled and bandaged hands resting on his shoulders. Both were dressed in rags, with matted hair and beards; neither had shoes.

'What am I meant to do with them, Tiberius?'

'Just do as they ask and have a little faith in yourself.'

'Faith?' He looked down at the two supplicants falling to their knees at the foot of the steps to the dais and then signalled to the magistrate.

'You may address your Emperor,' the magistrate said, not hiding his revulsion at the two ragged and filthy figures.

The blind man raised his head and held out his arms in roughly Vespasian's direction, beseeching him. 'Princeps, three months ago, I was struck by a curse of the gods; you can make me see again.'

'And you can heal my fingers, Princeps,' the other man said holding out his crooked hands, his expression pleading.

Vespasian managed to restrain an explosive guffaw by putting his hand to his mouth and turning the noise into a fit of coughing. When he had control of himself once more, he managed to affect a sombre countenance. 'What would you have me do?'

'Rub saliva in my eyes, Princeps.'

'Tread on my hands.'

This time the coughing fit was slightly more acute and was preceded by a loud snort; it was a few moments before Vespasian trusted himself to look back down at the two men and then another couple before he dared open his mouth to speak. 'My saliva?'

'Yes, Princeps. You are come from the East to save the Empire; you have the power to heal.'

Vespasian opened his mouth but bit back a sarcastic reply; he glanced at Tiberius Alexander, his eyes questioning. The prefect nodded almost imperceptibly and Vespasian realised what was going on and knew he had to play his part to make it work. He stood and addressed the crowd cramming into the forum. 'These men have asked me, your Emperor, to heal them. I make no claim to healing powers, nor have I made a claim to be the messiah from the East, long foretold, come to ease the cares of the world. I am a man who has risen to the Purple and no more. Should I, therefore, attempt to heal these men?' He held an arm out, gesturing for a reply. It was affirmative and unanimous. He looked back down at the two men, their heads bowed in supplication, and then to Tiberius Alexander who gave a faint conspiratorial smile and another slow nod. 'Very well, I shall try, but not in the sure knowledge of success.' He sat back down. 'Come!'

The two men crawled to the steps, and then, with the sighted one leading, ascended them on their knees.

'Come close,' Vespasian commanded as they reached the top.

Obedient to his word they shuffled forward; the stench of them reached Vespasian's nostrils and his face wrinkled. 'Take off your bandages.'

The blind man pulled his free as his companion fumbled with the soiled rags on his hands and then tugged on them with his teeth.

Vespasian leant forward to look into the blind man's eyes; they stared, vacant, at a spot in the far distance, showing no recognition that there was anything closer. Feeling that he had nothing to lose but everything to gain, if Tiberius Alexander had really somehow managed to set this up, Vespasian spat, with great ostentation, into the palm of his hand.

The crowd hushed, peering forward with tense anticipation.

Vespasian presented his spittle-covered hand to them and then wiped the liquid off with his thumb. 'Come forward, blind man.'

The man pushed himself forward until Vespasian could reach him; this close, his stench was almost intolerable. 'Stop.' Holding his breath, Vespasian smeared his saliva on first one eye and then the other; not a sound could be heard in the forum. Vespasian withdrew his hand and, realising that he had to go the whole way, got again to his feet. Swallowing his revulsion, he placed his hand on the man's head. 'See!'

The hush deepened.

Vespasian released the man's head and held a finger up before his face. The blind man turned his eyes towards it. Vespasian moved the finger left and then right; the man's head turned back and forth, following it.

The shocked gasp of so many thousands of onlookers felt like a physical blow to Vespasian as he helped the man up and turned him to face the crowd. 'What do you see?'

Slowly shaking his head in amazement, he surveyed the crowd. 'I see faces; a sea of faces.'

'He sees!' Vespasian cried. 'He sees!'

'He sees!' the crowd replied and then broke into adulation, praising their new Emperor as a miracle worker as the newly sighted man kissed Vespasian's hand and then with an incredulous expression walked down the steps without faltering.

With a shrewd idea of how the prefect had worked the last trick, Vespasian looked down at the deformed hands of the second supplicant and wondered if this attempt would be quite so successful. The fingers were swollen and curved like claws and seemed to be set rigidly in place.

Again the crowd quietened, although the silence was not absolute on this occasion as many congratulated the cured blind man as he made his way through to show off his new vision.

'Lay your hands on the ground,' Vespasian ordered the cripple. He turned to Tiberius Alexander to see whether he had any advice.

'Press down hard,' he mouthed.

With a mental shrug, Vespasian looked back down to the two disfigured hands lying palm-up on the wooden floor. He placed his right foot on one, forcing the man's fingers flat under his toes. He laid his hand on the cripple's head and then pushed down with the ball of his foot. He felt a series of clicks and the man shuddered as if restraining a cry. Vespasian then turned his attention to the second hand and, with the same preparation, pushed all his weight down upon it. This time the man did let out a stifled cry of pain and Vespasian could see his eyes watering.

Vespasian stood back. The man raised his hands and stared at them as if he had never seen them before. One by one he flexed his fingers; each digit moved independently with a full range of movement. Vespasian offered his own hand; the former cripple took it and was raised to his feet and turned to face the crowd.

'No longer is he cursed,' Vespasian cried. 'His hands are cured!'

The man held his arms aloft and clenched and unclenched his fists as the crowd melted into messianic adoration.

'So how did you do it?' Magnus asked, once he had got over his mirth. 'Not that I hold with miracles at all, mind you, they ain't natural.'

'Yes, Tiberius, how did you do it?' Vespasian asked, standing next to Caenis and looking out over the Great Harbour as the sun set; a light, refreshing breeze blew in his face, cooling him. High, to his right, smoke showed that the raging fire which would burn all night, taking the sun's place reflecting in the great bronze mirrors, was being stirred into life at the top of the Pharos.

'I can guess,' Caenis said, linking her arm through Vespasian's and watching a small flotilla of lanteen-sailed fishing vessels gliding out through the harbour mouth to ply their trade through the night.

'It was quite straightforward,' Tiberius Alexander admitted.

'The blind man said that he had been cursed by the gods, three months ago; in other words about the time you would have arrived back in Alexandria after promising a miracle.'

Tiberius accepted a glass of iced wine from a half-naked slave girl. 'I can see you have the basis of the matter.'

'So you paid him to pretend to be blind, and to make the deception easier he wore bandages over his eyes so that people couldn't see that he wasn't.'

'Precisely. And I made sure that he was well known, as a blind man, throughout the city by always having the Watch move him on roughly and generally treat him unkindly so that he became noticed and attracted a degree of sympathy. Everybody knew him as a blind man and no one questioned it. And I'm sure if you asked people how long he'd been around for, they would have said for ages and not just three months.'

'And the cripple?' Vespasian asked.

'Same again: I paid him. I had his fingers dislocated and then bound up. I have to say, I was amazed that they did pop back in when you trod on his hands; still, that was a risk I had to take as two miracles are far more convincing than one.'

'And now I'm the messiah,' Vespasian mused, 'how ludicrous.'

'How useful,' Caenis corrected.

'Here in the East, perhaps, but not in Rome. I shan't play on it there.'

'Quite right, love; don't play on it but don't deny it either. The rumours of what happened today are bound to travel and they can do you no harm if you just refuse to address them one way or another.'

Magnus did not seem so sure. 'Yeah, but what happens when these miraculously healed people start to boast about their exploits and the truth comes out?'

'Oh, I wouldn't worry about that,' Tiberius said with an unconcerned air. 'It's been given out that these two fortunate gentlemen have been taken to Rome as proof of the miraculous events here; no one will miss them in Alexandria. It's just such a shame that the Emperor cured them only for their ship to fall foul of a winter storm.'

'So they've taken ship already, then, if you take my meaning?'

'Yes, Magnus, they sailed for the necropolis a couple of hours ago. I can only hope they sailed with the satisfaction of the knowledge of a job well done.'

Vespasian pursed his lips in approval. 'Thank you, Tiberius; I have to say that it had crossed my mind that keeping them alive could leave us open to blackmail. Now the question is: do we leave it at that or am I expected to be performing miracles every day?'

Tiberius sipped his drink and contemplated the question for a few moments. 'Well, I've not got any more set up, Princeps, so unless you feel that you can *really* perform one I think that's it. What I will do, though, is start rumours of other miracles; you know how credulous the masses are, they'll believe anything if they want to badly enough.'

Vespasian gave a wry grin at the extent of Tiberius Alexander's cynicism as Titus came out onto the terrace, looking worried and holding a scroll. 'What is it, Titus?'

'A letter from Mucianus.'

'What does it say?'

Titus unrolled the scroll. 'He's at Aquileia with Hormus. There have been some negotiations between us and the Vitellians but no progress has been made. They have heard that a Vitellian army is marching north under Caecina; he had a debate with all the legionary legates as to what to do, in the absence of any new instructions from you, and they decided to stay put and wait. However, Antonius Primus, the legate of the Seventh Galbiana, stationed in Pannonia, has disobeyed Mucianus' orders and has marched to meet it because he felt that since Lucilius Bassus, the prefect of the fleet at Ravenna, persuaded his men to declare for you, the north of Italia is there for the taking. Mucianus thinks that the spilling of Roman blood by Romans in your name is now unavoidable.'

Vespasian thumped the balustrade. 'Antonius Primus? The fool! What does he think he's doing? I was absolutely clear that none of my troops should enter Italia until negotiations had proved fruitless.'

'But he has, Father; this letter is ten days old, so he may well have already met the Vitellian army.'

'One legion against an army? Surely no one is that rash?'

Titus looked back at the letter. 'He was and that's the main reason that Mucianus has written. He says that he had no choice but to follow Primus, as, if his single, unsupported legion were to be defeated, it would be catastrophic for your cause. The whole army of more than forty thousand men is in Italia and is heading for Cremona, just near to where Vitellius defeated Otho.'

'And is in all likelihood already there, my love,' Caenis observed. 'It may even be that that battle has already been fought and it could be another ten days before we know the result.'

'Ten days? Yes, you're right, Caenis.' Vespasian's already strained expression increased as he came to a decision. 'Prepare a caravan, get me a guide and have the camels loaded onto transport ships, Tiberius; it's time for me to go to Siwa and consult the god Amun.'

CHAPTER XIIII

'TAKE JOSEPHUS WITH you, Titus,' Vespasian said to his son as they both prepared to depart the Great Harbour of Alexandria, one to the East and the other to the West. 'He may be useful in negotiating Jerusalem's surrender. If that fails, which instinct tells me it will, then use all force possible. And once Jerusalem has fallen come directly to Rome and join me. Traianus can be left in charge of the mopping up operations until whoever I choose to conduct the siege of Masada arrives in the province.'

'Yes, Father,' Titus replied, grasping Vespasian's forearm. 'I expect to be there within the month. With luck I'll circumvallate it by—'

'Wait!' A thought struck Vespasian. 'If you plan to circumvallate it, it would be best to have as many of the bastards within the walls as possible, would it not?'

Titus grinned. 'In order to starve them out so much the quicker.'

'Exactly, my boy. Use the negotiations as a way of delaying until their feast of the unleavened bread sometime early in the new year; I've heard that often the city swells to a million and a half people at that time; let them try to feed all those mouths together.'

'That's brilliant, Father; that way we could kill tens of thousands of them.'

'The more the better.'

'Indeed, the more the better.'

Vespasian pulled Titus into an embrace. 'Make them suffer like they've never suffered before, so they won't dare to rise against Rome again.'

'I will, Father; I'll break their mothers' hearts.'

'And once you've done that we'll share a Triumph back in Rome. That should see us safely on our way to securing our position.'

'Provided Mucianus wins.'

'He will.'

Titus essayed a look of confidence; it did not convince Vespasian. 'I know he will, Father.'

'And even if he doesn't, we've still got the East, and we'll keep that, then take Africa and starve Vitellius out. I've already sent messages to the Governor of Africa and the legate of the Third Augusta there; if they refuse to come over to me then, when I get back from Siwa, I'll launch a campaign to take the province. We'll win in the end now that we've started, Titus; never let go of that thought.'

Titus returned his father's embrace. 'I won't.' He stood back and looked Vespasian in the eye. 'But tell me: what do you hope to gain from this voyage up the coast and then a two-hundred-mile trip across the desert to some remote oracle?'

'The same as Alexander when he came here: advice and guidance.'

'Come on, Father, there are plenty of other oracles which don't involve such an arduous journey.'

'That may be true, Titus; but I was there once and it was made clear to me then that I would return; and now the time is right for I know the question that I must ask.' He kissed Titus on both cheeks, turned and walked up the gangway of his quinquereme to where Magnus and Caenis waited for him on board.

'It no safe, master.' The guide was adamant as he and Vespasian stood on the summit of a coastal sand dune, looking to the south.

Vespasian glanced down at the brown-skinned, curly haired, wiry little Marmarides who reminded him so much of Magnus' former slave, Ziri, now lying forever in a river in Germania Magna so far from his parched homeland. 'How far away is it?'

The guide shaded his eyes and gazed towards the brown cloud looming on the horizon; he sniffed the air and muttered to himself as he calculated. 'Six hour, perhaps eight.'

Vespasian studied the dust storm for a moment; it was evidently huge, far larger than the one he had experienced the last time he had travelled to Siwa, which had buried more than a hundred of his men. 'Is it coming this way?'

The Marmarides shrugged. 'Maybe, maybe not, master; the sand-god's wrath come and go where he please. We say: "When sand-god blow, no further we go".'

'I'm with the desert-dweller,' Magnus said, puffing. 'Ziri knew everything about the desert and I'll wager that this frizzy little camel-botherer is in the same league. We stay here, with the ships, until that thing has gone.'

Vespasian, despite his haste, found himself agreeing. He turned and looked back at the three ships, bobbing at anchor fifty paces out on a calm, refreshingly blue sea. 'Very well, we'll camp on the beach; but we'll offload the camels from the two transport ships. It'll give them some time to stretch their legs after being at sea for three days.'

'Or we could just turn round and sail back to Alexandria,' Magnus suggested in a helpful tone.

Vespasian ignored the comment and, taking another quick look at the dust storm, walked back down the dune to the beach.

'What I don't understand,' Magnus said as he placed six fish, one by one, on a grill above a driftwood fire, close to the water's edge, 'is why you don't just take the two Egyptian legions and transport them over to Brundisium in southern Italia. With the fleet in Ravenna having declared for you there would be nobody in those waters who'd oppose the landing and you'd have Vitellius fighting on two fronts.'

Vespasian smiled to himself, lying back next to Caenis on the sand with his hands behind his head, looking up at the star-strewn night; the gentle rhythm of waves rolling ashore had relaxed him almost to the point of slumber in the time it had taken Magnus to set the fire. The smell of the grilling fish now completed the idyll. 'It's too late in the year to risk taking two legions on such a voyage.'

'It weren't when they first declared for you back in July. Mucianus arrived in Aquileia in September; you could easily have had those two legions on Italian soil by then and there wouldn't have been much for Vitellius to negotiate about other than the size of his annual wine allowance.'

'And what about Lucilius Bassus and the Ravenna fleet?' Caenis asked. 'We didn't know until recently that they had declared for us.'

Magnus dabbed some oil onto each of the fish. 'Yeah, well, surely that would have been a risk worth running? With the whole East supporting us, the Ravenna lads would have seen sense and left the landing well alone.'

'But I couldn't guarantee that, could I?' Vespasian heaved himself up and sat cross-legged; the fire warmed his face and chest as smoke, sprinkled with red sparks, swirled up into the sky, drawn by a strengthening breeze. 'It could well have been a bloody affair had the Ravenna fleet decided to oppose the landing and I probably would have ended up losing the best part of two legions to Neptune. The whole strategy of my campaign, firstly in Judaea and then in this year of civil war, has been to use negotiation wherever possible. It is only after that has failed that I resort to violence and then I make it as extreme as possible, as I don't see the point of half measures when you are trying to defeat someone.'

Magnus looked up from his cooking, the firelight reflecting bright in his glass eye, giving the impression that the flame burned within his head. 'I couldn't agree more. Hit the fuckers as hard as you can so that they go down before they get you down – that's what I used to do when I was in the legions and that's what I used to do when I was patronus of the South Quirinal Crossroads Brotherhood; but that is not what I see you doing now.'

'What do you see me doing, then?'

'I see you going in completely the opposite direction from Rome, across over two hundred miles of what we both know to be the most unpleasant desert, which has currently got a sandstorm raging in it big enough to make the one that nearly killed us thirty years ago seem like one of Juno's polite farts, in order to consult an oracle about something that, as far as I can see, you already know the answer to because it's so glaringly obvious.'

'What is?'

'The answer, that's what.'

'And what is this glaringly obvious answer?'

'Go to Rome as soon as you can and claim what is now yours.'

'Yes, that's the answer to the question: what should I do now? I grant you that. That's why I'm not going to ask that question, it would be a waste of everyone's time.'

'Then what are you going to ask?'

'That will be between the god and me; but I assure you, Magnus, that it will be well worth the effort of getting to Siwa. I need the answer to this question because it will put my mind at ease on a subject that will influence the way that I govern when I get to Rome.'

Magnus turned the fish with his knife. 'It had better be a really good question then, a nice tricky one to make all this worth our while.'

Caenis rolled over and lay on her side resting her head on a hand. 'I'm not complaining. Look how beautiful it is here. Do you imagine that we'll be able to have evenings like this when we're back in Rome? Of course we won't. These are probably our last few days of relative freedom before the responsibility of office and the magnitude of the task of rebuilding the Empire's finances precludes little holidays like this.'

'You've evidently never been across a desert, then,' Magnus surmised, 'not if you consider riding a fucking camel two hundred miles across one as a little holiday.'

'You're right, Magnus, I haven't, but then I haven't done much in my life other than watch people scheme and plot in Rome. When we went to Britannia eight years ago that was the first time I'd been to any of the provinces since the one time I went to

Gallia Belgica twenty years ago and since then I've been enjoying travelling: Achaea, Thracia, Judaea, and now Egypt. This will be my last chance to see these places because when we get back to Rome we will be too busy for this sort of leisure.'

Magnus grunted and tested one of the fish with the tip of his blade. 'Yeah, well, I'd just rather skip this bit of holiday and get down to whatever hard graft you seem to have planned back in Rome.'

'You don't have to come to Siwa,' Vespasian pointed out. 'You could stay here with the ships and have that lovely big cabin in the quinquereme all to yourself.'

'What, and miss the opportunity to watch you chatting with a god? Bollocks I will. I'm coming too.'

'Then stop moaning and serve the fish and pass the wineskin. Let's enjoy what may well be our last chance to have a peaceful meal on a beach, sitting around a glowing fire on a warm evening with good company.'

Magnus took a gulp of wine and then passed the skin across. 'Yeah, well, I suppose you've got a point. Who'd have thought that one day I would be sitting on a beach, cooking fish for an emperor?' He scooped a couple of the fish onto a plate. 'Mind you, who'd have thought that when I stopped you to offer the brethren's services, as your family entered Rome, all those years ago, that you would become emperor?' He broke a hunk of bread from a loaf, put it on the plate and passed it to Caenis. 'Not me, that's for sure; I wouldn't have even put money on you becoming a quaestor, a snotty youth like you, and yet here you are.' He shook his head in disbelief, chuckling to himself as he served up Vespasian's plate. 'It really ain't natural.'

Vespasian took a long suck on the skin and then wiped his mouth with the back of his hand. 'There, you see, Magnus, you're enjoying yourself already.'

'Six more hour,' the Marmarides guide assured them, pointing ahead, across the flat desert floor, ochre and dun, broken here and there by outcrops, large and small, of rough rocks of the same hues. 'Straight south.'

'And you're sure that there will be water at this well, Izem?' Vespasian asked, his thirst growing as he goaded his camel with a stick to keep it going forward.

Izem shrugged. 'I no know. If dust storm has blocked it like last well, then no. If we lucky, yes.'

Magnus grunted, dry-throated, and glanced up at the sky, burning bright, despite it being only the second hour of the day. 'Best press on, then; another day of this without water and we'll be having dreams of drinking each other's piss again.'

Vespasian turned to see the sixty riders of their escort still in column, two abreast. 'At least we're managing to stay together, no stragglers, as yet.'

'But if we don't find water at the next well,' Caenis said, wiping the sweat from her brow with the linen towel she wore over her head, 'we'll run out tomorrow and we've still got at least two days to go.'

'So, if the next well has also been blocked by the dust storm, the question would be: what is our best chance? Go forward uncertain whether we will find water again before Siwa, or go back because we know that there is a full well a day's travel away.'

'And then keep going for another four days back to the sea, my love, without doing what you came here to do? That would be a waste of time.'

'Yes, but we would still be alive.'

'We could survive another two days without water, surely?'

'Not all of us; we'd lose some to the heat.'

'Next well very big,' Izem said, grinning and nodding. 'Next well big enough for whole army to drink and fill waterskins.'

'Well, I can't imagine who would be foolish enough to lead an army through here,' Magnus said, taking off his floppy-rimmed leather hat and wiping the top of his head. 'Did Alexander, when he came?'

'No,' Vespasian replied, 'he came with a small escort like ours for that very reason. No one has dared to bring an army through here since King Cambyses of Persia sent an army towards Siwa, to claim it for Persia; it was never seen again. A whole army just swallowed up by the desert.'

Magnus replaced his hat. 'Well, if the desert can eat an army, then, with the way things are going, I'd say it's looking at us and considering us to be a tasty morsel, if you take my meaning?'

Vespasian did, but did not want to admit to it.

On they went, rocking to the camels' ungainly stride, staring at the sharp line of the horizon where sky-blue met desert-brown, as the sun climbed towards its zenith, burning down in fury upon all below it. Vespasian pushed visions of a parched death from his mind, arguing with himself that he had had worse desert experiences the last time he had crossed this barren land to Siwa from Cyrene, and then again in Africa on his way back from the Kingdom of the Garamantes.

'Now we stop,' Izem, said, holding up his hand as the sun neared its maximum height. 'Three hour then we go.'

Vespasian coaxed his camel down, forelegs first, and dismounted as the escorts busied themselves rigging a canopy under which they would all shelter from the ravages of the midday sun.

With care, he took a couple of sips from his almost-empty waterskin, swilling the warm liquid around his mouth in the hope that it would stay moist for at least a short while. Idly looking south for want of anything better to do as the shelter was set up, he squinted as something caught his eye. 'Are those hills, Izem?' he asked, pointing at what seemed to be a series of bumps on the line of the horizon now shimmering with the haze of the building heat.

'No, master, no hills between here and Siwa; just flat, hard desert and then a sea of sand dunes. No hills.'

'Then what is that?'

The Marmarides peered into the distance, shading his eyes from the almost vertical sun. He frowned as he saw the rise in the otherwise flat landscape. 'No hills,' he said, in a questioning tone more to himself than to anyone else. 'No hills.'

'Well, there are now,' Vespasian said. 'Quite big ones, by the look of it, and directly in our path. How far away would you say that is, Izem?'

Izem scratched his full beard, thinking for a few moments; as he did so his face fell and he turned to Vespasian. 'It not good, master; they must be big sand dunes made by dust storm. They about three hours away; they by well. Maybe they on well.'

It was with a sense of dread that the column approached the dunes as the sun fell into the west; news of the sighting and the probable location of the dunes had spread quickly through the men and the desire to know their fate had caused them to leave the rest stop half an hour early.

'That has to be the height of the Pharos,' Vespasian said as the true magnitude of the phenomenon became clearer the closer they came. 'Have you ever seen such enormous ones, Izem?'

The Marmarides shook his head, his eyes wide in awe. 'Never, master. I never dreamed there was so much sand in one place.'

'And we have to go up and over?' Caenis asked.

'Yes, mistress; if well still there, it on other side.'

'But more likely underneath,' Magnus complained as the ground began to rise.

Up they went, traversing the steepening dune in a series of long diagonals, climbing ever higher above the desert floor. Behind them, to the north, the desert grew in volume as their altitude pushed back the horizon, so that they had a sense of diminishing in size in relation to the huge mound they ascended and the vast, ever expanding vista in which it was set.

With increasing hardship the camels pressed on, their hoofs sinking further and further into the sand as it became looser towards the summit; drifts of it cascaded down in mini avalanches, forming irregular waves down the otherwise smooth side of the dune. Snorting their displeasure, the beasts were goaded on; their heads held high as they looked imperiously around them as if trying to understand just what the objective of such a hard climb was.

But the objective was the summit in order to see what lay on the other side and that summit was reached as the sun was no more than an hour from setting. Vespasian drove his camel on, accelerating now that the terrain had evened out more. Three, four hundred paces he rode across the top of the dune looking for the edge to see back down to the desert floor and to know one way or the other whether the well was still viable.

It was with a sense of confusion that he registered an anomaly as the further side of the dune came into view. For a few moments he could not process what he saw below as he approached the dune's lip: a dark shadow spreading across the land at least a mile into the distance. And yet it was not constant, there were lighter patches within it. He brought his mount to a halt on the very edge of the summit and gazed down at what should not have been there; and then his brain recognised it for what it was: a huge gathering of people, thousands of them, some sitting, some lying, and with them were camels and horses, they too lying down, mainly on their sides, and all were motionless, as if frozen in time.

And it was then that Vespasian realised that they were, indeed, frozen in time and his mouth opened as he understood the enormity of what he was looking at. 'The army of Cambyses,' he whispered to himself.

'What did you say?' Magnus asked as he and Caenis drew their mounts up to either side of him, eyes agog at the sight before them.

'The army of Cambyses,' Vespasian repeated. 'That's the army that disappeared five hundred years ago. It must have been buried by a dust storm like the one that struck a few days ago. Buried alive they were, just like we nearly were on our way to Siwa last time. Buried for all those years until four days ago.' Vespasian whistled softly.

Magnus spat and clutched at his thumb to avert the evil-eye.

'Shall we ride down to them?' Caenis asked, her voice breathless.

'Of course, my love; I'll not miss a sight such as this.'

There was no stench of death hanging in the cooling air above the countless lifeless bodies as Vespasian led the column down the far side of the dune, just the sweet smell of warmed leather. In silence they descended; even the camels seemed to sense the sombreness of the sight and kept their snorting complaints to a minimum. As they came down to just fifty feet above the desert floor the army filled their whole vision, such was its magnitude. Still, apart from the occasional cloak or plume, fluttering in a soft breeze, the army of Cambyses lay where it had been smothered five hundred years previously, men and beasts together exposed to the elements for the first time in half a millennium.

The bright reds, blues, yellows and greens of the men's trousers and knee-length tunics as well as the caparisons of the horses and camels were still vibrant after so long kept from the sun. Tanned, black or red leather boots, cuirasses, harnesses and headgear, whose warm smell thickened the closer they came, shone as if freshly polished and metal gleamed in the setting sun, burnished bright by infinitesimal grains of sand. As Vespasian rode between the first clumps of bodies it seemed to him that they were but freshly deceased as the appearance of their uniforms and equipment was next to immaculate. Beneath that it was a different story: all had suffocated seeking shelter beneath their cloaks whether lying flat on the ground or crouching or, even, kneeling over, and most remained like this, covered; but here and there the breeze had dislodged their protection and hands and faces were exposed, revealing the husks of men. Dry and stretched was their mummified skin; hollow were their eye sockets and their gaping nostrils were set above the thin-lipped rictus grins that were their mouths. Claw-like hands clutched at cloaks as if still attempting to keep the swirling sand from building up around their bodies. Horses, camels and mules shared the fate of their masters, lying on their sides or bellies, now little more than parchment-covered skeletons. An army of the dead both physically and literally and through the dead Vespasian rode with Caenis and Magnus to either side of him, followed by the guide and his escort.

Regiment upon regiment they passed, all frozen in the moment of their death, thousands upon thousands as well as the slaves who attended them. After a mile or so the volume of bodies began to increase as they neared the heart of the army. The richness of the men's costume and lavishness of their horses' decoration grew as their status increased the closer they were to the satrap commanding the doomed expedition. But high status or low, they had shared the same fate, entombed in a mountain of sand, suffocated and desiccated; the shrivelled husks of the army of the dead, dehydrated and frozen in time.

On they travelled through the silent host towards a large outcrop of rocks, saying not a word, for what comment could be made that did not sound trite in the face of such mortality, such serenity, such history and, yes, such beauty? And it was a beautiful sight in that it stirred Vespasian's heart as he witnessed first hand how the might of man can be defeated by an act of the gods; hubris would never be forgiven by deities.

And so they approached the outcrop at the heart of the camp; at least thirty feet wide and as tall as a man, it stood as the focal point of the army.

'Would this have been the well, Izem?' Vespasian asked, turning to the guide.

'I no know, master; the well I look for is buried under dune. Maybe this was well before sandstorm buried army years ago. I look.'

'There's no need to look,' a voice said as Izem coaxed his camel down. 'The well is here and has been preserved by Amun.'

Vespasian struggled for a few moments to make out the source of the remark; it was not until he moved that the man could be discerned. He stood wearing nothing but a white kilt, belted, and a tall hat with a long feather stuck in its crown. 'Welcome back, Vespasian, Amun is expecting you.'

Vespasian frowned and then, after a pause, recognised the man as the younger of the two priests from the Temple of Amun in Siwa when he had been taken there by the treacherous Ahmose all those years ago. 'I have come to consult the Oracle of Amun.'

'And Amun awaits.' The priest extended his arm all around. 'Amun has given you a demonstration of his power. "Amun, Thou wilt find Him who transgresses against Thee. Woe to him that assails Thee. Thy city endures, but he who assails Thee falls." Thus Amun defeated the army sent against his temple to claim it for Persia and now he shows you, Vespasian, the proof of it. "The hall of him who assails Thee is in darkness, but the whole world is in light. Whosoever puts Thee in his heart, lo, his sun dawns. Amun!'"

'Amun,' Vespasian found himself repeating.

'The well in these rocks has been covered for five hundred years and is still plentiful. Drink and fill your skins and then follow me to the Temple of Amun.'

CHAPTER XV

W ITH THE PRIEST leading the way the people parted for them as they walked, having left their camels at the gate, through the crowded streets of Siwa's main town, after two days' easy travel. Lined with farmers selling their produce on blankets or palm-frond mats laid out on the ground and with the smell of exotic spices and human sweat filling the air, the main thoroughfare made its way up a hill towards a temple built of sandstone, with a tapered tower protruding from its northern end, at the town's centre. As they approached it Vespasian recalled that the rows and rows of tiny figures carved into the stone walls were lists of priests and records of kings who had visited since the temple was built over seven hundred years before.

'It don't look like much,' Magnus said as they mounted the steps to the temple doors.

'Perhaps not,' Vespasian replied, clutching the bag that contained his gift to the god, 'but it contains a great power.'

'Yeah, well, anything that can bury an army and then dig it up five hundred years later has to be respected, I suppose.'

'You suppose right,' Caenis remarked as the priest opened the doors.

The temperature drop was considerable as they entered the building. Symmetrical rows of columns, three paces apart, supported the lofty ceiling, giving the impression of an ordered stone forest. From a few windows, cut high in the south wall, shafts of light, with motes of dust playing within them, sliced down at a sharp angle through the gloom of this interior, petrified grove. The musky residue of incense and the cloying smell of ancient, dry stone replaced the fresh scents of woodland in bloom. Through the temple the priest led them, never looking back to check they still followed, until they came to the chamber at the heart of the building; within was the surprisingly small statue of the god set upon an altar, lit by two flaming sconces, that Vespasian had knelt before on his last visit. Representing Amun seated, the statue showed him bearing a sceptre in his right hand and an ankh in his left; his face was that of a man, the mouth open and hollow. Across his legs was laid a sword in a richly decorated scabbard of great antiquity: the sword of Alexander the Great left here by him when he had come for the god's counsel three hundred and eighty years previously.

'Hail to You, who brought Himself forth as one who created millions in their abundance. The one whose body is millions. Amun,' the priest intoned as he halted before the statue.

'Amun!' the other three priests replied.

'No god came into being prior to Him. No other god was with Him who could say what He looked like. He had no mother who created His name. He had no father to beget Him or to say: "This belongs to me." Amun.'

'Amun!' the priests and Vespasian replied.

Again, the smoke of pungent incense wafting through the room began to make Vespasian feel very light-headed and euphoric. He turned to see Caenis and Magnus standing towards the rear wall of the chamber; Caenis smiled and nodded in reassurance.

Vespasian turned back to the god, taking Alexander's breastplate from its bag. He knelt and placed it leaning against the god's legs, beneath the sword, reuniting for the first time since his death the weapon that Alexander had used against his enemies and the armour that had defended him from them.

Vespasian held up his arms and raised his head to the god; the incense was becoming more intense and his vision began to swirl. He felt himself being lifted to his feet; oil was poured on his forehead and left to trickle down his face. He remembered how that had made him feel at ease and smiled.

'You who protect all travellers, when I call to You in my distress You come to rescue me. Give breath to him who is wretched and rescue me from bondage. For You are He who is merciful when one appeals to You; You are He who comes from afar. Come now at Your children's calling and speak. Amun.'

'Amun,' Vespasian repeated.

The word echoed around the room.

Then silence.

Vespasian stood staring at the god; around him the priests were motionless.

The room became chill. The smoke hung, still, in the air. The flames in the sconces died down.

Vespasian felt his heartbeat slow.

He heard a soft breath emanate from the statue's mouth and in the dim light he could see the smoke begin to swirl about the god's face.

Another breath, more rasping this time, moved the smoke faster; the low flames flickered.

'Are you prepared this time?' a voice asked.

Vespasian could not tell whether it was real or existed solely in his head; whichever of the two he knew that it was the voice of the god and must be answered. 'I believe so, Amun.' Again he could not tell whether he had vocalised or imagined these words.

'You have matched the gift; you may ask your question.'

Smoke swirled around the mouth of the statue yet all else remained still; there was no other sign that the god had really spoken.

Vespasian squeezed his eyes closed and drew a deep breath. 'Who should succeed me, my eldest son or the one whom I deem to be the best man?'

There was a silence, deeper than Vespasian had ever known, that stretched through a dozen or more slow beats of his heart, before the flames flickered again. 'The two are one.'

'Perhaps; but if I choose my son Titus, will his younger brother not plot against him so that he can take the prize? And that won't end until one kills the other.'

Again a silence in which, this time, even the smoke stood motionless. 'The younger son will always take that course of action, whoever you choose to succeed you unless you choose him; and that you must never do for he has ruthless and undeserving ambition and overbearing, preening pride. Already he is acting above his station and will resent being pulled back down.'

'Then what is my path?'

'You cannot kill your younger son, for Rome will see that as a return to the days of Nero and you will fall. Neither can you banish him, for pride and ambition will force him into reckless attempts at escape that will kill him as surely as you putting a knife in his heart, and, again, you will be seen as the father who killed his son. Nor can you overlook your eldest son, in the cause of family harmony, as he, too, has great ambition and pride but his is deserved; he will challenge whoever takes what he considers to be his by right of birth and war will be unavoidable. And yet you must go forward.'

'Then I must doom one of my sons to death by the hand of the other.'

'You must take up the duty that has fallen into your hands; this moment has always been foretold but what you should do now is not what you think.'

'I shouldn't go back to Rome as soon as possible?'

'By coming here, you have avoided making the mistake that both Galba and Vitellius made: getting to Rome whilst it was still in turmoil. This year you hold the East: stay and secure it; let Rome come to you and ask, plead even, that you return. Next year, with the grain the East produces, you will return to the West as a saviour as opposed to a conqueror. Now go; do not defy the will of the gods because you fear to spend your sons. The power that guides fate, our power, the power of the gods, is great, as was demonstrated to you with the army of Cambyses, so take what the gods offer you and think not of the consequences.'

Vespasian opened his mouth to ask another question but the smoke was rapidly inhaled into the mouth of the statue and the lamps began burning with their original intensity. He blinked and breathed deeply and then rose to his feet for he knew that the audience was over; his course was now set and he was helpless.

*

'Well?' Magnus asked as Vespasian turned away from the altar.

'Well what?'

'You know perfectly well what I'm talking about.'

'Didn't you hear anything?'

'It was as if Time's Chariot stood still, my love,' Caenis said stepping out of the shadows. 'I couldn't tell you how long we have been in here; it may be but a hundred heartbeats or a hundred hours; but what is sure is that we heard nothing and all we saw was you motionless before the altar.'

Vespasian remembered the same phenomenon happening the last time he had been here; the priest had told him that the words of the god were for him alone. 'The god spoke to me; at least, I think he did.'

'Well?' Magnus asked again, this time with more insistence.

'Well, he didn't give me any cause to feel at ease.'

'What did you ask him?'

Vespasian shook his head. 'That's between me and Amun. But what I can say is that I must embrace my destiny despite whatever personal or familial consequences there may be.' Vespasian's normally strained expression became painfully stressed as he contemplated those consequences.

'Are you all right, my love?' Caenis said, cupping his face in both hands.

'I will have to be as there is nothing I can do to avoid the inevitable; there is no other path to take other than the one that I'm on; the one that I was set on from the moment of my birth. I'm swept along by the tide of fate and my personal wishes are secondary and so therefore I have no choice but to keep going and pray that Titus stays safe.'

Magnus frowned in confusion. 'Titus?'

'Yes, Titus.'

Caenis' countenance darkened as she understood Vespasian's dilemma. 'Of course, my love; I'm amazed that we didn't see that earlier. We completely overlooked the consequences of Domitian not being your successor.'

'Ahhh.' Magnus mused as it too dawned on him. 'That is a nasty thought; that little shit has never been one to stand back and let others overshadow him. He has very different priorities and won't be afraid to have a stab at making rather a sharp point, if you take my meaning?'

Vespasian grimaced at the image. 'I'm afraid I do, Magnus.'

Caenis sucked on her bottom lip. 'So what can you do about it?'

'That is something that I will have to decide next September when I get back to Rome.'

'Next September?' Magnus said. 'I don't know if I'll last until then. Why not go as soon as the sea-lanes open in spring?'

'Because I was advised to let Rome come to me whilst I stay here to secure the East.'

Caenis nodded her approval. 'I think that would be sensible, my love; once Vitellius is either retired or dead, the Senate will have no choice but to support you. Let them send a delegation to plead with you to come to Rome so that you're seen as the Emperor who takes the prize that was offered him and not one who seizes it. Mucianus and Sabinus can run the city in your name until then.'

Vespasian looked down at the statue of the god, now no more than an inanimate carving and yet still an object to inspire awe, for, in a moment of clarity, he had realised the true benefit of doing the god's bidding. Now he understood why it had been so important for him to return here for he had just been prevented from making a serious political error in returning to Rome before the situation there was settled. 'Yes,' he replied, 'but more to the point it will be Mucianus who has to deal with the dissenters and outspoken supporters of Vitellius, not me; admittedly he'll be doing it in my name but I won't be seen as being directly responsible for my enemies' deaths or banishments. Mucianus will clean up the Senate; he will be the one to take the unpleasant decisions, not me. If I wait until late next year, once everything has settled down in Rome, then I'll be able to return to the city with no blood on my hands, and I'll be returning because the Senate has asked me to and no one will have cause to resent me.

My position will be far more secure that way than if I were to do the dirty work myself.'

'I came as soon as I could, master,' Hormus said without any preamble, as he was admitted into Vespasian's private quarters in the Ptolemaic palace of Alexandria. 'It's taken me nineteen days as my ship nearly foundered in a storm off Crete and we had to wait there for six days for the weather to improve.'

Vespasian kept his head back, resting on the back of the chair as Caenis scraped her razor up his oil-slick chin, shaving him close and comfortably. 'How did you find a trierarch willing to take you in the first place at this time of year?'

'I told him that we were to be the first to bring you the news of the Senate debating the letter you sent them and vote to recognise you as sole emperor.'

Caenis quickly pulled her razor away from Vespasian's throat; he sat up with a jerk. 'Vitellius?'

'Is dead, master; eleven days before the calends of January, thirty-three days ago. The Senate met the next day and voted you most of the titles that Nero had possessed. I went north the following day and reported the events to Mucianus and then travelled with his army down to Rome. We arrived on the calends and he is now running the city using your ring as authority. I left two days after that.'

'Thank you, Hormus; you've served me well.' Vespasian took a damp towel from Caenis and rubbed the excess oil from his face. 'Most of the titles, you say?'

'Yes, master; I have brought a copy of the law, the Lex de Imperio Vespasiani.' He handed Vespasian a scroll.

Vespasian handed the towel back to Caenis and unrolled the scroll; he took some time digesting the contents. 'This is not nearly as thorough as I need. I must be seen as being no different from the previous Emperors, I must have the same powers and I want them to be set out for all to see and understand. Who promulgated this half-hearted piece of legislation?'

'Mucianus is guiding the Senate in their decisions ...' Hormus let the sentence hang.

Vespasian looked at Caenis. 'Now we shall see just how far we can trust him.'

Caenis wiped her razor clean of stubble. 'He's always going to try to keep something back for himself; who wouldn't in his situation?'

'A consulship, no doubt.'

Hormus shook his head. 'No; in your absence, master, he had the Senate confirm you and Titus as the first two consuls of this year and has left it to you to decide how long you stay in position and who should take over as the suffects.'

Vespasian's surprise was clear. 'He does seem to be showing restraint.'

'Not in every aspect, master; he said to tell you that he has sent a couple of centurions to Africa to kill the Governor, Lucius Calpurnius Piso, in order to secure the province and its grain.'

'That makes sense; I wrote to both him and Calpetanus Festus, the legate of the Third Augusta, demanding their acknowledgement; I received a letter from Festus a few days ago assuring me of his support and that he was going to get the legion to swear the oath to me. Piso did not reply. What evidence did Mucianus have against him?'

Hormus shrugged. 'He didn't say, master; he just told me to tell you that Piso was to die and he was sure that you would be very pleased to hear it.'

'At least you didn't order the killing, my love,' Caenis said, placing her razor back in its box.

'Yes, that is something. Who else has died, Hormus?'

'Vitellius, obviously, and his seven-year-old son.'

Vespasian grimaced at the news and again felt relieved that he had not been the one to give the necessary order, for the boy had to die.

'Julius Priscus, the prefect of the Praetorian Guard, was commanded to commit suicide; and Piso's son-in-law, Calpurnius Galerianus, was taken for a ride out of the city and er ... *persuaded* to do the same. About another dozen lesser men also died before I left.'

'Mucianus is getting a lot of blood on his hands.'

And that was what Vespasian had been dreading ever since returning from Siwa to Alexandria in November where news of Antonius Primus' defeat of the Vitellian forces, at the second Battle of Bedriacum, had awaited him. This had been followed by the news that the entire Batavian auxiliary cohorts, under Gaius Julius Civilis, had taken to the field, ostensibly in Vespasian's name. He had written to the Senate immediately demanding that they recognise him as sole emperor.

After hearing of the Batavian revolt and of Antonius Primus' victory Vespasian had been frustratingly lacking in news due to the inhospitable qualities of the winter sea. Throughout the remainder of November, December and the first part of January two questions had played upon his mind: firstly whether Civilis was being opportunistic; Vespasian did remember him as being a prefect of one of the Batavian cohorts that had been attached to the II Augusta during the invasion of Britannia, and remembered liking and respecting him. If Civilis was genuine in his support for him then Vespasian would show his gratitude; but if he was not, he would be one of the first things to be dealt with once Vespasian had secured power. Either way, he had comforted himself with the thought that it was a useful distraction to have rumbling on along the Rhenus and would take troops away from Vitellius which he could ill afford to lose.

But what of Vespasian's troops? That was the second question that he had regularly turned to. That Antonius was marching on Rome, he could guess, but how quickly and with what precautions? As to Mucianus' whereabouts there had been no word and he could but assume that he was racing to catch up with Antonius in order to prevent the impetuous and ambitious general taking overall control of Rome. For two months he had waited and heard nothing; the silence from the West had rung in his ears and his inability to affect the course of events scared him and irked him in equal measure. He had begun to consider ignoring the god's advice and making preparations for a return to Rome as soon as the conditions permitted. But now, finally, the news that he had waited so desperately for had arrived; now he knew for sure that he was emperor, recognised by all. He also knew that his fears were being realised and that Mucianus was not holding back in his assertion of power; people were dying in Vespasian's name but not by his direct order and for that, at least, he was grateful.

'And what of Sabinus and Domitian?' Vespasian asked, having contemplated Mucianus' behaviour for a few moments.

Hormus paused, his eyes looking down at the fine mosaic that he was standing on. 'Domitian has been voted a praetor with the status of a consul.'

'A what? That's ludicrous for a boy his age; whose idea was that? Sabinus would never have let that happen, surely.' Vespasian stared at Hormus, waiting for his reply. The freedman said nothing; his eyes remained lowered. Vespasian felt his heart lurch as the realisation of the truth hit him. 'He's dead, isn't he?'

Hormus swallowed and raised his eyes so that they just met his master's. 'Yes, master; he tried to hold the Capitoline for you, waiting for Mucianus and Antonius to arrive. Vitellius' men stormed it and took it, burning down the Temple of Jupiter in the process. Domitian escaped but Sabinus was captured; he was killed on Vitellius' orders.'

Vespasian felt Caenis' hands rest on his shoulders, comforting him at the same time as restraining him. But he had no need of restraint and much need of comfort as images of his brother flashed through his mind: the beast who had tormented him as a child; the sneering young man who had returned from four years' service under the Eagles to belittle and humiliate him at every available opportunity. And then it had slowly turned around, beginning with their confrontation at the Oracle of Amphiaraos where Sabinus had admitted that he was scared of being eclipsed by his younger brother; and so had come the gradual acceptance over the years that this was to be so that culminated in Sabinus' appearance the previous year, bearing the breastplate of Alexander, urging Vespasian to grab the destiny that would, indeed, eclipse him, the older brother. And now that brother was dead, dying to ensure that his younger sibling would be the one to bring glory to the family; an unselfish gesture from a man Vespasian now realised that he had loved very much.

It was from deep within his core that the first sob erupted, almost choking him; a second and then a third and, before Vespasian was able to control himself, he had tears rolling down his cheeks and his chest was heaving erratically. How long he remained in a state of tunnelled grief he did not know for all he could focus on was his loss. Gradually he pulled himself back from the depths and began to master himself, becoming once more aware of the world around him: of Hormus standing before him looking uneasy in the face of his master's deep grief; of Caenis, her hands kneading his shoulders in an attempt to take the tension of that grief from his body.

It was with a couple of deep breaths that Vespasian mastered himself and looked directly at his freedman. 'Tell me what happened.'

Vespasian swallowed yet another sob and slapped the arm of his chair. 'So they exposed his body on the Gemonian Stairs?'

'Yes, master,' Hormus replied, his throat dry from long usage.

'And his head?'

'Paraded through the streets on a spear.'

'And Vitellius did nothing to prevent this outrage because my brother refused to ... well, of course he refused to.' Vespasian again slapped the arm of the chair, rose and headed to the doors opening on to the terrace with Caenis supporting his arm. 'But what was the point of killing Sabinus when Vitellius must have known that Antonius was camped at the Mulvian Bridge and would enter Rome the following day? Sabinus' life could have brought that idiot his own.'

'He wasn't in control, master,' Hormus said, following Vespasian out. 'He was weak; he had tried to abdicate but his followers wouldn't let him for fear of what would happen to them.'

'I'll kill every one of them,' Vespasian hissed, 'every one!'

'That's why it's best that you are not there, my love,' Caenis said. 'Had you gone into the city spitting vengeance all about you, you would soon have been perceived as a tyrant and your head would have ended up on a spear.'

'As did that of Vitellius,' Hormus said.

'Did it? Good.' Vespasian's voice was cold. 'Did he put up a fight at the end or was he his normal fat and slovenly self?'

'Antonius' army easily defeated the ragtag remains of Vitellius' troops which had been bolstered by armed citizens and gladiators; he pushed them aside at the Mulvian Bridge and swarmed into the city. There was fierce street fighting with the four Praetorian Cohorts still in Rome supporting Vitellius as emperor. I came in with Antonius, having been sent to him by Mucianus with a plea that he should delay the attack on Rome until he had caught up as he was only a couple of days behind.'

'But Antonius refused,' Vespasian said, picturing the situation.

'Yes, master; he saw that the city was virtually undefended and didn't want to share the glory.'

'What glory is there in the rape of Rome?'

'Again, another very good reason for you not to be there,' Caenis pointed out.

'Yes; and I can see that when the history of this is written Antonius could be made out to be the villain; him and Vitellius. How did Vitellius die?'

'He was dragged from his hiding place; he had taken over the Golden House, which had caused a lot of resentment, but they found him in there and he was hauled down the Sacred Way and on into the Forum. Some of his Germanic Bodyguards tried to free him but they were cut down. He was brought to the rostra where Galba had been murdered and then forced to watch his statues being thrown over.'

Vespasian gave a dark chuckle. 'That would have hurt his dignitas if he had any left to hurt.'

'I think he did, master, as just before the kill was made he said: "and yet I was once your Emperor." He was hacked to death; I saw it and it wasn't pleasant. His head was paraded through the city and his body exposed in the exact place that Sabinus' had been. But no one claimed it as they had claimed Sabinus' for burial and it was dragged on hooks and thrown into the Tiber.'

'And good riddance to useless blubber.'

'You will have to show more magnanimity than that about your predecessor when you return,' Caenis reminded him.

'Don't worry, my love; I shall be statesmanlike. I believe his daughter is still alive and will be of marriageable age soon; to emphasise the difference between Vitellius and me I shall provide her with a dowry. Will that be magnanimous enough?'

Caenis smiled. 'Perfect.'

Vespasian closed his eyes and sighed as he remembered the question he had yet to ask. 'And what did Domitian do in all this?'

'He appeared once all the fighting had died down, dressed in full uniform, and allowed himself to be hailed as Caesar and was then escorted by Antonius' troops to your house.'

'Hailed as Caesar?'

'Yes, master; the title has also been conferred on Titus.'

'Well, he perhaps deserves it. What's Domitian done since?'

'He presided over the Senate until Mucianus arrived and began the process of choosing a senatorial delegation to present the Senate's oath of loyalty to you, master.'

Vespasian shook his head, his expression one of disbelief, and looked out over the harbour. 'I'll wager he's puffed himself up with his own self-importance and is loving telling everyone what to do and making subtle threats, or not so subtle ones, as to what he will do to people who thwart him now that he has power – or at least he thinks he has power. I can see that I'm going to have to bring that boy down; right down, if only for his own good.' Vespasian looked at Caenis and wagged a finger at her. 'And don't you start saying things like be kind to him or don't be too harsh.'

'When it comes to Domitian, Vespasian, I hesitate to give any advice, and if I were to, it would certainly not be the sort that you just mentioned.'

Vespasian grunted and then turned back to Hormus. 'A senatorial delegation, you say?'

'Yes, master.'

'When was it due to leave?'

'I don't know, master; there was a lot of disagreement as to its composition but I believe that it was almost agreed as I left, so they should be only a few days behind me.'

CHAPTER XVI

'ALL I'M SAYING is that you should watch him,' Magnus said to Vespasian as they descended the last few steps of the echoing, marble stairway that thrust through the heart of the palace. 'He's come here because he knows that he overstepped the mark back in Rome and Mucianus would have had him executed. He's desperate and you know how unpredictable desperate men can be.'

'I do indeed.' Preceded by twelve lictors, Vespasian, in a purple toga and wearing a laurel wreath, turned left into a wide hallway with the busts of previous prefects of Egypt set on plinths alternating with flaming sconces on tripods in recesses on either side. 'But Antonius also did much for my cause, albeit often against my orders. Yes, he is an opportunist and would probably have done the same for Vitellius or Otho, had he seen how it could benefit him, but I can't be seen to punish him without displaying an astonishing lack of gratitude that would be a cause for concern for everyone else who backed me.'

Magnus drew a wheezy breath as he struggled to keep up with what was no more than a dignified pace marked by the steady clack of the lictors' hobnails on white marble. 'I understand that, sir, and I ain't saying that you should execute him, far from it. I just reckon that a man like Antonius should be closely monitored and kept from talking to anyone he may think can be more use to him than you are at present; and I would say that amongst the fifty senators here from Rome, there could well be one or two candidates. I for one would want to know exactly why Antonius turns up so soon after them; was it to see you or a member of the delegation, if you take my meaning?'

'I do indeed, Magnus; and I shall take your advice and give

orders for Antonius not to be allowed to mingle with the delegation once I have received it.'

Turning right at the end of the hallway, by a grand window overlooking the private palace harbour, they came to a corridor that was dominated by a series of statues of both male and female subjects of the line of the Ptolemys, all bewigged and painted in lifelike colours and clothed in real garments. Vespasian stopped at the first one, the founder of the dynasty, Alexander's general, Ptolemy Soter, and examined the breastplate attached to it and then grinned. 'It's still the duplicate one that we had made when I stole the original to use to replicate Alexander's. That seems like a lifetime ago.'

'Thirty years and I'm feeling every one of them.'

Vespasian admired the statues as they progressed down the corridor until they came to that of Cleopatra, the seventh of that name, and Vespasian again paused to admire her as the lictors turned left into the formal reception room of the palace. 'It was here that Flavia caught me gawping at Cleopatra's face the evening we met again after our first brief meeting in Cyrene three years before; she spoke to me from the room behind me and I turned to see someone far more beautiful than Cleopatra.' He took a few moments to remember his wife and the mother of his children who had been so brutally nailed up on a cross, by outlaws, four years before; Vespasian closed his eyes and shook his head as he remembered putting her out of her misery with a sword thrust to her heart. 'She was a good woman,' he muttered before entering the room.

Magnus kept his counsel as he watched Vespasian walk into where the senatorial delegation awaited him.

'Hail Caesar!' was the unanimous shout that greeted Vespasian as he faced the fifty-man delegation all draped in their senatorial togas and wearing military crowns or Triumphal Ornaments, if eligible, to add to the dignity of the occasion.

Vespasian glanced around the faces and found that he recognised each one. 'Conscript Fathers, you do me honour in making such a journey from Rome at this time of year; the weather has been far from clement.' He walked through the crowd to a curule chair behind which sat both Hormus and Caenis ready to record the minutes of the meeting.

'Princeps,' Gnaeus Julius Agricola, the leader of the delegation, said once Vespasian had indicated that he was comfortable and the meeting could begin. 'We offer the loyalty and support of the Senate and people of Rome.'

'And I am pleased to accept it,' Vespasian replied, keeping his expression neutral; now was not a time to show the relief that he was feeling. 'Brief me as to the situation in Rome and the West.'

'The civil war in Italia is at an end although it continues in other theatres. Three of the defeated Vitellian legions have been sent to Moesia to repel the latest Dacian and Sarmatian incursions from across the Danuvius; these started when Antonius Primus took his legion into Italia without consulting Mucianus, thus leaving Moesia vulnerable to attack. Mucianus had asked us to emphasise that Antonius' rash move caused the main body of your army to delay whilst the first wave of incursions was repelled, thus seriously imperilling your cause.' Agricola paused to let the implication of that sink in.

Vespasian did not react; he now knew just why Antonius had come running to him. He was going to enjoy his interview with the impetuous, self-seeking general later. 'So Moesia is holding; good. And the small rebellion in Pontus is being subdued by one of my auxiliary prefects; so what of matters further west?'

'There were rumours of a revolt by Venutius of the Brigantes in northern Britannia, just before we left Rome, Princeps; but the details were scarce. However the elements of the four legions in the province who had come south in support of Vitellius have been sent back so we hope that Marcus Vettius Bolanus, the Governor, can cope as we currently have no spare legions on the Rhenus to send to his aid.'

Vespasian understood the problem immediately. 'The Batavian revolt?'

'Yes, Princeps; the revolt by the Batavi, originally nominally in support of your cause, has been exposed for what it really is:

a rebellion against Rome. In the belief that our legions are busy fighting each other as well as repelling the Dacians and Sarmatians, the rebellion has spread to other Germanic and Gallic tribes. The latest news that we have from there is that Civilis has declared a Gallic/Germanic empire in the two Germanies, Gallia Belgica and Gallia Lugdunensis. We have despatched three legions, the Eighth Augusta, the Ninth Claudia and the Thirteenth Gemina, to reinforce the ones that the usurper, Vitellius, had sent north.'

Vespasian smiled inwardly at this reference to his predecessor as he knew that most here had supported him in some degree. 'And who has been placed in charge and who made that decision?'

'Your son-in-law, Quintus Petillius Cerialis, along with your son, Titus Flavius Caesar Domitianus, sharing the command. Cerialis was nominated by your deputy, Mucianus; and Domitian by Marcus Cocceius Nerva.' Agricola indicated to Nerva, standing next to him, who inclined his head a fraction. 'The decision was then voted on by the Senate.'

So that's what Mucianus has styled himself, Vespasian thought, as he returned Nerva's acknowledgement. Still, he kept his face neutral as he digested the news that the worst choice of generals had been appointed to subdue the nation with arguably the best auxiliaries in the Empire and a growing number of allies: Cerialis had, through inexperience and incaution, lost the best part of his legion, the VIIII Hispana, in the early stages of Boudicca's rebellion in Britannia; Vespasian had witnessed the debacle at first hand. As for Domitian who had absolutely no military experience whatsoever, that was just plain stupid, but he refrained from saying so. 'These appointments seem to have more to do with pleasing me than with the urgency of tackling the situation efficiently.'

There was an awkward silence as Agricola looked around his colleagues for support.

Nerva stepped forward. 'As you will recall, Princeps, you had asked me to look out for your younger son whilst you were away. I have merely done what you asked me to do. He is, after all, Caesar; and, as he has no military experience, it is time he should acquire some. Besides, he hasn't gone with the main army and will only go with the second wave once they've mustered.'

'Yes, but he'll still be nominally in joint command when he arrives; he'll be trying to make decisions.'

'The legates of the three legions are all men of great experience and Cerialis won't let him make a fool of himself; I've emphasised that to him on your behalf.'

'We apologise if this displeases you, Princeps,' Agricola said, his voice betraying a hint of nervousness.

Again Vespasian smiled inwardly as he now had the delegation exactly where he wanted them. 'From now on all such appointments must be referred to me.'

'But you were here in Egypt, Princeps.'

'And so I shall remain for a few more months overseeing the harvest and the delivery of much-needed grain to Rome. But all military decisions that involve imperial provinces as opposed to senatorial ones will be referred to me as only I have the power to make them. And speaking of power: I thank the Senate for the Lex de Imperio Vespasiani but I don't feel that it goes far enough. I want you to amend it and vote me a package of measures that shall detail my areas of influence as your Emperor, where I can act alone and where I need the backing of the Senate, so that in future there can be no argument as to where the power lies. I will not be returning to the days of Nero when it seemed that the Emperor could do as he pleased because everything was his possession. That will not be happening in my principate. I will draw up some recommendations that I think should be considered by you before you leave.'

Agricola inclined his head, looking pleased. 'We will do that with pleasure, Princeps.'

'Good, because we will have a lot of work to do. I believe, from my calculations, that to bring the Empire back to how it was before Nero and civil war bankrupted it will take something in the region of four thousand million sesterces.'

There was a collective sharp intake of breath.

'Which will have to be found; and we will all start looking for it as from now. I have already raised taxes here in Egypt but a lot of that money is going towards the war in Judaea, which will eventually pay for itself with the plunder from Jerusalem and the huge amount of slaves that we will capture, but until then Egypt's taxes go to that war. So, Conscript Fathers, the rest of the Empire is going to have to pay more.' He studied the gathering, every man there for what he could get from their new Emperor, and now he planned to ensnare them. 'I intend to replace many of my predecessors' appointments as governors with placements of my own.' He just controlled a flicker of amusement as the innate greed of the assembled senators displayed itself in the form of intense, wide-eyed interest. 'These men will naturally be people who have showed their loyalty to me over the past year and will be responsible for raising the maximum amount of tax from the province without sending it into revolt. Four thousand million, Conscript Fathers; let us get to work.'

Vespasian rose to his feet and strode from the room, leaving a sense of purpose and profit in his wake.

'What I did, I did only for you.' Antonius Primus was adamant.

And so was Vespasian. 'Bollocks!'

Antonius looked down at Vespasian, seated behind a large desk in the imperial study, surprised at his vehemence; through the window, the trireme that had brought him from Rome that morning rocked at its mooring in the palace harbour. 'But I did, Princeps. Time was crucial; it had to be a quick attack otherwise Vitellius would have been able to consolidate his legions.'

'Which he managed to do, Antonius; and Mucianus did not, because you had gone rushing ahead in order to snatch the glory. And in your haste you forgot that your legion's main function was meant to be guarding the Danuvius.' Vespasian looked up at the man standing before him in the uniform of a military peacock; handsome in a refined, slim-featured way, with calculating, dark eyes and tanned, smooth skin which looked to be in receipt of far too many oils and balms for Vespasian's taste. 'Or did you, Antonius? Did you forget? Because it seems to me that it was quite convenient that there should be an incursion across the Danuvius just as Mucianus was coming across the Hellespont; it meant that he had to send a substantial part of his force north into Pannonia to deal with it whilst he himself was obliged to remain close in Dalmatia until he was sure that his rear was secure before he moved on towards Italia.'

'But he was going to do what I did and take the Moesian legions with him, seeing as they had declared their support for you.'

'Don't make yourself look stupid as well as treacherous, Antonius. Vexillations of the legions; not the entire body, but four or five cohorts from each one so that they remain in position keeping that northern border secure. You left nothing to keep your section of the river defended; not one century. Now that, Antonius, could be construed as treachery and I could quite legitimately have you executed for that.'

'But I won you the Purple!'

'And thereby lies my problem; although, for the record, you did not win it for me single-handed, it was a combined effort. But I'm well aware that if I were to have you executed, it would look very shabby on my behalf; but if you think I'm going to reward you in the way that Mucianus will be rewarded, you can think again.' Vespasian paused and scrutinised the miscreant with a steady eye.

But Antonius was not to be intimidated. 'It was my troops that won the Battle of Bedriacum!'

'No, it was *my* troops! And it was *my* troops that you shamefully let sack Cremona; troops fighting for me, raping the wives and daughters of fellow citizens; it was as if I was humping each one myself, such is my reputation amongst the survivors. Why did you let it happen?'

A sly look inveigled its way across Antonius' face. 'Oh, so you haven't been told, have you? Didn't Hormus mention his part in the sacking of Cremona?'

'Hormus had a part in that disgrace?'

'The biggest, I would say; he ordered it.'

Vespasian was dumbstruck for a few moments. 'I don't believe you.'

'Then you had better ask him, Princeps; because I will swear that he came to me after the battle and ordered me in your name to sack the city to encourage other Vitellian strongholds to surrender rather than hold out.'

Vespasian could see the logic, but the action had gone right against the spirit in which he had wanted the war conducted. 'Very well, I will ask him, but that won't excuse your actions. I had explicitly ordered that there would be no invasion of Italia until negotiations had broken down. My brother was leading the talks for me and your pre-emptive action can be seen as being the catalyst for the violence that ended up costing Sabinus his life.' Vespasian put up his hand as Antonius went to rebut this statement. 'No! You will listen to me, Antonius, or by my guardian god, Mars, I'll have your head and fuck what everyone thinks. You have done nothing to deserve my favour despite professing to have nought but my wellbeing in the forefront of your mind. So I'll tell you what I'm going to do, Antonius: obviously you can never be trusted with a military command again but I don't want to be seen as not rewarding you.'

'A tricky situation,' Antonius said in a tone that implied he was enjoying Vespasian's dilemma.

'Not at all, Antonius. I believe that your home city is Tolosa in Narbonese Gaul; am I not correct?'

Antonius frowned. 'That's right, Princeps.'

'Well, I'm sure you would appreciate going home and spending more time with your family. I think that you will make the most suitable governor of the province seeing as you know it so well. I shall be expecting a substantial increase in the tax revenues as I'm sure you know all the little tricks that the locals use to conceal their wealth.'

Antonius looked at Vespasian in horror. 'But that will make me—'

'Very, very unpopular with your own people, Antonius. I know, but it can't be helped as you are obviously the ablest man for the job and, as you have assured me that you have my best interests at heart, I'm sure you won't mind making that little sacrifice.'

'But it's a senatorial province.'

'The Senate will grant me this one little favour so I wouldn't worry about that if I were you; you can count yourself safe in the position. Now get out of my sight before I change my mind.'

Antonius looked down at Vespasian with unconcealed hatred as he realised that he had got the best out of the Emperor that he could expect; without a word he spun on his heel and stalked from the room.

Vespasian watched him go with a slight smile and one hand stroking his chin whilst gently tapping the desk top with the forefinger of the other. As the door slammed his expression changed as he remembered what Antonius had said. 'Hormus!' he shouted.

'It's true, master, I did order the sacking,' Hormus said without any reservations.

Vespasian sat back in his chair, staring aghast at his freedman, unable to believe what he had just heard. 'And what makes you think that you had the authority to give such an order even had it been the correct thing to do?'

Hormus looked momentarily confused. 'I had your ring, master.'

'Mucianus has my ring; he is the only person I have authorised to use it.'

'That I didn't know; Mucianus lent it to me when he sent me after Antonius Primus to order him in your name to halt and wait for him.'

'And when Antonius refused you stayed with him rather than return to Mucianus?'

'Yes, master; that's what Mucianus wanted me to do in those circumstances.'

'He told you to stay with Antonius?' And then Vespasian saw it. 'Wait. It was him, wasn't it?'

'Who, master?'

'Mucianus. He told you to order Antonius to sack Cremona, didn't he? Because he knew that if Antonius did something like that in my name I would never forgive him, which I won't; and that way Mucianus manages to cancel out any military glory that he deems that Antonius has stolen from him. That's what's happened, isn't it, Hormus?'

'I don't know, master; I just did as I was told, thinking that it was all for the good of your cause.'

'Sacking Cremona was for the good of my cause!'

'It wasn't specifically Cremona, master; Mucianus told me to order Antonius to sack the nearest town to the first battle – it just so happened that it was Cremona. And I could see the logic of it as Mucianus said that one town's suffering could be the catalyst for many towns opening their gates to your armies and it would reduce the casualties in the long term.'

'And you didn't think that the murder of citizens and the rape of their wives and daughters was something that I'd care about?'

Hormus wrung his hands and looked with pleading, watering eyes at Vespasian. 'Mucianus had your ring, master; I didn't question his orders or his motives. As far as I was concerned, it was as if you yourself were telling me what to do and, as you know, I have never disobeyed you, nor would I ever.'

Vespasian knew that to be the case only too well and his ire retreated as he contemplated the man who had served him with such devotion for over twenty years. 'I'm sorry, Hormus; it's not your fault. That bastard Mucianus used you for his own purposes and perhaps, in a strange way, he was right to do so. Cremona's suffering may well have saved lives in the long term, but you try telling that to the survivors. I can see that I'm going to have to teach Mucianus a little lesson when I reach Rome.' Vespasian paused for a kindly smile at his freedman, whose face lit up with the relief of forgiveness. 'Find Caenis and Magnus and then come back here; we're going to work out the terms by which I return to the city.'

'I think that one of the two most important powers they should confer on you is to enable you to make treaties with foreign powers without having to consult the Senate,' Caenis said to Vespasian, having read the unamended Lex de Imperio Vespasiani. 'There's nothing about that in here and Augustus,

Tiberius and Claudius all managed to do that without a specific law enabling them to do so.'

Vespasian was thoughtful for a few moments, sitting behind his desk and contemplating the shipping in the royal harbour. 'Yes, you're right, my love, not to have that set down will make me seem an inferior version of them. The trouble is how would I justify it?'

'That is the trouble.' Caenis handed the scroll back to Hormus who was minuting the meeting.

'It's easy,' Magnus said, surprising Vespasian, Caenis and Hormus, none of whom thought that such a constitutional sleight of hand could be described as being such.

Vespasian gestured across the desk with a wave of the hand. 'We're all very eager to hear the workings of your sharp legal mind, Magnus.'

'Now you're mocking me again, sir, and I don't think that's very fair seeing as I'm just about to save you from ignoring the obvious.'

'Which is?'

Magnus placed his cup of wine down. 'Who controls the Empire's borders?'

Caenis' countenance brightened. 'Of course, Magnus, you're absolutely right: with the exceptions of Africa and Cyrenaica, all the provinces on the borders of the Empire are imperial, not senatorial, therefore it could be argued that the Emperor must have a free hand with foreign policy because it is his provinces that are directly affected should a war break out.'

Vespasian looked at Magnus as if he were seeing his old friend in a new light. 'You worked that out all by yourself?'

'I ain't too sure that I appreciate that tone, sir; the body may be slowly giving out and I don't trust a fart any more, nor can I afford to waste the occasional erection that comes my way, but the brain is still nimble. Yes, I did work that out myself and I'm surprised that you hadn't seen it, because if you're going to make a success of all these powers that you're trying to get then you're going to need to be able to see the obvious stuff like that.' Magnus pointed a forefinger at Vespasian. 'Being emperor is much like being the patronus of a brotherhood back in Rome: you have to keep ahead of all the people clawing at your ankles, trying to get your job or con you out of something that they have no right to. One of the most important weapons in that fight is the ability to see the right way to use what you already have, as, in general, that is all you have to play with since no one is going to freely give you anything else. So you'd best start making a mental note of everything you've got because I ain't going to be around to point out the obvious to you for much longer, if you take my meaning?'

'Oh, I wouldn't worry yourself unduly about that, Magnus. I can't see the Ferryman wanting anything to do with a cantankerous old sod like you anytime in the near future; he appreciates a nice quiet life on the banks of the Styx so I imagine that you'll be around to point out my failings for a good while yet.'

Magnus grunted and returned his attention to his wine.

Vespasian turned back to Caenis. 'You said there were two important powers in your opinion; what's the second?'

'Well, I would have thought that was obvious, my love.'

Vespasian grimaced. 'Not you as well, Caenis. Hormus, perhaps you would like to join in this new game of making the Emperor feel stupid.'

Hormus looked shocked and set down his stylus. 'No, master, I would never want to do that.'

'I'm pleased to hear it. So what would you say is the second important power?'

Hormus had no doubts. 'That you have the right to do whatever you think necessary for the good of the Empire.'

Vespasian paused, frowning. 'But that would mean that I would be able to do anything I wanted without having to refer to the Senate.'

'What's the point of being emperor if you can't, master?'

'And besides,' Caenis said, 'that can be disguised by the argument that for the good of the Empire you must be able to act quickly in reaction to any given circumstance wherever you are, and being tied to always consulting the Senate would not be for the common good.'

'Yes, suppose you're right, my love. So are there any other suggestions before I recap?' Vespasian looked at Caenis, then Magnus and then Hormus who all shook their heads; he smiled in triumph. 'Ha! You see, you're not the only politically sharp people in the room for I have one more clause to add at the end which will basically nullify the reign of Vitellius and the Senate's recognition of him. The final clause will be legitimising any action or decree I made before the Lex de Imperio Vespasiani became law, right back to the beginning of my reign.'

'But what difference will that make, my love? The Senate recognised you as emperor just a few days before they passed the first version of that law back in December.'

'Ah, but was that the real day that I became emperor? I seem to remember being hailed as emperor on the third day after the calends of July in Caesarea and the Egyptian legions had already proclaimed me on the calends. So I would argue that I came to the Purple on that date and not when the Senate finally caught up with events. Therefore their proclaiming of Vitellius was illegal and is, therefore, null and void, as is all the legislation that has been passed since. That should secure my position as it would make all my actions since the calends of July completely legal.'

Magnus whistled in appreciation. 'Perhaps you don't need my advice so much any more and I can stop worrying about you.'

'Thank you for that vote of confidence, Magnus; it was much appreciated. So now to recap. Thank you, Hormus.' Hormus passed over his notes; Vespasian glanced through them. 'There will be eight clauses. First, that I have the right to make foreign policy without reference to the Senate. Second, that I can convene the Senate whenever I require it. Third, that when the Senate is sitting at my command all laws it passes will be legitimate. Fourth, that whoever I put forward for elections should carry the vote. Fifth, that I have the power to enlarge the *pomerium*.' He looked up from his notes at Caenis, Magnus and Hormus, enjoying the power he felt as he spelt out his demands to the Senate. 'That clause is in solely because Claudius had the right to expand the religious boundary of the city of Rome, not because it's something that I plan to do; however, more than anything, it makes me really understand that I am Emperor of Rome.' With a brief, incredulous shake of the head he looked back down at the notes. 'Sixth, whatever I deem to be in the interest of divine, human, public or private matters ...'

PART IIII

❧ ❧

ROME, AUGUST AD 70

CHAPTER XVII

' . . . Private matters, there be right and power for him to undertake and do, just as there was for divine Augustus, Tiberius Julius Caesar Augustus and Tiberius Claudius Caesar Augustus Germanicus.' Mucianus, now the suffect-consul replacing Vespasian, paused to let the magnitude of this clause sink into the collective consciousness of the Senate.

Vespasian, sitting on a curule chair at the head of the meeting, cast his eyes around the five hundred and more members as they swallowed this declaration of absolute power, the first time that the full extent of the Emperor's authority had been set down as law. He smiled inwardly as he watched the Conscript Fathers register its import and wondered what their forefathers would have made of it.

Mucianus proceeded. 'The seventh clause: that in whatever statutes or plebiscites it is written down that the divine Augustus, Tiberius Julius Caesar Augustus and Tiberius Claudius Caesar Augustus Germanicus should not be bound by, from these statutes and plebiscites Caesar Vespasianus Augustus shall also be exempt; and whatsoever things it was proper for the deified Augustus or Tiberius Julius Caesar Augustus or Tiberius Claudius Caesar Augustus Germanicus to do in accordance with any law or proposed law, it shall be lawful for the Emperor Caesar Vespasianus Augustus to do all these things.'

Again Vespasian felt a surge of pride as he listened to the confirmation that he was an emperor of equal standing with Augustus.

'And, finally, that whatever prior to the passage of this law has been done, carried out, decreed or ordered by the Emperor Caesar Vespasianus Augustus or by anyone at his order or mandate, these things shall be legal and binding, just as if they had been done by the order of the people or of the plebs.'

As Mucianus carried on reading the final Sanction of the law, Vespasian closed his eyes and savoured his position. It had been a smooth transition from Alexandria to Rome; he had left once the second harvest had been brought in and the granaries were full. He had wanted to wait for Titus to successfully conclude the siege of Jerusalem and return together with his eldest son; however, the defence had been fanatical and much boosted by almost three hundred artillery pieces that had been captured from the XII Fulminata in the first stages of the revolt. With the news that Titus was through the first two walls and currently levelling the Antonia Fortress to facilitate his final assault on the Temple, Vespasian had decided that he could postpone his triumphant return no longer. He had achieved what he had needed to in the East and it was now time to fulfil the prophecy by taking the West with the bounty of the East.

With the grain fleets of both Egypt and Africa arriving before him, Italia was a place of plenty when he finally arrived at the port of Brundisium to an ecstatic welcome of a well fed populace who had recently had the dangers and insecurities of civil war lifted from above their heads. In state he had progressed from town to town towards Rome; the magistrates of each municipality received him with tedious speeches of loyalty and praise that Vespasian had sat through with his strained expression rigid upon his face as he played the part expected of him. Judgement he was asked for and judgement he gave as he settled disputes and took petitions on his road to Rome.

It had been Domitian, along with a senatorial delegation, who had been the first to greet him from Rome, travelling all the way to Beneventum. Having recently returned from delivering reinforcements to Cerialis for the conflict against the Batavi, his youngest son had attempted to treat him as an equal and take similar precedence as him but Vespasian had, with tact and firmness, relegated Domitian to the status of the senators who had accompanied him.

ROBERT FABBRI

Vespasian studied his youngest son, seated to the forefront of the senators, having received the status of an ex-praetor, and contemplated how he was going to keep him in check. Already he had heard the stories of Domitian dispensing patronage that he had no right to deliver and in doing so was building up a considerable client base; that was something that Vespasian needed to halt.

Mucianus it had been who had greeted him next, making the journey as far as Capua in order not to let Rome remain too long without governance in Vespasian's name. Vespasian had embraced him as an old friend rather than as a potential rival and the tensions between them seemed to melt away, especially as Vespasian used Tiberius' old trick of deferring to the position of consul, an honour that Mucianus had taken up in July at Vespasian's invitation – Cerialis had been made the suffect junior consul, but in name only as he was still engaged in the north with Civilis and his Batavian revolt, which had now widened to include the Lingones under Julius Sabinus and the Treveri under their chieftains, Julius Classicus and Julius Tutor, as well as units of Ubii and Tungri all now claiming loyalty to a Gallic empire based around the two German provinces and three of the four Gallic provinces.

And now, as the people of Rome, who had cheered him almost to delirium as he had entered the city only yesterday, gathered in the Forum to witness a piece of history, Mucianus called for the House to divide on the Lex de Imperio Vespasiani. Vespasian rose and moved to the right-hand side of the chamber along with all those who supported the new law.

'That is comprehensive, Father,' Domitian said, his dark eyes glinting with excitement. 'Never before have an emperor's powers been set down and we've been voted almost everything.'

Vespasian glanced briefly at his son as he acknowledged the greetings of senators close by. 'We?'

'Yes, we, Father; we're the new imperial house and as such we all share in the power.'

'And what would you do with that power, Domitian; if you were to have it, that is, which you don't?'

294

Domitian's eyes narrowed. 'I have every right to it, Father; I'm your son, and I helped hold the Capitoline Hill in your name and I have just returned from a victorious campaign against the Batavi.'

'Which is still ongoing and growing, judging by the reports I read.'

Domitian's face, which could be thought of as handsome if a touch ruddy, showed genuine hurt. 'I came back to welcome you, Father.'

Vespasian reproved himself, wishing that he could get a grip on his naturally antagonistic feeling to his youngest offspring. 'We'll talk more later,' he said and moved towards his nephew, Titus Flavius Sabinus, whom he had not seen since his return to Rome.

'Uncle,' the younger Sabinus said.

Vespasian put his hand on Sabinus' shoulder as all around him senators took on solemn countenances, knowing what was being discussed. 'You saw it, didn't you? Did he die well?'

Sabinus, so much his father's image, nodded. 'Very well, Uncle. He held his body firm and extended his neck; he didn't flinch as the blow came.'

'And yet you still accepted the consulship from Vitellius?'

'I had been promised it by Otho; Vitellius honoured Otho's appointments and I saw no reason to refuse just because he had executed my father.'

Vespasian considered this for a few moments as the final senators came over to support the law. 'You were right, of course, Sabinus; one must not mix the personal with business.' Vespasian frowned as a lone figure, unknown to him, standing on the other side of the chamber, caught his attention. 'Who's that?'

The younger Sabinus looked over. 'That's Thrasea's son-in-law, Helvidius Priscus, one of this year's praetors.'

'I wonder which of the two is motivating him then: politics or business?'

It was a sea of jubilant faces and a cheer that would drown the howl of any storm that greeted Vespasian as he emerged from the Curia into the Forum Romanum. Waiting for him, as had been previously arranged, was Caenis. Raising his arms to acknowledge the crowd's deafening accolade, he turned to the woman he had loved throughout his adult life and smiled. 'Come, my love.'

Caenis did not hesitate, but stepped forward, passing through his lictors, and took her place at his side; Vespasian slipped an arm about her and gestured to her with the other hand and the people of Rome responded, accepting the former slave as their Emperor's de facto wife, raising more than a few eyebrows of the senators witnessing the event. 'They were hoping to marry their daughters to me I should guess,' Vespasian said as he noticed some of the looks that the people's acceptance of Caenis had engendered. 'But don't worry, my love, you are safe; after all, the Senate has just voted me the power to do what I deem to be best for the state and I deem it best that you be by my side.'

Coquettish, she looked up at him. 'Is that the only position you deem it best for me to be in, my Emperor?'

Vespasian laughed and turned back to the crowd and with an extravagant overhead gesture signalled that they should follow him up to the burnt-out Capitoline.

Vespasian, standing between the blackened stumps of the columns of the Temple of Jupiter, pulled a fold of his toga over his head, in deference to the deity about to be invoked, and stretched his arms out, palms up. 'Jupiter Optimus Maximus, or by whatever name you wish to be called, whether you, for whom this precinct is sacred, are a god, or if you are a goddess, it is right to make an offering of a pig to you in atonement for clearing and enclosing this sacred place. Therefore and for these reasons, whether I or someone who I designate shall make offerings, may it be considered rightly done. I pray good prayers to you in regard to this endeavour, offering this pig in atonement, in order that you may willingly favour me, my house and home, and my children. On behalf of these things, may the offering of this pig in atonement honour and strengthen you.'

Mucianus' mallet slammed into the pig's head, stunning the beast, an instant before Vespasian slit its throat with a sharp tug of his blade. Blood gushed, splattering into the bronze bowl at the animal's feet. Stepping back to avoid an ill-omened splash on his toga, Vespasian watched the pig give itself up to death.

As its heart gave out, the pig was rolled onto its back by two acolytes from the temple and stretched out for Vespasian to make the incision and remove heart and liver.

With the heart sizzling in the altar fire, Vespasian placed the liver on the table next to it. With a damp cloth he cleaned the organ of blood and then leant down to scrutinise it. And there, just as it had been all those years ago on a sacrifice he had made as consul, was the mark he had half expected. Two veins rising to the surface and joining to form the letter 'V'; it was beyond a coincidence and now it made sense of all the signs and portents that had followed him – or, more probably, led him – all his life.

Vespasian lifted the liver and showed it, bearing its mark, to those members of the Senate closest to him, causing more than a few eyes to widen in religious awe. He then placed the liver down and turned to the crowd. 'Jupiter Optimus Maximus has given his blessing to our endeavour: today we commence the rebuilding of his city beginning with his temple and I, your Emperor, shall take the lead.' He crossed to where Caenis stood by an almost-full hod of rubble held upright by a public slave.

Caenis stooped to pick up a charcoaled piece of timber and held it in the air so that all could see before symbolically placing it in the hod.

Vespasian took the hod from the slave and smiled at Caenis. 'If only this moment could be the reality of what we have achieved, my love; but I fear that the mood will change as the practicality of what must be done to bring financial stability and to rebuild the city becomes clear. They think I'm bringing them peace, and so I do, but alongside it I also bring austerity.' He lifted the hod onto his shoulder and, staggering under the weight, carried the first load of rubble away from the blackened and ruined Temple of Jupiter.

*

'So to pay the troops off and send them back to their provinces without them feeling hard done by will cost one hundred sesterces per man,' Vespasian said, contemplating the problem whilst lying on a couch with his eyes closed and a damp cloth on his forehead. 'That is roughly half a million per legion so therefore fourteen million for all twenty-eight. And then there is the Praetorian Guard, the Urban Cohorts and the Vigiles, all of whom will expect something.'

'Don't forget the auxiliary cohorts,' Magnus said, rubbing a balm into his ankle which had begun to swell up as, through the window, a light rain fell on the Circus Maximus standing, resplendent and new, below the Palatine.

'I was coming to them. So if I give three hundred sesterces each to the guard and two hundred to the Urban Cohorts and fifty a piece to the Vigiles and auxiliaries, that is roughly another three million, plus eight hundred thousand plus three hundred and fifty thousand and then another seven million for the auxiliaries, making a total of ... Hormus?'

Hormus did a brief piece of arithmetic. 'Twenty-five million, two hundred and fifty thousand sesterces, master.'

'Let's call that thirty as there will inevitably be more, and that is just the army; we haven't begun to consider the fleets.' Vespasian sucked the air through his teeth in disbelief. 'Have they finished the inventory of what was left in the imperial treasury yet, Hormus?'

'It's still being done, master; but it shouldn't be much longer.'

'Unfortunately I don't think it's going to take as long as you might have wished for, if you take my meaning?' Magnus said, turning his attention to his other ankle.

'Indeed I do, Magnus,' Vespasian replied, rubbing his eyes and sitting up; the damp cloth fell into his lap. 'Tax, tax and more tax, but on what without slowing commerce? If I raise the purchase tax too much then fewer transactions are made and even more transactions are hidden. I can do a one-off poll tax as I did in Egypt but that is only a stopgap. Taxing luxuries brings in so little as, logically, only a few can afford them. I've written to all the governors ordering them to squeeze their provinces, and I've made sure that their procurators are of a rapacious disposition on the basis that more than a few of them will be too greedy and I'll be able to prosecute them and get their ill-found wealth off them when they return to Rome.'

Magnus grinned. 'I like that one; I think that's very clever. It'll be only what they deserve and quite lucrative.'

'Yes, but it's not going to fill the treasury.'

'No, so it won't. I think, sir, that you've got to start thinking a bit differently.'

'What do you mean?'

'Well, you're taxing purchases of everything from slaves and garum to statuettes of gods and glass beads, all the normal stuff that people buy, and you're right – if you raise the tax too much then they buy less or, at least, pretend to. No, sir, you've got to tax the stuff that people can't do without, so no matter what the tax is they will still pay it.'

'Like what? Water? Grain? A seat at the circus? There would be riots.'

'And rightly so if you were to bring in such foolish measures. But I'm sure there are some things.'

'Urine,' Hormus said.

Vespasian looked at his freedman in disbelief as Caenis came into the room carrying an armful of scrolls. 'What? Tax everyone for using the public lavatories? Make them pay each time they go? Or even better, tax their turds as well; make them shit on some scales and charge by the pound; or would it be easier to tax them on their length and width; or, perhaps, have a sliding scale of weight versus volume. Don't be silly, Hormus.'

'I was being serious, master; but you misunderstood me. I meant: tax the people who collect the urine: the tanners, the bleachers and the laundries. Every street has a barrel in which people piss and these traders take it away for free as well as emptying the cisterns of the public lavatories that don't have a drainage system. Why should they have one of the main tools of their trade for nothing when it's actually the city that provides it? They should pay a tax.'

A slow look of comprehension crept across Vespasian's face. 'Of course they should; they've been getting away without being properly taxed for years. Naturally, they'll pass the tax onto their customers and so their goods and services will become more expensive but then that will mean I'll raise more in the purchase tax and therefore gain both ways. The people's anger will be directed away from me because I won't be seen as the one who put the prices up. Hormus, that is brilliant; I shall tax piss.'

'And the good people of Rome shall piss tax,' Magnus quipped.

'Rome? No, Magnus, the whole Empire is going to piss tax.'

'Aren't you afraid that you'll be laughed at?' Caenis asked, placing the scrolls down on a table and warming her hands over a brazier glowing in front of the window.

'People can laugh as much as they like; the point is that it's a never-ending source of money.'

Caenis considered this for a moment. 'Yes, I suppose you're right.' She indicated to the scrolls, a good dozen of them, lying on the table. 'And this is something else that's never ending: correspondence from the provincial governors. Are you ready?'

Vespasian picked up the damp cloth, wetted it in a bowl of water and placed it back on his forehead and lay back down. 'Come on then, let's get this over with, but in future I'm going to deal with correspondence first thing in the morning when I'm fresh.'

'And finally from Marcus Suillius Nerullinus, the Governor of Asia,' Caenis said, picking up the final scroll as the clouds cleared outside and a late afternoon sun emerged to shine through the west-facing window, bringing with it the smell of evaporating rain and the chatter of birds rejoicing in more clement weather. "To Titus Flavius ..."'

Vespasian waved his hand. 'Yes, yes, my love, skip all that, and all the thanks for appointing him as well as the congratulations on my return to Rome and all the other flattery and sycophancy and get to the point of what he really wants, because what I really want is my dinner.'

'Now that sounds like a fine idea,' Magnus concurred. 'I expect your guests are arriving and we wouldn't want to keep them waiting, would we?'

Caenis scanned the rest of the letter and then put it down. 'He wants two things, Vespasian: firstly your advice as to whether he should start to limit the amount of Jewish captives being sold in the province's slave markets as the influx is causing the prices to go down, even for virgins, and so therefore the tax revenues are falling. Nerullinus doesn't wish you to be displeased with his efforts at raising taxes in one of the most profitable provinces.'

Vespasian considered the matter and then turned to Hormus, sitting at a desk with a stylus in his hand and a fresh wax tablet before him. 'To Marcus Suillius Nerullinus from Titus Flavius Caesar Vespasianus Augustus, greetings. I agree that something must be done to preserve the value of slaves and I shall write to my son, Titus Caesar, in Judaea and have him limit the amount of captives the slave-dealers can export in any one month. In the meantime impose a strict limit, as you see fit, on the number of slaves that are allowed onto the market each month in your province and ensure that the rest are kept in their pens and not shipped out to another province where the problem will just reoccur.' Vespasian looked back to Caenis. 'What was the second issue?'

'He's worried about the growing number of followers of this crucified Jew, Christus.'

'Yeshua bar Yosef? I thought that when Nero executed Paulus of Tarsus and his friend Petrus a few years ago, after the Great Fire, that this would go away.'

'According to Nerullinus it hasn't. He was obliged to crucify a few hundred when he arrived in the province and had the population swear the oath to you. Since then he fears that the canker is growing and that when it comes to reaffirming the oath in the new year there could be more that need to be nailed up.'

Vespasian sighed and sat back up. 'What to do about this? I'd forgotten about it whilst I was in Judaea dealing with equally unpleasant religious extremists.'

'If you want my opinion, sir,' Magnus said, 'kill them where you find them, these unbelievers, atheists, these deniers of the gods; it ain't natural. We've watched it grow and now it's your chance to do something about it. They won't be satisfied until everyone believes the rubbish that they believe, that much was obvious from that little shit, Paulus. Start here in Rome and carry on the good work that Nero began – at least he got one thing right.'

Vespasian shook his head. 'No, I'm not going to kill people for their beliefs; only if they break the law.' He turned to Hormus. 'Next sentence. As to the problem with the followers of Christus, I consider that you should make your own judgement on a case by case basis. Should they refuse the oath, apply the full weight of the law upon them. If they see sense and take the oath, then, so long as they do not break the law in any other manner, they should be free to get on with their lives.'

'I think you're making a grave mistake there, my love,' Caenis said as Hormus scratched away with his stylus. 'They won't reward your clemency.'

'And Myrddin won't thank you,' Magnus said.

Vespasian looked at his old friend and frowned, wondering what the immortal druid of Britannia had to do with the subject.

Magnus shook his head. 'Don't you remember why he wanted to kill you? You told me he said that one day you would have a chance to cut out the canker that is growing at the heart of Rome and threatening to kill the old gods and that you would fail to do it. Well, I would say that this is what he was talking about: you're doing nothing about the people who deny the existence of our gods. So perhaps you should think about that.'

'It's just a small sect, a passing fad; how can something like that destroy the true gods? No, I'll not go after them so long as they behave themselves. Compared to the Jews in Jerusalem, they are a minor threat to our way of life; but since the news of Titus being ready to storm the Temple they shouldn't be troubling us for much longer. Let's get rid of one set of religious maniacs first before we start turning another sect into fanatics ready to die for their nonsense.'

'Well, I'd say it's too late for that; you've seen how easily they die under the illusion that they are going to a better world. Bollocks, it is. Now, I for one am going to eat.' Magnus heaved himself out of his chair, grunting with the effort and then grimacing with pain; taking a sharp breath he supported his weight on the desk.

'Are you all right?' Vespasian asked, sitting up in alarm.

'Not really,' Magnus wheezed, clutching his side. 'It comes and goes; I've a feeling that I'm running out of fight and fuck, but I ain't complaining, I'm eighty and I've had plenty of both.'

'I'll get my doctor to have a look at you.'

'The fuck you will. What's he going to do? Feed me some foul-smelling concoction of crushed herbs and insects and advise me not to eat and drink so much? Where's the joy in that? No, sir, I shall go out as I've lived: enjoying myself and bollocks to everyone else; and if this evening's dinner doesn't kill me then I'll just have to try harder tomorrow.' Magnus straightened up, took a couple of steadying breaths, turned and walked towards the door, muttering.

'Helvidius Priscus will do everything he can to prove you an autocrat,' Mucianus said as the fruit and sweet wines were served.

'And he won't stop until he thinks that he has done so,' Nerva added, looking with interest as the after-dinner entertainment arrived in the form of half a dozen dancing girls and a troupe of female musicians. 'Which means that he'll question every decree you make and look for evidence of tyranny.'

'You should have him executed, Father,' Domitian said.

Vespasian dipped his fingers in a bowl of water and wiped them on his napkin. 'I don't kill a dog for barking.' He turned to Caenis, reclining next to him on the couch. 'Who organises the entertainment here?'

'I do; as do I set the menu and choose the wine.' Caenis rubbed his arm. 'We may not be married, my love, but I shall do all the things that a wife should and I won't even pester you to grant me the title of "Augusta".'

'I'm sure you'll find your reward in other ways.'

'Don't you worry, Vespasian, I do: I control access to the Emperor; that's worth a lot more than a mere title.'

Vespasian gave a wry chuckle. 'If you upped your prices then I might not have so many people petitioning me.'

'Don't you believe it, sir,' Magnus said, his one good eye fixed on the dancers as they took up their opening poses showing off lithe limbs to full effect. 'Price was never a hindrance to asking a favour.'

'Very true, Magnus; it looks like you're going to be a very wealthy woman, Caenis.'

'I already am, my love, from all the money that I made for charging for access to Narcissus and Pallas.'

A couple of beats of a drum brought the musicians together and a slow tune ensued to accompany the elegant gyrations of the dancers. Conversation slowed as the diners enjoyed the grace of the performance. Vespasian reached for Caenis' hand and squeezed it, taking in the magnificence of the palace triclinium. Originally built by Augustus it was then rebuilt after the fire by Nero in a surprisingly tasteful fashion, as he reserved his more extravagant tastes for the Golden House. It was a work of beauty: a high ceiling decorated with a geometrical pattern painted mainly in a strong red contrasting with sky- and deep-blue; thin bands of vibrant green and a bright yellow divided the squares and oblongs of strong colour. All four walls were frescoed with scenes from mythology containing a musical theme, reflecting Nero's love of the art; the double door, polished cedar wood, was a wonder in itself as it had glass panels inset within it that glowed with the lamplight of the equally impressive atrium beyond. 'It's all ours, my love,' he whispered in Caenis' ear. 'All ours. Who would have thought it on that day when our eyes met just outside the Porta Collina on the day I came to Rome, no more than a country boy with high ideals, rustic manners and a Sabine accent.'

'Just the gods, Vespasian; and they were trying to tell you all your life that this is what you were destined for; you just never stopped to listen to them properly.'

'I did; I just never believed them. Well, not until recently, in the last few years. Now it seems to have been blatantly obvious, and my parents knew it all along. As did Sabinus.' At the mention of his brother, Vespasian fell silent, watching the dancing and holding his woman's hand. He felt himself relax for perhaps the first time since he had displeased Nero by falling asleep during a recital for Tiridates, the King of Armenia; subsequently recalled from hiding by the Emperor and then placed in command of suppressing the Jewish revolt, he had had, since that time, no chance to let his mind rest and drain itself of angst. Yes, there was still much to worry over, especially in financial terms and the ongoing revolts, but now that he was here, back in Rome, supported by the Senate and the law, Vespasian felt secure; and it was a strange feeling and a rare one in Rome with its relentlessly competitive society. That sense of wellbeing flowed through his system as the music played and the delightful figures moved with elegance and poise so that, soon, his eyes began to rest and his head started to loll.

It was the door swinging open and the sound of feet walking with purpose across the mosaic floor that disturbed Vespasian's contentment; he opened an eye to see his steward approaching with a serious countenance. 'What is it, Varo?'

'Princeps, Marcus Ulpius Traianus is outside waiting to see you.'

'Traianus? But he's with his legion in Judaea, surely?'

'I apologise for not being clearer, Princeps, it's his son who has been serving as a military tribune with his father for the past six months. He has a letter from Titus Caesar.'

'You had better show him in, then.'

Varo signalled to a slave standing at the door who opened it. In walked a youth of no more than seventeen, smart in a tribune's uniform, round-faced and thick-necked with a prominent nose, a thin-lipped, straight mouth and the darkest, most piercing eyes Vespasian had encountered.

With a confidence beyond his years, the younger Traianus approached the Emperor of Rome, snapped to attention before Vespasian's couch and saluted with the crispness of a thirty-year veteran prefect of the camp. 'Princeps!'

'Yes, yes, there's no need for all that when I'm at dinner,' Vespasian said, hiding his amusement at the earnestness of the lad. 'You have a letter for me from my eldest son, I believe.'

'Yes, Princeps.' Traianus handed Vespasian a leather scroll-case and stamped to attention again.

'Please, tribune, relax; there's a spare place, recline and have some fruit and wine whilst I read this.' Vespasian slipped the letter from the case and unrolled it.

'Well?' Caenis asked after a short while.

Vespasian looked up from the letter. 'Well, my love, gentlemen, Jerusalem has fallen and the Temple has been destroyed. There is not a Jew left alive in the city and over a hundred thousand are in chains; Shimon bar Gioras, their leader, is being sent to Rome.'

There was a communal exhalation of breath at such momentous news.

Caenis pressed her hand onto Vespasian's forearm. 'But that's wonderful.'

'It is; I shall summon the Senate tomorrow and convey the good news and make it clear that I expect them to vote me and Titus a double Triumph.' Vespasian paused and frowned and then looked over to the young Traianus. 'Why did Titus send you, tribune? I told him to come himself as soon as the city fell and leave the mopping up to your father.'

'My father *is* mopping up, Princeps.'

'Then where is Titus, is he following you?'

'No, Princeps; he's gone, with Queen Berenice, to Egypt.'

Vespasian's blood froze. 'Egypt! How dare he? He hasn't got my permission.'

But Vespasian knew full well that Berenice would not be concerned by niceties like that, as she was leading Titus into temptation. One glance at Domitian told Vespasian that he too understood just what was at stake: Berenice was showing Titus how easy it would be to make himself King of the East; she was attempting to pitch son against father.

Vespasian's sense of security and wellbeing melted.

CHAPTER XVIII

'AND THAT BRINGS me to our dispositions along the Rhenus and Danuvius,' Vespasian said, his voice echoing around the Curia packed with senators who had heeded their Emperor's summons. 'Now that Cerialis has restored the west bank of the Rhenus to our control and the rebel leaders, Civilis, Tutor, Classicus and Julius Sabinus, have fled east and the incursions into Moesia and Pannonia have been repelled we have an excellent opportunity to reorganise our frontier defences in such a way that these outrages do not occur again. It is vital for the long-term development of the Empire that our colonists in those areas can feel safe to bring up their families in peace and therefore further Romanise those regions.' Vespasian gave way with a sigh as for the fourth time that morning Helvidius Priscus got to his feet to make an interjection.

'The *Imperator* seeks to gloss over an issue here, I believe: what about Civilis, Classicus, Tutor and Julius Sabinus? Not to mention the hundred and twenty-three other rebel petty chieftains who went with them into exile in Germania Magna; what about them, Conscript Fathers? Did they not revolt against Rome? Were they not the cause for much spillage of Roman blood? Did they not nearly succeed in splitting the Empire in two as the *Imperator's* own son is currently doing in Egypt, parading in a kingly diadem with a Jew-bitch queen on his arm? A new Cleopatra. How much more blatant can he be?' Puce with righteous Republican indignation, Helvidius Priscus cast his eyes about the chamber whilst adjusting his toga and posture to imitate the grandees of that period as they too railed against creeping tyranny. 'Yes, Titus has sent plunder and captives back to Rome for the Triumph he and the *Imperator* are due to share in three months in June, but will he actually be here? Or will he have become the new Marcus Antonius and declared himself King of the East?' With venom in his eyes he pointed an accusatory finger at Vespasian. 'Perhaps that's why the *Imperator* is unwilling to bring those Germanic and Gallic traitors to justice for rebelling, so that he can equally forgive his son for the same treason.' He sat down, bolt upright and eyes forward with his nostrils slowly flaring as he sucked in huge breaths after his tirade.

'Are you finished, Priscus?' Vespasian asked in a mild tone mixed with a touch of exaggerated concern.

Priscus was in too much of an advanced state of indignation to answer.

'Very well, I'll take that as a yes.' Vespasian cleared his throat as he looked down the rows of senators all awaiting his reply with eagerness; Titus had been the talk of Rome since news of his going to Egypt had reached the city six months previously. 'Of course I don't need to answer such accusations, but in this instance I will and I will take them one at a time. Firstly, the reason I do not punish Civilis, Classicus and Tutor is that they have accepted Roman hegemony and their auxiliary units have retaken the oath and are now fighting for us again and not against us. Four Batavian, two Tungrian, three Lingonian and four Nervian cohorts are already back in Britannia helping quell the Brigantian revolt in the north, and Cerialis, whom I have appointed as the new governor of that province, will be taking more with him when he goes, including Gallic and Germanic cavalry. If they've come to their senses, why upset them by killing their princes? Civilis is of noble blood, grandson of the last Batavian king; he is more useful to me alive than dead. The only one who will forfeit his life is Julius Sabinus, when we find him, as he termed himself Caesar and that can never be forgiven; the Lingones will have to suffer that or face further retribution. Does anyone question my thinking?'

There was a positive murmur from the gathering; with the exception of a seething Priscus, all present seemed to be in agreement.

Vespasian put up a hand to call for silence. 'As to my son and the situation in both Egypt and Judaea: Helvidius Priscus, a man of great principle, does have a point. However, he is mistaken. Titus Caesar did not seek permission from me to enter Egypt because the precedent for that was set by Germanicus fifty years ago when he, also the heir apparent in the terms of Augustus' will, entered Egypt without Tiberius' permission. He was not reprimanded—'

'No, he was murdered!' Priscus shouted in triumph. 'By Calpurnius Piso on Tiberius' orders; the act of a tyrant! Is that what you plan for your son?'

Vespasian struggled to keep his voice level. 'The idea is preposterous; shall we confine ourselves to reasoned argument rather than ridiculous theory? Titus is in Egypt with my blessing,' Vespasian continued, hoping that the unease he felt at the lie did not show on his face, 'and he will be here for our joint Triumph in June; long before then.' He tried to keep uncertainty out of his voice.

'But what's he doing there?'

'I would remind you, Priscus, that the amount of booty that he has sent to Rome is more than this city has seen in centuries. Indeed, a shipment of top-quality male captives destined for the arena and the mines arrived only yesterday; that is not the act of a man who is thinking about rebelling. Titus took so much gold from the Temple that the price has halved in the East. Contrast this with the Jews beginning to try to buy their brethren out of captivity, which means the price of slaves has not fallen, due to the huge glut that has just come on the market, as we had originally feared one time last year, but, instead, has remained stable and is now starting to rise again. That's what he's doing in Egypt, Priscus, negotiating the sale of Jewish prisoners to Jewish delegations paying with Jewish gold from all over the Empire who are meeting in Alexandria because it has the richest Jewish community. He is making sure that the fanatics stay enslaved, living out short and miserable, but useful, lives in the mines or arenas all over the Empire, and that the women, children and less dangerous men are bought for a decent price and do not go back to Judaea but, rather, are dispersed throughout Jewish communities both within the Empire and in Parthia and Armenia as well. Some may even go as far as the Jewish settlements in India.' Vespasian began to warm to his improvisation. 'So you see, he's selling slaves back to the Jews for twice the amount of gold that we could have expected because we took so much from the Jews that the price fell. I'd call that a much-needed act of genius which will, along with the rest of the plunder taken from Jerusalem, go a long way to balancing the budget. Now does that satisfy you, Priscus?'

'I shall believe it when I see it,' came the grudging reply.

Vespasian decided to waste no more time on the unsettling subject of his son. He had received very few letters from Titus in the six months he had been in Egypt and they had been vague in detailing his plans, although he had mentioned the idea of selling the Jewish prisoners back to the Jews. But more than that Vespasian did not know. His spies had confirmed that Titus had worn a diadem that he had received from the Alexandrians at various occasions both religious and civil, and he had been treating Berenice as his wife, a scandal to both the Greek and Jewish communities. Vespasian had written back, veiling his concerns about his son's loyalties with entreaties for him to return to Rome as soon as business allowed so that he could take charge of the organisation of their Triumph; but still he tarried.

'And now Conscript Fathers,' Vespasian resumed, 'if Helvidius Priscus is satisfied, I wish to return to the much more important subject of our borders. I will keep the number of Rhenus legions at eight, four in both Lower and Upper Germania. In the former, the Twenty-first Rapax will be stationed at Bonna and the Twenty-second Primigenia at Vetera where it will rebuild the fortress that was destroyed in the Batavian revolt. Novaesium will be the base of the Sixth Victrix, and the Tenth Gemina will construct a new camp in the north of the province. As Lower Germania was the centre of the Batavian revolt I shall boost the number of auxiliary cohorts in the province with the First and Second Civium Romanum, the Sixth Ingenuorum and the Second and Sixth Brittonum building new forts for them to garrison, making a total of twenty-seven forts in all with less than ten miles between each one. I think, Conscript Fathers, when you look at those dispositions you will feel that the province is well protected from attack as well as uprising.'

Most of the Senate, having served under the Eagles, saw the military sense in their Emperor's thinking and rumbled their agreement; Priscus, however, rose to his feet.

'What is it now?' Vespasian asked, failing to keep the irritation from his voice.

'What if we don't feel that these dispositions are adequate, would it make any difference? Could we argue the point or is your word final?'

'My door is always open to people who wish to offer me advice, Priscus; indeed, I made this plan for the defence of the Empire having consulted with many of this House who have served as governors of the frontier provinces or as legates in the legions involved. I myself have served in Moesia and Upper Germania as well as Britannia; remind me where you have served, Priscus; what is your area of military expertise? I believe you were a quaestor in Achaea, a tribune of the plebs and now a praetor.'

'I served under Corbulo in Armenia.'

'Then I shall consult you when I come to deploying legions to that client kingdom.'

'But we have no legions there.'

'Exactly!'

Amidst much sycophantic laughter, Priscus sat back down with as much dignity as he could muster, fuming at the manner of his put-down.

'Now for Upper Germania,' Vespasian continued. 'Moguntiacum will remain a double camp for the First Adiutrix and the Fourteenth Gemina, which will not return to Britannia. The Second Adiutrix, newly formed from marines, will replace them in order to blood the new legion. Argentorate will house the Eighth Augusta, and the Eleventh Claudia will replace the Twenty-first Rapax at Vindonissa; the auxiliary cohorts already in the province will all remain in place. The Thirteenth

Gemina and the Seventh Galbiana, which will now also be renamed Gemina, will garrison in Pannonia whilst the First Italica, Sixth Ferrata, the Seventh Claudia and Third Gallica will be stationed in Moesia. Since the concerted attacks that we have faced in that province, there have been calls for a full-scale invasion of the Dacian and Sarmatian lands across the Danuvius with a view to incorporating a province of Dacia into the Empire. Whilst I applaud the idea and can see its many advantages, I consider that now is not the time for such a venture and I will leave it to my successors to complete once the Empire's finances are back in order. For now we shall hold our borders as they are but there will come a time when we shall again expand, out of necessity, for I believe that a stagnant empire is a doomed empire. Therefore once we have rested and the wounds of this civil war are healed we shall go back onto the offensive.'

This was met by a bout of patriotic cheering and waving of scrolls and the loose ends of togas.

Vespasian indulged the sycophancy for a while; it was his stomach rumbling that caused him to call for silence so that he could finish his round-up of the state of the Empire's defences, his first and most important speech on the subject. 'Finally, I would like to announce the creation of two new legions on top of the Second Adiutrix in order to bring the number up to twenty-nine. One will take the survivors of the Fifteenth Primigenia which was almost annihilated at Vetera last year as well as the more worthy members of the Sixteenth Gallica, First Germanica and Fourth Macedonica legions, all of whom will be cashiered for their disastrous performance and cowardice in the Batavian revolt. These two new legions, Conscript Fathers, will be called the Sixteenth Flavia Firma and the Fourth Flavia Felix and will receive their Eagles from my own hand.'

'Vanity!' Priscus shouted.

'No, Priscus, that is not vanity. That is no more than my desserts having reached where I am; a legacy is the least a good emperor can expect and I intend to be a good and just emperor.'

'A tyrant, more like.'

'Priscus, even a good and just emperor has a limit to his patience, and mine is approaching. Now, before I adjourn this meeting of the Senate I have one more announcement: on part of the site of the Golden House, I intend to commence the largest public building project since the rebuilding of the Circus Maximus. Estimated by my architects as a ten-year construction, the Flavian Amphitheatre will be Rome's first stone amphitheatre and will be able to seat over fifty thousand people. And that, Conscript Fathers, will be forever my legacy.'

'Vanity!'

'He goes too far, Father,' Domitian said as he and Vespasian processed behind their lictors towards the colossal stature of Nero at the heart of the Golden House.

'He does, but at the same time he serves a purpose,' Vespasian replied.

'What? Making you look weak?'

'In a manner of speaking, yes: in that at least I don't look all-powerful; there is still room for a bit of dissent in the Senate.'

'A bit? He openly ridicules you and accuses you of being a tyrant.'

'Exactly, thus proving that I'm not. No tyrant would allow someone to openly accuse him of being so and let him live. Helvidius Priscus is doing me a great favour and making himself look ridiculous at the same time.'

'All the same, you should have him executed, or banished at the very least.'

'Then I really would look like a tyrant.'

'Does that matter as long as we keep a firm grip on power?'

'No one who rules by fear has a firm grip on power, Domitian. Power is like water: you can easily hold it in your cupped hands but if you try to grab it in your fists it runs away. I'm keeping my hands cupped.'

Domitian looked sidelong at his father and shook his head, disbelieving.

Vespasian thanked Mars that he had an older son in Titus but, again, as he did so, his unease as to what Titus was doing began to gnaw within him and he resolved to try to bring the matter to a head. 'Domitian, I need you to do me a favour.'

'What is it, Father?'

'It's your brother.'

'What about him? Are you afraid that he's going to steal the East?'

'You should be concerned about that too, Domitian, seeing as it affects you just as much. Where will you stand if he does divide the Empire?'

'Then I'll be your sole heir.'

'And you think that I will survive the division? If I preside over that, it won't just be Helvidius Priscus who will be speaking out against me. What is the West without the East? That's what they will ask. Take the richest provinces away and how will we cope for tax revenues and grain? Who will govern them, senators from Rome? I think not; so will Titus set up an alternative Senate in Alexandria and, in which case, who will it comprise of? Will families who have lived in Rome for generations move to Egypt so they have a chance of those lucrative posts? No, Domitian, the consequences of what your brother is contemplating would mean that you would be the sole heir of an assassinated emperor, and I would say that was not a very happy position to be in.'

Domitian's eyes narrowed as he followed through the logic in his head. 'But that would be terrible for me; I'd be dead.'

'More than likely.'

'You must stop this, Father.'

'How? If I write to Titus expressing my fears, I'll be admitting that I know what he's thinking of doing, which will force him to carry through the action because he'll think, rightly, that I can no longer trust him. Whereas—'

Domitian had no trouble finishing Vespasian's sentence. 'Whereas if I were to write to him telling him that you're concerned for what *might* be on his mind and I explain to him the full consequences of his action for his whole family, then he can still return without there being a breach of trust between you.'

Vespasian put his arm around his younger son's shoulders. 'Well done, Domitian.'

'I'll help on one condition.'

'I don't think you're in the position to make conditions.'

'That you give me permission to marry Domitia Longina.'

Vespasian took a deep breath. 'Well, what harm can it do now? All right, you have my permission.'

'I'll go and write the letter immediately.'

'That would be very helpful.'

'Having surveyed the whole site, Imperator,' Marcus Patruitus said as he and Vespasian looked out over the artificial lake that was the centre-piece of the grounds of the Golden House, 'this is the best place to build your amphitheatre. The lake is five hundred feet square and twenty feet deep, so already we have the basis for the foundations and the dungeons, thus making a huge saving already.'

Vespasian liked the man immediately. 'Very good, Patruitus.'

'And then, of course, we don't have to clear the site, saving even more.'

'Good, good.'

'On top of that, the lake is fed by an underground aqueduct so the infrastructure is in place to flood the arena; again, another huge saving.'

Vespasian rubbed his hands together, pleased with the prognosis. 'Excellent. When can you start work?'

'As soon as I have the manpower, Imperator.'

'There is a shipment of Jewish prisoners awaiting distribution in the slave-pens down in Ostia. My lanistas are choosing the best for the games that I'm holding next month; the rest are for my Triumph, but you can make use of them before and after. But I warn you, they are the more fanatical of the Jews and may not take too kindly to being forced to work.'

Patruitus smiled, dismissing the notion. 'Don't worry, Imperator; I'll nail a few up to encourage the others. They'll soon get the hang of it.'

'Yes, well, don't crucify too many, I want a decent number left to parade to the people.'

'I'll be sparing with them.'

'Good.' Vespasian looked out over the lake, trying to envisage the great construction that would soon stand there. 'When will the model be ready?'

Patruitus thought for a few moments. 'I'll have it at the palace in four days' time.'

'What do you think, Magnus?' Vespasian asked as they inspected the beautiful scale model of what was to become the Flavian Amphitheatre; six feet across its longest axis and five on the shorter, it stood four feet high, its arches and seating all painstakingly sculpted; on the sand were figurines of gladiators so that the scale could be appreciated as it stood in the middle of Vespasian's study.

Magnus put his eye to an arch and squinted along the corridor within. 'It's nicely done. I can really see how it's going to look; and you say that it's going to be flooded?'

'When required, yes.'

'Well, that should do it.'

'Do what?'

'Keep your name alive after you've had your rendezvous with the Ferryman. The Flavian Amphitheatre; that sounds good. I wouldn't mind wagering that it gets known as just the Flavian.'

Vespasian allowed himself to imagine the idea. 'It will be one of the sights of the world. When it's done I'm going to have that colossal statue of Nero moved to stand next to it.'

'You don't want a colossal Nero standing next to your amphitheatre.'

'No, of course not; I'm having the head removed and replaced with that of a god.'

'Which one?'

'I haven't decided yet; either Mars or Apollo, I should think.'

'Well, be careful who you choose as you don't want a colossal god to hijack the name and it becomes the Marsian or some such thing.'

Vespasian smiled at his friend and slapped him on the shoulder. 'I wonder if you'll ever see the positive side of anything?'

'Now, now, sir; I was just saying, that's all. Naming something is all very well but it's the nicknames that stick, the names that the people give, they're the ones that last.' Magnus looked away biting his lower lip and scratching the back of his head. 'I don't know whether I should tell you this or not, sir.'

'What, Magnus?'

'Well, it's a bit of a difficult subject, nicknames, if you take my meaning?'

'You mean, what people call me?'

'It's not so much what they call you, it's more what they call something else.'

'Why should that worry me?'

'Well, they use your name.'

'Vespasian? What for?'

'Well, since you brought that piss tax in they've started to say: "I'm going for a Vespasian" or refer to the public piss-houses as "Vespasians".'

Vespasian threw his head back in laughter. 'And there we were worried that my name might not live on, but a thousand years from now people will still be pissing in a Vespasian. I consider that to be quite an honour.'

'What are you finding so amusing?' Caenis asked, walking into the room.

Vespasian got his mirth under control. 'My urine tax has caught the public imagination, my love; I am now an object into which they piss.'

Caenis did not look impressed. 'I think you deserve a little more respect than that.'

'And I think that it's a mark of affection; something that I'm pleased to have so soon in my reign.'

'If you're happy with it then so be it.' Caenis proffered a scroll.

'What's that?'

'That, my love, is what you asked me for; it's the document that grants the town of Aventicum municipality status in recognition of its hospitality to your parents when your father set up his banking business there.'

Vespasian took the scroll and perused it. 'Just before he died my father said to me that if I'm ever in a position to grant the town this status he would consider it a favour to him if I would.

I didn't know what he was talking about; I put it down to the ramblings of old age. But of course, he knew what my destiny would be because he had seen the signs at my birth.' He took the document across to his desk and picked up a pen; dipping it into the ink pot, he signed at the bottom. 'The good people of Aventicum are probably not even aware that their former banker is the Emperor's father,' he observed as he held a stick of sealing wax to a flame. 'This will come as a big surprise.' The melted wax dropped onto the scroll. 'This is a debt that I enjoy paying.' He pushed his signet ring into the wax and fulfilled his father's dying request.

It had been a long morning of killing and still the people of Rome felt the need for more as they cheered themselves hoarse every time one of the Jewish prisoners was despatched. Forced to fight, with the alternative of being eaten alive by wild beasts, the once-proud fanatical defenders of Jerusalem shed their blood for the delectation of the people they had so implacably opposed in almost every aspect of life. But giving oneself up to the blade without a fight was not an option as the brother-in-arms opposing you would be subject to that mauled death on the circus sands; likewise any act of self-murder was punished with brethren dying in the maws of beasts. And so, it was for mutual benefit that the Jewish captives fought with such ferocity and valour the length and breadth of the Circus Maximus, dressed as gladiators but without the specialist training, fighting in pairs or groups with the lucky ones receiving a clean death after a crowd-pleasing contest.

Vespasian, seated in the imperial box, in the exact same place he had seen Tiberius on his first full day in Rome as a youth of sixteen, played his part as sponsor of the games as the blood flowed and the crowd roared. He stood, resplendent in purple and wreathed in laurel, and pointed to a captive whose efforts he considered to be inadequate. 'Take him to the beasts!' Although unheard over the quarter of a million-strong crowd, his gesture was clearly understood and the intensity of noise escalated. Screaming, the miscreant was hauled off to the beast-pen, fenced off with iron bars at the far end of the Circus, and without ceremony was pushed through the gate.

With a flurry of fur, claws and teeth, the starved black cats dismembered and disembowelled the prisoner whose fading eyes' last sight was of a feline killer gnawing on his severed arm. The intensity of the dozen or so conflicts along the length of the track rose as none wanted to share the same fate.

'Let me condemn the next one, Father,' Domitian, seated to his left, requested, his face twisted cruel with killing-joy and his arousal evident.

'If you wish.' Vespasian pointed to a Thracian and retiarius combat on the far side of the spina. 'Keep an eye on that trident-man; I think he lost his net deliberately and he seems to be pulling some of his thrusts.'

'How much longer are you going to stay, my love?' Caenis, seated to Vespasian's right, asked, her voice barely concealing her boredom.

'Until the end, and I'm afraid that you have to stay with me; we want the people to see just how much we enjoy pleasing them.'

'I'm trying to look as pleased as possible but it's started to make my jaw ache.' She smiled, broad and false, and rubbed the offending part of her face to prove the point.

Vespasian turned to the Praetorian centurion commanding the guards at the entrance to the box. 'Send a man to find out how many more prisoners there are to go, centurion.'

Snapping a smart salute, the centurion barked an order at one of his men as a man was shown in through the door.

Vespasian felt his heart jump and relief flood through him; he got to his feet and took both of the extended, proffered hands.

'Here I am, Father,' said Titus. 'Here I am.'

'I came straight to Puteoli, rather than to Brundisium,' Titus said by way of explanation. 'That's why you had no advance warning. I wanted to get here quickly.'

'And forego the triumphant progress all the way from Brundisium to Rome,' Vespasian mused, 'being greeted as a returning hero in every town along the way; feasted and eulogised. You must have been in a great hurry; why would that be?'

Titus looked down at the track as a murmillo shot a straight jab to the throat of his opposing secutor. 'You know well, Father, why I had to hurry.'

'Did you stop enjoying yourself in Egypt all of a sudden?'

'Don't toy with me, Father. I heard what you had done and needed to reach you as soon as I could to get you to reverse the decision.'

'What decision?'

Titus looked momentarily confused and glanced at his brother and then back to his father. 'That you had written me out of your will and that Domitian was your sole heir.'

Vespasian had to admire his younger son's device. 'Who told you that?'

'I had a letter from Domitia Longina telling me that Domitian had boasted to her that that was the case and asking me if it were true and I was going to stay out in the East. She said that she needed to know before she accepted Domitian's proposal of marriage.'

Vespasian turned to Domitian. 'Did you know about this letter?'

'No, Father.' The lie was perfect.

'Had you made this boast?'

'No, Father.'

'Don't you lie to me, boy.'

'Well, I may have said something of the sort when it looked as if Titus was going to grab the East.'

Vespasian did his best to look incredulous. 'Grab the East? Where did you get that nonsensical idea from? Not me, certainly.'

Domitian shrugged.

For once feeling pleased with his younger son and knowing that self-interest would prevent Domitian from telling the truth, Vespasian turned back to Titus. 'There, you see; it was just in your brother's mind and nothing to do with me.'

Titus frowned. 'So you didn't suspect me of going back on my word to you, Father?'

'Suspect you? Of course not; I just assumed that you were dealing with the business of selling the slaves back to the Jews and having a bit of a rest with Berenice. Where is she, by the way?'

'She went back to Tiberias. I wanted her to come with me but she said that she couldn't be witness to me celebrating a Triumph over the Jews.'

'Good; that's one problem out of the way.'

'So none of this is true then; I'm still your heir and retain your trust?'

'Of course you do, Titus; why should you think otherwise? In fact, to show you just how much trust I place in you I'm going to make you the prefect of the Praetorian Guard.'

'Me? But that post always goes to an equites.'

'And I'm going to change that as I plan to change the Guard by reducing it back down to nine cohorts of five hundred men of our choosing. We need to consolidate our power and by having you in command of a smaller, loyal Guard means that there is one less threat.'

Titus digested that for a few moments before nodding and looking Vespasian in the eye. 'You're right; thank you, Father.'

But with one glance at Domitian, Vespasian could see just what his younger son thought of the power that his forged letter had brought to his sibling.

CHAPTER XVIIII

'ONE FAMILY; ONE extended family!' Helvidius Priscus ranted, his face ruddy, with a hand above his head, forefinger pointing at the Senate House roof. 'One extended family has gathered to it all the power that should, according to the ways of our ancestors, be shared amongst the senatorial and equestrian classes. In announcing next year's consuls six months before the end of this year the *Imperator* has shown himself for what he really is.'

'And what am I, Priscus?' Vespasian interjected, his patience straining under the constant attacks that he had been subjected to since making Titus prefect of the Praetorian Guard.

'A power-hungry monster who revels in self-aggrandisement, and to prove my point you're not satisfied with your Triumph tomorrow, so you're also taking yet another consulship next year along with the prefect of the Praetorian Guard.' He turned to Titus, seated next to Nerva in the front row of the lines of senators. 'Who has ever heard of such a thing: a consul being also the prefect of the Praetorian Guard? It's an outrage. And then to make matters worse the suffect-consuls are Titus Flavius Sabinus, Vespasian's nephew; Marcus Ulpius Traianus, related by marriage; and then, for the third time, Caius Licinius Mucianus, a former bum-boy of his.'

Vespasian jumped to his feet, all magisterial dignity gone. 'That is quite enough, Priscus. Withdraw that assertion.'

'Certainly; I withdraw "former".'

Vespasian restrained himself from charging across the floor of the House to strangle his constant adversary. 'You know exactly what I mean, Priscus. Withdraw!'

'Or what? Or you'll have the senior consul evict me from the chamber?' He looked at Domitian, chairing the Senate. 'The senior consul,' he sneered. 'Senior? He hasn't even reached his twentieth birthday and you mock the institution of the consulship by not only making him consul twenty-three years early but also making him "senior"! Don't you see just how foolish it makes you look?'

'No, Priscus; as your Emperor, voted by this House, I have been given the power to nominate whoever I wish to be consul and it behoves my younger son to be given the dignity of the rank, whatever your petty jealousies make you think.'

'Jealousies! How can one be jealous of a tyrant?'

'Tyrant!' Titus exploded, jumping to his feet. 'You call my father a tyrant to his face and you don't see just how foolish that makes *you* look? Well, be careful what you wish for, Priscus.'

'I *am* careful what I wish for and I wish for a state without tyrants. What is more, a tyrant with illegitimate sons.'

'Illegitimate! How dare you?' Titus stormed across the chamber, his strides full of purpose.

'I dare for it is the truth. Your mother was the daughter of Flavius Liberalis, a freedman with Latin Rights, not full citizenship. He was freed after she was born, which makes her a freedwoman and not a citizen as she claimed and we all know the law about senators not being able to marry freedwomen. And should they have progeny from the relationship then the offspring are illegitimate and are certainly not citizens.'

'Enough!' Vespasian roared, his temper finally broken. 'Flavia was a Roman citizen and her father was the son of a freedman not a freedman himself. I will hear no more of such slander.'

'And I demand freedom of speech.'

'Which is exactly what I shall offer you,' Titus called over his shoulder as he paused at the door.

'I would be amused to see that.'

'And I will share your amusement, Priscus,' Titus said as he signalled for the Praetorian centurion commanding the Guard detachment outside to step in. 'And bring two of your men, centurion.'

Helvidius Priscus looked in outrage at the armed soldiery invading the Senate House. 'What is the meaning of this?'

'This, Priscus, is granting both your wishes: I'm calling for your banishment.' Titus looked over to Vespasian. 'What do you say, Father, shall we give him his wished-for tyrant?'

Vespasian steepled his hands and pressed them to his lips in thought. 'Yes, Titus,' he said after a few moments. 'Yes, I shall act the tyrant for him, which will no doubt please him thoroughly; take him away and then grant him his wish of a solitary life on an island where he won't be in any danger of being ruled over by a tyrant and will be free to say what he wishes.'

'You can't do this!' Helvidius Priscus shouted as the guards grabbed him by the shoulders.

'I can and I will because you made me and you will have plenty of time to contemplate that in the future; now go, Priscus, and should you wish to come back all you have to do is write a letter of apology.'

Priscus' mouth opened and closed, spluttering at the thought of such a demeaning task. 'Tyrant!' he yelled as he was dragged through the door.

'And now, Conscript Fathers,' Vespasian said as the cries diminished, 'before this House rises and prepares for the festivities tomorrow, I wish to address the report of the commission I set up last year to return property looted during the recent civil wars to its rightful owners. Not the act of a tyrant, as I'm sure you will agree.'

'And finally from Cerialis,' Caenis said, squinting at the letter in the light of a couple of smoking oil lamps at each end of the desk.

'What does he want?' Vespasian asked, dipping a chunk of bread into a bowl of olive oil. He smeared garlic onto the bread as Caenis read the letter.

'He's arrived in Britannia with the Second Adiutrix and seven more auxiliary cohorts and has engaged the Brigantes with great success and expects them to be subdued by the time you receive this letter.'

'I hope that isn't Cerialis' normal overconfidence,' Vespasian said through a mouthful of his breakfast. 'Anything else?'

'Once he's defeated the Brigantes he's planning on moving even further north and wants your advice on the subject.'

Vespasian chewed his bread in contemplation, his face more strained than was the norm; he turned to Hormus as he broke off another piece. 'To Cerialis and fill in all the pleasantries. I congratulate you on a speedy resolution to the Brigantian revolt and thank you for bringing the final conflict raging within the Empire to a conclusion. Whilst I admire your desire to complete the conquest of the island by taking on the tribes to the north, I would urge you not to just yet. We have had almost three years of wars and rebellions in every corner of the Empire and I feel that it is time for a period of peace and reflection. I intend to, if I can, close the doors of the Temple of Janus.' He paused for another mouthful of bread. 'Add some more pleasantries at the end, Hormus.'

'Yes, master,' Hormus said, finishing off his shorthand note on a wax tablet. 'But I won't have time to do all these before the Triumph begins.' He indicated to the double pile of wax tablets that had been the end result of Vespasian dealing with his correspondence.

'Give them to the clerks; they can read shorthand.'

'But I like to do them myself, master.'

'And I want you to start delegating; you are more than my private secretary, you're my freedman who now has equestrian status as a reward for your loyalty, and you need to start behaving as such. Leave the menial tasks to those suited to them.'

'Yes, master.'

Vespasian scrutinised his former slave, satisfying himself that Hormus had understood that it was now time for him to behave with the dignity of his rank. 'Good. Now go and tell the steward to let my clients in for my morning *salutio*.'

'Hail, Titus Flavius Caesar Vespasianus Augustus, I bid you good morning on the day of your Triumph,' Marcus Cocceius Nerva said, formally, taking the seated Vespasian's proffered forearm.

'Thank you, Nerva.'

Nerva nodded at both Titus and Domitian standing to either side of their father's chair. 'And I wish the joy of the day to Titus Caesar and Domitian Caesar.'

Titus smiled broadly at Nerva as Domitian scowled at the thought that he would enjoy a day where he was to play a lesser role than his brother.

Vespasian attempted to ignore his younger son's mood which had been thus since he had been informed that he would only be riding a horse in the procession and not a Triumphal chariot since he had done nothing to merit the honour.

'My father asked me to send his greetings,' the young Marcus Ulpius Traianus said as Nerva moved off into the milling crowd of senators and equites and his turn to salute the Emperor came. 'And to thank you for the privilege of a consulship next year; he was honoured when he received your letter informing him of the distinction.'

'I look forward to seeing him in Rome soon, Traianus.'

'And he looks forward to returning.'

'Tell him to call on me at his earliest convenience, we shall dine together.'

The young Traianus inclined his head and moved off with a brief acknowledgement of Titus and Domitian whose scowl had not improved.

'Greetings, master,' Titus Flavius Josephus said, stepping in front of Vespasian, 'see now the real truth of my prediction.'

Vespasian chuckled. 'You scurrilous Jew, you; that wasn't a prediction, it was either a very well-informed guess or a desperate gamble. But I think none the less of you for it.'

Josephus inclined his head in acknowledgement without giving any indication whether he thought Vespasian right or not. 'I have a favour to ask as your freedman, master.'

'Name it.'

'As I'm sure you are aware, I cannot go back to Judaea after what has happened. I was present at the storming of the Temple and its subsequent destruction; I saw the flames and I saw the sacred ornaments and scrolls taken from the Holy of Holies by Gentiles and I did nothing about it. I can never go back.'

'So you stay here in my household.'

'That is what I had hoped, master; however, should I do that I need something to occupy myself.'

327

Vespasian scrutinised Josephus with a degree of suspicion. 'If you're asking for a position in—'

'No, master; I would never presume to that. I know how difficult it would be for a Jew to be accepted here in Rome as a person with power. No, master; I ask for something different: permission to write a history of the Jewish War which has now inextricably bound our lives.'

Vespasian considered the matter. 'Very well, but on one condition: that you emphasise just how much of the killing was done by Jews. Many, many more Jews died at Jewish hands than did by Roman. I want you to write a book that shows that the Jews were responsible for their own fate, not Rome.'

A gleam came into Josephus' eyes. 'That, master, is the very book that I intend to write.'

'I will be the one to judge that when it is complete. Keep me informed of your progress. In the meantime, I want you to have the scrolls that were removed from the Temple; they are no good to me but, as a Jew, you might derive some benefit from them.'

'I am in your debt; thank you, master,' Josephus said, putting his arms across his chest and bowing his head to take his leave.

'Hail, Caesar,' Agricola said, taking Josephus' place in front of Vespasian.

'My love, you had better come quickly,' Caenis said, surprising Vespasian by coming up behind him and whispering in his ear.

Vespasian turned to her, frowning. 'Why? What is it?'

Caenis' face was full of concern. 'It's Magnus. He collapsed as he was ... well, as he was, how did he put it? As he was making use of one of the occasional erections that come his way.'

'The old goat. How is he?'

'Not good. He's asking for you.'

Vespasian felt his stomach sink and hurried to the call of his old friend.

The room was gloomy with the sound of soft, female sobbing in the far corner and slow, irregular, rasping breaths coming from the large bed set under a closed window; the first thin light of dawn crept through the cracks in the shutters.

'Magnus?' Vespasian called as he stepped through the door with Caenis following. 'Magnus, are you all right?' He walked across the floor trying to make as little noise as possible, although for what reason he could not say. 'Magnus?'

'Is that you, sir?' Magnus wheezed, stirring in his bed.

'Yes. I hear you've been exerting yourself a bit too much.'

Vespasian halted at the side of the bed and looked down at his old friend's face; even in the dim light he could tell it was pale and the skin seemed stretched. His glass eye was lying in a bowl on the table next to the bed.

Magnus winced and put a hand to his chest. 'Yeah, well, I thought it would be a shame not to make use of it seeing as I woke up with such a magnificent one, so I invited Caitlín to hop on, if you take my meaning?'

Vespasian glanced over to where Magnus' slave was slumped, crying on the far side of the bed. Caenis moved across to comfort her.

'She blames herself for being too athletic; I must admit, it was quite a ride. But I felt something go inside, as it all came to a conclusion,' Magnus grimaced again, 'in the same place where I've been having a lot of pain recently.' A coughing fit took him.

Vespasian put his hand under Magnus' head, supporting him as the bout reached a retching crescendo and wiped his mouth with a cloth; there was blood in the phlegm. 'I'm calling my doctor.'

'No you ain't; I'll not have him near me.' He paused for another couple of strained coughs. 'I'm done, sir, and I want my last moments to be pleasant and not subjected to the proddings and pokings of some Greek with about as much knowledge of medicine as a Vestal has of testicles.'

'That's not fair; he's very well trained.'

'I'm very pleased for him.' Magnus winced again with pain and shuddered out a few more coughs. 'But I ain't having him in the room. Now, sir, look after Caitlín for me; she's been good to me over the years and didn't nag overmuch and mostly did what she was told without needing to be slapped.'

'Of course I will, Magnus; I'm sure Caenis will be only too happy to have her join her household. But who said anything about you leaving us?'

'Haven't you been listening? I did; and I should know.' He closed his eye, squeezing it tight as another explosion wracked his body. 'I've got quite a bit stashed away with the Cloelius Brothers' bank in the Forum. I've left half to her in my will. Hormus drew it up for me.' His breaths were getting weaker with each series of coughs and his voice thinner. 'The rest I've left to the South Quirinal Crossroads Brotherhood, the only place I could ever call home, apart from the army, that is.'

'And here with me, Magnus.'

'Well, it's more of a palace than a home, sir; but I take your meaning. And, well, I suppose I've always looked upon you as a son.'

Vespasian smiled. 'And I've always considered you to be a grumpy old man – even when you were younger.'

Magnus laughed, swallowing a cough; his chest heaved. 'Now, sir, you're mocking me again.'

'I'm going to have to stop that.'

'You will.'

Vespasian suppressed a sob as the truth of the statement sank in. 'I know.'

'I'm sorry to do this on the day of your Triumph.'

'Yes, I was thinking that it was rather selfish of you.'

'It makes up for all the times you mocked me.' Magnus reached up and took Vespasian's hand as another fit shook his body. 'Juno's puckered arse, that hurts.' He took a couple of weak breaths. 'I'll be well out of it, sir; and I ain't got no regrets about life. I lived it to the full and fuck everyone else, so I'm happy enough to go now.'

A tear slipped from Vespasian's eye.

'Come on, sir; a man shouldn't do that; it ain't natural.'

'It is, Magnus; I can assure you it's the most natural thing in the world.' He looked down at his friend; he could tell the life was leaving him. 'What shall I do with your ashes?'

'Build me a nice tomb at your estate in Cosa; I always liked getting out to the country.'

'I will.'

'I just have one bit of advice for you, sir.' Magnus' voice was frail and fading. 'Something that now you're emperor you might forget because you won't like it.'

'What's that?'

'Well, it's to open your purse a bit more often; people rarely see the inside of it, in fact I think its forgotten what sunlight looks like.' Another convulsion seized him and blood trickled from the corner of his mouth. 'But you'd better overcome your tightness and people will love you the more for it.'

Vespasian nodded, tears now flowing free. 'I will, Magnus.'

'Good lad. It don't do to be a wealthy corpse.' Another bout of coughing juddered through his whole being. 'If you take my meaning?'

'I do, Magnus; in fact I always have.' He squeezed Magnus' hand but it was limp. Leaning over he brushed a hand over Magnus' eye, closing it.

Caitlín wailed as Caenis took her from the room.

Vespasian looked down in disbelief at the motionless features of his oldest companion and let the grief pour from him. And so it flowed until Caenis came back into the room and placed both her hands on his shoulders. Stifling the sobs, Vespasian wiped the tears from his cheeks; with a smile at the memories that they shared, he leant forward and kissed Magnus' forehead and then pulled up the sheet and covered his face. 'Goodbye, old friend.'

'There you are, my love,' Caenis said, smearing on the last of the pigment with a cloth, 'the red face of a god.'

Vespasian looked at his reflection in the polished bronze mirror and saw the visage of Jupiter peering back at him; Hormus completed the image by placing a laurel wreath on his head. He adjusted his purple Triumphal toga and stepped back to take in the full picture. Despite the deep sadness he felt at the thought of Magnus lying cold just a few rooms away his pride almost burst from him as he looked at the classic image of a Triumphal general. 'Today is my day.'

Caenis kissed him on the lips. 'Today is also Titus' day, my love.'

Vespasian grunted. 'True. So today is the House of Flavius' day. That sounds better.'

'I don't think Domitian would agree.'

'Some of the glory rubs off on him too, although granted he has never, nor will he ever, been satisfied with just some of the glory. No doubt he will find a good excuse in the future to celebrate a Triumph, but not whilst I'm around. I wouldn't trust him with an army: both how he'd command it and what he'd do with it.' He adjusted his wreath so that it tilted further back on his head. 'Where's Titus, Hormus?'

'He said he would wait for you downstairs in the atrium so that you could travel together to the Theatre of Pompey in a covered carriage.'

Vespasian, sitting next to Titus, peeked through a gap in the curtains, shielding the passengers from the outside world until the moment of their Triumph, as the carriage rumbled down the Palatine in the direction of the Campus Martius. The people of Rome were in festive mood and rightly so: kitchens had been set out throughout the city ready for the feast that would follow the parade.

Vespasian sniffed the air. 'Mmm, baking bread, so much better than the normal smell of the city.' He looked over at Hormus sitting opposite him. 'How many loaves did you pay for?'

Hormus consulted his ledger. 'Two million, four hundred thousand, for a total price of three hundred thousand sesterces.'

Titus whistled softly, his pursed red lips looking almost comic. 'That is a lot of bread; can Rome really produce that in one day?'

'Every bakery in the city has been working at full capacity since yesterday afternoon and they should reach the target by the time the Triumph commences.'

'And how much is all the food and drink distributed by the kitchens costing?'

Hormus looked at the ledger again. 'Including the bread, the total bill is just shy of six million sesterces.'

Vespasian shook his head, biting back words of complaint as he remembered Magnus' dying advice. 'Time to raise more taxes.'

Titus turned to Vespasian. 'Yes, Father; what is this that I hear about you taxing urine? I've heard a lot of sniggering in corners by some very influential people since I've been back; it's become a joke.'

Vespasian held out his hand. 'Hormus, pass me your purse.'

Vespasian emptied the contents into the palm of his hand and showed the coins to Titus. 'Smell them.'

Titus sniffed at the pile.

'Well?'

'Well, they smell of coinage.'

'And yet they come from piss.'

Titus looked up and caught Vespasian's eye twinkling. 'When it comes to money you just don't care, do you?'

'On the contrary, Son, I care very much.'

They both broke into laughter as the carriage passed through the gates of the city and out onto the Campus Martius.

The fanfare echoed around the precincts of the Temple of Pompey as Vespasian and Titus appeared at the top of the steps, beneath the portico decorated with flowers and flags for the occasion; prayers had been offered and sacrifices made within and now it was the moment of Triumph. The roar of the crowd was mighty and they stood, bathing in the adulation for many beats of their hearts. Vespasian felt Caenis' hand brush the back of his as she came out with Domitian and his new wife, Domitia Longina, to stand just behind the Triumphal pair.

Vespasian cast his eyes around the Campus Martius, decorated and packed with people of all stations as the parade, which had been assembling since the early hours of the morning, prepared to set off. The leading musicians were already waiting at the Triumphal Gate, only ever opened on these occasions and for the lesser Ovation, in readiness to lead the procession through the city. Following them were the ragged bands of captives, all in chains and showing the lick of the whips that had been used on them to keep them docile. Behind them were many carts piled high with captured weaponry followed by wagons with tableaux of scenes from the war being played out by actors showing the two Triumphing generals in a very positive light, smiting Jews, storming towns and tearing down city walls with their bare hands. After these came the gold and silver; so much of it, from coinage and jewellery to the great seven-armed menorah of solid gold taken from the Holy of Holies when the Jewish god's temple had been destroyed and he made homeless, a wandering wraith. Piles of gold and silver plates as well as bullion taken from the Temple treasury, the stored wealth of the Jewish people for the last hundred years since Pompey Magnus had cleared it out, formed the next part of the parade.

Then would come the Senate but at this moment they waited within the pomerium, behind the Triumphal Gate so that they could accept the surrender of command of the returning generals. A form of words had been agreed to get over the slightly embarrassing fact that both Vespasian and Titus had been in the city for some time and had therefore already technically given up their commands; but no one was going to let such a small detail spoil the day.

Vespasian descended the steps to one of the two four-horse chariots awaiting the party side by side; as he did so he caught Titus glancing over his shoulder at Domitia Longina and sharing a look with her; he hoped Domitian had failed to notice but knew that to be a small hope as Domitian noticed most things that affected him personally, and his older brother making eyes at his new wife would most certainly affect him personally.

At the bottom of the steps, Vespasian's and Titus' lictors waited formed up in two columns, their fasces wreathed in laurel for this special day, so that the Triumphviri passed between them, heading for their vehicles. As Vespasian and Titus stepped into their chariots a public slave followed each of them in.

Vespasian and Titus both picked up their reins in one hand and raised the fists of the other into the air and then brought them down in unison. A bucina rang out, crisp and clear, cutting through the cheering crowd; its call was taken up by another stationed further along the parade and then another until the signal reached the musicians at the front. It was with a crescendo of percussion that the band struck up and the Triumphal Gate swung open.

The height of Vespasian's career was about to be achieved and the crowd roared his and Titus' names.

In step the musicians marched, slow and with great dignity befitting the occasion, to the pounding of massed drums and the sonorous notes of many horns, filled out by intricate melodies plucked in unison by a century of harpists and then all rounded off by the deliberate, wheezed notes of many water-organs mounted on low carriages interspersed throughout the rest of the musicians.

Gradually the column began to move forward as the slave-masters whipped their charges forward to be pelted with refuse by the crowd whose cheers turned to jeers as the wretched Jews came into view. Rank after ragged rank of the once-fanatical holy warriors were whipped into the city whose myriad of gods had combined to vanquish their mono-deity. And the people of Rome gave thanks that their many different ways of life were safe from the threat from the East that these religious fundamentalists had posed; they revelled in the misery of the captives, laughed at their humiliation and abused them all in any manner possible. There was no pity, for none had the Jews shown, either to their own kind or the legions that had been thrown against them.

In they were herded, weighed down by chains and misery until at last the weapon-carts and tableaux could begin their journey. Mules and oxen were goaded into movement and wheels creaked on goose-fatted axles and the long line of loaded vehicles crept forward.

And still Vespasian waited, his four horses stamping and snorting with impatience, their halters held by stable-lads. Domitian sat behind him on his mount with some of the senior officers of the legions who had partaken in the war, his face a picture of seething humiliation as he stared at his older brother in his moment of triumph. Behind the officers, before another large section of musicians, came the standards of the defeated enemy, mainly black flags with religious text embroidered onto them in white, promising destruction to the enemies of the one true god; accompanying them were two pure-white oxen, garland-decked and with gilded horns, an offering to Jupiter at the climax of the day.

With joy, Vespasian watched the Triumphal parade enter the city through that historic gate until it came the time for him and Titus to urge their teams forward.

'Remember you are but mortal,' the public slave riding with him in the chariot whispered in his ear. And Vespasian did, for he had witnessed death just that morning and it did not need a public slave to remind him of mortality, and he knew that should he die now he would die happy and fulfilled.

As he and Titus reached the Triumphal Gate, Lucius Flavius Fimbria, the suffect senior consul and, uncoincidentally, a kinsman, and Caius Atillius Barbarus, his junior colleague, waylaid Vespasian before he could enter.

'Your command, Imperator,' Fimbria demanded.

Vespasian reached into the fold of his toga and brought out the symbolic baton of command that he had awarded himself that morning; Titus produced his, and again it was but a gesture to the formalities of a Triumph. With the command set down the Triumphing generals were free to cross the pomerium and enter the city, with the Senate leading them and their troops following behind, to the rapture of its citizens.

Waving the colours of their racing factions, red, white, blue and green, they welcomed in their Emperor and his son as if they had not seen them for many a year. Fronds and flowers hurtled into the air to rain down on the chariots, filling the atmosphere with sweet smells that augmented the baking bread, roasting meats and wafts of perfumed incense.

'Remember you are but mortal.'

And how could Vespasian forget? A god does not feel the thrill of being worshipped as they consider it to be their due; but a man … yes, Vespasian felt his mortality as the city worshipped him and he revelled in it. They worshipped him for subduing the

East, for pushing back the Sarmatians across the Danuvius, for crushing the Batavians and the burgeoning Gallic Empire in the north, for suppressing the Brigantian rebellion and many other smaller flashpoints that had coincided with the beginning of his reign; but mostly they worshipped him for being the last man standing after a civil war in which tens of thousands of Rome's citizens had perished. And it was for this and the stability that he had returned to them that they roared themselves hoarse as he and Titus passed along the Triumphal Way towards the Circus Maximus, around that and then onto the Sacred Way in the afternoon, before arriving in the Forum Romanum as the sun began to cool. Ten, twenty deep they crowded along the route and with thousands more mounted on statues or leaning out of windows, or perched in far more dangerous and precarious vantage-points, all wanted a glimpse of their new Emperor and his son coming to them in Triumph.

As they approached the Capitoline the prisoners due for ritual execution by garrotte were led into the Tullianum to their fate by the gaoler and his hirsute companion who capered with excitement at the slow death he was about to administer to the deserving. The rest of the prisoners were whipped back out to their pens on the Campus Martius for distribution to whatever torment they had been allocated for the rest of their lives.

With the Senate processing with great dignity, military crowns, Triumphal Ornaments and all the other baubles of rank being displayed to the full, Vespasian and Titus made their way up the Capitoline Hill to the partially rebuilt Temple of Jupiter. Parked before the temple were carts containing the most valuable portion of the booty: the contents of the Holy of Holies; the menorah, the shewtable, the beautifully crafted vessels as well as the priestly vestments and other gold and silver items that had been sacred to the Jewish god.

To thunderous joy, the oxen were brought forth to climb the steps and disappear into the dim realm of Rome's guardian god. Dismounting, Vespasian and Titus followed them up to an altar with a fire burning upon it. They turned and surveyed the crowd, not so many in the cramped confines of the Capitoline, but packing the Forum Romanum below and then on throughout the city. Again they raised their arms and again they were praised, with the Senate leading the chorus as they gathered around the cartloads of booty, glistering in the evening sun.

Vespasian signalled for silence; it was soon manifest on the summit of the hill as the cheering continued throughout the city. 'Conscript Fathers, this bounty has come to restore our city's fortunes.' He gestured to the plunder of untold wealth, the gold of the Temple. 'This hoard will be the start of the refinancing of the Empire; my reign will be seen as the beginning of a time of peace and prosperity where the law is upheld, a man's rights are secure and the currency is stable. That is the mark of a civilised society; that is what we shall strive for. This gold is the beginning of a new Rome.' He pointed to the menorah and all the beautifully crafted Temple vessels. 'Melt them down, all of them; they have caused enough trouble in this world and now it is time for them to do some good.'

EPILOGUE

AQUAE CUTILLAE, 22 JUNE AD 79

Titus Flavius Caesar Vespasianus closed his eyes as his father, the Emperor Vespasian, groaned in pain and shot out another stream of diarrhoea into the bed-pan held by Hormus. A sweet stench of decay filled the room off the courtyard garden of the farmhouse on the Flavian estate at Aquae Cutillae; a house that Titus, like his father, had known all his life.

'Are you squeamish?' Vespasian asked as the bout drew to a close.

Titus opened his eyes and looked at his father, who had lost much weight since this sickness had come over him down in Campania, ten days previously. Vespasian had returned to Rome and then decided that he would rather begin his final journey on the estate he had loved all his life. And now the commencement of that journey seemed to be close. 'I'm sorry, Father; I was just trying to preserve your dignity.'

'Dignity? Ha! I lost that when I started pissing shit out of my arse uncontrollably. Where does it all come from? That's what I'd like to know.' He looked down at the slopping contents of the bed-pan. 'Blood?'

Hormus peered in, his nose wrinkling at the stench. 'Yes, master, I think it is.'

'Of course it is.' Vespasian shook his head and lay back down, breathing in swallow gulps and sweating despite the cool temperature in the room. 'Well, that's it then; I'm nearly done.'

'You'll get better, Father.'

Vespasian's smile was weak. 'No, I won't; and nor would you want me to. Your time has come now, my son, and you'll not want me hanging around to delay it.'

Titus did not reply as he knew it to be the truth. His father had reigned for ten years; good years; years of peace and reconstruction and relative harmony between the Emperor and the Senate. Vespasian, the Emperor who taxed urine as he would be forever known, had been a just emperor, Titus could concede, and now his turn was coming and he would be judged by his father's standards. They had shared a joint censorship in which they had completely reorganised the senatorial and equestrian classes, but that as well as the overseeing of the construction of the almost complete Flavian Amphitheatre and the first consulship of the year for eight out of the ten years of the reign, were the only endeavours they had shared. The rest of the time they had travelled on different paths: Vespasian as a benign emperor and Titus as a feared prefect of the Praetorian Guard, shielding his father from implication in the darker side of maintaining power. Vespasian was loved but only because Titus had made it so; now that was about to change.

Vespasian, weakening with each breath, reached up and took his son's hand. 'For four years, since Caenis died, you have been my support and strength, Titus; not your brother, you. Where is Domitian? He'd rather stay in Rome and plot than be here at my death bed.' He paused for a few laboured breaths.

Titus squeezed his hand; it was clammy. He could hear the low murmur of the household slaves talking outside in the garden as they awaited news of their master; from beyond them came the shouted orders and *lituus* signals of the Praetorian cavalry escort ala drilling in the stable-yard. 'Rest, Father.'

'I'll have plenty of time for that very soon; now listen to me. I have executed very few people, Helvidius Priscus and a few others, but you on the other hand, as prefect of the Praetorian Guard, have not been so restrained, and I know that I have cause to thank you for that. But, Titus, you are hated now as well as feared. Anyone who aroused your suspicions was executed or murdered. You even had Aulus Caecina invited to dinner and then stabbed in the triclinium as soon as he had eaten.' Vespasian groaned. 'I've soiled myself.'

'Let me change your tunic and loincloth, master,' Hormus said, coming forward.

'No, Hormus, there's nothing to do about it, it'll just happen again; it's just the final indignity that I shall have to bear.' He looked back up at Titus, his eyes bloodshot, eyelids flickering. 'You're hated; you're hated for pulling men from the theatre, the baths, their own homes, sometimes even as they were sharing a meal with their wives and children. I know you thought that it kept us safe, but you earned their hate whilst your high-handed actions kept me their love. But I am dying and you will inherit; and you will inherit as a hated man. So what of Domitian, what of him? He has too much pride and anger within him to allow that to happen. And he has done nothing to earn people's hate; he would have their support if it came to it. So what will you do?'

'I will not kill Domitian, Father; I will not have fratricide added to the accusations against me.'

'But he would not fear that label.'

'I know.'

'And one of you must bear it; can't you see that to be the truth?'

'No, Father; I see that only to be a possibility. But I'm not stupid; I will be careful and I will watch Domitian. And I will be a different emperor to the prefect that I have been; I will re-engage their love. I will be generous to the Senate and extravagant to the people; the opening of our amphitheatre will be the greatest spectacle Rome has ever witnessed.'

'Yes, I'm sorry to miss that.' Another spasm wracked Vespasian's body and the sound of spilling bowels rumbled on.

Titus held onto his father's hand as his face contorted with pain, his breath coming in short gasps. His eyes closed but his breathing continued, just. 'He's passed out, Hormus; wipe his brow.'

Hormus did as he was asked, his tears now flowing.

Titus waited, watching his father fade, feeling the weight of the approaching transition of power and resolving to be good to his word to his father; his reign would be just and long and he would thwart all of his brother's plots and still keep him alive, no matter what he tried.

Another explosion from beneath the sheet brought Vespasian round; with a sudden jerk of his chest, his eyes flicked open. He looked around as if he knew not where he was and then, focusing on Titus' face, pushed himself up. 'Help me, Titus; an emperor should die on his feet.'

On weakened legs, Vespasian struggled to stand, Titus supporting one arm and Hormus the other; his soiled tunic noisome but neither noticed.

Titus looked at his father: his eyes were fixed into the distance as if he saw his destination far away.

Vespasian slumped and a thin smile quivered on his lips. 'I think I'm turning into a god.' His head lolled and his knees gave way.

With suppressed sobs Titus and Hormus lay his body back down on the bed. As the tears began to flow, Titus knelt down next to his father and kissed him on the mouth. He closed the sightless eyes and then stood looking down at the corpse of the New Man from the Sabine Hills who had become the ninth Emperor of Rome, his father, Titus Flavius Vespasianus.

AUTHOR'S NOTE

This work of fiction is based, once again, on the works of Tacitus, Suetonius, Cassius Dio and Josephus.

Tacitus gives a good account of the first Battle of Bedriacum and it is much as I have described; as is Otho's suicide and Vitellius' reaction to seeing so many dead citizens. Tacitus also tells us that Vitellius did believe Paulinus and Proculus' protestations of treachery and cleared them of all suspicion of loyalty; I find it hard not to chuckle when I'm reading him.

The elder Sabinus did take the Capitoline in Vespasian's name but was forced out, very much as shown, and then captured and executed. The final conversation between him and Vitellius is my fiction as I wanted to complete what I had already set up, all those years ago, in *Rome's Executioner*.

Josephus gives us a fantastic account of the Jewish revolt including the siege of Jotapata, his prophecy as to how long it would last, his cunning way of escaping death and his subsequent surrender to Vespasian and prophesying that he would become emperor. How much of that he embellished is up for speculation. However, he did become, firstly, Vespasian's slave before being his freedman and taking the name Titus Flavius Josephus.

The father of the future Emperor Trajan was the legate of the X Fretensis under Vespasian's command. Vespasian was wounded in the foot – or the knee, according to Suetonius – at Jotapata and the Jews did use sheep disguises to get in and out of the town and increased the height of their walls behind ox-hide screens.

The murderous in-fighting between the Jewish sects, both within Jerusalem and around the province, is attested to by Josephus. The various groupings of fanatics spent more time killing each other than the real enemy; and alas, as we have seen throughout the centuries, even to this very day, it was ever thus where religion is peddled by the ignorant and intolerant.

Tiberius Alexander, the Jewish prefect of Egypt, was the first to have his legions swear loyalty to Vespasian; that he did so because he owed his life to Vespasian is my fiction.

Mucianus did also support Vespasian, more than likely because he himself had no children and could not offer such stability. However, it is hinted that his interest in Titus was not irrelevant to his decision.

What Titus' reasons were for going to Rome on Galba's ascension are unclear; perhaps it was in the hope of being adopted. He did, however, turn back upon Galba's death and went via Cyprus to hear what Venus' oracle had to say about his future; the news was good.

King Malichus' part in going to Rome and then to Parthia on Vespasian's behalf is my fiction; however, Vologases did offer forty thousand horse archers to Vespasian so someone must have travelled east to see him.

Titus' affair with Berenice is well documented and subject to much literature and poetry. Suetonius tells us of Titus' behaviour in the East and Egypt and for a while it must have been a worry to Vespasian; he did, however, come back to Rome, leaving Berenice behind.

Sabinus coming to see Vespasian in Judaea is my fiction but he was removed as prefect of Rome by Galba and then reinstated when Otho came to power so, theoretically, had the time to travel.

Vespasian was said to have performed miracles in Alexandria; I have changed the location of them to the forum there to make it even more public. Whether they were staged or not we shall never know – although we can take a shrewd guess.

Vespasian going to Siwa to consult with Amun is my fiction; I also could not resist him coming across the army of Cambyses on the way – one day, perhaps, who knows, the sands might deliver it up.

As to his dying words, Suetonius gives us those and to me it shows what a marvellous sense of humour the great man had. That line is what drew me to Vespasian in the first place and is why I love him so much.

ACKNOWLEDGEMENTS

As this is the final Vespasian book I won't name names but, rather, I would like to give my thanks and heartfelt gratitude to everyone who has in some way contributed to the publishing of the series. Some of the people I know and some I don't but I'm well aware just how important each part of the process is; so thank you all.

Now that I've come to the end of Vespasian's story, a story that I started exactly ten years ago today, on 8 February 2008 – at 11.08 a.m., if you really want to know – I realise just how much I shall miss him; it's been a fabulous journey and I'm so pleased, dear reader, that you came along for the ride.

Robert Fabbri
Berlin
8 February 2018 – at 11.08 a.m., if you really want to know.

Read on for an exclusive extract from

ALEXANDER'S LEGACY:

TO THE STRONGEST

PROLOGUE

BABYLON, SUMMER 323 BC

'TO THE STRONGEST.' The Great Ring of Macedon wavered in Alexander's dimming vision; his hand shook with the effort of raising it and then speaking. Emblazoned with the sixteen-pointed sun-blazon, the ring represented the power of life and death over the largest empire ever conquered in the known world; an empire that he must bequeath so early, too early, because he, Alexander, the third of that name to be King of Macedon, knew now that it was manifest: he was dying.

Rage surged within him at capricious gods who gave so much and yet exacted so high a toll. To die with his ambition half-sated was an injustice that soured his achievements, augmenting the bitter taste of death that rose in his gorge; for it was but the east that had fallen under his dominion; the west was yet to witness his glory. And yet, had he not been warned? Had not the god Amun cautioned him against hubris when he had consulted the deity's oracle in the oasis of Siwa, far out in the Egyptian desert, nigh on ten years ago? Was this then his chastisement for ignoring the god's words and reaching further than any mortal had previously dared? Had he had the energy, Alexander would have wept for himself and for the glory that was slipping through his fingers.

Without an obvious, natural heir, who would he allow to follow him? To whom would he give the chance to rise to such heights as he had already attained? The love of his life, Hephaestion, the

2

only person he had treated as an equal, both upon the field of battle and within the bed they shared, had been snatched from him less than a year previously; only Hephaestion, beautiful and proud Hephaestion, would have been worthy to expand what he, Alexander, had already created. But Hephaestion was no more.

Alexander held the ring towards the man standing to the right of his bed, closest to him, the most senior of his seven body-guards surrounding him, all anxious to know his will in these final moments. All remained still, listening, in the vaulted chamber, decorated with glazed tiles of deep blue, crimson and gold, in the great palace of Nebuchadnezzar at the heart of Babylon; here in the gloom of a few weak oil-lamps, for little light seeped through the high windows from the early-evening, overcast sky, they waited to learn their fate.

Perdikkas, the commander of the Companion Cavalry, so far loyal to the Argead royal house of Macedon but ambitious in his own right and ruthless with it, took the symbol of ultimate authority from his king's forefinger; he asked his question a second time, his voice tense: 'To whom do you pass your ring, Alexander?' He glanced around his companions before looking back down at his dying king and adding: 'Is it to me?'

Alexander made no attempt to reply as he looked around the semi-circle of the men closest to him, all formidable mili-tary commanders capable of independent action and all with the human lust for power: Leonnatus, tall and vain, model-ling his long blonde hair in the same style as his king, aping his looks, but whose devotion was such that he had used his own body to shield Alexander when he fell wounded in far-off India. Peucestas, next to him, already was showing signs of going native in his dress, having been the only bodyguard to have learnt Persian. Lysimachus, the most reckless of them all, was possessed of bravery that was often a hazard to his own comrades. Peithon, dour but steadfast; unquestioning in his execution of even the most cruel orders, when others might quail. And then there were the older two: Aristonous, who had been Alexander's father, Phillip, the second of that name's, bodyguard; the only survivor of the old regime, whose counsel was infused with the wisdom of one old in the ways of war. And finally, Ptolemy; what to make of Ptolemy whose looks hinted at him being a bastard brother? At once gentle and forgiving and yet capable of ruthless political adroitness should that part of his nature be abused; the least competent militarily but the most likely to succeed in the political long game.

Alexander looked past the seven, as Perdikkas repeated the question a third time, to the men beyond the bed; men who had followed him, sharing the dangers and the triumphs, on his ten-year journey of conquest, silent in the shadows as they strained to hear him answer. Passing along the dozen or so faces he knew so well, his weak gaze rested on Kassandros standing next to his younger half-brother, Iollas, and Alexander thought he detected triumph in his eyes; his sickness had started the day after Kassandros' arrival from Macedon as his father, Antipatros' messenger; had Antipatros, the man who had ruled as regent in the motherland for the past ten years, sent his eldest son with the woman's weapon of poison to murder him rather than obey the summons that Alexander had sent? Iollas was, after all, his cup-bearer and could easily have administered the dose. Alexander cursed Kassandros inwardly, having always hated the ginger-haired, pock-marked prig whose loathing had been returned in equal measure and augmented by his humiliation at having been left behind for all those years. His mind turned back to Antipatros, a thousand miles away in Pella, the capital of Macedon, and his constant feud with his, Alexander's, mother, Olympias, scheming and brooding back in her native Molossia, a part of the kingdom of Epirus; how would that resolve without him playing off one against the other? Who would kill whom?

But then, half obscured by a column at the far end of the dying-chamber, Alexander glimpsed a woman, a pregnant woman; his Bactrian wife, Roxanna, three months from full term. What chance would a half-caste child have? Not many shared his dream of uniting the peoples of east and west; there would be few Macedonians of pure blood who would rally behind a half-breed infant born to an Eastern wildcat.

So it was with certainty, as he closed his eyes, that Alexander foresaw the struggles that would mark his passing, both in Macedon and here in Babylon and then throughout the subject Greek states, as well as among those of his satraps who had carved out fiefdoms of their own in the vast empire he had wrought; men such as Antigonos, The One-Eyed, satrap of Phrygia and Menander, satrap of Lydia, the last of Phillip's generals.

Then there was Harpalus, his treasurer, whom he had already forgiven once for his dishonesty, who, rather than face Alexander's wrath a second time, had absconded with eight hundred talents of gold and silver, enough to raise a formidable army or live in luxury for the rest of his life; which would he choose?

And what would Krateros do? Krateros, the darling of the army, a general second to only Alexander himself, now somewhere between Babylon and Macedon, leading ten thousand veterans home; would he feel that he should have been named Alexander's successor? But Alexander, weakness creeping through him, had made his decision and, as Perdikkas once more put the question, he shook his head; why should he give away what he had won? Why should he give the chance to another to equal or surpass him? Why should not he, alone for ever, be known as 'The Great'? No, he would not do it; he was not going to name the Strongest; he was not going to give them any help.

Let them work it out for themselves.

Opening his eyes one last time, he looked up at the ceiling, his breathing fading.

All seven around the bed leant in, hoping to hear their name.

Alexander twitched one last smile. 'I foresee great struggles at my funeral games.' He gave a sigh; then the eyes, that had seen more wonders than any before in this world, closed.

And they saw no more.

PERDIKKAS,
THE HALF-CHOSEN

THE RING FELT heavy in his hand as Perdikkas' fingers closed about it; it was not for the gold of which it was wrought but for the power in which it was steeped. He looked down at the still face of Alexander, as beautiful in death as it had been in life, and felt his world teeter so that he had to steady himself with his other hand on the oaken bedhead, alive with ancient animalistic carvings.

He drew breath and then looked to his companions, the six other bodyguards sworn to the death to the king who was no more; on the countenance of each was evidence of the gravity of the moment: tears on the faces of Leonnatus and Peucestas, each heaving their chest with irregular sobs; Ptolemy, rigid, eyes closed as if deep in thought; Lysimachus clenched and unclenched the muscles of his jaw, his hands in white-knuckled fists; Aristonous struggled for breath and then, forgetting dignity, squatted down on the floor with one hand supporting him. Peithon stared at Alexander, his eyes wide, dead to emotion.

Perdikkas opened his hand and gazed at the ring. Now was his time – should he dare to claim it as his own; Alexander had chosen him to receive it after all. *And he chose well, for of all here in this room I am the most worthy; I am his true heir.* He picked it up and held it between thumb and forefinger, examining it: so small, so mighty. *Can I claim it? Would the others let me do so?* The answer came quick, as unwelcome as it was unsurprising. In

6

the second group, beyond the bed, his younger brother, Alketas, standing between Eumenes, the sly little Greek secretary, and the grizzled veteran, Meleagros, caught his eye and slowly shook his head; he had read Perdikkas' mind. In fact, all in the room had read his mind as all eyes were now upon him.

'He gave it to me,' Perdikkas affirmed, his voice imbued with the authority of the symbol he held before him. 'It was I whom he chose.'

Aristonous got to his feet, his voice weary. 'But he did not name you, Perdikkas, although I would that he had.'

'Nevertheless, I hold the ring.'

Ptolemy half-smiled, bemused, shrugging his shoulders. 'It's such a shame, but he half-chose you; and a half-chosen king is just half a king. Where's the other half?'

'Whether he chose anyone or not,' a voice, gravelled by the shouting of battlefield commands, boomed, 'it is for the army-assembly to decide who is Macedon's king; it has ever been thus.' Meleagros strode forward, his hand on his sword-hilt; his beard, full and grey, dominated his weathered face. 'It is for free Macedonians to decide who sits on the throne of Macedon; and it is the right of free Macedonians to see the body of the dead king.'

Two dark eyes stared at Perdikkas, daring him to defy ancient custom; eyes that were full of resentment, as he knew only too well, for Meleagros was almost twice his age and yet remained an infantry commander; Alexander had passed him over for promotion. However, it was not through ineptitude that he had failed to rise, it was because of his qualities as a leader of a phalanx. It took much skill to command the sixteen-man-wide-and-deep Macedonian phalanx unit; it took even more to command two score of these two-hundred-and-fifty-six-man *speira* in conjunction, and Meleagros was the best – *with the possible exception of Antigonos One-Eye*, Perdikkas allowed. To ensure the right pace as the unit manoeuvred over various terrains so that every man, wielding his sixteen-feet-long sarissa, pike, was able to keep formation could not be learnt in one campaigning season. The phalanx's strength was its ability to deliver five pikes for every one-man frontage; armies had broken on it since its introduction by Alexander's father, but only because of men like Meleagros knowing how to keep it ordered so that the front five ranks could bring their weapons to bear whilst the rear ranks used theirs to disrupt missiles raining down upon them. Meleagros kept his men safe and they loved him for it and they were many. Meleagros could not be dismissed.

Perdikkas knew that he was beaten, for the moment at least; to realise his ambition he needed the army, both infantry and cavalry, on his side and Meleagros spoke for the infantry. *Gods, how I hate the infantry and I hate this bastard for blocking my way – for now.* He smiled. 'You are, of course, right, Meleagros; we stand here debating amongst ourselves as to what we should do and we forget our duty to our men. We should muster the army and give them the news. Alexander's body should be removed to the throne-room so that the men can file past it and pay their respects. On that, at least, do we all agree?' He looked around the room and saw no dissent. 'Good. Meleagros, you call the infantry and I'll summon the cavalry; I'll also send out messengers to every satrapy with the news. And let's always remember we are brothers with Alexander.' He paused to let that sink it, nodded at them and then made for the door, wanting only some time to himself to reflect upon his position.

But it was not to be; as a dozen conversations broke out around the corpse of Alexander, echoing around the cavernous chamber, Perdikkas felt someone fall into step beside him. ·

'You need my help,' Eumenes said, without looking up at him, as they walked through the door and into the main central corridor of the palace.

Perdikkas looked down at the little Greek, a whole head shorter than him, and wondered what it had been that made Alexander give him the military command left vacant when he, Perdikkas, had replaced Hephaestion; there had been much disquiet when Alexander had rewarded Eumenes' years of service, firstly as Phillip's secretary before transferring his allegiance to Alexander upon his assassination, by making him the first non-Macedonian commander of Companion Cavalry. 'What could *you* possibly do?'

'I was brought up to be polite to someone offering a service; in Kardia it is considered good manners. But, I grant you, we do differ in many ways from Macedon: for a start, we've always enjoyed *eating* our sheep.'

'And we've always enjoyed killing Greeks.'

'Not as much as the Greeks do themselves. But be that as it may, you do need my help.'

Perdikkas did not reply at first as they marched, now at speed, along the corridor, high and broad, musty with age, the geometrical paintwork fading and peeling in the humid atmosphere that afflicted Babylon. 'Alright; you've made me curious.'

'A noble condition, curiosity; it's only through curiosity that we can reach certainty as it causes us to explore a topic from all angles.'

'Yes, yes, very wise, I'm sure, but—'

'But you're just a blunt soldier and have no use for wisdom?'

'You know, Eumenes, one of the reasons that people dislike you so intensely is—'

'Because I keep on finishing their sentences for them?'

'Yes!'

'And there was me thinking that it was only because I'm an oily Greek. Oh well, I suppose one can't help but learn as one gets older, unless, of course, one is Peithon.' A sly glint came into his eye as he looked up at Perdikkas. 'Or Arrhidaeus.'

Perdikkas waved a dismissive hand. 'Arrhidaeus has never learnt a thing in his thirty years other than to try not to drool out of both sides of his mouth at the same time. He probably doesn't even know who his own father is.'

'He may not know he's Phillip's son but we all do; as does the army.'

Perdikkas halted and turned to the Greek. 'What's that supposed to mean?'

'You see, I told you that you needed my help. You said it yourself, he's Phillip's son which makes him Alexander's half-brother and, as such, his legitimate heir.'

'But he's a halfwit.'

'So? The only other two direct heirs are Heracles, Barsine's four-year-old bastard, or whatever is lurking in that eastern bitch Roxanna's belly. Now, Perdikkas, where will the army stand when presented with that choice?'

Perdikkas grunted and turned away. 'No one would choose a halfwit.'

'If you believe that then you're automatically ruling yourself out.'

'Piss off, you Greek runt, and leave me alone; you can make yourself useful by mustering your cavalry.'

But as Perdikkas walked away he was quite certain that he heard Eumenes mutter: 'You really do need my help and you will get it, like it or not.'

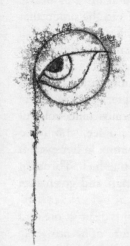

ANTIGONOS,
THE ONE-EYED

G ODS, HOW I hate the cavalry. Antigonos,
the Macedonian governor of Phrygia,
muttered a series of profanities under his
breath as he watched the lance-armed,
shieldless, heavy-cavalry on his left wing
attempt to form up on rough ground, far
further from the left flank of his phalanx
than he had ordered. The error left too much space for his
peltasts to cover once they had finished driving off the skirmishers from the scrubland protecting the enemy's opposite
flank; it also pushed his javelin-armed, mercenary Thracian
light-horse too far away for them to be able to respond with alacrity to any signal he might send. However, he hoped to finish
the day's work with one mighty blow from his twelve-thousand-
eight-hundred-strong phalanx. All his adult life Antigonos had
been an infantry commander, leading his men from the front
rank, looking no different to them, wielding a sarissa whilst
shouting orders to the signaller six ranks behind; at fifty-nine he
was still taking joy in the power of the war-machine that his old
friend, King Phillip, had introduced. And, as such, he knew the
value of cavalry to protect the cumbersome flanks of the phalanx
from enemy horse; but that was why he disliked them so much
as they were constantly boasting that the infantry would be dead
without them. Annoyingly, that was the truth.

'Go up there,' Antigonos bellowed at a young, mounted
aide, 'and tell that idiot son of mine that when I say fifty paces I
don't mean a hundred and fifty. I may only have one eye but it
is not totally useless. And tell him to hurry up; there's no more

11

than an hour of daylight left.' He scratched at his grey beard, grown full and long, and then took a bite from the onion that passed for his dinner. Despite his youth, his son, Demetrios, showed promise, Antigonos conceded, even if he did favour the cavalry as it far better suited his flamboyant behaviour; he just wished that he would take more heed of orders and reflect more upon the implications of doing as he pleased. A lesson in discipline was what the boy needed, Antigonos reflected, but he was constantly thwarted by his wife, Stratonice, who doted on him to the extent that he could do no wrong in her eyes; it was to drag Demetrios away from her skirts that he had brought his fifteen-year-old son on his first campaign and given him command of his companion cavalry.

Chewing, Antigonos examined the rest of his disposition from his command post on a knoll behind the centre of his army. He swallowed and then washed down the mouthful with strong, resonated wine; emitting a loud burp, he handed the wineskin to a waiting slave and took a deep breath of warm, late-afternoon air. He liked this country with its ragged hills and fast-flowing rivers; rock and scrub, hard land, land that reminded him of his home in the Macedonian uplands; land that chiselled a man rather than moulding him with gentle hands. But however good the land might be for the forming of a man's character, it was a liability to the conduct of smooth military operations. And it was with both those considerations in mind that he studied the Kappadokian satrap's army facing him, formed up with a river, a hundred paces wide, spanned by a three-arched stone bridge to its rear. He scanned the ranks of brightly robed clansmen, whose colours were enhanced by the sinking sun, clustered around a centre of a couple of thousand Persian regular infantry, in front of the bridge, stringing their bows behind their propped-up wicker pavises. In embroidered trousers and long bright-orange and deep-blue tunics and sporting dark-yellow tiaras, they were the original satrapy garrison that had helped Ariarathes, Darius' appointment, to hold out against Macedonian conquest for the ten years since Alexander, after a brief foray as far as Gordion, bypassed central Anatolia, taking his army south by the coastal route.

But now Antigonos had cornered this warlord of the interior who had preyed upon his supply lines and left a trail of his men writhing on stakes throughout the country; or at least cornered his army for he had no doubt that whatever the result of the coming conflict, Ariarathes would escape. It was a shame after the effort of having force-marched from Ancyra along the King's Road, the mighty construction that linked the great cities of the Persian Empire with the Middle Sea. The speed of his move had caught Ariarathes' army as it attempted to cross the narrow bridge over the River Halys back into Kappadokia after their latest raid. Caught in a bottleneck, Ariarathes had no choice but to turn and fight as he tried to extract as many of his troops as possible from the precarious position; only the setting of the sun could save him. As he watched, Antigonos saw many scores of the rebels streaming over the bridge and he had no doubt in his mind that Ariarathes would have been the first across. *But I'll trim his wings today, whether he survives or not.* He looked behind towards the westering sun. *Provided I do it now and quickly.* A glance up to his left told him that Demetrios had finally formed up in the correct position; satisfied that all was in order, Antigonos stuffed the rest of the onion into his mouth, jogged down the knoll and then, rubbing his hands together and chuckling in anticipation of a good fight, made his way through the phalanx to his position in the front rank.

'Thank you, Philotas,' he said, taking his sarissa from a man of similar age. 'Time to drown as many of these rats as possible,' he added with a grin. Taking his round shield that had been slung over his shoulder, he threaded his left hand through the sling so that he could grip his pike with both hands and still rely on a degree of protection from the shield even though he could not wield it as a hoplite would his larger hoplon. Without looking behind, he shouted back to the horn-blower. 'Phalanx to advance, attack pace.'

Three long notes sounded and were repeated all along the half-mile frontage of the phalanx. As the last call rang out in the distance the first horn-blower took a deep breath and blew a long shrill note. Almost as one, the men of the front ranks stepped forward to be followed by the file behind them; with rank after rank rolling forward, giving a ripple effect like breakers surging to the shore, the army of Antigonos closed with the foe.

It was with the same pride that he always felt when advancing at the heart of a phalanx that Antigonos tramped forward, his great pike held upright so that he could keep his shield covering as much of his body as possible as they neared the enemy. *Gods, I could never tire of this.* He had fought in the phalanx ever since its inception, firstly in Phillip's wars against the city state of Byzantion and the Thracian tribes to secure his eastern and northern borders; there the tribesmen had skewered themselves on the hedge of iron that protruded from the formation so that very few managed to close into the individualistic hand to hand combat they favoured. But it was in Greece that the new, deeper formation had really been tested; Phillip gradually expanded his power south until it was to Macedon that the Greek cities deferred and the days when Macedonians were publicly derided as being no more than barely civilized provincials of questionable Hellenic blood were gone – those thoughts were now shared only in private. The heavier phalanx had crushed the hoplite formations and the lance-armed Macedonian cavalry swept their javelin-wielding opponents from the field. Antigonos had loved every moment, never happier than when he was in the heart of a battle.

However, he had been left behind by Alexander soon after he had crossed into Asia and defeated the first army that Darius had sent against him at Gaugamela; but it had not been a dishonourable dismissal: Alexander had chosen Antigonos to be his satrap in Phrygia precisely because of his joy of war. The young king had trusted him to conclude the siege of the Phrygia's capital, Celaenae, and then to complete the conquest of the interior of Anatolia whilst he went south and east to steal an empire. Ariarathes was the last Persian satrap to still resist in Anatolia and Antigonos thanked the gods for him for without him he would have nothing more to do other than collect taxes and hear appeals; in fact, sometimes he wondered to himself whether he had allowed Ariarathes to hold out on purpose just so that he would always have a good excuse to go campaigning. But now that news had reached him that Alexander had returned out of the east and had recently arrived in Babylon, Antigonos had decided that a very real attempt should be made to rid this part of the empire of the last rebel satrap; he did not want to face the young king, for the first time in almost ten years, without completing the task he had been entrusted with.

With the thunder of twelve thousand footsteps crunching down on hard ground in unison, the phalanx pressed on and Antigonos' heart was full. To his left he could make out the peltasts, named after their crescent, hide-covered-wicker *pelte* shields, drive the archers threatening that flank from the scrubland in which they had taken cover; blood had been spilt and life was good. With a final volley of javelins, aimed at the backs of the retreating skirmishers, the peltasts rallied and withdrew to their position between the phalanx and the covering cavalry that advanced, as ordered, at the same pace as the infantry. *Gods, I do so love this.* Antigonos' beard twitched as he smiled behind it; his one good eye gleamed with excitement and the puckered scar in his left socket, which gave him a fearsome countenance, wept bloody tears. *One hundred paces to go; gods this will be good.*

Looking out from behind their pavises, the Persian infantry aimed their bows high; a cloud of two thousand arrows rose into the sky and Antigonos' smile grew broader. 'Keep it steady, lads!' And down the arrows plunged, clattering through the swaying forest of upright pikes; their momentum broken, they did little harm; here and there a scream followed by a series of curses as the casualty's comrades stepped over the fallen man and struggled to avoid getting their feet caught on his discarded pike. Some gaps would open, Antigonos knew, but they would soon be filled as the file-closers pushed men forward; he did not need to look round to make sure that was happening.

Again, another shower of iron-tipped rain fell from the sky and again it was mostly soaked up by the canopy over the phalanx's heads, the missiles falling to the ground as if twigs broken off in a tempest. *Fifty paces, now.* 'Pikes!' Another signal blared out and was repeated along the line, but this time the manoeuvre did not need to be completed in unison; from the centre, spreading left and right, pikes came down as a wave, the front five ranks to horizontal and the rear ranks to an angle over the heads of the men in front, shielding them still from the continuing arrow-storm.

Hunching forwards, Antigonos counted his steady, even paces, impatient for each one, as the enemy neared; now the Persian aim was more direct and arrows began to slam into the front rank's shields that rocked with the impacts as they were not held secure with a fist gripping a handle but just slung loose over the arm. Now the casualties began to mount; unprotected faces and thighs became targets; screams of pain became commonplace as, with the wet thuds of a butcher's shop, iron-tipped missiles pierced flesh and came to a juddering halt on bone. Shaft after shaft hissed in and Antigonos smiled still; he had not been touched since one had taken his eye at Chaeronea when Phillip had defeated the combined forces of Athens and Thebes. Since then he had been blessed of Ares, the god of war, and felt no fear walking into a blizzard of arrows. Now he could see the Persians' eyes as they aimed their shafts. An instinct made him duck his head; an arrow clanged off his bronze helmet, making his ears ring; he raised his face and laughed at the enemy, for they were going to die.

Taking up their pavises to use as more conventional shields, the Persians jammed their bows back into the cases on their hips, pulled long-thrusting spears from the ground and stood shoulder to shoulder, dark eyes staring at the oncoming phalanx, bristling with life-taking iron-points. Antigonos' laugh turned into a roar as he trudged the final few steps, the muscles in his arms aching with the strain of holding the pike level. His men roared with him, natural fear flowing from them to be replaced by the joy of combat.

And then he was there and now he could kill; with a power that filled him with joy, Antigonos thrust the pike forward at the hennaed-bearded face of the Persian before him, each man in the front rank judging the timing of the killing blow for himself;

the Persian spun away from the pike-tip and grabbed the haft, attempting to yank it from Antigonos' grasp, but he pushed on, along with the rest of his men, forcing their way forward, so that within two paces the second rank sarissas were coming in under those in front of them at belly height. On they pushed, pace by pace, working their weapons, still well out of reach of the enemy who now struggled, as the third rank's points came into range, with the multitude of weapon-heads ranged against them.

A couple of Persians, braver than the rest, charged forward, their spears over their shoulders, twisting between the wooden hafts, making for Antigonos, whose pike point was now lost to view; but still he kept stabbing forward, blind, as the Persians approached to within range of their weapons. But Antigonos did not flinch for he knew the men behind him; out of the corner of his eye he saw a pike being raised as the fourth-ranker lifted his arms and thrust his weapon forward. With a scream, a Persian doubled over the wound in his groin, fists pulling at the pike embedded in it as another comrade behind Antigonos, with a sharp jab, dealt with the second man. And still they moved forward, the pressure mounting with every step, but the weight of the phalanx was what made it so difficult to stand against and all along the line the enemy floundered as their frontage buckled. It was the Kappadokian clansmen, to either side of the Persians, tough men from the mountainous interior, who turned first; unable to face the Macedonian war-machine with only javelins and swords they ran, in their thousands, towards the river for they knew that a Macedonian phalanx could not chase its quarry with any speed.

With pride Antigonos looked to his left and saw exactly what he had hoped to: his son, purple-edged white cloak billowing behind him, leading the charge, at the head of the wedge formation so favoured by the Macedonian Companion Cavalry, which would achieve what the phalanx could not. And it was with speed and fury that they swept into the broken Kappadokian ranks, the wedge increasing pressure the deeper it drove, crashing men aside and trampling many more beneath thrashing hoofs as lances stabbed at the backs of the routed, dealing out wounds of dishonour. It was then that the right flank cavalry hit, boxing the beaten army in; the Persians now knew they could not possibly hope to extricate themselves across the bridge to safety and they too turned in flight.

Antigonos raised a fist in the air; a horn rang out once more. The phalanx had done its work and would halt, resting, whilst it watched the glory-boys of the cavalry do the easy part of the action: murder the vulnerable.

All were driven before them as the heavy-cavalry swept through from both flanks. Further out, light-cavalry patrolled in swirling circles, picking off the few fortunate enough to escape; Antigonos had indicated before the action that he had no interest in prisoners unless it be Ariarathes himself as he had a particularly wide stake ready for the rebel to perch on. Only the enemy cavalry managed to escape with their mounts swimming to the far bank.

With the phalanx precluding any flight to the west, those who could not get on to the bridge, now heaving with a stampede of the desperate, had but one choice to make: certain death on the point of a cavalry lance or the river. And so the Halys churned with drowning men, each trying to survive at the expense of others as the current washed them away, sucking them under. Some, those with the luck of their gods on their side, managed to cling to one of the two great stone supports sunk into the riverbed, although many were hauled off by others grabbing at their ankles as they swept past. A few managed the climb up to the parapet but none made it over into the crush of humanity swarming across but were, rather, thrust back down into the river by men who saw that another person on the bridge would lessen their own chances of survival.

Antigonos laughed as he watched Demetrios and his comrades spear fleeing Persian infantrymen as they attempted to push their way onto the bridge. Their Boitian-style helmets, painted white with a golden wreath etched around them, glowed warm in the rays of the setting sun as, sitting well back on their mounts and gripping with their thighs, their feet hanging free, they controlled their beasts with a deftness born of a life in the saddle. Calf-length leather boots, a boiled-leather or bronze muscled-cuirass with fringed leather *pteruges* beneath it, protecting the groin, and tunics and cloaks of differing hues, red, white, dun or brown, they made for a fine sight Antigonos was forced to concede. And, as they slaughtered their way through to the crush attempting the bridge, few turned to oppose them for most had discarded their weapons as they fled.

Antigonos slapped Philotas on the shoulder as Demetrios' lance broke and he reversed it to use the butt-spike. 'The boy's enjoying himself; he seems to be getting a taste for Easterners' blood. And it's about time: Alexander was roughly the same age when he led troops in battle for the first time.'

Philotas grinned as Demetrios' flanker took a Persian's hand off as he attempted to drag the young lad from the saddle. 'Caunus is looking after him, so he shouldn't come to any harm. You'll just have to stress to him that it isn't always quite so easy.'

'He'll learn that soon enough.'

Demetrios' unit, an *ile* of one hundred and twenty-eight men, was now at the bridge, the leading six hacking and stabbing their way forward as the press of the vanquished thinned out and flight became swifter; and still they killed and still men fled before them. On they drove and the smile faded from Antigonos' face the further they went. *The little fool.* He turned to the signaller. 'Sound the recall!'

The horn blared rising notes that were repeated throughout the formation yet Demetrios led his men on until there were none left on the bridge to kill and he burst out onto the eastern bank and, in the last of the light, slew all he could find.

'If a Kappadokian doesn't kill him,' Antigonos muttered, 'then I will when he gets back.'

'No you won't, old friend; you'll cuff him round the ears and then give him a hug for being a fool, but a brave one.'

'My arse I will; it's foolish behaviour like that that gets people killed unnecessarily. He's either got to learn discipline or resign himself to a short life.'

'In my experience it's not always the foolish that suffer as a result of their actions.'

Antigonos' face darkened. 'If my son ever does that again, Philotas, I pray to Ares that you're right and he doesn't kill himself.'